ABIGAIL'S PEACE

a novel

PEGG THOMAS

Spinner of Yarns Publishing
Ossineke, Michigan

Copyright @2022 by Pegg Thomas
https://peggthomas.com/
Published in the United States of America

ISBN: 979-8-9850278-4-6

Cover Design and Interior Formatting by Hannah Linder
www.hannahlinderdesigns.com
Cover Art Copyright by Spinner of Yarns Publishing

More Books

BY PEGG THOMAS

This novel is dedicated to those who work to preserve and appreciate our history for what it was and how it shaped us rather than holding it up to a 21st Century standard. May we look at our history with clear eyes and learn from those who came before. They were not perfect—and neither are we—but their struggles and choices and consequences formed our world today. They used the tools and knowledge and courage they had to survive and thrive in a world far different from the one they left for us. To every historian, museum curator, librarian, teacher, and author who keeps it real: I thank you.

Fans of historical fiction will fall in love with Abigail Aldridge, an unlikely heroine, as she arrives at Fort Niagara with high hopes to create an independent life for herself. Pegg Thomas' careful attention to detail brings richness and reality to pre-Revolutionary America, and the setting adds to the tension of constant danger for both those within the fort and those outside of its walls. History, adventure, an unexpected romance, edge-of-the-seat suspense...*Abigail's Peace* has it all!

—SUZANNE WOODS FISHER
Award-winning, bestselling author of *Anna's Crossing*

In *Abigail's Peace*, author Pegg Thomas pens another moving story of love and resilience in a time of colonial frontier warfare. In this, her third book in the *Forts of Refuge* series, Thomas offers an atypical heroine and an unexpected hero who behave truly to the period, their cultures, and each other. Set during the brewing conflict at Niagara and subsequent massacre at Devil's Hole, the rich historical detail brings to life an aspect of Pontiac's War most have forgotten. Readers of heroic, frontier love stories will devour this new offering in *Abigail's Peace*—as real as it is romantic.

—NAOMI MUSCH
Author of *Song for the Hunter* and *Season of My Enemy*

In *Abigail's Peace,* the third book of her *Forts of Refuge* series, Pegg Thomas gives us a moving vision of what might have been had the white settlers and the native peoples sought to live together in peace. Initially fearful of and even repelled by the Indians she encounters at Fort Niagara, Abigail Aldridge nevertheless finds herself increasingly drawn to two young Seneca women, and then to their brother, Koyengquahtah. A Seneca scout for the fort's British garrison, Koyen, as the soldiers call him, is equally distrustful and contemptuous of the Whites invading his people's lands. But Abigail and Koyen are increasingly thrust together as Pontiac's War spreads from Fort Pitt and Fort Detroit, both under siege, to also threaten Fort Niagara. And with each encounter, they begin to respect, and then to admire each other, feelings that lead to deeper emotions. *Abigail's Peace* is beautifully written and historically accurate, featuring well-drawn characters both Native and White that readers will open their hearts to. An engaging storyline with a solid faith theme makes *Abigail's Peace* a perfect addition to this outstanding series.

—J. M. HOCHSTETLER
Author of *The American Patriot Series* and,
with Bob Hostetler, of *The Northkill Amish Series*

Abigail's Peace is a well-researched, delightfully told story of pre-Revolutionary War America. Pegg Thomas' appealing characters bring this era of conflict and danger to life with honesty and hope.

—JAN DREXLER
Award-winning author of *The Amish of Weaver's Creek*

Acknowledgments

This is the point where authors sweat bullets dreading the thought of forgetting to mention someone who was or is vital to their world of writing. Or to their world in general. But I wish to thank those who really make it all possible—the readers. To everyone who purchases, is gifted with, or borrows this book and reads it... you are my hero. Without you, my stories would remain in my head or possibly in my computer, but would not see the light of publication. You rock!

Author's Forenote

The story's heroine, Abigail Aldridge, has a bad stammer. For this story, I chose to only use three letters at the beginning of words to illustrate it, just enough to give the reader a feel for her affliction, but in no way does it attempt to mimic an actual person's stammering pattern. I wrote it that way to give the reader a sense of her speech without slowing down the story more than necessary.

The Seneca in this story speak to each other in their own language which I have not tried to write as any sort of dialect but used common English for the interpretation. When they speak English, I have removed what Abigail calls the "little words" that make English such a difficult language for others to learn. I hope this makes it easier for the reader to understand when switching between the languages.

Hand talk—or Native American sign language—is also used. I interpret it in the story using common English and setting it apart in italics.

Koyengquahtah (KOY-en-QUA-dah) is the name of an actual historical Seneca chief who was born in 1760, but the Koyengquahtah in this story is completely fictional.

When I began writing Abigail's Peace, I reached out to the Seneca Nation in New York. I was shuffled from one contact person to another but found no one interested in reading this book for accuracy. Any mistakes or misconceptions are entirely my own. This is a work of fiction, but I did my best to keep it as authentic as I could via my research of the time and place and the people who lived there.

ABIGAIL'S
PEACE

Chapter 1

Abigail Aldridge crossed her arms and submitted to be carried from the pathetic excuse for a transfer boat—little more than a fat canoe—to the shore of Lake Ontario. With no proper dock jutting into the waters off Fort Niagara, she and the other women were subjected to the undignified manhandling of smelly sailors who waded through thigh-high waves in the shallow waters.

Speaking to her uncle about getting a dock constructed would be first on her list of things to do. After all, it wasn't fitting for a young woman of her standing to be treated in such a fashion. With nothing short of a heave, as one would a sack of turnips, Abigail was dumped onto the shore. The sailor grinned at her with what few teeth he owned, as if expecting her to be thankful. She turned her back to him and ignored his grunt.

She did her best to straighten her skirts while brushing a cloud of gnats away from her face. By the female grumblings going on around her as the other ladies were similarly dumped on the shore, she wasn't the only one feeling poorly used.

Fort Niagara spread before them, where an imposing stone

1

building commanded her attention. In Boston, she'd heard it called the French Castle, and she could see why. It was impressive in size, devoid of adornment to the point of being austere, with numerous dormers jutting from the steeply pitched lower roof edge, typical of French architecture.

The double gate in the palisade stood wide open. Beyond the castle, its attending outbuildings, and the parade grounds rose a great dark forest of massive trees. The fort truly did represent the last bastion of civilization before the untamed frontier.

She swung around. The newly built schooner *Huron* bobbed on white-topped waves in Lake Ontario, the fat canoes already halfway back to its side to fetch the women's trunks and other supplies for the fort sent from Boston.

"'Tis not what I assumed," Mrs. Waterman said, a hesitancy in her voice. But then, the woman was timid about everything.

"And no one to greet us," said Mrs. Morland, the quartermaster's wife. "But I suppose we should become used to that, should we not, ladies?"

Abigail was a bit intimidated by her. If her husband ordered the fort as well as his wife had shepherded the rest of the officers' ladies on their journey, they'd discover everything in fine shape behind the pointed log walls.

"'Tis very…" Mrs. Spooner, a lieutenant's wife and closest in age to Abigail, wrinkled her nose as she fumbled for the right word.

"'Tis p-p-perfect." Five faces turned toward Abigail, and she mentally kicked herself for trying to say a word beginning with *p*. She'd been careful along the journey. How could she have been so careless at this moment? Heat flooded her face, but she lifted her chin.

Fort Niagara was perfect—for her. If the rest of the women didn't agree, that was their affair.

Trunks, crates, and boxes were hauled ashore from two more

of the crude canoe-like boats and dumped onto the sand. Uncle Corne should talk to the commander about that, too. A proper British fort, be it on the edge of civilization or not, should keep to certain standards.

Abigail grabbed her small satchel, the one thing she would need most from Boston, and started toward the imposing stone building.

Mrs. Morland barked orders to the officers' wives and then caught up with Abigail. "I dare say 'tis far from perfect, but 'tis home for the summer, at least."

"Indeed." Abigail restricted herself to the one word she could reliably get out intact and ignored the older woman's questioning glance.

Boston was far behind her. There would be no drawing rooms here. No disapproving matrons with scowling faces. No need for Deloris, her well-meaning sister-in-law, to finish Abigail's sentences, or worse, to answer for her as if she were an imbecile. No need for Bartlett to make excuses for her, nor for Susanna to pretend she didn't exist. Her older half-siblings would have been happier had she never been born. They viewed her as little more than a disgrace to the family.

Fort Niagara was as far away from them as Abigail could get. Uncle Corne's posting to the fort had provided her the perfect escape. Being able to travel with the officers' wives, the perfect opportunity. Her brother and sister-in-law traveling out of town the same day as the *Huron* departed, the perfect timing. Everything had come together nicely. And Uncle Cornelius would be happy to have one of his family close by.

She hoped.

3

Koyengquahtah pressed farther into the shadows of the stockade. The unexpected British schooner had been sure to unload supplies—but women? And not just any women by the look of them. The fort had its camp followers, dressed in drab garments with many patches. They washed or cleaned or tended the gardens, as women should.

Those gathered on the beach, however, wore the oddest clothing he had ever seen in colors bright enough to challenge the soldiers' red coats. And so much of it. It was no wonder the sailors had to carry them ashore. If all that cloth had gotten soaked, they would have drowned.

Maybe it would have been for the best.

Among the Seneca, select women—clan mothers—wielded more power than the white women he'd seen. Perhaps he hadn't seen their clan mothers before. Perhaps these were such women, come to add their voices and their wisdom to the men in the fort.

How would that impact his people?

"Koyen!" Sergeant Morland pounded toward him, brow furrowed and mouth a grim slash, several soldiers in his wake. "Give us a hand with these newly arrived ladies."

"I am scout." How many times would he have to remind them of this? "Not soldier."

"I care not if you be the queen of Egypt." Morland stopped in front of him and jabbed a thumb toward the beach. "Those are *ladies*, and we will escort them to the castle and tote their belongings."

Koyen didn't answer as Morland stormed off, but he fell in step behind the soldiers. He would admit only to himself that he was curious what kind of women had landed on the shore. Curious, and a little apprehensive. He could almost feel a change blowing off the lake with the breeze.

But what sort of change?

Sergeant Morland stopped in his tracks. The young soldier following bumped into him without earning a reprimand. They waited the space of several breaths before one word exploded from the sergeant.

"Dinah!"

The woman in the lead, the older of the pair, raised her head in response.

Sergeant Morland whipped off his hat, knocking his wig askew, before hurrying on.

"Sergeant Morland." The woman's voice was stiff with disapproval, even at the distance. "We must discuss the manner of transportation I was forced to endure."

A woman of power.

Morland nodded, then flung his hand in the direction of the other women following from the beach and shouted at the soldiers. "Escort the others."

Koyen eyed the younger woman beside the one Morland called Dinah. She was fair, as they all were, with hair the dusty brown of a mourning dove and eyes almost the same color. Her hair was piled atop her head and covered with a white cloth cap except for two wisps which escaped to frame her face. Her eyes were widely spaced, divided by a short but straight nose above a rounded chin. A pleasing face, if too exotic for his taste.

He reached for the satchel, but she pulled it away from him with a slight gasp.

"'Tis fine, mistress," Morland said. "He will carry it for you."

"I am quite contented w-w-with my own s-s-satchel, thank you." She spoke to the sergeant, not to Koyen.

"As you wish." The sergeant inclined his head while the older woman wrapped her hand around his arm. "Koyen, bring the trunks to the castle."

They moved past, the younger woman with her face straight ahead, never glancing his way. That one was too young to have much influence, but she thought highly of herself even if nervous enough to stammer.

He moved down the beach, passing the other five ladies, their faces also averted. He grabbed the first trunk he came to and hoisted it onto his shoulder, the metal workings along its edge digging into his skin.

"Let it not worry you, Koyen." George Swan, an ensign who sometimes joined Koyen on scouting duties, shouldered another trunk. "'Tis your state of undress that unnerves them."

Koyen glanced at his leggings and breechclout.

George laughed, and several of the other men stopped to stare.

Koyen ran his hand across his bare chest, the spring breeze off the lake raising pebbles across the otherwise smooth skin.

"'Tis not their way back east, to see a man unclothed."

"Other women in fort not unnerved," Koyen said.

"They would not. Most have seen a man considerably less dressed than that." The younger man gave an exaggerated wink before resettling his trunk. "These ladies are from Boston." He moved on toward the castle.

Koyen followed.

The one the sergeant had called Dinah must be a clan mother. That would explain the deference she'd been shown. But the younger woman beside her? Perhaps a daughter or a younger sister. Did not his own sisters stay near to their mother who was herself a clan mother?

But that one, Mourning Dove, she looked nothing like the older woman.

One thing was certain, the women who had just arrived marked a change at the fort. And not to the benefit of his people.

AS IF BEING LUGGED ASHORE BY A FILTHY SAILOR, HIS hands on parts of her person never before held by a man, were not enough, to then be confronted by a half-naked savage... Abigail pulled her shawl tighter across her shoulders. She would have swooned for certain if not for the soldiers surrounding her. Fort Niagara was at the edge of civilization, of course, but it was a proper British outpost. There were standards to be kept, after all.

Yet, was it not those very standards from which she was running?

Before she could ponder that thought, the door to the castle opened and Mrs. Morland entered on the arm of the man who must be her husband. Formal introductions would come in time. Three men in officers' uniforms awaited them, including—

"Uncle Corne!" Abigail scooted past the older couple and raced across the vestibule toward her uncle.

He did not open his arms to her, but perhaps that was due to the other officers standing nearby. The paleness of his face in the dim interior could be awarded to any number of reasons. However, the downturned slash of his mouth slowed her approach to a sedate walk.

Uncle Corne took her arm and steered her away from the others. "Abigail? What are you doing here?"

Tears pressed against the back of her throat. Of course, he'd be surprised to see her, but even in her doubtful moments, she'd never envisioned him to be so thoroughly displeased.

"I have come to s-s-stay w-w-with you, Uncle."

"Have you lost all good sense, then?" His brows, dark beneath his powdered wig, drew into a single line above his high-bridged nose, an expression so like her mother's. As it should have been, his being her twin.

"No, indeed." She glanced around the room, which was

filling with the rest of the women and their belongings. "But p-p-perhaps w-w-we could s-s-speak of this elsewhere?"

He let out a snort that fluttered the ruffles on her linen cap. "I have no idea what to do with you. There are no women's quarters here."

Her heart leaked a bit of the confidence that had driven her since escaping Bartlett's house seven days prior. Had she erred? Had her impulsive nature overruled good sense again? Was she not to be welcomed by her most beloved uncle after all? She blinked back rapidly swelling moisture.

"There, there." Uncle Corne took her hand and patted it. "We shall arrange for something. After all, there is a gaggle of you."

"The rest are w-w-wives of the officers."

He closed his eyes with a sigh, then opened them again and placed his palm on her cheek. "You are the very likeness of Elizabeth. Grown now, but I would have known you anywhere."

Abigail summoned a wobbly smile, although in truth she often struggled to remember her mother, who'd been dead for nine years.

Uncle Corne's brows drew to a line again. "What was your brother thinking—?"

"Half-brother."

"Do not interrupt."

She offered him a meek nod, but truly, she preferred not to think of Bartlett any other way.

"How dare he put you on a boat and send you here without so much as a letter?"

"He did not."

A pause followed that cut through the chatter of the other women greeting their husbands after a winter of separation.

"Abigail, what have you done?"

Chapter 2

"I am sorry, my dear, but there is nothing for it." Uncle Corne looked as uncomfortable as Abigail felt. She surveyed the tiny room with its single window facing Lake Ontario. At least she'd be afforded a breeze on hot days. There was nothing else good to say about the chamber.

"'Twill be fine, Uncle." She did her best to add a lightness to her tone. "After all, I did not come to be a cosseted, but to join you and s-s-serve you however I might."

"About that—" Uncle Corne eased the door closed, leaving them barely enough space to turn around. "Sit." He gestured to the narrow bunk with its lumpy ticking.

Abigail perched on the edge while he gingerly seated himself on the only chair in the room, a ladderback made of stripped branches rather than milled boards.

"Tell me how you have come to arrive at the fort."

How much could she tell him without breaking down and embarrassing herself? He'd always been the uncle on the other end of the letters, seen in person only as he had leave. It'd been five years since she'd seen him last. Yet he wrote faithfully. In every way that mattered, he was her closest and most loved relative. She could be no less than honest with him.

"Bartlett and Deloris left town for a fortnight to visit her family in Connecticut. Days p-p-prior, I had learned of Mrs. Morland's p-p-plans to bring the officers' ladies to the fort." She pressed her lips together and glanced out the window at the water so far below. "I inquired of her to allow me to join them, and s-s-so to join you."

"She agreed?" His voice rose, whether in amazement or disapproval she couldn't be sure.

She turned back to him. "I may have led her to believe that it w-w-would be your w-w-wish for me to come."

He opened his mouth, then snapped it shut and let his head fall into his hands, elbows supported on his knees. "What have you done?" came his muffled response.

"I have escaped a p-p-prison."

"Prison?" He jerked upright, eyes boring into hers. "What do you mean?"

"Uncle." She swallowed against the tightness in her throat, against the verge of despair should he turn her out. "You know that I am unable to s-s-speak p-p-properly. My days consisted of s-s-staying out of my half-brother's w-w-way." She shrugged. "Deloris took me on calls w-w-with her, of course, but s-s-she rarely allowed me to talk. S-s-she answered for me, s-s-spoke for me, treated me like a child or... w-w-worse."

"My dear girl." He blew a loud breath, then rubbed his nose with the back of his hand. "I know society can be harsh—"

"Do you?" How could he—a respected officer in His Majesty's army? "Have you ever been treated as if you have not a thought w-w-worth s-s-sharing? Have you ever been told to s-s-stay home and avoid talking to p-p-people? Do those w-w-who s-s-should love you look down their noses at you?" In spite of her best efforts, the last words trembled as they left her lips.

"But, Abigail, whatever shall I do with you *here*?" A matching anguish filled his voice.

"I can w-w-write." She tapped her satchel. "I brought all my own s-s-supplies. You must have need of letters w-w-written, reports transcribed, and other s-s-such duties."

"'Tis not that simple, my dear." He rubbed his hand over the back of his neck. "This is a fort filled with men, not all of whom are the gentlemen you are accustomed to."

"Like the s-s-savage w-w-who met us on the beach." She hadn't meant to say that aloud.

Uncle Corne's face pulled into grim lines. "Those too, but the rank-and-file soldiers are often no better, it pains me to say."

"S-s-surely, being your niece w-w-will afford me the p-p-protection I need?" The gravity in his eyes did little to reassure her.

"We can hope, of course." He stood, pushing off the chair like an old man. "I will leave you to unpack your things." He grimaced. "I am sorry we have no lady's maid to assist you, and that you must endure this tiny room. Ensign Tharp was hastily removed to new quarters in the barracks that you may have it. 'Twas the best I could do. My room is directly across the corridor."

"At least 'tis not one of the dormers under the eaves w-w-with the s-s-servants." She summoned a smile.

"Those are not rooms, my dear. Those are gun dormers for the cannons."

The notion of being in a fort had seemed romantic in her spacious bedchamber in Boston, where no cannons were needed in the attic. She stood and took a tentative step toward him. This time, he opened his arms, and she all but fell into them.

"'Twill be well enough, I suppose." He patted her back. "We shall make it work until I can obtain passage for you to return to—"

"No, Uncle, I beg of you. Allow me to s-s-stay w-w-with you."

"'Tis not proper or fitting for you to be here, my dear. However difficult things are with your brother" —he lifted a finger to stop her from correcting him— "'twill be even more difficult for you here. You must trust me in this." Then he gave her a gentle squeeze before handing her a key. "Lock the room at all times, whether you are in it or not." With that warning, he left.

Abigail sank back onto the bed and stared at her unpacked trunk. Not that there was any place to unpack it to. No armoire, dressing table, not even a desk, only crude wooden pegs driven into the walls. Most of her belongings would have to stay in the trunk. For how long? How much time did she have before Uncle Corne sent her away?

She pressed her lips together and glanced out at the water again. It'd taken Mrs. Morland weeks to arrange transport on one of the new ships that sailed this far west. It may take more weeks before it returned. Weeks in which she would find a way to surprise her uncle and make herself useful to him. Indispensable.

She glanced at the trunk again, allowing herself only the tiniest moment to wish a maid hovered outside the door awaiting her instructions. Then she sighed and lifted the lid.

A good beginning would be to learn to be indispensable to herself.

HIS MOTHER'S LONGHOUSE WAS FILLED WITH WOMEN busy at their evening tasks. Koyen approached and sat near her fire. She handed him a gourd filled with tea she kept warm in a kettle near the fire, its metal reflecting the light of the low flames.

A device of the white man.

As was his musket, his knife, his hatchet, and even the beads decorating his shot bag. All things brought here by a people who were determined to stay. A people who outnumbered the Seneca and probably every tribe across the land. Perhaps all of them combined, if the stories the soldiers told were true.

"You have deep thoughts this evening." His mother handed him a hardened clay bowl with a shiny surface, another product of the white man. The scent of early dandelions and stewed fish rose from it, smothering his urge to throw it away from him. So many changes the white man had brought among them.

He took a drink of the broth, flavored with the herbs his mother harvested in the fall and dried. At last, something steeped in the traditions of his people.

"Women came to the fort today."

His mother nodded. As a clan mother, she would have heard already.

"Not like the other women there."

She gave the stew a stir, then set the dried gourd ladle aside. "How are they different?"

"They wore much more clothing and of bright colors like the meadow in spring."

"Hmm." She settled across the fire from him and folded her hands in her lap. "What did you think of them?"

"That their clothing would have drowned them if not for the sailors who carried them ashore."

His mother laughed, a pleasant sound and one that took him back to his childhood, when she'd been carefree and accountable only to her family. Before she'd been named clan mother and absorbed the responsibilities of that position.

He grinned at her and then smacked his chest. "They did not approve of my lack of a shirt."

"White ways are strange to us. So much clothing to make, to

tend, to repair, and for what? To make more and tend more and repair more." She shook her head.

He took another gulp of the stew, chewing on the fish and enjoying the fresh taste of the dandelions. Soon they would have plentiful greens from the forest and their gardens both. Spring was his favorite time of year. The time of fresh food. The time to fill in after a winter of leanness.

Not that Koyen had been in want during the winter. They fed him midday at the fort when he was there, and he was there daily as much as possible, giving his mother one less mouth to feed at her fire. Sometimes the baker woman, Lurana Quinn, gave him a loaf of bread to bring back to the longhouse as a treat for his sisters.

"I think these may be their clan mothers."

That got her attention. He grinned as he scooped the last of the fish pieces out of the bowl and chewed them.

She frowned at him. "You should have told me that first."

"I know." He set the bowl down. "But it was fun to watch your reaction."

"Such a tease." She scolded half-heartedly. "Why do you think they are clan mothers?"

"Sergeant Morland showed the oldest one great respect, and their clothing was not only much and colorful, but seemed to have more significance, I think." He tipped his head, remembering. "He called them… ladies."

"You know the English words. What does that mean?"

"I thought it just another word for woman. The English have many words for the same thing." As if their language wasn't confusing enough. "But it wasn't the word so much as the way he said it, with a reverence. Like we say clan mother."

She stared off into the longhouse, but he doubted she saw anything, one finger tapping against her teeth as she often did when deep in thought.

"Koyen!" His sisters had adopted the shortened version of his name that the British soldiers used. Red Beads and Shining Day scampered to the fire, one settling on each side of him as if they were still youngsters and not old enough to accept a husband. At least Red Beads was old enough, even if she didn't act it.

Shining Day, as she must, remained silent, but Red Beads chattered away about their adventure in the forest. She plopped a basket filled with mixed edible greens near her feet so her hands could move in the graceful hand-talk of their people as she spoke.

He listened with half an ear while plucking a few tender shoots from the basket and munching on them.

"And then we saw the English women being carried off the boat," Red Beads said.

He paused mid-chew. "You were there?"

"And we saw you." Her dark eyes glittered in the firelight.

Shining Day's hands moved in response, but she didn't smile. She must have seen the way Koyen had been snubbed by the English women, for a frown marred her lovely face as her hands wove the story of her contempt for them.

Red Beads reached across Koyen and grabbed their sister's hands, stilling them. Then she released them and grinned at him as she spoke and gestured. "Did not our brother show them who was the best man by choosing the largest box to lift and carry to the castle?"

Their mother gave a soft snort, proving she'd been listening.

"I had no wish to impress those women." He ignored the lift of their mother's eyebrows. "I wished to help George Swan. He is a decent man—for an Englishman—and not large enough to carry such a box."

While his sisters signed back and forth to each other, Koyen shifted his position to see out the open doorway rather than acknowledge the speculation in his mother's eyes. He had not been tempted to show off for the women. But now that his sisters had put the notion in his head... The one he thought of as Mourning Dove, would she have been impressed by his strength if she had looked at him?

Not that he cared what an English *lady* would think.

———

THE HALL WHERE THE HIGHER-RANKING SOLDIERS ATE was long and dark even with candles flickering from sconces on the walls. The stones seemed to drink in their light, leaving little to shine on the long tables and uniformed men.

As Abigail stepped into the room, heads swiveled in her direction, hands paused halfway to mouths, and a hush filled the space.

"Abigail." Uncle Corne strode toward her, offering her his arm.

She placed her fingers against the thick wool of his coat sleeve and kept her face forward as they passed the benches of the soldiers. A few made to rise as she passed, but Uncle Corne waved them down. At the far end, another set of tables was laid more formally for the officers and their wives.

Mrs. Morland looked down her nose at Abigail, but Mrs. Spooner gave her the briefest of smiles before Uncle Corne seated her at his left side and sat in his chair.

He leaned near her. "There is another staircase on this end of the hall for your use, my dear. Forgive me. I did not think to mention it before."

"'Tis fine, Uncle." She kept her voice low as well. "I w-w-will learn. You w-w-will s-s-see."

"I say, Hayward." The man at the center of the table banged his tankard on its surface. "Introductions are in order."

16

"Major Wilkins." Uncle Corne rose again. "May I present my niece, Abigail Aldridge." He then introduced the commanding officer and the rest of those assembled.

Abigail had only to nod and murmur what an honor it was to meet them. She used few words and only those she could manage reliably, happy that her stammer didn't give her away on the first evening. And, of course, she knew all the ladies from the schooner, even though she'd kept mostly to herself on the journey.

Once she could turn her attention to the meal in front of her, Abigail felt the eyes of the soldiers on her. Uncle Corne's warning about the men made it hard to swallow the mouthful of fish she'd bitten into. *The rank-and-file soldiers are often no better...* No better than the half-naked savage on the beach? They were men honorably in service to the king. Why did their furtive looks and outright stares make eating her dinner so difficult?

For the first time since she'd overheard Mrs. Morland talking about the journey to Fort Niagara, she wondered at the wisdom of her rash actions, and doubts filled her stomach more than fish.

Chapter 3

H and lifted to knock on Uncle Corne's door, Abigail gasped as the thick wooden panel opened. A tall young man in the less-ornamented uniform of an ensign blocked her view of the inside. With his reddish, unpowdered hair and matching mustache drooping from his lean face, he resembled the Vikings she'd once seen depicted in a painting.

"What is it, Tharp?" Her uncle's voice came from the far side of the room that served as both his bedchamber and office.

"'Tis your niece, sir." The young man stepped to the side to allow her entrance.

"Abigail." Uncle Corne looked up from his desk. "Come in. Dismissed, Tharp." The last came out a full command, with a snap to the words.

Abigail stepped into the room and waited for the ensign to leave.

"What can I do for you, my dear?"

"'Tis the w-w-wrong question, Uncle." She laced her fingers at her waist. "The question is, w-w-what I can do for you?"

A long moment stretched between them, then Uncle Corne leaned back in his seat. "As I said when you arrived yesterday, there is naught here for a young lady such as yourself."

"And as I s-s-said before, I am w-w-well able to w-w-write and have a good head for numbers. S-s-surely there is s-s-something you need assistance w-w-with?" There had to be. She must prove her worth at the fort.

His long sigh that followed gave her little hope.

"I have nothing at present, but perhaps Mrs. Morland would have a suggestion, hmm?" The rise in his voice at the end was a kinder dismissal than the ensign had received, but no less final.

"Indeed, Uncle. I s-s-shall locate her and inquire."

He beamed his approval before his elbows hit the desk, and his attention turned to the papers strewn across it.

Abigail backed out and shut the door quietly behind her. She turned and nearly walked into the young Viking, a gasp escaping her.

"My apologies, Miss...?" He let the word draw out, obviously waiting for her to supply her name.

"Aldridge." She'd half a mind not to tell him. But this was Fort Niagara, not some drawing room in Boston. There were no matrons seated at the windows willing to perform an introduction. For that matter, there were no windows on this long stretch of stone corridor along the second story of the castle. And Uncle Corne had addressed him as Tharp, so 'twas likely he was the one her presence had pushed from the room she'd been given. For that alone, he deserved her name.

"Miss Aldridge." He inclined his head in an informal bow.

"I am terribly s-s-sorry that you w-w-were p-p-put out of your room by my arrival." His reaction to her stammer was much as she was used to, the raised brows and slight drawing back. But perversely, rather than do her best to avoid it, she had purposely used the letters that forever tripped her tongue.

"'Tis of no matter, truly." He bowed again. "Can I be of any assistance to you today?"

Could he? Abigail folded her hands at her waist. "P-p-perhaps you could escort me to Mrs. Morland?"

"I would be delighted." He crooked his elbow for her hand.

Not without a little hesitation, Abigail laid her fingers on his sleeve. After all, Uncle Corne hadn't warned her specifically away from this man, and he'd been in Uncle Corne's room when she'd arrived. He'd also surrendered his chamber for her. Although likely he'd had no say in the matter, he also did not seem offended by it.

They moved to the end of the corridor, where the ensign tapped on a door that looked like every other door they'd passed.

"Enter," came the muffled reply.

Ensign Tharp opened the door and stood aside for Abigail to enter, then closed it behind her with a slight click.

Crowded into the room and perched on the same type of chair that Abigail had in her room were Mrs. Morland, Mrs. Waterman, Mrs. Spooner, Mrs. Reynolds, and Mrs. Lewes, the same women she'd traveled with from Boston. All wives of officers in the fort. Most frowning at Abigail's intrusion.

Then the youngest in the group, Mrs. Spooner, rose. "Miss Aldridge, you are welcome." She looked around the room. "We have no more chairs, but perhaps you could sit on the crate by the window and join us in mending uniforms."

"As she's not married," said Mrs. Morland, "she can start on the unmarried officers' uniforms."

Several others nodded.

As neatly as that, she was reduced in their esteem already. Abigail lifted her chin and her skirts and picked her way past the others to the crate by the window. She may not have the most comfortable seat, but at least she'd have the best light.

Before the day was done, she'd also produce the best stitches and mend the most garments. She'd show these women that she was not someone to be looked down upon. She'd show Uncle Corne that she was needed in the fort. She'd...

Do her best not to be utterly miserable.

KOYEN FINISHED THE TRIP FROM LOWER LANDING with a sprint to the fort. He'd caught the whiff of bread baking even before the palisade had been visible through the trees. After he delivered the dispatch to Sergeant Hagerman—the sergeant in charge of scouts—he'd wheedle an entire loaf from Lurana Quinn. He almost grinned as he tapped the contents of his pouch.

Hagerman took Koyen's dispatch and then dismissed him. It was well past midday, but the bake house still puffed its yeasty aroma across the parade grounds. Koyen opened the door and poked his head in.

The slight woman in front of the huge brick oven didn't turn or acknowledge him as she wielded a flat wooden paddle and removed two long loaves of crusty bread from the dark opening. His stomach rumbled. She repeated the process, drawing out four more loaves before she shoved a thick wooden door over the opening, dusted off her hands, and turned to him.

"You are here to rob me of a loaf of bread, are you, Koyengquahtah?"

Lurana Quinn was half Onondaga and half Scottish. Her smooth skin of an indeterminable age was neither light nor dark but somewhere in between. Hair as dark as any Onondaga, yet it curled and wisped in ways foreign to that tribe. She wore it braided and pinned up as a white woman might. She was lean, short, and a force to be reckoned with. Had she elected to return to her tribe when her husband had been killed, she would have been a respected clan mother.

But she had chosen to remain with the British army.

Part of Koyen wanted to resent her for that, but the other part wanted the loaf she pushed across the wide table in his direction.

"Take it. I suppose you have earned it already this day."

"I have." He slid the loaf into his pouch. "I have run to Lower Landing and back."

"Mmm." She cocked her head at him. "And did you learn anything worth the trip?"

He frowned and glanced out the open door. Not that any British who might be listening would understand their words in the trade language used among the Iroquois tribes. "I only carry the messages. They are not told to me."

"And what would you do if they were?"

He snapped his eyes back to her. "It would depend on the words."

"Be careful, Young King, lest you let your heart overrule your head."

"My heart beats for my people, and my head listens to it."

Lurana Quinn sighed. "Sometimes we need our heads to keep our hearts from going wrong."

"My heart tells me that the white man is not good for my people, and my head tells me the same."

"And yet,"—she looked him up and down—"you accept their pay and their bread."

"You know why."

She nodded. "But do not be misled into thinking that all white men are bad and all Iroquois—all Seneca—are good. It is not so."

Of course she would think that way, having been married to a Scotsman who was reported to have treated her well. He'd died at the hands of an Onondaga warrior, which might explain why she'd elected to remain at the fort. But it was said she held no bad will against her own people for the act. It was said she held no bad will toward the British either, for sending her husband into the fight.

Lurana Quinn was a mystery. A mystery who baked the best bread Koyen had ever tasted. It was the one thing he would miss when the British were driven from the land.

Four days of sitting for hours in an overcrowded room that had been hastily cleared for the women's use and mending a pile of uniforms that only grew taller as more men brought in their neglected clothing had left Abigail in a foul temper.

Uncle Corne was gracious at mealtimes and unapproachable at others. She knew that his duties to the fort were his priority, that his time was allotted to the army first and foremost, but she had expected to see more of him. To have more of his attention.

His affection.

The letter-writing and doting uncle she'd loved for so long was a stranger to her. Instead of sitting at his side and penning neat letters as she'd hoped, she was stuck in a stuffy little room with stuffy little women mending stuffy clothing for men she'd been ordered to avoid.

It was almost—but not quite—as intolerable as Boston. Already, she'd limited her responses to the other women to single words and only those she was confident she could pronounce clearly. If she didn't find another occupation soon—

"I say." Mrs. Waterman eased her back with the flat of her hand. "The smells from the bake house are near to intoxicating this afternoon."

Indeed, the open window at Abigail's elbow allowed its heavenly aromas into the room. Abigail drew in a long breath, as did several other women.

"Scones would do nicely with our tea, I dare say." Mrs. Morland dropped her mending to her lap. "'Tis moments like this when I miss my maid. I suppose one of us must fetch them if we are to have any."

"Indeed." Abigail stood and placed her mending on her crate. Any excuse to leave the room, even for such a short errand.

"That is very kind of you, Abigail." Mrs. Spooner gave her a gentle nod. Of all the women, only that one had shown any signs of friendship. "If not scones, whatever is available would be lovely."

Abigail nodded and fled the room. Her soft-soled slippers made barely a whisper on the wide flagstones of the upper corridor. She wasn't likely to meet anyone at this hour, but if she did, she didn't care. For a few moments at least, she was free.

Down the stairs, across the wide vestibule with its indoor well, and out the main door she went. The sun shone on the parade ground in front of her, more bright than warm in early May. The breeze swirled around the castle, carrying the scent of the lake and its coolness. But the open windows of the bake house brought the best smells.

Abigail hadn't been in the building before. She followed it around to the narrow door on its south side. Did one just enter? Or was a knock expected? The door stood open, so she stopped short of the threshold, her hand raised to knock on the lintel.

Words reached her. At least, she thought they were words. She didn't understand them, but they had the cadence of speech. She peered into the building—to the broad, naked back of an Indian.

"Who have we here?" A diminutive woman stepped from behind the Indian. She wore a simple dress covered with a huge apron, her dark hair braided and pinned to the back of her head was not covered with a mob cap. Dark eyes took Abigail's measure but gave no hint to her findings.

"I have come for s-s-scones for the ladies' tea." Abigail ignored the half-naked savage who turned toward her—the same one she'd seen at the beach—and kept her eyes on the woman.

"As it happens, I have some keeping warm. How many are there?"

"S-s-six, in total."

"Then I shall put in a dozen." The little woman whisked the scones into a cloth-lined basket and handed it to Abigail but kept her grip when Abigail took it. "And see that the basket comes back to me, or there will be no more scones from my bake house." Dark brows drew together. "Understand me?"

Abigail's emotions vacillated between outrage that a baker—a common tradeswoman—would speak thus to her, and half-panic that the Indian's eyes had not left her since he'd turned around. Eyes even darker than the woman's and filled with something she couldn't define. Something she didn't want to define.

"I w-w-will return your basket, ma'am." Abigail clutched the bowl-shaped item.

The little woman nodded, and the Indian placed his hand on his bare stomach, then bent his leg and performed as courtly a bow as any Abigail had ever seen in Boston. Basket pressed to her middle, she fled the bake house.

"Young King, what are you playing at?" The woman's words reached Abigail as she scurried away, thinking the stuffy room upstairs overlooking the parade ground wasn't as disagreeable as she'd imagined it earlier.

At least it held no mocking, shirtless savages.

Chapter 4

I t had rained for two days, the kind of rain needed to prepare the ground for seeds the women readied for the planting moon. Koyen used a stick to scrape the bottom of his moccasins before entering the longhouse. The kind of rain that turned pathways between the forts to clingy mud.

But he'd paid it little mind on his run back from Fort Schlosser, too full of the news he had heard.

The soldiers told him little, and nothing of importance, but there had been other scouts at the fort, Iroquois scouts from the Mohawks. They had been south for many days, scouting for the soldiers and keeping their eyes and ears open.

As Koyen did.

"You look pleased with yourself, my son." His mother looked up from where she squatted by the fire. "What has your eyes so bright?"

He dropped to the low sleeping platform, keeping his feet away from his mother's furs and blankets. The rest of the longhouse was buzzing with the normal fireside talk of early evening. He leaned closer and kept his words soft.

"I spoke with a pair of Mohawks at Fort Schlosser today."

She dusted off her hands before joining him on the platform. "And what excited you about their words?"

"Rumors." He frowned at her wince, and then continued. "Rumors with truth behind them, they were sure, of plans to attack the fort where the mighty rivers join."

"What do they call it now that the British have taken it again?"

"Pitt, after some Englishman or another."

"Ah. I have heard that name."

"The Ottawa chief, Pontiac, has sent some of his warriors into that area. Many from other tribes are listening to them." He dropped his voice even lower. "Many agree that the British must be driven away."

His mother nodded, her eyes on something in the distance that she probably didn't see. "And if they are driven away"—she blinked, then glanced at him—"who will replace them?"

He pulled back, sitting straighter. "Why would anyone replace them?"

"My son, what happens when you scoop a handful of wet sand from the lake's edge?"

What did that have to do with driving out the British? But he knew better than to ask. "More sand fills the hole with the next wave."

"It is so."

"But these are white men, not grains of sand."

"The principle is the same. Remove the French and the English come. Remove the English and who will fill in the hole?"

"We would." They'd have to. They couldn't allow their lands to be overrun again. "The Seneca and our Iroquois brothers."

"My son, there are not enough people in the tribes to fill the hole the British would leave."

He pointed to the fort. "The Seneca alone outnumber the soldiers."

"Ah, but the British are more than just their soldiers." She cocked her head at him. "Did you not tell me of women arriving not long ago?"

Mourning Dove came to his mind. Her ignoring him on the beach. Her eyes avoiding him in the bake house. Her stiff back as she hurried away from him, clutching the basket. Anger churned deep inside him at being dismissed in such a way. "I did."

"Then more will follow, and children will arrive. Families that need space to grow." She shook her head, eyes clouded. "They will be a wave that replaces the hole in the sand."

"How can you be so sure?"

She looked at him then, her eyes cleared of sadness, sharp with knowledge that sometimes left him in awe of her. As it did then.

"We know of their villages to the east that they call cities. Places where the trees have been removed and houses that make our longhouses seem small cover the land. We know of their great canoes that can cross the salt water to lands our mothers knew nothing about. They are a mighty people in numbers and clever in their workings." She lifted one of the shiny clay bowls she prized, then nodded to his musket still strapped across his back. "If they leave us in peace, perhaps it is best for our people that we leave them in peace as well."

Koyen bit back the protest that clawed the back of his throat. One did not argue lightly with a clan mother. He would need to think through his argument in favor of following Pontiac's lead and driving the British from Seneca lands.

No good could come from allowing them to stay.

28

THE RAIN—AND THE MEMORY OF THE MOCKING HALF-naked Indian—had kept Abigail inside for days. Days of boredom and loneliness, even crammed in a little room full of other women. The mending all finished, they'd turned to needlepoint.

Abigail detested doing needlepoint. And even had she enjoyed it, what would she do with it when she was finished? The cushion cover she'd been working on would be a ridiculous addition to her primitive quarters, assuming she'd be able to obtain anything to fill the cushion with.

Oh, why wouldn't Uncle Corne listen to her? Why wouldn't he budge on her offer to write his letters? Or even... even clean his room? Did he not see that her offer to act as a common servant had been proof of her devotion to him? Her unswerving desire to stay with him? She resisted the urge to stamp her foot.

She tucked the edges of her fichu into the front of her gown before stooping to retrieve her shoes. A flash of something brown caught her eye as it dashed from under the bed, ran across Abigail's foot, and scurried under her trunk.

Abigail screamed and jumped onto the bed.

Someone pounded on the door. "Miss Aldridge?" came Ensign Tharp's voice.

With another little shriek, Abigail rushed to the door, unlocked it and pulled it open. She clutched the ensign's arms and all but dragged him into the narrow room, pressing close against his chest.

"What has happened?" His expression hovered somewhere between scandalized and alarmed.

Abigail pointed to her trunk. "A mouse!"

"In your trunk?"

"Under. It-it-it ran across my foot!"

"What is going on here?" Uncle Corne's booming voice filled the corridor.

Ensign Tharp snapped to attention, his face a peculiar shade of red. "Your niece encountered a mouse, sir."

Mrs. Spooner appeared at the door next to Uncle Corne. "Oh, dear."

"Stand aside, Tharp." Her uncle commanded. "Abigail, did you not have plans this morning?"

"Indeed, w-w-with Mrs. Spooner."

He let out something between a sigh and a snort. "Get along then. Tharp and I will see to the rodent." He gave a pointed look to her hands still clutching the ensign's arms, and then to her stockinged feet.

Abigail dropped the fistfuls of uniform sleeve, grabbed her shoes, and squeezed past the men.

Mrs. Spooner gathered her close, an arm around Abigail's shoulders, and led her to a bench down the corridor where she could sit and buckle on her shoes.

"I daresay, that was enough excitement for one day, and 'tis hardly past daybreak."

"Indeed. Far too much excitement." Abigail pressed her fingers against her hot cheeks. "'Twas s-s-so s-s-startling."

"And upsetting, to be sure. But 'tis over and done now. Are you ready?" Mrs. Spooner asked, the handles of a basket secure over her arm.

"I am."

"Have you no shopping basket?"

She didn't. Shopping was something the servants did back in Boston, or if she and Deloris ventured out, a servant accompanied them to carry their purchases. "I hope to p-p-purchase one at the s-s-sutlers."

Mrs. Spooner took Abigail's hand and tucked it under her arm. "Then let us be on our way. And please, you must call me Judith. Surely we know each other well enough for our Christian names, do you think?"

"Indeed." Abigail relaxed and let herself be escorted down the stairs. "And I am Abigail."

"I have always loved the name Abigail. It somehow mingles strength with a decidedly feminine air. At least, I believe so."

"I have never thought of it that w-w-way." But she liked it very much. "Judith is a s-s-stalwart name, yet musical."

"'Twas my mother's mother's name." Judith flashed her a wide grin. "She was a fearsome old woman, but I loved her dearly."

What must it be like to have a relative to love dearly? Abigail had thought she loved Uncle Corne dearly—albeit from a distance—but he was turning out to be a great disappointment. Why had she thought he'd tolerate her and her infernal stammer any better than Bartlett?

She shoved the dark question aside as they stepped into the sunshine. It was a warm morning for mid-May, and everything smelled fresh after the rain. Even the soldiers drilling on the parade ground failed to raise any dust. A good day to explore the sutlers' tents that lined the eastern wall of the fort.

Judith strode out smartly, and even though Abigail was taller by a few inches, she had to hustle to keep up. She was a bit out of breath by the time they arrived, but Judith appeared unfazed. Perhaps Abigail needed more exercise, more time out-of-doors.

The tents were a ramshackle collection of canvas and hides, with men and women dressed in a similar combination of cloth and buckskin. There was a blacksmith on one end with his foul-smelling forge belching black smoke. Another man displayed an impressive number of knives with handles of bone, antler, and stone. A woman in a drab dress worked a spinning wheel behind a table covered in stacks of cloth, several jars of buttons, hanks of yarn, and a box of spooled threads. In front of the middle tent was a portly man rubbing his whiskers with a dirty hand and scowling at a pair of young Indian women.

The women wore buckskin skirts and cloth shirts—which brought Abigail a sense of relief, having heard that it wasn't uncommon for Indian women to also walk around bare-chested in the summer. One appeared about Abigail's age, the other slightly younger. They both held colorful woven baskets.

"As I told you last week, I have no buyers for your baskets." The man made a shooing motion. "Let me be. I have customers to attend."

Other than Judith and herself, there were only two men poking around the knife table. Judith was busy sorting through the button jars, but Abigail stepped closer to the Indian women. They had understood the sutler, so they should understand her.

"May I s-s-see your baskets?"

The older one turned, something like hope in her expression. She touched the arm of the younger one, who aimed a frown at Abigail.

The older one held out her basket.

Taking it, Abigail turned it over in her hands. It was beautifully worked and tight enough it might even hold water, not that she needed it for that. It was the size of a small wash kettle and would be nice for storage in her chamber. She could hang it by its handles, well above the floor and… mice.

"May I have a look at the other?"

The young woman didn't respond, but the older one made some sort of motion with her hands and then took the basket and gave it to Abigail.

It was the perfect shopping basket, with two handles long enough to loop around her arm, and about half the size of the first. Both were perfectly suitable for her needs. Abigail tapped her embroidered pocket with its stash of coins, coins her mother had left to her. Bartlett hadn't known about the money, so it was hers to spend as she wished. But how much did baskets like this cost? Abigail had never paid directly for anything other than sweets at the confectionery.

"W-w-what are you asking for them?"

The older one shot the sutler a glance, then back at Abigail. "Threepence each."

Judith had moved closer and shook her head. "Maybe for the larger basket, but no more than twopence for the smaller, I should think."

Relief flooded through Abigail. She'd have to learn more about handling money on her own, that much was certain.

The older Indian's hands wove in a type of pattern, and whatever it was, the younger must have understood, because her scowl lessened, and she gave a brief nod.

"Agreed." The older one extended her hand, palm up.

Abigail dug into her pocket, fishing for a pair of small coins, aware of the sutlers' eyes on her. She may not be worldly, but she knew better than to draw out a handful that would command their attention. She pressed two Bay Colony coins into the dark-skinned hand.

The young woman closed her fist around them, grabbed the other girl's arm, and hurried away.

"Perhaps we should return to the castle," Judith whispered. "The sutlers do not appear pleased with your purchasing from the Indians."

Sure enough, several faces glowered at her as Abigail took a firmer hold on her baskets and allowed Judith to shepherd her back to the castle. Well, if they'd bought the Indian baskets, Abigail could have purchased from them. But they hadn't.

A part of Abigail was thrilled to have cut them out of her transaction. Thrilled to have helped someone being bullied. She pulled in a breath and squared her shoulders. It made her feel in charge of herself for the first time in... possibly ever.

Koyen waited by the gate, arms crossed and feet planted in the damp soil. Red Beads and Shining Day almost careened into him when they finally noticed him blocking their escape from the fort.

"What were you doing near the sutlers' tents?"

Red Beads grinned at him, one hand clenching the other at her waist. "We sold two baskets to a woman from the castle." She opened her hands and showed him two coins.

He leaned closer. Two coins, and not pennies. He shot a glance at the castle. He'd recognized Mourning Dove as she'd spoken to his sisters. She had paid them a fair price.

Learning about the white man's money had been one of Koyen's first lessons. He'd been younger than Shining Day when he'd taken pennies for a stack of furs he'd worked for all winter.

"You did well—this time—but I do not want you to go to the sutlers' tents alone. I do not trust them."

"It was not a sutler who bought them." Red Beads clenched the coins in her fist again, her chin up and eyes flashing.

No. It hadn't been. "But you approached one of them first."

His sister hung her head.

"Tell me when you wish to go again, and I will see you there and back."

Red Beads nodded and grabbed Shining Day's hand. They ran past him and into the woods., no doubt to proudly show their mother the coins.

British coins.

Another change from the traditional ways. Yet it was easy to exchange coins for other items they wanted. His sisters would wish for the thick blankets or maybe cloth for more clothing. It didn't wear as well as good buckskin, but it was colorful and soft, and the women enjoyed it.

He shot another glance at the castle. Why had the woman who would not look upon him pay a fair price for his sisters' baskets?

Chapter 5

"I desire to s-s-speak w-w-with my uncle." She could not spend another week in that room, cooped up like a silly chicken, listening to the other women prattle on for hours about nothing.

"He is occupied on official business, miss." Ensign Tharp remained straight as a post beside her uncle's closed door. "He does not wish to be disturbed."

"I am hardly a disturbance, ensign." She pulled her shoulders back and matched his stiff stance. "I am his niece."

The man had the grace to flush, at least. The memory of his uniform against her cheek while she'd clutched him after the mouse incident threatened to bring on a blush of her own.

"Miss Aldridge, were it within my power, I would admit you at once. You have my word." He gave a slight shrug. "'Tis not, however."

"P-p-perhaps you could just s-s-step aside for a moment?"

"No, miss. That would render me derelict in my duty."

The door was wrenched open from within. "Abigail, stop badgering the man." Uncle Corne wore an expression she'd never seen on him before. It made him look... older.

She took a step back. "Uncle Corne—"

"Let her in, ensign." He turned and stalked to his desk.

Abigail entered, startling when Ensign Tharp shut the door behind her. Perhaps it hadn't been such a good idea after all.

Or maybe it was an opportunity.

"Uncle, I can s-s-see how busy you are." She gestured to the cluttered desk as he took his seat behind it. "As I have s-s-said before, I w-w-would be more than happy to—"

"Sit down." It was a command, not a polite request.

Her bottom connected with the hard wooden chair before she'd made the conscious decision to obey.

"My dear." He steepled his fingers and stared at her over the top of them. "As I have told you, I do not have time to entertain you during the day."

Or in the evenings or any other time except for supper, but she held her tongue.

"There are things brewing west of here that will..." He let his sentence trail off and shook his head. "I have done my utmost to find a ship to return you to Boston, but to no avail. Nor does it appear there will be one anytime soon. I wish there were another way to return you to safety, but overland is out of the question."

She schooled her lips not to respond to the excitement bubbling inside of her. At least, not yet. He was obviously not pleased by his failure, in direct contrast to her delight. Things at the fort were not as she'd hoped, but they were still better than Boston. If she could only convince Uncle Corne to let her assist him, they would get even better. She leaned forward and kept her face and voice serious.

"S-s-since I am to s-s-stay, and you are horribly overworked, w-w-why resist my offers of assistance? I do not boast when I s-s-say that I can w-w-write an excellent hand." She straightened and folded her hands on her lap. "My s-s-stammer does not inhibit my intelligence nor my p-p-penmanship, I assure you."

He grasped his temples with the forefinger and thumb of one hand and then pulled the hand down his face. "I never thought it did."

Then he was the only one.

"But, my dear, what I am reading and writing about, 'tis not fit for your delicate sensibilities."

"I am much s-s-stronger than you think."

"I seem to recall an episode with a mouse…"

Abigail's face warmed, but she plunged on with her argument. "'Twas the unexpectedness of it. It raced across my foot. But w-w-with you nearby, I w-w-will be quite s-s-safe."

"There are times I will be away, or with the major, or—

"I truly am s-s-strong enough, Uncle."

He blinked, then studied her for a long moment. "Perhaps you are. Heaven knows your mother was. She outlived two husbands and I have little doubt would have buried a third had the fever not taken her." A shadow crossed his features. "Taken her far too young." They'd been close, her mother and him. Abigail had understood that even as a little girl. Grief pulled at the wrinkles on his cheeks, and an answering grief tightened her throat.

He slapped his hand on the desk, and Abigail flinched.

"If you are sure"—he cocked an eyebrow, and she nodded—"then I suppose we can give it a go." He smacked the desk again. "Tharp!"

The ensign opened the door.

"Fetch something to serve as a writing desk for Abi—Miss Aldridge. Straight away."

"Yes, sir." The words were barely out before the door closed again.

Uncle Corne snorted. "Good man, that one. Doesn't waste time or ask foolish questions." He pointed a finger at her. "The same I will expect from you."

"Of course, Uncle. I w-w-will not disappoint you." She rose. "I w-w-will fetch my w-w-writing case and return." She all but skipped across the corridor and snatched up her satchel. Finally, she would have her chance to show her mettle.

She paused only a moment at the door to her chamber. After all, it was what she'd wished for. Planned for. It was her new beginning. No more drawing rooms. No more needlework. No more inane chatter that benefited no one.

She would use her gift of the written word to forge her way into the future.

THE SCOUT CROUCHING IN FRONT OF HIM MOTIONED Koyen down. They both dropped to the forest floor. The scent of new growth mingled with the lingering decay of old leaves on the damp trail they followed. Not a main trail, just an animal track that traced along the river.

They'd left Fort Niagara seven days prior to scout out rumors that had reached Major Wilkins. Rumors of the possible siege on Fort Pitt.

But that fort, its British flag snapping in the wind, sat at the point where two great rivers merged, soldiers visible along the palisade walls. It appeared to be a hive of activity. Perhaps too much activity.

That wasn't what had Tall Otter motioning them down, however. On the far side of the southernmost river came a long line of canoes filled with warriors. They hugged the shore, probably to stay out of range from the fort's muskets, but they made no attempt to hide from those on the palisade walls.

Lenni Lenape by the look of them. Yet only that morning, Koyen and Tall Otter had seen Mingo and Ottawa warriors squatted around campfires northeast of where they watched the river.

When they'd arrived in the area the previous evening, they'd seen smoke—thick pillars of smoke—rising from three different places. It didn't take much to imagine the cause, settlements burned out by the Indians roaming the countryside, tightening the ring around Fort Pitt.

Preparations to take the fort.

Koyen tapped Tall Otter and motioned behind them. They eased back into the denser cover of some bramble bushes.

"It is true." Koyen allowed a wolfish grin. "Pontiac of the Ottawa has joined the tribes together for a fight against the British."

Tall Otter, older by a handful of years, grunted as he scanned the area around them. "It is a fool's errand."

Koyen tightened his grip on his musket. Why did so many Senecas resist what was forming in front of them? Had they grown soft? Were they afraid of the white man with his metal knives, guns, and bullets? He glanced at the musket in his hand. Part of him wanted to toss it away. The more prudent part knew he'd need it if he were to join the fight.

And he intended to do exactly that.

Tall Otter pointed toward the river. "Those warriors out there are few. The soldiers are many. And more will follow."

"But joined with the Ottawa, Mingo, Shawnee, Hurons, and our Seneca, we would be many as well."

The older man cut a glance at him. "You think this a fight we could win?"

"I do."

"I might have"—Tall Otter shrugged—"once."

"What changed your mind? Working for the British?" Despite Koyen's best effort, his contempt must have leaked into his voice, for the older man frowned at him.

"As do you."

Koyen shifted on his heels, crouched, ready to spring into action as needed. "Not to assist them, but to learn."

"And yet, you are here, with me, scouting for the major."

Koyen bit back the retort that sprang to his tongue. He may be scouting for the major, but he was also learning. Learning what Pontiac was doing and with the help of which tribes. Information he'd take back to the major, but information he'd also share with the Seneca chiefs and clan mothers.

He may be scouting for the British, but he did so to help his people—not theirs.

"MIND YOU NOT WASTE A SCRAP OF PAPER," UNCLE Corne told Abigail for at least the hundredth time since she'd begun working with him eight days ago.

Eight very long days. Abigail stretched her back and canted her neck to the side until it popped. She was tempted to rub her sore backside, but she couldn't deviate from her Boston upbringing enough to do that, no matter how hard the chair and how long the hours.

Aside from being able to put her talent to use—even Uncle Corne had admitted her penmanship was exceptional—she'd also developed a new understanding and respect for her uncle. He hadn't neglected her upon her arrival. The man had barely two moments to himself from sunup until well past sundown. Officers and soldiers tromped through his room like waves along the lake, splashing in and ebbing out.

Yet he didn't become flustered or cross with any of them. Oh, maybe a bit sharper with some than with others, but always as the officer in charge that he was. Always the gentleman in uniform. That the men respected him was plain to see.

He paid her scant attention through it all, as if she'd become a part of the makeshift desk Ensign Tharp had hastily fashioned for her. It was functional but less than comfortable. Perhaps she should find time to finish that needlepoint cushion and apply it to the seat of her chair.

Instead, she took the paper—a precious commodity in the frontier fort—and hunched over her desk again, ready to pen Uncle Corne's words.

Someone knocked on the door.

"Enter," Uncle Corne barked from his desk.

Ensign Tharp opened the door. "Two scouts have returned from their journey to the southwest, sir. Major Wilkins wishes them to brief you on their findings."

"Show them in."

The ensign stepped inside, holding the door open, as two half-naked savages entered the room. One was the same man who had approached her on the beach and then mocked her at the bake house. Abigail bowed her head, concentrating on the blank paper before her and not their bronzed chests and muscled arms.

"Abigail." Uncle Corne's voice was soft, lacking any of the force of command it usually had. "I am sure you could use a walk to stretch your legs after a full morning at that desk. Ensign Tharp will accompany you."

Abigail corked her inkwell and wiped her pen dry. Feigning calm, she strode past the two men without looking at either and hurried to the door.

"Have her back within the hour, ensign."

"Yes, sir."

Abigail stepped into the corridor and gulped in a breath.

Ensign Tharp offered his arm. "They can be intimidating up close."

"Indeed." She took hold of his arm, happy for the support.

"Our army needs to use them. They are valuable for gathering information." He glanced at her. "But I apologize if they have distressed you."

She pulled in another deep breath, then shook her head. "I am adjusting to life here, and the s-s-savages are p-p-part of it. I must adjust to them as w-w-well."

"You are adjusting amazingly well, if I may be so bold. Your handwriting is a vast improvement over your uncle's, I assure you. I have heard the major himself remark upon it."

Bold indeed, but her cheeks warmed at his words. To be recognized for what she could contribute was gratifying.

"P-p-perhaps I may w-w-wr-wr—"

"Write?"

Abigail bit the inside of her cheek. Nothing frustrated her more than someone finishing her words for her when she struggled with them. He meant to be helpful, she was sure, but it still felt demeaning.

"Indeed. P-p-perhaps I may assist the major s-s-sometime."

"He has all the assistants he needs."

He stepped ahead of her and opened the castle's main door. It was a gray and dreary day. While no drops fell, murky clouds hid the midday sun, and the scent of rain carried on the cool breeze.

"Shall we circle the fort and end our stroll at the bake house?" he asked. "Perhaps Lurana Quinn will have something special set aside when we arrive."

Abigail took his arm again and nodded. "W-w-why does everyone refer to her by both names, and not as Mrs. Quinn?"

"That is what she prefers."

"That s-s-seems odd."

"For us, it may, but Lurana Quinn is Onondaga."

"She is an Indian?" Abigail thought back to the black braid

and dark eyes of the diminutive woman in the huge apron who spoke impeccable English. "But she runs the bake house."

"Half Onondaga, I should say. Her father was Scottish. She was also the wife of a British soldier."

Abigail turned her face away from the ensign and let his words register. Of course she knew there were people who inter-married with the savages. Who hadn't heard the stories? Men who went into the frontier and found an Indian woman to keep as a wife. Marriage probably wasn't the correct term for those unions, and she'd been given to understand by juicy bits of gossip picked up over the years that most of those same men had a proper family back in the towns along the coast.

Scandalous, to say the least.

But she'd never thought about it from the women's point of view. Had Lurana Quinn's husband also kept a proper family back east?

They were passing by the gate facing the forest when two Indian women entered. The same two Abigail had purchased her baskets from. She tugged on the ensign's sleeve and stopped.

"Hello."

The older one flashed her a smile. "Hello."

The younger one scowled.

Ensign Tharp cleared his throat. "Miss Aldridge, we should—"

She raised her hand to silence him, still looking at the smiling woman. "We did not exchange names, but we have met before. I am Abigail Aldridge." If the savages preferred both names, she would adjust to that.

"I Red Beads, my sister Shining Day." Her English was oddly accented and missing words, but perfectly understandable.

"Your baskets have been indispensable to me. I do not know how I w-w-would manage w-w-without them."

Her grin broadened. "You wish more?"

"I have no room for another at p-p-present."

The other woman glanced down at the basket in her hands.

Abigail thought fast. She knew disappointment when she saw it. "P-p-perhaps I could s-s-speak with the s-s-sutlers on your behalf?"

"Miss Aldridge, I do not think your uncle—"

"My uncle s-s-said I needed a w-w-walk and for you to escort me. W-w-which you are. And now you can escort the three of us to the s-s-sutlers' tents." She turned back to the Indian women. "Come. Join us."

She couldn't say why, exactly, but she felt a pull to help these sisters. Maybe it stemmed from thinking about the Indian women misused by men who already had families. Or maybe she was simply responding to the friendliness in the older sister's face.

A bare-chested man was one thing. A smiling woman her own age… that was something altogether different. It was an opportunity. She'd made a place for herself inside the castle, perhaps she could make a place for herself outside it as well.

Chapter 6

They hadn't waited for him as Koyen had instructed. He fumed inwardly as he watched his sisters' progress across the fort's grounds, with Mourning Dove and the soldier Captain Hayward had sent out with her.

"Are those your sisters?" Tall Otter asked.

"They are."

"With the woman who left the room upstairs. Interesting."

"She purchased baskets from them several days ago." Which in no way excused their disobedience to him. He'd been very firm about it. They were to stay outside the fort until he came back for them.

Of course, if he and Tall Otter had come straight to the fort last night instead of returning to their village to await the morning, his sisters wouldn't have been with him at all. He ground his teeth. He would have to make it plain to their mother that her daughters needed to remain in camp. It would be too dangerous for them to wander about on their own before long.

When full-fledged war broke out.

It wasn't just the white men who would make it dangerous, either. Warriors from other tribes would be in their area. Tribes with only a loose relationship to the Seneca. Tribes not

46

connected to the Iroquois Nation. Best to keep Red Beads—and especially Shining Day—in their mother's longhouse.

Until the British were beaten back and the other tribes returned to their own lands.

Koyen left Tall Otter and strode toward the sutlers' area. His sisters were closer and arrived before him. He came behind them as they spoke with a rotund man in front of one of the tents.

"As you can s-s-see..." Mourning Dove held one of his sisters' baskets. "The w-w-workmanship is w-w-without flaw." She turned the basket over in her hands, showing the man something.

Why did she do this? She was stammering as if in fear, but stood at ease, as if in command.

The soldier eyed Koyen up and down, stepping to the side to keep him in sight. Not a bad move. Koyen returned his regard. A capable soldier, which was no doubt why the captain had entrusted Mourning Dove to him.

Koyen snapped his attention back to the British woman as she continued to speak. Was she the captain's woman? She was much younger, but sometimes older men acquired a young wife to produce children. Was that why she had come to the fort?

Shining Day caught sight of Koyen, her eyebrows raising. She lifted her hand toward Red Beads, but he shook his head, and she let it drop.

"Good s-s-sir, if you cannot appreciate the quality of the w-w-workmanship and value of these p-p-pieces, then I s-s-shall s-s-search out one w-w-who can. I assure you that in Boston, these w-w-would fetch a handsome p-p-price."

"We are not in Boston, miss. And no high-bob stammering woman is going to badger me into purchasing something I do not want. So be off with you."

The soldier stepped forward and, to his own surprise, Koyen moved with him.

Red Beads, her eyes snapping, also took a step forward. Koyen grabbed her arm and pulled her behind him. The basket in her hands tumbled to the ground.

Mourning Dove snatched it up and faced Koyen. "Let go of her. You have no right to manhandle—"

"Red Beads, take Shining Day to village. Now." He didn't take his eyes off the British woman in front of him.

"Now s-s-see here." She drew herself up like a partridge preparing to drum its feathers, her eyes on his face, not looking away. "This is none of your affair."

The soldier stepped between them and faced Koyen. "No harm was done here. We need to return to the castle."

"Are you going to let him order those p-p-poor girls around, Ensign Tharp?" Her voice rose in a challenge.

"They my sisters. My responsibility. Not yours."

She blinked, her oddly colored eyes clear as her brows puckered above them. Then she turned to Red Beads, who hadn't moved. "Is this true?"

"Yes." His sister's voice was barely a whisper.

To his astonishment, Mourning Dove's mouth twisted, and she stepped around the soldier and took Red Beads by the hand. "I have a brother as w-w-well. If you ever need anything, you have only to ask me. If I can assist you, I s-s-shall."

Red Beads nodded, then took Shining Day by the arm and urged her toward the fort's gate with a look over her shoulder at Koyen.

Mourning Dove lifted her chin and faced Koyen again. "I meant only to assist them in s-s-selling their baskets."

The soldier took her by the elbow. "We really must be on our way, Miss Aldridge."

Miss Aldridge—Mourning Dove—lifted the hem of her ridiculously wide skirt and pivoted away from Koyen.

He should have followed his sisters, but he stood like an oak tree planted beside the river, watching the sway of her skirts as she marched to the castle.

ABIGAIL'S HANDS WERE STILL SHAKING AS SHE entered her uncle's room and took her seat. His door had been open, so she hadn't needed to knock, and he'd barely glanced up when she'd entered. Just as well. He didn't need to notice her undoubtedly flustered appearance.

She took a moment to let her breathing settle and then picked up her pen. She'd have to be careful not to spatter any ink. And why?

All because she'd spoken to a bare-chested man in full view of several witnesses and while under the protection of Ensign Tharp. A savage, no less. Although, he hadn't sounded like a savage. His words were oddly accented, his sentences missing a few words but perfectly understandable, just like his sister's.

The one sister, anyway, Red Beads. The other had never spoken. That one frowned and looked anything but pleased.

A friendly sister, a scowling sister, and an intimidating brother with broad shoulders, dark eyes, and a fierce expression that put his little sister's to shame.

"Uncle?"

"Hm?" He didn't look up from the map spread across his desk.

"Do all the s-s-savages s-s-speak English?"

"Hm? What?" He looked up then and blinked at her. "No, of course not. Whyever would you ask?"

"I met three today, and two of them s-s-spoke English. P-p-

49

perhaps the third did as w-w-well, but s-s-she did not s-s-speak at all."

"Where did you—Tharp!"

The ensign stepped into the room, having taken up his post when they'd returned. "Sir?"

"Where did you take my niece that she was exposed to Indians?" The growl in his voice was unmistakable. No wonder the ensign's Adam's apple bobbed.

"Uncle, the ensign did not take me anywhere. W-w-we s-s-strolled around the inside of the fort."

Uncle Corne waved a hand at her. "Let him speak."

"As she said, sir, we strolled around the fort. Two young Indian women joined us at the forest gate, and then Scout Koyen came for them when we were at the sutlers' tents."

"Koyen?"

"Indeed, sir. 'Twould appear the young women are his sisters."

"Hm." Uncle Corne slipped one finger under his wig and scratched. "He's a top scout. Brought us good information." He then pinned Abigail with a hard stare. "I hear he learned English as a lad from Moravian missionaries."

"Is he a friendly Indian, then?" she asked, not even sure there was such a thing.

"Friendly? What?" Uncle Corne waved Tharp from the room, the man easing the door closed behind him. "No, my dear, I do not believe he is friendly. Useful? Indeed. Especially considering the news they just brought in. But I believe any of them would as soon slit our throats as take our coin." He waved a hand at the paper still on her desk. "Do you have what you need to compile those lists?"

"I do. Thank you, Uncle."

"Finish them quickly. I have need to send a letter off—two copies—ready to go at first light. We have no time to dawdle."

"S-s-straight away."

As soon slit our throats as take our coin. That phrase kept flitting through her mind as Abigail created the lists her uncle needed. Red Beads's brother, perhaps. He certainly looked wild enough. But the young women? Red Beads had seemed so open, trusting even. Had things been different, someone Abigail would have been happy to call a friend.

Her pen stopped, poised above the paper.

Everything *was* different. She was at the edge of civilization with only her uncle and a stack of paperwork. No Boston busy-bodies. No conventional rules. No social norms. Well... not too many, anyway. She brushed the quill's feathered end against her cheek. Should she see Red Beads again, Abigail had every intension of reaching out to her. In friendship. Across the divide of white and red skin. Just two young women who—if they searched—might find commonality. They certainly had one thing in common.

Overbearing brothers.

As soon slit our throats as take our coin. Indeed, that seemed to fit Red Beads's brother. Abigail suppressed a delicate shiver. He was all male in a way she'd never encountered before. In a way that made Bartlett appear a fop in comparison.

In a way she would never trust.

THE VILLAGE CHIEFS SAT FACING THE FIRE AND listening, faces unreadable, as Tall Otter finished his report of all he and Koyen had seen and heard. Koyen itched to add more detail, but as the youngest man in the circle, it was not his place to speak unless spoken to. The clan mothers sat to one side, also listening, faces no more readable than the chiefs'.

"Koyengquahtah, do you agree with Tall Otter?" one of the chiefs asked.

Koyen stood. "I do. I would add that there was much activity around the fort now called Pitt. Many people, and most not wearing red coats."

One of the clan mothers leaned forward. "What do you think of that?"

"The burned cabins in the surrounding area may mean the whites who survived took refuge in the fort."

The eldest chief grunted. "A wise observation."

"Meaning more guns," another chief spoke. "More men to keep watch."

"And more mouths to feed," Koyen said.

His mother nodded at him. They'd already had a similar discussion around her fire the evening before.

"Tall Otter." The oldest chief turned to the other man. "Do you agree?"

The older scout nodded. "The tribes there may be able to wait until those in the fort are hungry enough to come out. Or until they run out of bullets for their muskets and shot for their cannons."

"Which would not work at the fort here." Many eyes turned to Koyen then, so he continued. "Fort Niagara is backed by Lake Ontario. The British have ships to bring them food and ammunition. To bring them more soldiers. Even if we sent out many canoes, the cannons in the castle would tear them apart before we could reach a ship to take it over."

He let the truth of his words settle onto the wise heads around him.

"We must take time to think on all you have told to us." The eldest chief waved his hand in dismissal.

Tall Otter and Koyen left the fire.

"What do you think they will decide?" Koyen asked.

"It is hard to tell. There is much wisdom in that circle." He cut his eyes toward Koyen with a smirk. "And much procrastination."

"If they would join us to the tribes rising with Pontiac—"

"They would be going against the rest of the Iroquois Nation."

A weight settled on Koyen's chest. As much as he wished his tribe to join with the Ottawa chief to the west, it would come at a price. The Iroquois Nation had been together for generations. His father's father's father would not have remembered its beginning. They lived in peace together, the Seneca, Mohawk, Oneida, Cayuga, Onondaga, and Tuscarora, joined by a common language, traditions, and understanding. To be the tribe that pulled away from the others... would not be a small thing.

The other tribal leaders had already made it plain that the Iroquois should stay out of Pontiac's war. But what if they had it wrong?

Koyen strode off by himself, going to a favorite place in the forest, where he sat on a large rock to think. Between the leafy branches, wispy pines, and bristly spruce, he could see the great lake, the sun gleaming off its rippling waters.

The fort was not in sight, but he could picture it, bustling with soldiers drilling, others working, the clang of the blacksmith's hammer, the yeasty scent of the bake house, the imposing structure of the castle. Once it hadn't been there. Once this had all been Seneca land.

As it should be.

There were stories—very old stories—of a people who lived here before the Seneca. So old the truth of them was lost. Perhaps a people had been here before, but the Seneca had claimed the land for more generations than the Iroquois Nation had existed. It didn't belong to them as a pair of moccasins belonged to a man, but it belonged to them as a place to live and use and watch over. A place to be in peace.

Until the white man had come with his guns and metal and cloth, changing forever the ways of the Seneca. Did not the chiefs and clan mothers wear metal knives at their belts? Woven cloth against their bodies? Did not each chief have a musket as well as an iron-tipped lance?

As much as he hated to admit it, the white man had brought many things to the Seneca that made their lives easier. But was easier better? That was the question he wrestled with. His father had hunted with a bow and arrows. He'd provided for his family, both meat and hides. Before the war, when the French had passed out muskets to all, his father had sat by the fire in the winter months chipping stones to make arrowheads, hardening shafts, and drying fletching. Rarely had Koyen's family gone hungry.

When he'd died, the responsibility to provide had fallen to Koyen.

Instead of chipping stones, and because he'd learned the English language, Koyen had gone to scout for the British. What did that make of him? Could he provide for his mother and sisters without the British coins he earned? Without his musket? His stomach twisted into a sour knot.

If they did not beat back the British and reclaim who they were—or who they had been—the Seneca would not survive. At least, not how they'd been for generations upon generations. Koyen wanted to be the type of warrior his father had been.

But could he?

Chapter 7

The commotion outside reached Uncle Corne's open window, pulling Abigail from her work. She rose and stretched, walking to the window behind her uncle's desk. He'd stepped out for a while. She leaned against the frame but could see nothing other than the milling of soldiers on the grounds around the front of the castle.

A lot of soldiers, several of whom led mules.

A tendril of fear worked its way up her back. Abigail had written the letters for her uncle relaying the scouts' reports of Indians massing to attack Fort Pitt. Uncle Corne had assured her that Fort Pitt was many days' travel away from Fort Niagara, and that the Indian tribes involved were not those surrounding them.

She shuddered. Indians surrounding them.

But they were safe in the castle. The building even had an indoor well. If forced to withdraw to the stone fortress itself, the soldiers could defend it for weeks, having enough stored provisions and a supply of fresh water. The cannons under the dormers would drive away attempts to storm the building.

They were quite safe at Fort Niagara.

But who were the men below? Where had they come from?

Uncle Corne burst through the door, and Abigail jumped.

"Push whatever you are working on to the side, my dear. We must pen letters, with all haste."

"W-w-what is happening, Uncle?"

He pivoted to face her, lines etched across his forehead under the white wig. "Poor news, I fear. Dire. Fort Detroit is under attack by the Indian chief called Pontiac."

Abigail gasped.

"Now, now, 'tis a long distance from us here."

"As far as Fort P-p-pitt?"

"Farther, and I fear 'twill make getting assistance there even more difficult." He pulled out his desk chair and dropped into it. "But we must try. Pen these words."

Abigail hurried to her chair and grabbed a fresh sheet of paper, barely getting her quill in her hand before Uncle Corne's words rolled over her. Dire words, indeed. She forced her hand not to shake as she penned them, forced her breath to remain even and measured.

Forced herself not to think of those in a far-off fort, surrounded and outnumbered by a mass of savages, requesting help from hundreds of miles away.

By the time she'd completed the letter and started copying it to send up the chain of command, she was exhausted. Not physically, but emotionally. And for the first time, she almost wished herself back in Boston. Back where news of the frontier was just something printed in the daily paper. Where the thought of men and women living in forts seemed romantic. Where danger was something far away and slightly thrilling to contemplate.

A quick rap sounded before Ensign Tharp opened the door. "Sir, Scout Koyen to see you."

"Send him in." Uncle Corne didn't even glance up.

Abigail shouldn't have either, but she couldn't help herself.

Shirtless, as usual, the man entered the room on silent feet.

He approached Uncle Corne's desk, but not before his onyx eyes met hers.

A shiver worked its way across her skin, leaving gooseflesh in its wake. What was there about this man—aside from his constant state of undress—that bothered her so? After seeing him with his sisters, she might think it was a resemblance to Bartlett, albeit not physical, except that she'd felt the same before she'd met his sisters.

He stood in silence before Uncle Corne. Even in stillness, his presence radiated strength and danger.

Ensign Tharp must have noticed it as well, for he stayed in the room, watching the scout from behind.

Uncle Corne set aside the missive he'd been reading and looked up at the scout. "What other bad news do you have for me?"

From the side, it looked as if his lips twitched. In humor? Or something more sinister?

"I want return with men to Fort Schlosser. Hear more from others from sloop."

"Do you think we have not heard the whole truth of the matter at Fort Detroit?" Suspicion filled her uncle's voice.

"I answer better when I return."

Uncle Corne steepled his fingers and peered over them at the scout. "If Sergeant Hagerman has no other use for you, I have no objection."

The scout had made it almost to the door, passing in front of Ensign Tharp, when Uncle Corne's words stopped him.

"Speak to the other scouts while you are there. Find out how many tribes are massing around Fort Detroit. We need to know who and how many we are up against."

The Seneca man turned and met Uncle Corne's stare. "This I do."

Uncle Corne nodded, the scout left, and Ensign Tharp followed him out and closed the door.

"Uncle Corne?"

"Um?"

"You said that scout was useful."

"He is." Her uncle pressed a finger and thumb against the bridge of his nose. "I hope to God he remains on our side."

Abigail suppressed a gasp. "You think he might not?"

"At the moment, my dear, I know not what to think. At the moment, I wish you were back in Boston with your brother." He sighed. "But returning you is impossible now that we are at war again."

At war with men like the one who had just left the room, the one whose dark eyes had seemed to see right through her.

MOURNING DOVE'S EYES HAD BEEN SHADOWED WITH fear as Koyen entered the captain's room. While he should have been happy to see it there, happy to know that the British understood the war was underway, for some reason, he wasn't.

He left the stone building, entering into the bright sunshine to the bawling of mules and shouting of men. Men in red coats, men in buckskins, and several other scouts with bare chests. Koyen joined Tall Otter.

"Did you speak with the captain?" the older scout asked.

"I did."

"And will you go to the lower fort"—Tall Otter tipped his chin toward the milling crowd—"with them."

"If Sergeant Hagerman will spare me." Koyen turned to face him. "Will you go with me?"

"To what end?"

It wasn't really a question. Tall Otter was well aware that

Koyen's loyalty didn't lie with the British. But Koyen answered anyway. "To learn more from the scouts from Detroit who came on the sloop."

"Do you think they left them behind at Fort Schlosser for a reason?"

Did he? Maybe. The level of urgency was understandable, but the undercurrent of something more pulled at him. He couldn't know unless he spoke with them. "I would find out."

"You may hear something you do not wish to know."

Koyen cut a glance at the crowd, then back to Tall Otter. "What do you mean?"

"I am not sure." The other man shrugged. "Something about this feels... off."

"Then you will go with me?"

A long moment dragged out between them. "I will."

Koyen strode toward the sergeant, somewhat surprised that Tall Otter followed.

Martin Hagerman was a small man with a big temper. He was dressing down a soldier who had mismanaged loading a mule's pack saddle. Koyen waited until the little man ran out of words, then stepped forward.

"Tall Otter and I want go to Fort Schlosser with them." He tipped his chin toward the soldiers.

"Why?" The single word came out at almost a shout, while the sergeant scowled at them.

"Learn from scouts there."

He ran a gloved hand over his whiskery face. "Might not be a bad idea, at that. Go." Then he turned and tested the mule's reloaded pack saddle.

Koyen caught the look of a pair of men who'd overheard them. Men from Fort Schlosser or maybe Fort Detroit, men he didn't know. They were not from Fort Niagara. They didn't look happy, but then, if they'd arrived from Fort Detroit—a fort surrounded by Pontiac's gathered forces—they had little to be happy about.

And would put little trust in the Indian scouts, no doubt. It was good that Tall Otter had agreed to join him. To watch his back.

Within the hour, accompanying twenty laden mules and twice as many men, they started on the long overland trail to the lower fort. Koyen hefted one of the many packs, as did Tall Otter.

Canoes were impossible to use on the river. Its length was full of rapid waters, rocks, and falls that would tear the vessels apart. The overland trail had been worn down by Indian moccasins for countless generations, but the British had nearly finished the process of widening it for wagon use. Soon they'd be moving far more goods and materials between the forts, including the weapons of war like gunpowder, lead, cannon balls, and even the weighty cannons themselves. And food to feed the army, like the barrels of salted pork and wheat flour loaded on the mules ahead of him.

The British with their roads and supplies could outlast Pontiac's forces... unless the Seneca put a stop to it.

———

"You must need a break, Abigail." Uncle Corne waved a hand at her without looking up. "Go. Take a walk. Breathe some fresh air. Tell Tharp I said to escort you."

"Thank you. I w-w-will." She stood and stretched, first her shoulders, then her neck, and finally her fingers. She pulled her shawl from the back of her chair and wrapped it around her shoulders before stepping into the hall. "Ensign Tharp—"

"I heard." The young Viking touched his ear. "Anyone on this floor would have."

Abigail forced a wan smile. Any other day, his humor would have made her laugh, but after writing the letters…

Ensign Tharp offered his arm, and she took it gladly. "Thank you."

"Where would you like to go?"

"S-s-somewhere w-w-without p-p-paper or ink." Her voice must have conveyed her weariness, for his expression turned sympathetic.

"He is working you too hard."

"Oh, no." She couldn't have him thinking her weak. "'Tis only that the news from the w-w-west is s-s-so dire."

He patted her hand. "It can be harsh on the frontier. We are fortunate to be here at Fort Niagara, so close to civilization."

So close? How many days had she and other women sailed on the *Huron* before reaching the fort? How long had it been since they'd arrived? She searched her memory for the last date she'd written on a letter for her uncle.

Four weeks. Not quite a month. And so much had changed for her.

Before landing on the shore behind the castle, she'd never have consented to walking around the fort escorted by a man she barely knew without so much as a maid in tow and in full view of whoever might be looking out the windows. Not only had she consented—again—but her uncle had suggested it. A month before, such a thing would have been scandalous.

After writing letters about the uprising at Fort Detroit, recounting the random killings that had occurred, the foiled plot for Pontiac's warriors to gain the fort, and the urgent need for more men, ammunition, and supplies, the stroll around the fort with Ensign Tharp seemed trivial at best.

Smoke from the bake house permeated the air. She drew in a long breath in appreciation, which started her stomach growling. She pressed her hand to her middle.

"Perhaps we should start at the bake house." There was an underlying tone of humor in the ensign's voice.

"No, let us finish there instead." The need to walk outweighed her need to eat. And it was peaceful with all the mules and men gone. Had Red Beads's brother left with them? "Let us w-w-walk near the w-w-water."

"As you wish." He managed a rather courtly half-bow without letting her hand slip from his arm.

They strolled to the far side of the castle, which was backed by loose sand. A refreshing breeze from over the lake blew through the wide gates of the palisade. So much water, and so clean. Boston's harbor was noisy, dirty, and reeked of brine. It was also overpopulated with unwashed sailors and language saltier than the sea. She'd never set foot there, and tended to pull the carriage curtains rather than view it when they needed to drive past.

She could spend the entire day in front of the view before her. It was... glorious.

Or it would have been, had not the dark shadow of an Indian uprising lurked to the west.

She shivered.

"You are cold. Let us return to the castle."

She wasn't cold, not on the outside, but she allowed him to escort her to the bake house.

Lurana Quinn wielded a huge wooden paddle against a mound of dough, glancing up as they entered. "What can I do for you?"

Abigail's stomach rumbled the answer for her.

The half-Indian woman grinned. "I know that sound. What is your pleasure today? I have fresh scones with dried apple or bannocks or"—she held up one floury finger—"shortbreads."

Abigail's mouth watered at the mention of shortbreads. The buttery sweet biscuits had always been her favorite. But she needed more than that to fill her empty middle. "May I have one of each? I w-w-will s-s-share w-w-with my uncle, of course."

Lurana Quinn wrapped the baked goods, including four of the shortbreads, in a cloth.

Abigail reached for the offering when something brushed her skirts against her ankles. "Oh!"

"There now," Lurana Quinn said. "Leave the lady be."

Ensign Tharp chuckled.

Wrapping around Abigail's ankles was a huge gray cat—not a mouse—with eyes the color of pure amber. Abigail tucked the cloth-bound baked goods in one arm and knelt to touch the cat. The animal arched its back and then butted its head against Abigail's hand as if insisting on more attention.

"She is demanding, that one, but I could not run the bake house without her."

"What does s-s-she do?" Abigail had never touched a cat before. Her brother disliked them and refused to allow one on their property. She knew no one in Boston who allowed such an animal in a building other than a barn. And those cats scattered when people came near.

"She keeps the mice away from my flour bins." Lurana Quinn approached and lifted the animal, holding it against her aproned front. "She is worth her weight in gold, as her babies will be."

"S-s-she is expecting?"

"They are already here. Come and see."

Abigail followed the baker woman into the farthest corner of the large room of the bake house. In a box lined with soft cloths curled a colorful assortment of furry lumps. They didn't look like cats. They looked more like the mice they would one day help keep away from the flour bins.

"How many are there?"

"Seven. Too many to keep them all here, but I will select one.

A female." Lurana Quinn let the mother cat down. It went to the babies and fussed over them.

"W-w-why a female?"

"In the cat world, 'tis the females who hunt. The males, they are too lazy to be bothered."

"I s-s-saw a mouse in my chamber the other day. P-p-perhaps I need a female cat as w-w-well."

The little woman's eyebrows rose. "Then one is yours as soon as they are old enough to leave their mama."

Ensign Tharp cleared his throat. "Your uncle might not agree, Miss Aldridge."

She flashed him her best smile. "Or then again, he might."

Lurana Quinn grasped Abigail's free arm. "Never you worry. I will teach you how to care for one, as my husband taught me."

Abigail returned to her uncle's room with her cloth full of nourishment and her heart full of hope. She wasn't sure why, but the prospect of having a cat of her own made life in the castle seem... brighter, somehow.

Chapter 8

The trek up from Fort Schlosser was much quicker than the journey down. With no balky mules or heavy burdens, Koyen and Tall Otter covered the same trail in less than half the time the next day. But while his feet moved swiftly, Koyen's mind churned with unhappy news.

The French would not return.

One of the scouts, a stout Huron with an impressive display of tattoos, had whispered of a letter—read to Pontiac by a captive British soldier—from the Great Father in France. The letter said the French soldiers would return no more to fight the British.

Pontiac had taken the letter and hidden it away. The leader of the Ottawa wished for the French to return. His purpose in the war was to clear the path for that to happen. He still considered the French and Ottawa to be as brothers.

Tall Otter slowed and stopped next to the cliff that fell away into a deep gorge hiding a cave that was supposed to house an evil spirit. Koyen had been taught as a boy, as were all young Seneca, to avoid the gorge and the cave. It was told that voices could be heard there, and that only one man had ever lived to tell what they said, but he had been driven out of his mind.

"You are deep into your thoughts." Tall Otter's words brought Koyen back to the present.

"I cannot stop thinking about what the Huron told us."

"The letter."

Koyen nodded.

"Why does it disturb you?"

"What if Pontiac decides not to fight?"

Tall Otter moved to the base of a tall tree and squatted beside it, resting his back against its rough bark. "Then he will decide not to fight. It does not concern the Seneca."

"But it should!" Koyen paced in front of the other man. "If he can bring the tribes together, then we could be a part of it. We"—he thumped his fist to his chest—"could join in the fight to push the British back to the sea."

Tall Otter nodded, his face unreadable, his eyes focused on something behind Koyen. Or maybe on nothing at all. "When I was a young man, I dreamed of a great fight to remove the white man." His attention snapped back to Koyen. "When the French came and asked us to fight beside them against the British, I thought it was the answer to my dream."

"You fought with the French, as did so many of our warriors."

"We lost that fight. The French left. They are not coming back."

Koyen squatted in front of him. "Then we must drive away the British by ourselves, the Seneca and the tribes who will fight beside us."

Tall Otter's mouth pulled to the side, as if he'd tasted something sour. "If we could not best the British with muskets, gun powder, and lead given us by the French, then how will we do it without those things?" He glanced toward the forest. "How would we feed our families without the French providing barrels of salted meat and corn? We cannot hunt food and British at the same time. Our numbers are too few."

"If the Iroquois tribes come together—"

"They will not."

Koyen jerked back as if he'd been slapped by the words. "How do you know this?"

"Sir William Johnson."

Koyen dropped the rest of the way to the ground. Sir William Johnson was a much-trusted man. Even though he was British, he had always dealt fairly with the Iroquois tribes. He'd even taken a Mohawk woman as his wife, and they lived among the Mohawk. The man would not turn against his own people, however deeply ingrained he was with the Iroquois. And he was deeply ingrained enough to command respect… and loyalty. The Mohawk would listen to him.

Leaves fluttered in the tops of the trees, branches swayed, and a gust of wind rushed across the wide expanse of the gorge, creating a mournful sound. One that matched Koyen's mood.

"Come, before the wind awakens the evil spirit below." Tall Otter rose and broke into a relaxed run, a pace he could keep for many miles, if needed.

Koyen followed but glanced back at the gorge. Was it just the wind that made the noise? Or was there something more sinister below? He kept his attention on the trail ahead. Better to concentrate on what he would tell the chiefs and clan mothers upon their return.

Whether Pontiac fought on or not, Koyen wanted to see the white men out of Fort Niagara and away from Seneca lands. He wanted life to go back to how it was supposed to be. How it had been. He adjusted the strap across his chest that held his musket to his back.

He wasn't ready to let go of that piece of the white man's influence… yet.

A SHARP RAP ON THE DOOR INTERRUPTED ABIGAIL'S train of thought as she diligently transcribed some of the more boring documents for her uncle. Tedious reports of the provisions used and needed by the soldiers in the fort.

"Enter!" Behind his desk, Uncle Corne's voice was sharp, but then it had been since the news from Fort Detroit. All the officers were concerned for the contingent of ninety-six men who'd left Fort Niagara, bound for Fort Detroit, a fortnight before word had come of the hostilities there. A unit of British soldiers and rangers led by Lieutenant Abraham Cuyler.

Ensign Tharp entered, tossing her a glance as had become his customed before placing a sealed letter on Uncle Corne's desk. Then he turned to leave.

"Wait." Her uncle removed a knife from his belt and slit the thick wax. "This may require an answer." He scanned the document before letting it fall to the desktop. He planted his elbows on the desk, and let his head fall into his hands, fingers covering his face.

"W-w-what is it, Uncle?"

When he raised his face to hers, she wished the question back.

"Fort Sandusky has fallen. The garrison there... slaughtered."

Ensign Tharp's breath whistled from the doorway.

Abigail gripped the soft fabric of her fichu near her throat. It was one thing to know war was brewing in some faraway place. It was another to see the anguish on her uncle's face. To realize he probably knew some of the men who had died. She shivered.

Slaughtered.

"I am sorry, my dear." He rose and came to her desk, taking her hand. "I should not have blurted it out so abruptly. Such a shock." He patted her knuckles. "Do you need to retire? Perhaps lie down for a while?"

Abigail rose to wobbly legs. Perhaps she did need to get a bit of air. "I believe a w-w-walk w-w-will do me good."

"Then go. Tharp, escort her."

The ensign opened the door, and Abigail pushed past him into the corridor. She didn't slow her pace, but he caught up to her with long strides. She all but ran down the steps, across the vestibule, and out the door of the castle. The warm June sun hit her like a slap in the face. It should have been gray, cloudy, dreary. How could the weather be fine and agreeable when so many men lay dead on the ground?

"What is it, Miss Aldridge?" The ensign touched her sleeve and halted her headlong flight.

"They are dead. All the men at that fort."

He stepped closer to her and glanced around as if expecting danger in the fort. "'Tis a possibility all soldiers face."

She grasped his sleeve and looked at him directly. The color had leached from his face. "'Tis an awful thing. Did you... did you know any of them?"

"I did."

"I am s-s-so s-s-sor-sor..." She hated that being flustered or distressed made her stammer that much more pronounced.

"Sorry. As am I."

She couldn't bring herself to resent him finishing her sentence. The grief on his face was plain to see. He looked at the barracks, then back to her. "Miss Aldridge—"

"Go. There must be others you w-w-wish to tell the news. Others w-w-who s-s-should hear."

"You will stay by the castle?"

"I w-w-will visit Lurana Quinn." She gave him a little shove toward the barracks. "Go."

"If you are sure—?"

"I am."

He sprinted away, and Abigail turned to the bake house. There were no delicious aromas floating on the breeze. Lurana Quinn did not fire the ovens every day. If the woman wasn't there, at least Abigail could visit the kittens.

She pushed open the door to the ever-present muted scents of yeast and spices that must have clung to the very walls of the structure.

"Hello?"

Nobody answered. Abigail continued to the far corner and knelt beside the kittens' box. It had been less than a week since she'd met the kittens, but they'd changed. Tiny ears now perked at her voice, and two of them blinked cloudy eyes at her. They were an assortment of colors, from a rich ginger to the stormy gray of their mama. One in particular caught Abigail's eye. It had both gray and orange and even a smidgen of white on its nose and chest.

"Who has left my door open?" Lurana Quinn's voice entered before her. "Come, girls, and we will see what I have left over, if my larders have not been robbed in my absence."

Abigail stood.

"Ah, 'tis not for my bread that you came, but for the kittens, aye?" A smile spread across the small woman's face.

"I hope I have not overstepped—"

"Nay." The baker woman waved away Abigail's attempted apology. "Visit them as you wish. 'Twould be good if you formed a bond with one." Then she turned and urged someone to enter the bake house. "Come. The lady will not bite you."

Through the door stepped Red Beads and Shining Day.

"'Tis good to s-s-see you again." Abigail meant it. She'd thought of the girls almost daily since their brother had practically run them off from the fort.

"You know each other?" The baker's eyebrows and voice both rose.

"She buy baskets," Red Beads said.

Shining Day scowled and crossed her arms over her chest.

"Beautiful baskets." Abigail stepped forward. "And I have need of another now."

Red Beads grinned and wove her fingers in that strange way she had. Whatever it meant, the scowl on her sister's face lessened.

"Lurana Quinn is giving me a kitten." She pointed to the box. "When they are old enough. I will need a basket for the animal to sleep in." It hadn't occurred to her until that moment, but it would give her an excuse to spend more time with the Indian women.

"An excellent idea." Lurana Quinn rubbed her chin, the other hand planted on her slender hip. "I could use another basket or two here in the bake house. Then I would not have to threaten those who borrow one to return it with all haste."

Red Beads's fingers flew.

"W-w-what is that you are doing?" The words left Abigail before she could think of how impertinent they were. But the others didn't seem offended.

"'Tis hand-talk," Lurana Quinn answered, also moving her hands.

Shining Day nodded, her fingers as nimble and graceful as the others.

"For w-w-what purpose?"

"Sister not hear. White man's red spots stop her ears. She very young."

"I am s-s-so," Abigail concentrated to get the next word out, "s-s-s-sorry."

"'Tis not uncommon," the baker woman said.

"No, 'tis not, even among my p-p-people. S-s-scarlet fever

outbreaks are heartbreaking." She faced Shining Day. "I w-w-wish it had not happened to you."

Red Beads's fingers flew, and Shining Day watched them, but she did not answer. What resentment must she harbor against the people who had brought the disease from across the ocean? Abigail had read enough, and heard enough, to know that many such diseases had taken a terrible toll on the Indian population. Such a tragedy.

Like the tragedy to the west, where an entire garrison had been wiped out.

By Indians.

"Miss Aldridge, are you well?" Lurana Quinn's voice came from a distance, piercing the panic that had made Abigail flee the castle in the first place.

"I am. 'Tis just..." She pressed the back of her wrist to her forehead. "P-p-perhaps I w-w-will return to my chamber and lie down for a w-w-while."

Abigail fled the bake house and didn't stop until she'd shut and locked the door to her chamber behind her. How did one make sense of it all? Hundreds of miles away, Indians had killed —slaughtered according to her uncle—the garrison at Fort Sandusky. But in the bake house, Abigail had chatted with two Indians—or two and a half with Lurana Quinn—as if they were neighbors and friends.

It made no sense.

In Boston, one knew the rules. One stayed in her own social circle. Or was shunned by it for a stammer. Abigail dropped onto her bed and buried her face in her hands.

Somehow, she had to come to grips with a world much more complex—and dangerous—than she could have ever imagined from the frilly four-poster bed in her half-brother's house.

She raised her head and squeezed her hands together until they ached. Red Beads had seemed friendly enough each time they'd met. Perhaps that was the place to start. Perhaps Lurana Quinn would assist. Because somehow, Abigail was going to make a place for herself at Fort Niagara, and that meant learning to reach out to those already living there. Even the army knew that, or they wouldn't hire men like Red Beads's brother to scout for them.

A shiver skittered across her skin as she remembered his last visit to her uncle. That he was dangerous, she had no doubt. Perhaps she was already learning to discern the difference between Indians.

Or perhaps she knew nothing at all.

Chapter 9

T he night air was filled with tobacco smoke and long-winded voices. The gathering of so many near Koyen's village was rare, but the activity to the west demanded they make a final decision. Koyen sat on the outer ring of those in attendance, listening and watching. Waiting for someone to stand up and declare that the Seneca should join with the forces in the west, the Ottawa and Huron and Pottawatomie, to remove the white man forever from their lands. What better time? Surrounding him were the chiefs from several different clans, important men who could sway those too timid to make the decision.

As each speaker spoke in circles, like a bee trying to find the perfect stalk of clover, Koyen's hopes sunk ever lower. He contemplated leaving, and would have, except it might have reflected poorly on his mother. She sat to the side with the rest of the clan mothers, also watching and listening.

There was a pause, and then a chief unfamiliar to Koyen stood. He was a large man, neither young nor old, straight as an arrow, with muscles that rippled beneath his bronze skin. A man to be reckoned with. A man to listen to.

With fiery words and expressive gestures, the man told those listening why the Seneca—the Keepers of the Western Gate—should join with Pontiac to push the British from their lands. Koyen restrained the whoop of agreement that boiled inside of him. In a less solemn gathering, he would have jumped to his feet and let it loose. Instead, he leaned forward, as did several others around him.

The man laid out the argument for the cause of fighting. How the British ignored the Seneca's claim to the land. How they had beaten the French and then closed their storehouses to the Seneca, forcing them to purchase items the French had freely given in exchange for the use of the land Fort Niagara rested upon. No more gifts had arrived to honor the chiefs. The British were not interested in being as brothers to the Seneca. No, the British cared only to rule over them. To treat them as a conquered people.

Koyen hung on every word—agreed with every word. When the man sat, it was as if Koyen had run many miles, so tight were his muscles.

The meeting broke up after that, each returning to his own clan.

Koyen strode to their longhouse and made his way to his mother's fire, which had been moved outside with the summer's heat. Red Beads and Shining Day worked with reeds, bending, twisting, and securing them into intricate patterns for baskets.

"Is it over?" Red Beads set her work aside and stirred the kettle over the fire, sending out the aroma of stewed fish.

"It is."

"Are we going to make war?" Shining Day's hands flicked the words at him.

"Perhaps," he signed back to her.

Their mother joined them before they could ask him more

questions. She ordered the girls to serve the meal first, and they would speak after.

Koyen barely tasted what he chewed and swallowed, his mind reliving the big man's words. Not just the words, but the way he delivered them. So confident in what he'd said, so dignified and yet fervent. The type of man other men paid attention to. He shot a glance at his mother. And clan mothers too.

"Come. Walk with me, Koyen," his mother said.

He hadn't expected that, but he rose and joined her on the trail that led to the big lake. It was all he could do to hold his silence as they moved beneath the trees. The crashing of waves against the sand greeted them as they arrived at the beach well east of the fort.

Once they stopped, he couldn't hold the words in any longer. "Why have we come here?"

"To talk. To think." She motioned to the water in front of them. "To appreciate the things that do not change." Then she settled onto the warm sand, tucking her feet beneath her skirt.

Koyen joined her so that they faced each other. "What did you think of the last man's speech?"

She smiled, more of a resigned look than a happy one. "I knew you would ask about him first."

"Do you know him?"

"I know of him. His name is Farmer's Brother."

He leaned forward, forearms resting on his crossed legs. "He is a man to be listened to." Surely she must have heard it, the sincerity in his voice. His logical arguments. His assurance that they could be part of something bigger than just the Seneca.

"I listened." But her voice was soft, almost melancholy.

"How could you not agree with his words?" At her raised eyebrows, he settled deeper into the sand. "I mean no disrespect, but he spoke from the heart." He slapped his open hand to his own chest. "And he spoke to mine."

"I know." She glanced to the water, the crash of the waves filling the silence that grew between them for long, uncomfortable moments. Then she turned back to him. "I also know that the war he spoke of will mean women without men at their fires, children without fathers, and more hardship for our people."

Her words also found their way to his heart, cooling some of the ardor left after Farmer's Brother's speech.

She had become that woman without a man at her fire. As his sisters had become children without a father when his father had died fighting alongside the French. That same loss had left him, barely a man, with the responsibility to care for them and their mother.

"To clear our lands of these white men, we must make sacrifices."

"Must we? Or could we negotiate a way to live together in harmony?" Her voice was still soft, but with a thread of strength woven through it. "Would it not be to the advantage of all to learn to live together?"

He shook his head before she'd finished her words. "Our people wish for different things, believe in different ways, and hold different values."

"Ah, yes." The smile she gave him then was more genuine, more the type she'd have given him as a young boy who had achieved something to be proud of. "You understand the difficulties." She held up her hand when he opened his mouth, so he snapped it shut. "But war is difficult as well. Its consequences last for many years, perhaps even many generations. We must think with both our heads and our hearts in this matter."

"I have—"

"I know your desire, my son. I ask only that you wait for the decision of the chiefs and clan mothers before you join this fight."

As much as it galled him, he nodded. To go against his clan mother was almost unthinkable.

"And know this, I allowed your sisters to go to the fort while you were gone south."

"Mother, it is not safe for them there."

"Since many of the men were gone, I allowed them to visit Lurana Quinn. While they were there—not at the sutlers' tents —the woman who had purchased their baskets before asked for another one."

Mourning Dove. Why did she take such interest in his sisters and their baskets?

"When they are finished, I will be sure they return in your company to deliver it."

Was that to be his life going forward? The guardian of his sisters, the provider for his mother, a warrior content to sit by the fire and... what? That was no life for a warrior.

ABIGAIL'S UNCLE HAD BEEN OUT FOR MOST OF THE morning, attending meetings with the rest of the senior officers. She had finished the work he'd left for her, still warm from his praise of her efficiency and diligence. She spread sand over the last words she'd penned, then brushed the paper clean once it had dried.

Someone knocked at the door. It was not Ensign Tharp's sharp rap, but somewhat more muted. Perhaps one of the women was looking for her. She rose and pulled the door open.

Red Beads and Shining Day filled the entrance, which would have brought a smile to Abigail had not their hulking, shirtless brother stood behind them. She averted her eyes from his chest to Red Beads's grin, then spread her hands.

"To w-w-what do I owe this unexpected visit?"

The Indian woman held out a square basket with six-inch sides, beautifully woven of some sort of sturdy reeds that had been dyed a mellow gold and two shades of green.

Abigail took the basket and retreated into the room. "Come inside. My uncle is away." They crossed the threshold, and she took the basket to examine it, turning it over in her hands. "'Tis exquisite craftsmanship. I am s-s-sure the kitten w-w-will find it a most comfortable bed. How much do I owe you?"

Red Beads cast a quick glance at her brother, then back at Abigail. "Twopence fine."

"Nonsense. 'Tis as large as the first, and I requested it s-s-special." But her money was secreted away in her chamber, and not in her pocket. It didn't seem right to leave them here in her uncle's room while she crossed the corridor, nor would it be proper—with their brother glowering at her—to invite them to her room.

"What is going on here?" Ensign Tharp's voice brought the answer to her dilemma.

"These young w-w-women have brought the basket I commissioned." Abigail strode to the door. "I need to fetch the coins for it. P-p-please see to their brother w-w-while I do." She turned back to Red Beads and Shining Day. "Come w-w-with me."

Ensign Tharp backed out of the doorway and allowed them to pass, then stepped back into the opening as if to block the scout's view of them. Abigail stifled a shiver at the mental image of the Viking and Indian meeting in battle over a doorway.

She slipped the key from her pocket and opened her chamber.

"You live here?" Red Beads asked, taking in the narrow bed and single chair with Abigail's dresses hanging from pegs in the wall.

"I do." She moved to her trunk and felt along its side to the stash of coins she kept there.

Shining Day fingered one of the dresses, a satiny burgundy Abigail should have left in Boston. She'd never have use for it in a frontier fort. But there'd been much she hadn't known when she'd packed for her impulsive journey. How differently she'd have packed and prepared if she'd known anything about the frontier.

She pulled the coins from their pouch and handed them to Red Beads, then looked around the cramped room. "W-w-where do you think I s-s-should p-p-put the basket for the kitten?"

That graceful dance of hands and fingers happened again, with Shining Day pointing to the corner nearest the window.

"Of course. On cold days, the kitten w-w-w-w..." She stopped and took a deep breath. "'Twill enjoy the s-s-sunshine."

Red Beads cocked her head. "Abigail Aldridge, one in our village speaks as you. She make hand-talk like Shining Day, understand better. I teach you?"

Abigail pressed her hand to her throat, robbed of any words for a moment. She knew this for what it was, an overture of friendship. Could she accept it? Boston Abigail would have laughed at the very idea, but Niagara Abigail was determined to change and fit in at the fort, and it gave her the courage to nod. "I w-w-would like that, very much." Even if she could only use it with the girls in front of her and Lurana Quinn.

Red Beads hands must have interpreted Abigail's response, but Shining Day frowned, then left the room.

"I sorry. Sister carries much anger."

"Because she lost her hearing?"

Red Beads nodded. "Father too."

"I am s-s-so s-s-s-s," Abigail gritted her teeth.

"Like this." Red Beads made a smooth motion. "Means same as sorry." She did it again.

Abigail repeated the motion, but Red Beads took her hands and repositioned them, guiding them through the next attempt. On the third try, the Indian woman nodded her approval.

It was a small thing—but it was a good start.

THE NIGHT SKY WAS CLEAR AND BRIGHT, EVERY STAR vying to outshine those around it. Night insects clicked, deep-throated frogs boasted to one another, and bat wings snapped on the breeze. Koyen was aware of all but not attending to any of it.

His mind tossed the words of Farmer's Brother against the words of Hill Woman, his mother and, perhaps more importantly for the moment, his clan mother.

He'd come out to his thinking spot on the big rock to wrangle his thoughts into submission. He'd promised his mother that he would not join the fight until a decision had been made by the elders, but once it was made, he was free to do as he saw fit.

In his heart, he wanted the white man gone. In his heart, he wanted things to return to how they had been for more generations than could be counted. But in his mind, his mother had planted doubt, doubt that had taken firm root.

And then there was Mourning Dove. Why the woman would pay attention to his sisters puzzled him. It puzzled him because she was obviously someone of importance to her people, and because her attention seemed genuine.

Years ago, a pair of Moravian missionaries had come to the Seneca to speak of their God and urge Koyen's people to join with their beliefs. Their attention had also been genuine. They had taught English to several of the young men and encouraged them to teach the words to any others who wished to learn.

Koyen had been eager, wide-eyed over the men who'd brought gifts to his people, who knew their language, and who had befriended them and lived among them. It had crushed him when they'd left—after the Seneca had chosen to fight alongside the French.

Was that crushing disappointment coloring his view of the white man still? Was it also the loss of his father to a British musket during the war? And was it the loss of Shining Day's hearing to the red-spotted disease the white man had brought to their shores?

He picked up a stick and used it to scratch his back.

More Seneca would die if they joined with Pontiac. His mother was wise to point that out. But how many would die of disease or British muskets or hunger from sharing their hunting grounds even if they didn't join the war?

That was the question. A question whose answer Koyen could not know.

Chapter 10

"Abigail, we are at war." Uncle Corne thumped his hand on his desk.

"I know w-w-we are." She took a deep breath and moved to stand before his desk. "But p-p-perhaps if w-w-we reached out to the Indians around us, w-w-we might not be embroiled in the w-w-war here." She pointed to the flagstone floor. "At Fort Niagara."

He dropped his elbow to the desk and leaned his forehead into his palm. "You do not understand the way of things, my dear." He raised troubled eyes to her. "You were gently reared in Boston, as you should have been. In truth, 'tis where you should still be." His voice rose as if gaining momentum with his argument. "There is no room for women's frippery aboard one of His Majesty's schooners. If I could put one more thing aboard the *Huron*"—he pointed at her—"'twould be you."

Abigail cringed inwardly. Her argument to ship the Indian women's baskets east might backfire and land her on the boat instead. The last thing she desired, even though at times life here had been... unnerving.

"'Tis not, however, possible," he said. "The vessels are running full of soldiers both ways with so many taking leave, stricken with illness, or mustering out. On the way here, 'tis reported the men are sleeping in the open on deck. There is not a cabin to be had for a young woman traveling alone." He skewered her with a pointed look. "And less room for the baskets of some heathen women."

"'Tis just that I w-w-wished to help them, Uncle, but I s-s-see the w-w-wisdom of your w-w-words."

His face softened. "You have a soft heart, my dear. A compassionate heart. While that is a desirable thing, it may yet cause you grief." He waved a hand toward the window. "The Indians are not like we British. They do not think as we do. They do not believe as we do. They do not have a society with structure as we do. Therefore, 'tis best not to get too involved with them."

Not get involved with them, when they lived all around the fort? When they came to trade and purchase? When they scouted for the army?

The brother of Red Beads had come only that morning to speak with her uncle, his cold eyes flicking past her as if she were nothing more than a spot on the wall.

She shivered and returned to her desk.

Perhaps where he was concerned, her uncle was correct. But Red Beads was another matter, and Abigail intended to enlist the aid of Lurana Quinn in building a friendship with the girl. She wove her hands in the movement that meant *sorry*. It'd been a week, and not a day had gone by that she didn't hunger to learn more of the Indian hand talk.

And poor Shining Day. While Abigail had been put off by the younger woman's perpetual scowl and ill humor, she couldn't imagine what it must be like to be deaf. And worse, to be able to blame that deafness on someone. The British—which included Abigail. How much more bitter would she be if she could blame her stammering on something or someone?

Oh, to be able to talk without stammering...

Even if it meant using her hands and only with the Indians.

———————

KOYEN JOINED THE CIRCLE OF YOUNG MEN AROUND A cold fire pit away from the village. He recognized about half of those gathered, but he'd heard that some came from Seneca villages a full day's run to the east.

The one who drew his attention and kept it was Farmer's Brother. He couldn't have been much older than Koyen, but he exuded an aura of leadership that was unmistakable. The same commanding presence that had brought them all to listen.

The man entered the middle of the circle and raised his hands. "My brothers, it is time we took action. It is time to strike at the soldiers who live in the fort, who squat on our land without gifts to acknowledge our claim to it."

A low murmur rippled through the crowd, tightening the tension across Koyen's chest. These warriors were ready, like a musket primed to fire.

He mentally shook himself. He needed to think like a Seneca —not a white man. He closed his eyes and envisioned a bow string pulled to its limits, an arrow notched, a glistening stone arrowhead chiseled to perfection, and fletchings from a turkey aligned for a perfect flight. His blood pumped faster, warmer, stronger. He opened his eyes, and looked directly into those of Farmer's Brother.

"You are a scout at the fort," the big man said, for it wasn't a question.

"I am."

"And you are here with us." He glanced around the circle then back at Koyen. "This is good. You will continue there unnoticed and will tell us when parties of soldiers are to leave the fort."

He turned to the whole gathering again. "We will be waiting, and we will strike when the soldiers are outside the walls. When they are exposed. When they do not expect us."

The murmuring broke into a long discussion of how they would accomplish the strikes. Who would contact whom and where Farmer's Brother would be. That he was the leader went without question.

His mother's words gathered into a knot in the back of Koyen's head, but he pushed them aside. He would not be taking up his musket—or arrows—against the British. Not joining the fight. His lot was to feed information to the others.

To be a spy.

He shifted on the hard ground.

Others spoke of their future prowess, how many British they would kill, and their plans for the British they captured. They spoke of things that would bring them honor.

There was little honor in spying.

That morning, he'd gone to Captain Hayward's room. Mourning Dove had been bent over her desk, the quill in her fingers flicking across the paper in front of her. She'd glanced up, and those oddly colored eyes that fascinated him had rested on him for only an instant before she'd lowered her head again.

She feared him.

He could sense it, almost smell it, when he was around her. And yet, she had not left the room. She had courage, for all her halting, stammering speech.

But she needed to fear him.

Soon, he would be plotting against her people. Against her.

Why did that bother him? Was it because he wouldn't earn the same honor as those who fired the shots? Those who wielded the knives? He shifted again, and pushed the thoughts away. Spies were necessary in war. They always had been. They always would be.

The meeting broke up, and men melted into the forest without sound. Farmer's Brother approached Koyen as he stood.

"What we ask of you is no small thing."

"I know."

"But you would rather be in the fighting, am I right?" The man smiled, a genuine expression of understanding.

"I would, but I understand."

Farmer's Brother clouted him on the shoulder and moved on to speak to another.

Koyen headed back to the village, having gone no more than the length of a longhouse when Red Beads joined him.

"What are you doing here so late at night?" She needed a tether. He must speak to his mother about her again.

"I saw you leave."

He stopped and grasped her upper arms. "I will come and I will go, and you are not to follow me. Do you understand?"

She raised her chin. "Are you really going to spy for that man?"

She'd heard. He ground his teeth together and fought the urge to shake her.

"If I am, it is no concern of yours. Your concern is to help our mother until a man claims you for his wife. May that happen soon."

Her lips firmed into a straight line. "Maybe I have no wish to be a man's wife."

It was neither the time or the place to have that discussion with his willful, rebellious sister. Why couldn't she be more like Shining Day? That one was the dutiful daughter and sister.

"We are returning to the longhouse," he said. "I will be speaking to Mother about you."

That had her tucking her chin. Good.

"And you will tell no one what you have heard here"—he released her arm and waved a finger under her nose—"even

Mother. If you do, I will find a man to speak with Mother and bring bridal gifts. Do you understand?"

She nodded, not meeting his eyes.

Good. That threat should keep her silent. She was willful, but not stupid.

And she was his sister, so he had to trust her.

"Lurana Quinn?" Abigail called from the doorway of the bake house, still getting used to using the woman's full name rather than a more formal address.

"Who is there?" The smaller woman came from around a stack of barrels. "Ah, have you come to choose your kitten?"

In truth, she'd almost forgotten the box of furry creatures, so distracted she'd been by the idea of learning the Indian hand talk. She'd have been in the bake house days earlier had her uncle been able to spare her the time.

"Indeed, I w-w-would like that."

Lurana Quinn motioned her to follow. The kittens had doubled in size and no longer resembled rodents. Round eyes blinked back at Abigail, and when she touched the first kitten, it arched its thin back. Its delicate tail pointed to the rafters.

"They are darling."

The other woman nodded.

"W-w-where is the mother?"

"She hunts all the time now to keep them fed."

"You do not feed them?"

The baker woman looked around, although there were only the two of them present, then lowered her voice. "The mama cat can care for her babies, but sometimes I sneak them a bit of milk, and sometimes I soak a little bread in it." She pressed her finger to her lips.

Abigail giggled. There were only six cows to supply the fort with milk for butter and cheese. She knew that from the reports she'd copied for Uncle Corne. There would be many who would berate the baker for feeding any of it to a box full of kittens. But not Abigail.

"Your s-s-secret is s-s-safe w-w-w-w…"

Lurana Quinn touched her shoulder, and Abigail met her eyes. There was only kindness there, not condemnation. Then the other woman made a graceful gesture.

"It means, thank you. I thank you for keeping my secret."

Hope blossomed in Abigail. "W-w-will you teach me more of the hand talk?"

"When I can, but I am a busy woman." She mopped her forehead with the back of her hand. "I am in need of an assistant. Or maybe two. I should speak to Hill Woman, mama of Red Beads and Shining Day."

"W-w-would you?" Hope spilled over into her voice.

"Once a week, I think. Yes. On Fridays." The older woman nodded. "But today, you should choose your kitten. That John Stedman has been after me to take the rest to his stable. Says the mice eat as much of his feed as the horses." She squatted beside the box. "The first choice is yours."

"A female. You s-s-said that w-w-would be best."

"Yes." She lifted out the gray-and-orange kitten that had caught Abigail's eye before.

The kitten wrapped itself around Abigail's hands as it was placed there, its tiny claws leaving pinpricks on her skin. A rusty rumble vibrated against her fingers. "S-s-she is beautiful." She looked at Lurana Quinn. "W-w-what s-s-should I call her?"

"Call her?"

"W-w-what do you call her mother?"

"Cat."

Abigail grinned. "I w-w-will think on it and name this one s-s-something more original. Can I take her w-w-with me today?"

"Best to leave her with her mama for another fortnight. Cat will teach her to hunt, and that is what you wish her to do, yes?"

That had been her initial motivation, but as the furry creature climbed the front of Abigail's dress and nestled onto her shoulder, it claimed a bit of her heart. She'd never had a pet. Bartlett wasn't a hunter and so never kept a hound. They hadn't even had a bird, although there'd been a gilded cage stored in the attic from some ancestor or another. Bartlett kept a riding horse and a pair of high-stepping carriage horses, but the stableman had always looked down his nose at her and her stammering, so she'd avoided the stables.

She unhooked the kitten's claws from her fichu and placed it back in the box. "S-s-soon, little one."

"I baked singing hinnies to go with tonight's meal. I will send some back with you. The officers will not miss a few."

"W-w-what are s-s-singing hinnies?"

"They are bread rounds fried on a griddle. They were a favorite of my husband." A faraway look came over the older woman's face. "When I make them, I think of him."

Abigail took the still-warm bread and thanked the baker. She'd hoped to persuade the woman to help her learn hand talk, but Lurana Quinn had suggested the perfect solution.

If only their mother would be receptive to Red Beads and Shining Day helping at the bake house on Fridays. And if Uncle Corne could spare her.

Or be convinced to.

Chapter 11

The woods were strangely silent as Koyen waited for Walks Fast to arrive. It was almost dark, the sun having dipped below the tree line, leaving its graying rays to smudge the sky above the forest. He was in the right place, and it was the agreed upon time. Where was the courier for Farmer's Brother?

The softest brush of leaves against buckskin was all that alerted him to Walks Fast's arrival. The fellow Seneca was shorter than Koyen, and more slender. He came from a different village, a different clan, but they were brothers nonetheless.

"You have news?" the other man asked.

"More soldiers arrived on a boat yesterday."

"How many?"

"It took six of their fat canoes to bring them all ashore."

The other man grimaced. "They spread like fleas on a dog."

Koyen took a deep breath. "A work party will leave the fort in the morning, heading for Lower Landing."

"How many men will go? How well armed will they be?"

Koyen shook his head. "I did not hear all the plans, only as much as I have told you."

Walks Fast pointed toward the fort. "We need details."

Frustration brewed in Koyen's middle. "If I appear to be listening, if I appear to be in places I should not be, then no one will speak in front of me." He squeezed his fists and then relaxed. "You must trust me on this. I will do what I can."

Walks Fast grasped Koyen's shoulder in a firm grip. "I do." And then he melted back into the forest.

Koyen headed for the longhouse, his middle grumbling with both hunger and dissatisfaction. While he'd always listened, watched, and learned during his time inside the fort, that it had become his mission changed everything.

It did not bring him the satisfaction he'd thought it would.

He went to his mother's fire outside the longhouse. She was not there, but Shining Day moved to the kettle that had been left close enough to keep whatever was in it warm. She scooped something into a bowl.

Once her hands were empty, she signed, *"Do you bring no bread today?"*

He shook his head, but instead of looking disappointed, she smiled and signed, *"Tomorrow, Red Beads and I will bring back the bread."*

He put aside the bowl and signed, *"You are not to go to the fort without me."*

"Our mother has agreed to allow us to help Lurana Quinn every seventh day, on the day she calls Friday."

No. He couldn't allow that. He rose, bowl forgotten, and signed, *"Where is our mother?"*

Shining Day's face turned sullen, a look she wore far too often. *"She will not change her mind. She has given her word to Lurana Quinn."*

Koyen stomped toward the longhouse, knowing Shining Day was correct but needing to speak his mind anyway. He'd reached the longhouse door when his mother left another dwelling, walking his way. He stood, arms crossed and legs braced, waiting for her.

"My son has much on his mind this evening," she said when she stopped in front of him, an empty basket in her arms.

"Your daughters cannot go to the fort."

Her eyebrows rose, but the rest of her face remained unmoved. "And who has said this in my absence?"

"I have." He put all the confidence he could into his words, but it didn't alter her expression.

"Did I miss the ceremony when you were declared chief?"

He rocked back on his heels and glanced at the dark forest surrounding the village.

"Come. Walk with me, my son." Setting the basket by the doorway, she turned and headed down the wide path to the lake.

He followed, for what else could he do? Not for the first time, he wished his mother had not been chosen a clan mother. He was proud of her, of course, and sometimes in awe of her wisdom, but...

"What have you done, Koyengquahtah?"

"As you have asked, I have *done* nothing." The words came out with more force than he'd intended.

She stopped and faced him then. Rising barely to his shoulder, she was still a force of nature as sharp-eyed as the eagle.

"Something has changed. You have decided that you can give me orders now."

He bit back the denial of her words, because they were true. He'd overstepped. Badly. And by the look in her eyes, she'd not stop probing until she knew the extent of his doings. And since there was none he trusted more than the woman standing before him—

"I am watching the soldiers and reporting their activities to Farmer's Brother."

A long moment stretched between them, filled only with the rustle of leaves in the breeze.

"For what purpose?"

He swallowed the knot that threatened to silence him. "He will begin strikes against the British."

"At the fort?"

"No. When soldiers move outside of it."

"Ah." She looked past him, with that expression that said she was weighing all he'd said, and understanding what he'd left unsaid.

That her son was a spy.

When she turned back to him, her eyes were clear and her voice was firm. "I have given my word to Lurana Quinn. Your sisters will attend to her on the days she calls Fridays. You will see them to and from the fort each time, so that they will not run into trouble outside of its walls. If Farmer's Brother has no plans to attack the fort itself, they will be safe inside." She poked his chest with a stiff finger. "And if he decides to attack the fort, you will tell me immediately. Am I understood?"

He may have been able to deny his mother, but not his clan mother. "I understand."

"Then let us return and sleep well tonight. Tomorrow you will escort your sisters."

And tomorrow night, he'd have to make plain to Walks Fast that he must have advance notice of any attack on the fort. They may irritate him greatly at times, but Red Beads and Shining Day were still his sisters and under his care.

ABIGAIL BUCKLED HER SHOE AND WAS TIGHTENING the garter of her stocking when someone knocked on her door. She paused, hand to her chest. No one had knocked on her door in the weeks she'd been there. Taking the key from top of her trunk, for she'd heeded her uncle's warning from that first day, she unlocked and opened the door.

Judith Spooner's vivid blue eyes and sweet smile greeted her.

"Hello." Abigail's tentative friendship with the youngest of the officer's wives had been abandoned once she started working with Uncle Corne. But they still spoke at meal times and if they passed in the corridors.

"I have something for you." Judith held out a sealed letter.

Abigail took it, her stomach dropping at her half-brother's familiar handwriting spelling out her name.

"Thank you." Her words were breathy.

"I hope 'tis not bad news." Concern etched lines in the other woman's brow.

"I am s-s-sure 'tis not." Not the way Judith would think, at least. "I w-w-was just on my w-w-way to my uncle's—" She pointed across the corridor.

"Of course, I shall not detain you." Judith backed away from the door as Abigail exited the room and locked it again. "I have missed your company at our gatherings."

That brought Abigail's head up with a snap. Someone had missed her? Truly? Judith's face mirrored only sincerity, and something in Abigail warmed even more to her.

"P-p-perhaps, if my uncle could s-s-spare me, I may join you again s-s-sometimes."

Judith's grin broadened. "I should like that very much." Then she retreated down the corridor.

Abigail stared after her for a moment.

"You received a letter?"

Ensign Tharp's voice made her jump. He was such a fixture outside her uncle's door, that she hadn't even noticed him.

He chuckled. "I did not mean to frighten you."

"You did not. I w-w-was a million miles away."

"Because of the letter?"

She looked at the sealed missive, almost forgotten in her hand. "Yes." It was easier than explaining how much Judith's renewed offer of friendship had meant. "If you w-w-will excuse me?"

The ensign rapped on Uncle Corne's door and opened it for her at the man's bark of, "Enter."

She went straight to his desk. "Uncle Corne, I have received a letter. 'Tis from Bartlett."

"Oh?"

"Might I be excused from my duties here this morning to read and respond to it?" And visit the bake house, but there was no need to go into that. Bartlett had given her the perfect excuse to take the morning away from her desk.

Uncle Corne leaned back in his chair, fingertips steepled together beneath his chin. "Indeed. Of course. I should not want to work you all the time, my dear. You need some time to yourself. Indeed." He made a shooing motion. "Go."

She slipped around the desk and hugged his shoulders. "Thank you, Uncle."

"You will tell me if he says anything I should know, will you not?"

A sigh escaped before she could stop it. "I w-w-will." When his eyebrows almost met his wig, she added, "I p-p-promise."

Then she scurried from the room before he could say more, stuffing the letter into the pocket tied at her waist. Whatever her half-brother had to say, it could wait until after her trip to the bake house.

"YOU WILL NOT, UNDER ANY CIRCUMSTANCES, LEAVE the fort without me at your side." Koyen spoke and signed the words, glance sweeping from one round-eyed sister to the other. Perhaps he'd been a little more forceful than needed, but a group of soldiers exited the fort's gate as they emerged from the forest.

Farmer's Brother knew about the excursion. Would he and the young Seneca who followed him strike fast or wait until later in the day?

Koyen walked to the bake house with his sisters and entered behind them.

Lurana Quinn turned from the oven, one of the flat bread paddles in her hand. "Ah, my help has arrived." She greeted them in their Iroquois language.

"They know nothing of baking the breads you make." Koyen's voice cut through the room. "Why have you requested them?"

Without a glance at him, Lurana Quinn waved the girls toward her. "So they can learn."

"The Seneca do not use ovens such as these."

The little woman faced him squarely then, hands on her hips. "They have not in the past, but who knows what will happen in the future. It is a good skill to know."

"Oh!"

The exclamation came a heartbeat before a hand pushed against Koyen's back.

Mourning Dove backed away as he turned, her face the color of a fall apple. "I am s-s-so s-s-s-s…"

"Move out of the way, Koyengquahtah," ordered Lurana Quinn in English. "She would not have run into you had you not been blocking the doorway. Go. Leave us to get on with our work."

He didn't take his eyes of Mourning Dove. "I leave my sisters in your care."

She put a hand to her throat and sidled away from him, but at the same time, gave the slightest of nods.

It shouldn't have reassured him, but oddly enough, it did. He left the building and went in search of Sergeant Hagerman to get his orders for the day. Orders he would complete as if he were still employed by the British... because he was.

Spy or not.

Sisters in the bake house or not.

Mourning Dove with her stammering words, her dusty-colored eyes, and her soft hand that had burned its touch on his back... or not.

———

"WHY MY BROTHER SAY WE IN YOUR CARE?" RED BEADS asked, leaning close to Abigail as they both tried their hands at shaping the unwieldy bread dough into something resembling a circle.

Why indeed? But Abigail had scarcely been able to pay attention to Lurana Quinn's instructions, so much did those parting words affect her. "I am s-s-sure I do not know."

"Not like him."

Whether it was or wasn't, Abigail had no idea. It wasn't as if she knew the man at all. She'd seen him several times, of course. Even spoken to him at the sutlers' tents that day weeks ago, but he'd singled her out before he'd left with that statement, *I leave my sisters in your care,* as if... as if he expected something might go awry. But what? What mischief could the sisters come to under the baker woman's watchful eyes?

Abigail slapped the dough onto the wooden table, and a puff of flour rose like a cloud, clinging to the borrowed apron and undoubtedly to her sweat-dampened face.

"Gently, as you would treat a small child." The baker's face was pulled into a frown.

Shining Day giggled. So she could make sounds. And she

knew enough without hearing to know that Abigail hadn't done well learning to shape loaves. Unlike the Indian girl's nimble hands and fingers that had pressed her dough into the desired shape on the first attempt.

Red Beads turned her face away, but not before Abigail caught the twitch to her lips.

Lurana Quinn handed her a cloth. "Mop your face and try again."

It was on the tip of her tongue to ask why, since she'd never intended to learn to make bread with the Indian sisters, but what else could she do? She'd agreed to be responsible for them. And she wanted to learn their hand talk.

She did not, however, want to learn to bake bread.

With a sigh, she wiped her face clean and tackled the mound of dough again. It was hot in the bake house, but the chatter of Red Beads and Lurana Quinn made it bearable. Made it... friendly. Even Shining Day smiled a few times at whatever her sister motioned to her.

Probably laughing at Abigail's pitiful attempts.

Boston Abigail would have turned up her nose and stormed out of the building. Niagara Abigail firmed her lips and flexed her hands before attempting to shape a loaf. The room quieted, but she hardly noticed until she placed her slightly lopsided loaf beside the dozen or so others on the rising board.

Lurana Quinn nodded. "You did well."

Not exactly high praise, but Abigail sensed that from the baker woman, it actually was. She grinned in response.

"While they rise, we will learn some of the hand talk." Lurana Quinn looked at the sisters, hands moving as she spoke. "That is what Abigail Aldridge wishes to learn, not the baking of bread."

Red Beads nodded in eagerness, while Shining Day slipped

back into her familiar glower. But Abigail ignored it, so excited she was to finally start learning to speak with her hands.

The morning flew by, Abigail learning more of the hand talk than she'd thought possible. It wasn't like English, using far fewer motions than words. She lost herself in the lessons until the bugler sounded the noon meal.

"I must leave." Abigail slipped off the apron and hung it on the peg she'd seen the baker take it from. "My uncle will expect me at the table."

"Off with you then." The baker glanced at the sisters. "I will watch over them until he returns."

So Lurana Quinn had overheard the strange comment as well.

Abigail glanced at the sisters who were busy tidying the workspace. She lowered her voice. "W-w-what is his name? I heard you s-s-say it, but I did not understand it."

"Koyengquahtah is his name, but the soldiers shorten it to Koyen."

Through the door left open due to the heat, Abigail caught sight of a group of soldiers heading for the castle.

"I must go." She resisted the urge to hug the woman. "Thank you, thank you s-s-so much."

"Come again next Friday, and we will learn more."

Abigail signed, *"I will see you again,"* then dashed out the door. Lurana Quinn had explained that there was not an equivalent to the English *goodbye* in the Seneca language. Next Friday, she would learn more. A full week to wait. But even as she ran, she practiced some of the motions she'd learned that morning. It wasn't enough to talk much—yet—but she would learn.

Imagine how surprised Koyen would be when she was able to answer him with her hands. She stumbled at the thought.

"Miss Aldridge." Ensign Tharp appeared beside her, his steadying hand on her elbow. "Have a care."

"Thank you." He'd kept her from flattening herself in the dirt outside the castle's door. Instead of thinking irrational thoughts of the Seneca scout, she entered the building on the ensign's arm.

His strong, capable, and fully clothed arm.

Chapter 12

All day he'd waited, ears and eyes alert for anything amiss, skin practically crawling with tension he hid from the others. Koyen pushed away from the wall of the fort, glancing one more time around its interior as the soldiers who had left that morning dispersed to their own ends.

Then he approached the bake house. Mourning Dove had left at midday, hurrying to meet the red-haired soldier who waited on the captain. The one the captain entrusted her to when she left the room. He still didn't know how they were connected, Mourning Dove and the captain, but she didn't appear to be his wife. Maybe his daughter or a much younger sister.

She hadn't returned to the bake house.

That disappointed him. He'd charged her with looking after his sisters, and she'd agreed. But why he'd done so made no sense, and her agreement made even less. That exchange, as well as the waiting, had him in a foul mood. He did his best not to show it as he entered the building.

Shining Day's hands flew when she spotted him. "*See what we have made. It was not difficult. And it tastes as good as it looks.*"

Red Beads lifted two round loaves and grinned. "We will eat well tonight."

"They are quick learners," said Lurana Quinn. "I look forward seeing them next Friday."

"Perhaps."

His sisters' faces froze at his terse word.

"You think they might not come?" The baker's eyes bored into him, and he stifled the urge to fidget beneath them.

"These times are uncertain."

"Finish wiping the table and tidy the rack," she said to his sisters. Then her dark eyes narrowed to slits, and her voice dropped to a whisper as she stepped closer. "What do you know?"

He met her stare for stare. She would have been a fearsome clan mother, but she wasn't. And he owed her no allegiance. "Very little. Yet."

"Stay out of it." She shook her head. "Nothing good will come of a war with the British. Nothing good at all. Not for your people or mine."

"Who are your people now?"

She stiffened, the top of her head barely rising to his shoulders. "I am still Onondaga, Koyengquahtah. I wish only the best for my people. They cannot defeat the British any more than the Seneca can."

"If we band together with Pontiac and his Ottawa—"

"All will be defeated."

Frustration built inside him, and his words came out too sharp and too loud. "How do you know this?"

Red Beads and Shining Day both turned.

Lurana Quinn crossed her arms. "Speak with Hill Woman, your mother. See if she agrees with me."

From the set of her mouth, she already knew the answer. More frustration kept him from saying anything. He motioned for his sisters to follow and strode out of the building.

They entered the forest and walked in silence until Red Beads tugged on his arm.

"Why are you angry?"

The uncertainty in her voice plucked at him. After all, his frustration had nothing to do with her. It had to do with an attack that never happened. With being relegated to spying. With a meddling baker woman who didn't believe in her people —or his. And with a British woman who took up too much time in his thoughts.

Mourning Dove. One of his enemies.

―――

How could she have forgotten the letter? The excitement at the bake house learning hand talk must have blocked it from her mind. But it was time to read it. Abigail scooted out of bed and padded over the cold floor, cringing with each step lest another mouse appear and scurry across her bare feet. But she hadn't seen a rodent since that day weeks prior, and Lurana Quinn had said Abigail could bring her kitten back to her room next Friday.

She reached into her embroidered pocket and pulled out the sealed envelope.

Abigail Aldridge c/o Captain Cornelius Hayward, Fort Niagara, New York.

Even Bartlett's penmanship looked disdainful.

She crept back to her bed and angled so that the fading light from the window fell across the paper. Having no letter opener to hand, she dug her thumbnail into the hard glob of red wax marked with Bartlett's ring and pried the seal open.

The paper was cool and crisp against her fingers. Thick and smooth, it was much higher quality than what the army allowed her uncle. But she was only examining the paper to further delay reading his words. With a sigh, she read.

May 15, 1763

Boston, Mass

Abigail,

No salutation. Just her name, stark on the page. But then, what else could she expect?

Your disgraceful disappearance has caused all manner of a stir in our lives. At present, it is perfectly impossible for me to come and fetch you home. I have written also to Uncle Cornelius, although I expect he is doing everything within his power to obtain return passage for you with all haste.

Deloris has been beside herself with worry. In her present condition, it is unforgivable that you would put her through this.

In her condition? Deloris was expecting? Their first child—and they'd not told Abigail. A twist of something, disappointment or perhaps resentment, gripped her chest for a moment. Then she continued reading.

'Tis my hope that by the time you read this, you will have learned a valuable lesson and return with all humility to your place with us. Deloris will require assistance in the months ahead, and being an unmarried sister, 'tis your duty to be at her side.

"Unmarried half-sister."

He'd signed the letter Bartlett Coffin. His full name, as if she might not know who he was. If ever she'd regretted her rash decision to escape Boston and flee to Fort Niagara, his signature made it plain that she'd done the right thing.

The urge to mash the letter into a ball and fling it out the window was strong, but Uncle Corne's caution to save every scrap of paper prevailed. Bartlett had left more than half of the page blank, after all.

She tucked her feet underneath the covers, despite the warm night, and pulled her knees close to rest her arms upon them.

Uncle Corne hadn't mentioned getting a letter, but then, perhaps it hadn't arrived yet. Or perhaps he had kept it a secret.

Come to think on it, he hadn't appeared at all surprised when she'd told him of *her* letter.

She rested her cheek against her crossed arms.

Did no one want her? A tear slipped onto the back of her hand, but she ignored it. Crying did nobody any good. Yet it hurt that Uncle Corne wanted her gone, and that Bartlett wanted her only to attend to Deloris.

I will leave my sisters in your care.

She jerked upright, the words so fresh in her ears that she almost heard them again. Hand pressed to her chest, she looked out the window at the waves curling into ghostly white tops. Could it be that the only person not unhappy to see her was the bare-chested heathen who spiked her heart with fear? The man whose name she couldn't begin to pronounce. With her stammer, it would never come out as it should. Koyen, though, she could say.

Koyen hadn't looked down his nose at her that morning in the bake house. Instead, he'd given her charge over his sisters.

Which she'd passed on to Lurana Quinn.

Next time—if there was a next time—she wouldn't do that again.

WALKS FAST APPEARED AT THEIR MEETING PLACE OUT of breath. He bent over, hands to knees, and pulled in long gulps of air.

Koyen waited for the runner to recover enough to speak.

"What have you learned?" Walks Fast asked, voice still thready from exertion.

"There will be more men traveling between the fort and

Lower Landing in the next two days."

Walks Fast eyes flashed at the news. "Tomorrow or the day after?"

"Perhaps both. They wait for the blacksmith to finish his work. He makes new, stronger iron pieces to reinforce the gates there."

"How many men?"

Koyen shrugged. "As I know, so I have told you."

The other man snorted.

"To ask many questions would raise suspicions. I never asked such questions before."

"Maybe you should have."

"To what end?" Frustration clawed at Koyen. "To be turned out altogether?"

Walks Fast frowned. "Farmer's Brother wishes for more details."

"Tell him that is my wish as well."

"I will." The man turned to leave, but Koyen caught his arm.

"My sisters will be in the fort the day after tomorrow."

"We have no plans to attack the fort."

Koyen let him go but leaned closer. "See that you do not. Not without telling me first."

Walks Fast nodded and disappeared between the trees.

Koyen sank to a crouch in front of a towering maple. Its rough bark pressed against his shoulder blades. Would Farmer's Brother move against the British when the information reached him? And if he did, how would a strike outside of the fort convince the British to leave it? Would it not more likely see them entrenched? Would they not sharpen their defenses and double their guard?

The combined tribes at Fort Pitt and Fort Detroit were striking against those forts. They kept food and other provisions from reaching the soldiers there. In time, they could starve out the soldiers.

But how long would it take? And how many Indian children would go hungry during the winter months for not gathering, harvesting, and drying enough food during the summer?

He growled low in his throat as he rose and headed for the longhouse. Should he speak with his mother as Lurana Quinn had all but challenged him to do? Or should he follow his heart —or was it his loyalty to his people?

In his heart, did he want war? No. Not any more than his mother did. He wanted peace. But he also wanted the white man gone. He wanted life to go back to what it had been. What it should be.

Didn't he?

THE LONG WEEK HAD FINALLY PASSED, WITH ABIGAIL practicing hand talk every evening in her room. She'd secured the entire day off, even convincing Uncle Corne that she'd like to take her midday meal in the bake house. He'd been shocked, of course, to learn that she'd taken an interest in baking. But better that than explaining her desire to learn hand talk from the Indian sisters and Lurana Quinn. Best he didn't know that she engaged with Red Beads and Shining Day at all.

To add to her excitement, she would fetch her kitten back to her room when she returned. The baker woman had given her a heavy box and explained how to fill it with sand. She'd need that until the kitten was old enough to be let outside for its necessary functions. The idea of carrying the heavy box filled with the kitten's leavings was repugnant but perhaps Ensign Tharp could be prevailed upon to assist. He seemed ever at her elbow when she least expected him.

Likely following the orders of her uncle to keep an eye on her.

She pulled her plainest dress over her shift, petticoats, and stays. Neither the ensign nor her uncle would be watching over her in the bake house, and it didn't matter what she looked like. She'd be covered with an apron and dusted with flour before long.

As soon as her shoes were buckled, she skipped down the wide stone steps and made her way outside. She nodded a quick greeting to several of the soldiers who touched their hats to her, but she didn't slow down, so she arrived at the bake house slightly out of breath.

"It is about time." Lurana Quinn pointed to the aprons hanging on the wall. "Cover yourself and start kneading the next batch." The baker loaded a large tray with a pile of steaming scones. "I will return shortly." She whisked out the doorway with her burden. The officers and their ladies would eat well that morning.

Abigail's stomach growled, but she did as she'd been directed. She was elbow-deep in the sticky dough when someone darkened the doorway.

It was him.

Her heart fluttered behind her stays, but she strove to keep her face calm.

He scanned the inside of the bake house, then stepped through the doorway, followed by his sisters. Red Beads and Shining Day set their baskets aside and donned aprons as Koyen approached Abigail.

"You work here now? Not with captain?"

Abigail swallowed against the dryness of her throat. "My uncle has p-p-permitted me to come here on Fridays."

He grunted, looking around the building again as if he

expected someone to jump out from behind a barrel. "Good. You watch sisters."

She stopped kneading and faced him, her flour-covered arms resting on the dough. "I w-w-will s-s-stay until you return. I could not last w-w-week, but I w-w-will today."

His eyes met hers with the slightest lift of one brow. Then he scanned the room one last time before he left.

"He is the odd one."

"Sometimes." Red Beads giggled, and Abigail realized she'd spoken aloud.

"I meant no disrespect to your brother."

The other woman shrugged, then opened a barrel of flour and dusted the table. "He strange, but all men strange, yes?" She signed her words as she spoke. Abigail understood a couple of the movements.

Shining Day laughed at her sister's comment. She should laugh more. It was a pleasant sound and made her look like the girl she was, instead of older and bitter. But then, now that Abigail understood the root of that bitterness, she would go out of her way to be more pleasant. It might not help with Shining Day, but perhaps Red Beads would appreciate her efforts.

And maybe Koyen would too.

Plunging her hands into the dough once more, she lowered her face so that the others wouldn't notice her heated cheeks. She'd spoken to him. Boldly. More boldly than she'd spoken to men her age back in Boston. Of course, those men had avoided her if at all possible.

None of them wished to be seen by a matron as paying her attention. It could be misconstrued as interest. Interest in a woman who stammered and stuttered. Who would wish that?

She punched the dough.

"More gently, Abigail Aldridge." Lurana Quinn stepped through the doorway. "Bread responds to a loving touch, as do most things." As if to prove her point, the baker woman touched Shining Day's shoulder, and then Abigail's as she passed and set her empty tray on the sideboard.

Abigail dusted off her hands and arms, then signed, *"I am sorry."*

Red Beads clapped, sending flour dancing into the sunbeams that slanted through the window. "You do well."

"Thank you," she signed again.

Shining Day scowled and turned her attention back to the dough.

Some things would take time. Learning hand talk. Learning to make bread. Winning over Shining Day.

Proving herself trustworthy, even to a half-naked savage.

Chapter 13

Nerves stretched to the breaking point, Koyen did his best to listen to Sergeant Hagerman. He was going over the recent scouting reports and asking several of Koyen's fellow scouts for clarification. The clerk who wrote down their spoken reports sometimes missed the finer details.

"You spoke to the scouts from Fort Detroit when you accompanied the provisions to Fort Schlosser, Koyen?"

Koyen snapped his wandering attention back to the sergeant. "Yes."

"I do not see your report in this pile." He shuffled the stack of papers, frowning at them. "Did you report to the clerk?"

"Day after I return."

Hagerman's head jerked up. "Why the day after?"

"Return long after dark."

The sergeant glared at him for a moment, then back at the paperwork. "Go over the details with him again."

Koyen nodded, but the man had already moved on to the next paper report before eventually dismissing them.

Tall Otter joined Koyen as they departed the cramped office. "What is eating at you?"

"What do you mean?"

The older man gave him a look that said more than many words. "I am not a fool. Something distracts you today."

Koyen glanced at the bake house as Mourning Dove emerged and shook a long cloth, a white cloud releasing with each flap.

Tall Otter's eyebrows rose. "It is that one, is it?"

"My sisters are there. They learn from Lurana Quinn how to bake bread."

"Lurana Quinn and the lady from Captain Hayward's room."

Koyen didn't think so. He'd watched the baker woman enough to know that Mourning Dove's actions had not been as sure, as competent. No, that one was learning along with his sisters.

But why?

The captain, a powerful man in the fort, was her uncle. Oddly enough, that pleased him. But as he understood things in the British world, women of a powerful family had others to do the everyday work for them. Yet Mourning Dove was in the bake house. It was puzzling.

That wasn't what occupied his thoughts, however. There had been no attack the day before, which meant that if Farmer's Brother and the others were planning one, it would happen soon. The soldiers on the work detail had departed shortly after Koyen had delivered his sisters. Nothing had happened then, but where would the Seneca choose to strike? How close to the fort?

Why hadn't he asked Walks Fast? Although, the man wouldn't have had the answer. Wouldn't have known a plan until he'd spoken with Farmer's Brother.

The sun's rays slanted over the west wall of the fort. If they followed the same pattern as the day before, the soldiers would return before long. If they followed the same pattern, and if Farmer's Brother had men watching—

"What are you worried about?"

"I worry about nothing." Koyen headed toward the bake house. "I must see my sisters back to their mother's fire."

Tall Otter stopped, letting Koyen continue on alone. It was just as well. He didn't wish to tell the man about spying. He didn't wish to tell anyone about that. It still rubbed him wrong. It felt... dishonorable.

Mourning Dove noticed his approach. She waited, watching him with those oddly colored eyes. When he stopped in front of her, she tilted her chin to look up at him.

"I have s-s-stayed with your s-s-sisters, as I s-s-said I w-w-would."

Muskets fired outside the walls, not close, but then shouts reached them, followed by more muskets.

Lurana Quinn appeared in the door, Red Beads and Shining Day behind her. His youngest sister held a kitten against her chest.

"What is it?" the older woman asked.

Koyen's stomach tightened. "Attack."

"Oh!" Mourning Dove clutched her hand to her throat. "W-w-what s-s-should w-w-we do?"

The Seneca would not enter the fort, but what if those inside the fort retaliated against the Seneca within its walls? He glanced at his sisters.

Mourning Dove touched his arm. "I w-w-will take them to my room." As if she'd read his thoughts. "They w-w-will be s-s-safe there."

Would they? But what other choice was there? Koyen couldn't take them outside the fort, where shouts continued and shots peppered the air.

"Go."

Mourning Dove took the girls by the arms, but Shining Day pulled away. Koyen signed for her to go with the British woman.

His sister balked but a moment, and then Red Beads half-dragged her toward the castle, kitten still clinging to her.

"Do you know what is happening?" Lurana Quinn, having moved to his elbow, asked softly.

"An attack."

Her sharp eyes sought his, letting him know that wasn't enough answer, but he left her there and returned to Tall Otter's side.

Men had scattered to the heights, and muskets answered from the fort's walls, but the Seneca scouts stood in a loose knot near the barracks. They would not be asked to take up arms against their own people. It did not escape Koyen's notice that several soldiers watched them from the heights as well.

As they should.

Bile rose in the back of his throat. To be fighting outside the walls would be honorable. Fighting to remove the British, to restore his people to all their lands. That was a noble thing. As much as he'd tried to convince himself that spying was necessary and therefore also honorable, he'd failed.

He had a choice to make, stop scouting and join the warriors outside, or stop scouting and return to his village. He glanced at the castle but had no idea which window might hide his sisters and Mourning Dove.

Even as he plotted the downfall of her people, that one sheltered Red Beads and Shining Day.

Her actions were more honorable than his.

———

A KNOCK SOUNDED ON HER DOOR. ABIGAIL MOTIONED Red Beads and Shining Day to be silent. "W-w-who is it?" She couldn't suppress the tremble in her voice.

"Ensign Tharp. The captain wishes to know that you are safely in your room. He remains below with the other officers."

"Assure him that I am, ensign. And thank you."

She waited for his footsteps to subside, then opened the door and peeked into the empty corridor. They could see nothing from her room, but Uncle's window overlooked the front of the castle. She motioned for the sisters to follow her, and slipped across to her uncle's room, closing the door behind them before she hurried to the window.

The gunfire had stopped shortly after they'd reached her room. Soldiers rushed across the grounds on different errands, and across the way, near the barracks, were the Indian scouts. Including Koyen.

Red Beads joined her at the window.

"There is your brother." Abigail pointed.

The other woman frowned. "Soldiers keep scout there, all together?" A hint of uneasiness threaded her voice.

As well it should. Indeed, it looked as if soldiers were watching the scouts. Soldiers with muskets in hand. But why? The scouts were inside the fort, not part of whatever was happening outside the walls.

What if they were not allowed to leave? Koyen escorted his sisters to and from the fort. Abigail knew this from their chatter in the bake house. If he could not do so, what would become of them? Would they be set upon if they tried to leave?

The kitten made a noise from Shining Day's lap, providing a needed distraction for the moment.

Abigail turned to Shining Day, who sat at Abigail's desk. "S-s-she needs a name." She spoke as well as signed as much as she could.

The kitten meowed again, and Shining Day dangled the ends of her long hair within its reach. The kitten stood on its hind legs to try and catch the shining black braid. A rare smile brightened Shining Day's face, as if to live up to her name. Then her hands wove a message too quickly for Abigail to follow.

Red Beads said, "She say kitten name She Who Dances."

"S-s-she W-w-who Dances?" Never would Abigail have thought to name the animal that way, but watching it make another attempt at the braid, it seemed very fitting indeed. However, words that began with S and W always caused Abigail grief. "S-s-she is a s-s-small cat, let us s-s-shorten it to just Dance. Dance is a p-p-perfect name. How w-w-would I s-s-sign it?"

Distracted from the window, Red Beads showed her, and Abigail practiced it several times before a commotion outside drew them back to the window. Men entered their line of vision from the direction of the forest gate. Some walking and some being carried.

Some covered with blood.

Abigail clutched the window frame and fought a rising tide of panic. *Abigail, we are at war.* Uncle Corne's words came back to her. She'd assured him that she knew it. But looking at the bloodied and bedraggled men below, she realized how naive she'd been.

She knew nothing about being at war.

Men died—everyone knew that—but they spoke of the dead in terms of honor and glory and duty. Never of bloodied, broken bodies. Never of being carried across another man's shoulders, head limp and arms dangling.

Hand pressed to her mouth, Abigail turned away from the scene.

"Koyen." Red Beads pointed, and Abigail had to look.

The scouts, six in total, were being herded toward the castle. Soldiers followed with muskets fixed on them. As they neared, Koyen looked up. Abigail took a step back. What did it mean? It meant she had to get Red Beads and Shining Day out of the fort lest they be taken into custody too.

But how?

KOYEN FOLLOWED THE REST OF THE SCOUTS INTO THE castle. He'd gotten a glimpse of Mourning Dove and Red Beads in the window before they entered. Enough to know that his sisters were safe.

Mourning Dove had kept her word.

Instead of comforting him, the thought pecked at him. He didn't have time to ponder it as they were brought before Sergeant Hagerman. The soldiers who had taken their weapons before bringing them to the castle filed in behind them and stayed, muskets in hands.

"Tell me everything you know about what just happened." The man's voice sounded off the stone walls around them.

The scouts said nothing. No one shifted a foot. The silence of the stones was the sergeant's only answer.

"Swan," the sergeant barked. "What do you know?"

The soldier who was often with Koyen and other scouts stepped forward. "All scouts were inside the fort at the time of the attack, sir."

"Did you detect anything prior to the attack that made you suspicious? Or witness any behaviors exhibited by the scouts that seemed out of place?"

Koyen felt the pressure of the next few heartbeats as George Swan faced the sergeant. "Not that I can recall, sir."

The sergeant walked down the line of scouts, so close that Koyen could smell tobacco on his breath. "None of you will talk?" He swung around and glanced back down the line. "Three of His Majesty's finest are dead, and none of you knows anything?" His voice rose. "Am I supposed to believe that?"

No one spoke.

"Lock them up, the whole lot of them." Sergeant Hagerman turned and stomped from the room.

"Sorry, lads." Swan pointed to the doorway with the muzzle of his musket. "You heard the sergeant. Look lively."

Even if he'd played no part in the attack, he'd have been locked up with the rest. But it offered no comfort knowing his sisters remained upstairs in the castle. He should have insisted they stay in the village. He had let them down.

He glanced at the window again as they passed by the front of the castle, but there were no faces.

He was Koyengquahtah, the young king. He almost laughed out loud. Who was he to think he could save his people, when he could not keep his own sisters safe? The bitterness of his thoughts soured his belly.

He'd been a fool.

"ENSIGN THARP, I MUST S-S-SPEAK W-W-WITH YOU." Abigail held her chamber door close to her, the opening no more than a hand-span.

The ensign stepped across the corridor. His blue eyes earnest, he sketched a short bow. "How may I assist?"

How indeed? At least, how without bringing down the wrath of her uncle. On both of them.

"My friends are here." She eased the door wider, allowing him to see Red Beads and Shining Day, who cuddled Dance at her chest. "But they need to return to their village."

"Miss Aldridge—"

"I know 'tis a terrible inconvenience, but their brother is one of the s-s-scouts under guard. They must have s-s-safe p-p-passage."

"Your uncle, the captain—"

"Is, of course, far too busy for me to approach. W-w-which is w-w-why I called you over." She blinked at him, allowing her eyes to grow misty. "There is no one else I w-w-would trust." It was a ploy, and she knew it even as she executed it, but she didn't care. She must get the sisters to their village. She'd promised Koyen she'd watch over them.

And so she would—one way or another.

"Miss Aldridge—"

"After dark, p-p-perhaps w-w-we might s-s-slip out of the castle and—"

"We?" His eyebrows hiked to his hairline. "By no means would your uncle approve of you setting foot outside the castle after dark. By no means at all."

"Then w-w-we s-s-shall not tell him."

The ensign's mouth dropped open beneath his drooping mustache, making him look like a dumbfounded Viking.

Abigail squeezed around the partially opened door, glancing both directions of the corridor to be sure they were alone. "I w-w-would not let them be harmed, you s-s-see."

"Why would anyone harm—"

"Because of their brother." She blinked again, as if working to keep tears at bay. "W-w-we cannot hold his s-s-sins against them, now can w-w-we?"

"Miss Aldridge, I would do anything…"

She grasped his forearm with both hands, still gazing into this face. "Oh, thank you, ensign. I knew I could trust you. Knock s-s-softly after dark." She smiled and slipped back into her room, closing the door before he found his tongue again.

Red Beads covered her mouth with both hands, not quite

suppressing a giggle. Even Shining Day wore a less-hostile expression than normal.

"Do you think he will come?" Red Beads asked.

"I do." Because even though she had little experience in such matters, it was clear that the ensign was not averse to her company. That he might even overlook her affliction enough to see her as possible wifely material.

At one time that would have thrilled her, at least privately. She'd given up all hope, back in Boston, of a young man viewing her in that way. A young man in her social circle, anyway. And while Ensign Tharp wasn't in that circle, he was obviously well thought of by her uncle and making a name for himself among the junior officers in His Majesty's army. There was much to be said for that.

Boston Abigail would have fixated on the possibility of a romance between them.

Niagara Abigail was using him as a means to an end. Deep inside, she wasn't proud of that, but it wasn't stopping her. After all, Red Beads and Shining Day needed her.

That anyone actually needed Abigail Aldridge was an entirely new concept. It brought with it a very heady feeling indeed.

Chapter 14

"A re you s-s-sure this is the w-w-way?" Abigail asked Ensign Tharp. He'd taken several twists and turns down corridors and staircases in the castle she was unfamiliar with.

"'Twould be most imprudent to try and walk out the front door." The exasperation in his voice was unmistakable. That he was taking her, Red Beads, and Shining Day at all should be marked up to a minor miracle.

"Indeed." She glanced back at the sisters, following on her heels in the darkness. In places, no light had reached them, and her hand on the ensign's elbow had been all that kept her from walking into something. The sisters seemed to fare better in the darkness than she, but perhaps that was to be expected, them living…

How? How did they live? The thought had never occurred to her before. Lurana Quinn lived in a small room sectioned at the back of the bake house. But the Indians? They could sleep in trees or under rocks, for all she knew. But it was the wrong time to ponder their living conditions. The urgency was to get them free of the fort.

Ensign Tharp stopped, then the creaking of hinges in need of oil broke the silence. Light filtered in, the weak light of a partial moon veiled by fog. In the distance, waves lapped the shore, but no breeze brought the scent of the lake. Everything was still and damp, humidity hanging in eerie swirls of gray.

Any other time, Abigail would have retreated to her chamber and locked her door.

Red Beads touched her shoulder, then she signed, *"Why do we wait?"* At least, that was Abigail's best guess from the motions.

"Ensign—

"Shhh!" His reply was swift and low.

They waited together, huddled outside the door, until Ensign Tharp took Abigail's arm and led her away. She glanced to make sure the sisters followed. It took a long time to reach the forest gate, creeping between buildings, along the walls, and pausing many times. It was obvious that the ensign knew how to move undetected in the dark.

When they neared the gate, he pushed his face close to Abigail's and whispered. "I will get the guards to open the gate and distract them. You see that the Indians leave as quickly and quietly as they can. Then wait for me here, and I shall escort you back to your room." He may have added, "Before your uncle learns of this," but she wasn't sure. He'd already turned away.

The Indian women's dresses blended into the darkness. Abigail had donned her darkest clothing, even omitting her fichu for an overly warm blue wool shawl to cover her shoulders and neck. In the sticky air, it clung to her skin, prickling in the heat. She'd also removed her linen cap, feeling almost indecent without her hair covered.

"Ensign Tharp! What brings you out?" someone called.

"A walk around to report back to the captain."

"Ah, that I had your luck. I be stuck out here watching for savages in a fog too thick to see me hand at the end of me arm."

"Do you think they are still out there?" the ensign asked.

"I doubt it." It sounded as if the man spit, of all things.

"Did you hear that?" Concern colored Ensign Tharp's voice.

"Hear what?"

A pause. "That."

"I heard nothing."

"Open the gate, Baldwin. Let us have a look."

"A look? In this fog?"

"Open it." The command in the young officer's voice was unmistakable, followed by the thump and creak as the gate was unbarred and swung open.

"Come with me." Ensign Tharp's voice reached them as he led the man through. "You men on the wall, watch carefully to the east."

Clever of him. Abigail had learned that the Indian's village was to the west.

Abigail motioned the sisters to move, and she followed them to the gate, but instead of remaining inside, she slipped out with them. With any luck, she'd be back before Uncle Corne knew she'd left.

"Koyen!"

His name roused his thoughts back to the crowded room they'd been locked in. He rose and made his way to the door, careful not to step on his fellow scouts.

The red-haired ensign appeared in the doorway. "Come with me."

When the door closed behind Koyen, a cold sweat formed across his back. Why was he being singled out? Had his part in the attack been discovered? Would he be killed outright? Or beaten with a whip as the British often did, even for minor infractions by their soldiers?

He was not afraid of torture, but only a fool would welcome it.

The ensign strode at a fast clip and didn't stop until they reached the captain's door. He rapped on it and pushed it open without waiting for a command.

"Stay, Tharp." The captain paced behind his desk like a cougar overlooking a cliff. A very angry cougar.

Koyen stiffened, his head high. He was a warrior, even if reduced to spying. He would take whatever punishment this British captain would mete out.

Captain Hayward came around the desk and didn't stop until he was nose to nose with Koyen. "Your sisters left this fort a quarter of an hour ago. My niece went with them. Where would they have gone?"

Mourning Dove got his sisters out, but she went with them? Torture he could have met stoically, but he knew his face registered his shock. "Sisters go to village, to mother's fire."

"And my niece?"

"She go with them?" It was a question he couldn't make sense of. The British woman had no idea what lurked in the forest beyond the fort. It was dangerous for his sisters with the unrest and unfamiliar warriors, but it was much more so for Mourning Dove. And it was his fault. He'd charged her with watching his sisters.

"My thought precisely." He whirled to the ensign. "You will accompany Koyen and retrieve my niece. Do not return without her. Am I clear?"

"Yes, captain. How many men—"

"None." The captain wagged his finger between the two of them. "No one else must know of this, am I understood?"

The red-haired man stood straight and tall, but the end of his words came out as if strangled. "Yes, sir."

So it wasn't Koyen who was in danger. It wasn't Koyen

who'd been found out. Yet that didn't bring any relief because his sisters and Mourning Dove were in the forest.

Unprotected.

And somewhere out there were Farmer's Brother's warriors... filled with the blood lust of battle.

Instead of fearing the British, at that moment, Koyen was fearful of his fellow Seneca and what they might do.

SHINING DAY'S HANDS AND FINGERS FLEW IN motions too broad and jerky to be anything but angry. And too fast for Abigail to hope to follow. With each jabbing stab of a finger in her direction, she fought the urge to flinch. It was the third time they'd stopped and waited, listening for sounds of pursuit. And then the younger sister had launched into the tirade.

Red Beads turned her back on her sister, stepping between her and Abigail. "Sister angry you follow. Not want you go to longhouse."

"I p-p-promised your brother that I'd w-w-watch out for you."

"Inside the fort, yes. But here"—she waved a hand at the trees and fog surrounding them— "in the forest we are safe. You are not."

Abigail gripped the sweaty wool shawl at her chest. "I must s-s-see you home, w-w-wherever home is."

Red Beads crossed her arms, her brow furrowed. "You not walk into our village. Not safe."

"I mean no harm."

"This I know. Others—Sister—not trust British."

And Abigail was undeniably British, from her fair hair to her buckled leather shoes. "W-w-what s-s-should I do?"

"Return fort."

By herself? The enormity of what she'd done slammed into her like a white-topped wave crashing against a rocky shore. How was she to get back into the fort? The gate would be locked. The castle may even be locked. And somewhere—she glanced around them—somewhere were the Indians who had killed the three soldiers.

Once again she'd done the imprudent thing.

She put her hand out and leaned against the closest tree, pulling in several long breathes. What had she been thinking?

That her new friends needed her and that she couldn't let them down. Them or their brother, who even now remained in the fort, locked away somewhere with armed soldiers on guard.

"I do not know w-w-what to do."

"Go home."

Abigail jumped at the masculine voice so close behind her.

Red Beads gasped. "Koyengquahtah."

"Come, Miss Aldridge."

The unmistakable red hair and drooping mustache of Ensign Tharp brought Abigail a sharp stab of relief. But it lasted barely a heartbeat. Face pulled into severe lines, eyes creased at the corners, and a frown that made his mustache droop even farther, the austere man before her only vaguely resembled the ensign who awaited her uncle's command outside his door. And then he clamped a hand around her upper arm in a very non-gentle-manly fashion and yanked her to his side.

Koyen stepped toward her. "I thank you for watching sisters. Forest no place for you. Go." Then he took his sisters by the arms and they melted into the dark and fog.

"I—

"It would be better all the way around, Miss Aldridge, if you refrain from speaking until we reach your uncle."

The edge to his voice, more than his words, convinced her he was correct. Then he strode off, towing her by the arm as one might tow a mule. She gritted her teeth and grasped a handful of her skirts with her free hand, lifting them enough that she could keep up with his long steps.

If Uncle Corne was half as angry as the ensign...

WHEN RED BEADS OPENED HER MOUTH, KOYEN shushed her with a slash of his hand. Then he signed, *"Be silent. There may be others nearby."*

Her eyes grew large in the darkness, and Shining Day searched the murky forest. Good. They should be afraid. It might keep them at the longhouse.

It might keep them safe.

He moved off the familiar path, picking his way along a narrow trail frequented by deer and small animals. There was no need to avoid those who guarded their village, but he had no idea where Farmer's Brother's warriors were. And no desire to encounter them in the dark.

He'd known the trail his sisters would take, but seeing Mourning Dove in her ridiculous British dress on the path had jolted him. A part of him had not believed she would have gone into the forest with his sisters. Why would she put herself in such grave danger? It was dangerous enough for Red Beads and Shining Day, but a British woman?

She was either a fool or crazy.

Then why had his pulse raced at the sight of her? Why had he wished to escort her back to the fort rather than turn her over to the ensign?

It made no sense.

Before he could untie the knot of his thoughts, he spied one of the guards and signaled to him. The man nodded, and Koyen led his sisters into the village. There were men outside the long-houses, but no women. And the men wore knives and toma-hawks at their waists, muskets across their shoulders or in their hands. No fires lit the area.

Koyen nodded to several before entering the longhouse behind his sisters. His mother sat on the sleeping platform, but her head snapped up when they entered the dwelling. Her face relaxed, and she stood.

"You are safe."

Red Beads and Shining Day rushed to her side.

"We might not have been, but Abigail Aldridge took us to her room in the castle," Red Beads said. "She kept us there until after dark. Then she bribed a soldier to sneak us out of the fort."

"And the fool woman came with them," Koyen said.

His mother darted a glance at the longhouse opening, her brows furrowed.

"She returned with the soldier she'd bribed."

"It is good she kept my daughters safe." She looked up at Koyen. "And good that you are here."

"I am only here because of them." Something in his voice must have alerted her.

"What happened?"

"You know of the attack, of course." That was why the guards were alone outside, the reason for the lack of fires to draw unwanted attention. The clan mothers would have already met to discuss how it would affect their village. "All the scouts were taken into custody. We were locked in a room in the barracks."

"But you did not join the attack." It wasn't a question, but a lingering doubt flickered in her eyes.

"None of us did."

She closed her eyes, nodded, then glanced back to him. "They released you when they learned you had no hand in it?"

Koyen glanced away. "No. They released me when it was learned that the captain's niece had left the fort in the company of my sisters." Then he turned back to her. "You must keep them home now. It is too dangerous for them to return to the fort. Lurana Quinn will understand."

"I am sure she will." His mother ran her hands down the long braids of his sisters, then shot him an unreadable look. "I wish I did."

A wish that echoed deep inside of Koyen, but for a different reason.

"'TIS PAST MIDNIGHT!" ABIGAIL'S UNCLE BELLOWED AS he rose from behind his desk. His wig was gone, his equally white hair in disarray as if he'd combed it with frustrated fingers. His face reached an alarming shade of red. "Have you any idea of the danger you put yourself in this eve?"

"Uncle, I—

"Leave us, Tharp. I will deal with you in the morning." His voice dropped back into a command rather than a shout.

The door's latch clicked behind her.

"'Twas not Ensign Tharp's fault—

"Well enough I know where the fault lies." He plowed his fingers through his hair. "You are as headstrong and stubborn as my sister ever was." He dropped into his chair, the wood groaning in protest. "And tonight you proved thoroughly irrational."

"I am s-s-sorry. 'Twas thoughtless of me. I s-s-should never have entangled Ensign Tharp in my p-p-plan, but how else could I have gotten Red Beads and S-s-shining Day out of the fort?"

He raised weary eyes to her. "You should have come to me."

"Oh." Why hadn't that occurred to her? The hurt on his face

was unmistakable. She hurried to his side and knelt on the flag-stone floor, grasping his arm. "I am s-s-so s-s-sorry. You are right. I s-s-should have come s-s-straight to you. I w-w-was foolish."

He covered her hands with his. "My dear, if anything had happened to you..." He sighed. "You must never leave the fort again without a proper escort and my permission. Promise me."

"I do." And she meant it. She never wanted to cause this man such grief again. "But Uncle? P-p-please do not p-p-punish the ensign. I quite tricked him into assisting me."

"A soldier who cannot deny the wiles of a woman is no soldier at all." He squeezed her hands. "But I will take it into consideration when I decide his punishment. Go to bed, sleep while you may. The morning will be hectic for us all."

She nodded and rose, then leaned down and kissed the top of his messed hair. "I love you, Uncle."

He waved her off, but his expression lightened, and his eyes softened. "Good night, my dear."

She padded across the hall and unlocked her door. The kitten greeted her with a loud meow. Abigail scooped it off the floor and cuddled it close for a moment. Then she sat it on her bed and slipped out of her dress, stays, shoes, and socks. She stretched on her side next to the kitten—Dance. The basket on the floor was forgotten as the furry animal curled into the curve of her belly and exhaustion overcame Abigail.

Chapter 15

K oyen scratched in the dirt near the fire outside the longhouse where his mother had prepared their morning meal. It was too hot for fires and cooking inside, even in the early hours of the day.

"As Koyen has said, Lurana Quinn will understand." His mother sent a very pointed look toward her eldest daughter. Red Beads chafed at not being allowed to return to the bake house. Shining Day, on the other hand, brightened at the prospect of staying in the village. That one would make a Seneca warrior a fine wife, if a man were willing to overlook her deafness.

"And what are you doing this fine day, my son?"

Koyen dropped the stick and rubbed the grit of its bark from his fingers. "I have no plans."

"It would be a good day to dry fish or meat. It would give your sisters work to do." His mother raised her brows.

He stood, her message too clear to be missed. "Which do you prefer?"

She tapped her finger against her teeth for a moment. "Meat, I think."

He fetched his bow and arrows from the longhouse, leaving the musket on his sleeping pallet. The noise might bring unwanted attention to his whereabouts, but it was more than that. It was the feel of the wood against his palm and the age-old tradition of Seneca warriors providing for their families that filled him with pride. It was good to hunt as his people had hunted for generations beyond counting.

Half an hour's run from the village was a place he'd often hunted as a boy, tagging along behind his father. It took no real thought to turn in that direction. Leaves brushed his face and hair as he wove along a little-used path, his moccasins pressing into the earth, the scent of pines spicing the air. It was good to feel the pull of breath in his lungs and the flex of muscles in his legs.

For the past week, he'd stayed close to the village. Tall Otter and the other scouts had not returned from the fort. If he'd gone back, it was likely he'd have been locked up with them again. At least, Koyen hoped they were still locked up. That they hadn't been killed. As far as he knew, he was the only one who'd had any foreknowledge of the attack.

He'd met with Walks Fast the day after his return. The man had been full of questions and unsatisfied with Koyen's answers. But he could not report that which he did not know.

He wouldn't be reporting anything now that he was no longer in the fort.

But the urge to join those following Farmer's Brother had cooled, and he wasn't sure why. Maybe it had been seeing his sisters there in the fort while hearing the attacking just beyond the walls. Maybe it had been seeing Mourning Dove in the forest in a foolish attempt to protect his sisters. If the warriors had found her...

Koyen came to a halt at the top of a rise. A hawk flew high over the meadow below. A creek snaked its way to the west to join with the river there. It was a peaceful place. He hunkered down and watched the hawk for a few moments. It didn't flap its wings as the smaller birds did. It kept them open wide, allowing the wind currents to carry it where they would.

The hawk was like the Seneca used to be. Free to do as they pleased without fear of the white man's diseases or bullets. Not that they hadn't warred with other tribes, but they had warred on equal footing. With the British, they faced an enemy with deadly weapons both seen and unseen.

How did a people fight against that?

His mother's words came back to him. *"My son, what happens when you scoop a handful of wet sand from the lake's edge? If they are driven away, who will replace them?"*

How many people lived across the great salt water? How many would cross it if the British left? Koyen knew of the French and British—including the Scots—and had heard of a people called Dutch and another called German from the missionaries long ago. Were these people also more numerous than the Seneca?

Would they band together with the other whites as Pontiac was banding together tribes with old hostilities against the British?

So much thinking made his head hurt. What he wanted spread before him. The forests and clearings, trees and rivers, and wildlife to sustain his family. Perhaps a woman of his own in time.

Mourning Dove's face came to mind, but he closed his eyes and worked to replace it with the image of High Clouds. His mother would approve of a marriage with the Turtle Clan woman. She was of the same age as Red Beads, old enough to be a wife. Yet Koyen had dragged his feet about approaching her. She was pleasing to look at and worked without complaint beside her mother. Her clothing was well made and decorated with dyed porcupine quills and bits of shells. There was no reason not to approach her.

Yet he hadn't.

A twig cracked behind and to the side of him. He remained unmoving, tucked beneath the great branches of an oak tree. Another scuffle against the ground, then a soft snort. Whatever it was, it tried to catch his scent, but there was no breeze to move the air around him. He waited, hand wrapped around the grip of his bow.

The cautious creature took its time but finally emerged from the forest. The deer was old, its muzzle long and silvered. His mother would not appreciate meat so tough as that. With another soft snort, the creature picked its way across the top of the hill. Then, bounding behind it came a half-grown fawn, its spots still barely visible on the reddish fur. Koyen didn't raise his bow until the next deer stepped into the open. It was likely the old doe's offspring from the year before.

He waited until the deer turned its head away, then slipped an arrow from his back and notched it. Careful as he'd been, the animal must have sensed him, for it startled and swiveled to face him.

The arrow left his bow with a *snick* and pierced hide in a killing shot.

The old doe and her young fawn raced down the hill to the meadow below, white tails flagging their journey.

Koyen watched them for a moment before approaching the deer he'd shot. He stood over it and uttered the words his father had taught him. Words of thanksgiving for the bounty of meat that would sustain his family during the winter months.

His mother would be pleased. He was pleased. He lifted his arms to the sky for a moment and let the sun warm his face.

He was Seneca.

It wasn't fair. Abigail stewed even as she stroked Dance's soft fur, the kitten's purr vibrating beneath her fingertips. During the past fortnight while she'd been confined to quarters—Uncle Corne's term for her punishment—when not in her uncle's room, the kitten had consoled and comforted her. But it was Friday again, and Abigail ached to join Lurana Quinn in the bake house and learn more of the Indian hand talk.

She shifted on her bed for a better view of the parade grounds outside her window. Uncle Corne was in meetings all morning. Ensign Tharp remained at his post across the corridor, however. Whatever punishment he'd been meted out, she hadn't learned, but standing guard over her appeared to be his new assignment. His silent assignment. All attempts to speak with him had failed. He was as polite as a young officer should be, but any spark of friendliness had evaporated.

That was her fault, of course, for her rash actions and dragging him into them.

A commotion below caught her eye as raised voices reached her open window. Two soldiers appeared in her line of vision, each held an arm of the Indian between them.

Abigail gasped. It was Red Beads.

She set Dance aside. "S-s-stay here."

The kitten mewed in protest but stayed on the bed while Abigail rushed to the door. At least her uncle had never locked her in. He'd threatened to, but she'd been spared that indignity.

So far.

She wrenched open the door and rushed through, barely glancing at the ensign as she headed for the stairs.

"Miss Aldridge!"

She ignored his call and ran faster, her skirts firmly in one hand as she reached the stairs and raced down.

"Miss Aldridge!" His voice carried a note of desperation. As well it might if she managed to escape him. His booted foot-steps pounded behind her.

A group of soldiers congregated near the stone well in the vestibule. "Pardon me." They parted, and she slipped between them.

"Stop her!" shouted Ensign Tharp. Before they could react, for such an order aimed at the captain's niece must have flummoxed the lot of them, Abigail made it through the front door and sprinted toward the corner of the castle where the two soldiers stood with Red Beads.

"A moment!" she yelled.

Ensign Tharp arrived at her side as she stopped in front of the soldiers.

"Ensign, this is the young w-w-woman w-w-who assists Lurana Quinn in the bakery." She panted out a breath. "Ask these men w-w-why s-s-she is being treated thus."

The ensign glanced at Red Beads, then back to Abigail. "Come away, Miss Aldridge. This is none of your affair."

Abigail stomped her foot in the dust. "'Tis most certainly my affair. I have w-w-worked alongside Red Beads. S-s-she does not deserve to be manhandled in s-s-such a w-w-wa-wa—"

"Way."

She ground her teeth. Must he do that? Finish her sentences for her as Bartlett had?

"Your uncle—"

"S-s-should know about this w-w-with all haste." She crossed her arms. "I quite agree. I w-w-will w-w-wait with Red Beads w-w-while you inform him."

His nostrils flared, refusal written on his face.

"I s-s-shall, of course, remain with these two"—she motioned to the soldiers who looked more uncomfortable by the moment—"until you return w-w-with his response."

"Response to what?"

"W-w-why, to the indignant w-w-way this young w-w-wo-wo—

"Woman."

Oh, she wanted to smack him, but she sucked in a deep breath and plunged on, "W-w-woman is being manhandled, of course."

He shifted his feet, glared at the soldiers who remained mute, then back at her. He pointed at the ground. "Do not move from that spot until I return." He snapped his glare back to the soldiers. "See that she remains." Then he pivoted and strode to the castle.

Abigail hadn't agreed to his demand, but she wasn't foolish enough to ignore it either. She signed to Red Beads, *I am sorry.*

The other woman couldn't sign in return with a soldier hanging onto each arm. "I come work with Lurana Quinn. Learn bake bread soldiers eat. They not believe me."

"If that were true, why was she sneaking around behind the castle?" one of the soldiers asked.

"'Tis true." Abigail addressed the men. "I w-w-worked beside her myself, and w-w-with her s-s-sister."

Red Beads nodded, but neither man loosened his hold. They were soldiers, after all, on duty to protect the fort and those in it. Even while she was angry for Red Beads's sake, she allowed they were only doing their duty.

Another man, not in soldiers' garb, leaned against the back wall of the bake house and watched. Abigail's eyes met his for a moment, and the man had the gall to touch his hat brim and grin at her. She stepped to the side and turned, presenting him with her back.

"W-w-where is S-s-shining Day?"

The Indian woman looked down, her dusky cheeks darkening as she lifted and let drop one shoulder.

The soldiers exchanged a look.

Oh, would she never learn to curb her stammering tongue? What if Shining Day were outside the fort? What if she'd escaped the men? What if they decided to go after her next?

"I come without her," Red Beads raised her eyes. "Our mother not wish us come again. She not trust…"

No wonder she had been drawn to Red Beads from the start. A fellow rebel in a world that did not tolerate them gladly.

"What is happening here?" Lurana Quinn's voice broke the tension. Or perhaps added to it, the soldiers straightening at her approach. One thing Abigail had learned early on was how much the little woman was revered by the soldiers. Uncle said they would walk over hot coals for her… at least as long as she kept them well-supplied in breads and tarts and scones. Without her, their only bread would be rock-hard ship's biscuits or crumbly corn cakes cooked over their own fires.

"These men are holding Red Beads until Ensign Tharp returns w-w-with w-w-word from my uncle."

"Are they, indeed?" She glared at the soldiers who were looking anywhere else. "When I have bread to bake and no help for it?"

Uncle Corne, followed by the ensign, emerged from the castle. By the force with which his boots stuck the dirt, her uncle wasn't happy. Not happy at all.

"Abigail!"

She flinched but stood firm. "Uncle?"

"Why are you not in your room?"

She gestured to Red Beads. "I s-s-saw this injustice from my w-w-window and knew I needed to address it."

"Injustice?"

"'Twould appear so," Lurana Quinn said.

Uncle Corne jerked in her direction, as if he hadn't seen her on his approach. And he probably hadn't, so intent had he been on Abigail.

"What do you know about this?" His words lost their bark while addressing the little baker.

"Red Beads—as well as your niece—has been assisting me in the bake house." She wiped her hands on the apron that enveloped her. "I do not know how much longer I will be able to produce the extra bread you require to feed the new troops that continue to arrive without their help."

Uncle Corne's mouth firmed into a hard line. "And you swear that this woman is here only for that purpose?"

Lurana Quinn inclined her head. "I do."

He huffed out and breath and waved off the soldiers. "Let her go." Then he pointed at the baker. "But know this, you are responsible for her. If anything goes wrong—

"Nothing will." She cocked her head at him. "And your niece?"

Uncle Corne looked between Abigail and Lurana Quinn, then shook his head. "I suppose she may join you as well." He pointed again. "But you are also responsible for her, understood?"

The woman inclined her head again, every bit as regal as a matriarch back in Boston.

Her uncle harrumphed and turned, stomping his way back to the castle. "Tharp! They have no need of you in the bake house."

The ensign followed at a brisk pace, obviously preferring to be anywhere Abigail wasn't. It shouldn't have hurt, but it did… a little.

"Thank you." Red Beads rubbed her arms once the soldiers had released her. The men retreated in the opposite direction from the castle as if their boots were on fire.

What was it with men, anyway? Even the one who had been lurking behind the bake house was gone.

"Come." Lurana Quinn marched toward the bake house

leaving Abigail and Red Beads to scurry to keep up. "We have drawn enough attention for one morning."

True, but at least Abigail was out of her room and once again in the company of the two people who could teach her what she most wished to learn.

Chapter 16

I t was foolish to run so fast through the woods, making enough noise to wake a hibernating bear, but Koyen couldn't stop himself.

Red Beads was inside the fort. She had to be, for she was nowhere else that she should have been.

Their mother was beside herself with worry—as was Koyen —but the worry didn't completely squash his urge to wring his sister's neck. Why couldn't she be more biddable, like Shining Day? That sister would never have run off as soon as their mother's back was turned. No one was exactly sure when she'd gone missing. She'd lied—lied—to both their mother and their sister, keeping either from realizing her whereabouts.

But she'd begged again that morning to return to Lurana Quinn's care and teaching. That plus some moccasin prints leading away from where she should have been washing clothes, leading toward the fort, had sent Koyen on the run.

He had no idea how he was to extract her from the fortress once he arrived, which increased his ire tenfold. At least.

He glanced at the sky through the tops of the trees. The sun was well past its zenith and heading west. The days were long and hot in the middle of summer. He'd have no darkness to hide him. Any plan he came up with, he discarded with the next stride.

He was one man against an army.

Maybe he should leave her there and let her get a taste of her foolishness. They must have caught her—or perhaps let her in— but why would they release her? They still held the scouts, and it had been a fortnight. It would serve her right to be locked up with them.

But even as the thought swirled around him, he mentally swatted it away.

Because the answer was clear. The only way he would free Red Beads was by an exchange of prisoners. Himself for her. He could endure whatever the punishment would be. His sister, however... what they might do to her...

He slowed as he approached the palisade, pressing the heel of his hand to his side and breathing in long pulls of humid air. Giving himself a few moments, he caught his breath and then sneaked as close to the gate as he could without being seen.

Soldiers with muskets manned the heights. The massive gate was shut. Hammers rang against metal inside. A man shouted orders. In the distance, waves washed against the sand. And in a branch high above his head, a mourning dove cooed.

Mourning Dove. The woman was too often in his thoughts for comfort. The British lady who had befriended his sisters to the point of risking her own life to see them to their village. It had been a foolish gesture, of course, but that she'd made it said something about her. Something he tried not to think about.

Koyen secreted himself in a good location to be able to see both the gate and the path that led to the river. Work crews would come back along that path. If one came in toward evening, there might be a soldier he knew with it. One who might be able to bring his sister out to him. It was his best chance—perhaps his only chance—to avoid being taken prisoner again.

The sun dipped lower, but the heat didn't dissipate.

The faintest rustle caught his attention. It came from behind him, not from the path. The brush of pine needles against buckskin.

Koyen whirled.

Walks Fast grinned from no more than two strides away. Then he signed, *"It is good you watch. What have you seen?"*

Koyen shook his head. *"I come for my sister. She is inside."*

Walks Fast rubbed his chin. *"Very smart."*

"She does not watch." Red Beads could not be a spy. Her face was easier to read than deer sign in a mud flat. Which is why he should have known she'd come back to the fort. *"She learns from the Onondaga woman inside."*

"Lurana Quinn?" Walks Fast's voice was soft, but full of surprise.

"Yes."

"That one, she is too much British to be trusted." The other man frowned. "It would be better for your sister to stay away from her."

"I have told her the same."

Koyen ducked as metal hinges squealed. He flattened himself to the forest floor.

Walks Fast sprawled beside him, watching, his musket in one hand between them.

Red Beads appeared in the opening with… Mourning Dove.

The sun's rays picked up a hint of gold in the British woman's hair where it escaped the white linen cap. Her face was drawn, serious, as Red Beads stepped outside of the fort, turning to wave before heading toward the village.

The gate's hinges squealed again, closing Mourning Dove from his sight.

He hissed at Walks Fast, "Go, before she sees you."

The man crept away.

Koyen rose and worked from tree to tree, keeping out of his sister's sight until she was on the main path to the village. Then he stepped in front of her.

She gasped, hand flying to her chest. "Koyen!"

"Yes. It is your brother." He crossed his arms. "This time you are lucky."

"I—

"You will not be so lucky when you face our mother."

She hung her head, but her shoulders remained straight and proud.

She needed a husband—and soon. But if he said as much, it would prompt his mother to urge him to visit High Clouds and her family. And he wasn't ready for that. Not yet.

Not when Mourning Dove visited his dreams too many nights.

Ensign Tharp burst through the door, and Abigail jumped, barely preventing the ink on her quill from spattering on the paper before her.

Uncle Corne rose from behind his desk. "What is the meaning—?"

"Captain, sir, the woodcutters are under attack!"

Uncle started toward the door, then jabbed a finger at Abigail. "Into your room and remain there. Lock the door."

She wiped the nib of her quill and set it down before following. Her uncle and the ensign were already disappearing down the stairs when she entered the corridor. She was opening her door when Judith approached from the other direction, a basket full of needlework in her hands.

"What is happening?" the other woman asked.

The entire building shook from the roar of a cannon overhead.

"'Tis another attack." Abigail raced back into her uncle's room and rushed to the open window. Shouting, feet pounding, and then a distant scream. She wanted to press her hands over her ears but restrained herself.

Judith went to the other side of the window. "Another one." Her voice trembled. "How many will we lose to those savages this time?"

Something tugged at the back of Abigail's dress. She twisted and plucked Dance from halfway up her skirt, then cuddled the trembling kitten under her chin. The poor dear was terrified.

How many men would die? A normal detail of woodcutters would be six. She knew that much from keeping her uncle's records. And she'd heard during dinner one evening that they were to remain close to the fort, removing trees not only to burn but to push the forest farther from the fort's walls.

So this attack was close.

Several soldiers on horseback raced across the parade ground toward the forest gate. Abigail held her breath as the gate squealed open, as it had two evenings past when Red Beads had left.

Oh. She sank onto Uncle Corne's chair.

"Are you well?" Judith hovered over her. "You have gone quite pale."

"I am w-w-well. 'Tis just the s-s-shock."

"Naturally." The other woman brought Abigail's chair close and sat. "We are all shocked by such heathen behavior." She pressed the back of her hand to her brow. "What sort of people attack others who are simply gathering firewood?"

Red Beads's sort of people.

Something twisted in Abigail's chest. She couldn't align the vivacious dark-haired woman, her arms coated in flour, eyes dancing with humor, with the attack happening outside the palisade. She stroked Dance, her little head buried against Abigail's neck.

Not by Red Beads herself, of course. Yet the Seneca woman had been inside the fort just two days before. The timing was—

"I suppose this is what comes of allowing them into the fort at all," Judith said. "Even those young women who help in the bake house."

Abigail cringed inside. If Judith had drawn that conclusion, then surely Uncle Corne would as well. But they were wrong. Nothing had been said on Friday about any woodcutting detail, not in the bake house, not in front of Red Beads. Abigail had been at her side the entire time she'd been in the fort, had even walked her to the gate.

Had wished Koyen had been there waiting to see his sister home. Had worried about her safety. Had wished he'd seen that she'd looked after his sister while in the fort.

As he'd asked.

Gunfire erupted outside the walls, followed by more distant shouts. They didn't last long, and then the horsemen returned, several with men riding double. Two with men draped across their laps, arms and legs dangling on either side of the horse.

"Oh, my." Judith had risen and leaned against the window frame. "'Tis not good, I fear." She turned to Abigail. "I must join the other wives."

"Of course." After seeing her friend to the door, Abigail returned to her perch and watched the activity below. The two bodies were left on the horses—they must be dead or they would have been taken to the fort's surgeon straight away—but the other men riding double dismounted and walked off. Probably to report to Uncle Corne and the other officers.

Would he insist Abigail discontinue her friendship with Red

147

Beads? Of course he would. On the one hand, Abigail couldn't blame him. He was charged—along with the other officers—with keeping the fort safe. And it had been attacked two days after Red Beads had returned. But the first time, the Seneca woman and her sister been inside the fort during the attack. Surely that meant Abigail's friend wasn't guilty of spying.

Did it not?

———

COOL WATER LAPPED AGAINST HIS KNEES WHILE THE sun warmed Koyen's face, but every muscle in his body tensed, spear held steady, waiting for the exact moment to strike. A motion, slight but telling. Another ripple, and he launched the lance toward it, thrusting with enough force to pierce through to the other side. With a flick and a jerk, he pulled the flailing fish from the water, his spear bending under the weight.

His bare toes finding purchase amid the slippery rocks, he brought his prize to the riverbank and added it to the three fish already in his basket. They would eat their fill that evening.

"Well done."

Koyen whipped around toward the voice, the empty spear held poised to strike. "Tall Otter." He lowered the weapon. "Have you escaped?"

"No. They released us."

"That is good."

The other Seneca man stretched his arms out and then up. "It is good to have room to move again."

"What made them change their minds?"

Tall Otter wagged his head. "Who knows the thoughts of the white man? But we are not welcome to return. That was told to us. Our scouting days are over, my friend."

148

It came as no surprise. Koyen dropped to the ground beside the fish basket.

"Are you still wanting to join with Farmer's Brother?" Tall Otter sank beside him.

"Do you? Has this changed your mind? Are you ready to fight now?"

The other man plucked a blade of grass and smoothed it between his fingers. "No. For the same reasons. The Seneca would lose." He twisted to face Koyen. "We have lost enough, I think."

"My mother agrees with you."

"And you?"

It was a good question, one he'd been mulling over for days. "The thirst to fight has left me, but the anger has not."

It was true. He still rebelled at the changes the white man had brought to his people, but he had no desire to see the empty longhouse cots or hear the weeping of widows and children. And for nothing. He'd come to agree with his mother and Tall Otter. The Seneca would not come out of open conflict victorious. They would come out even more changed—and far fewer.

They rested without speaking for a while, listening to birdsong and the spotted frogs that thrived along the river, and swatting at mosquitoes.

"There may be a way you can help our people battle the British without musket, tomahawk, or knife."

Koyen sat up straight. "I am listening."

"Farmer's Brother and his followers will battle in the old way, the way of our fathers. But our ways need to change."

"Our ways were good enough for our fathers and our grandfathers."

"You are as good with a bow as anyone." Tall Otter nodded toward the basket. "And better than most with the spear. But a bow and a spear have not the deadly reach of a musket. The white man's weapons we cannot create for ourselves."

"Farmer's Brother has muskets and bullets and gun powder. He will meet the British with equal weapons."

The older man cocked an eyebrow at Koyen. "And how long do you think they will continue to sell us those things once we turn them against the soldiers?"

Koyen looked across the river. Tall Otter was right, but it still angered him.

"The French were happy to give us these things to use against the British—their enemies. But the French are gone. They will not return. The British know this even if Pontiac refuses to believe it."

"Then what can we do?" Koyen asked.

"If the British are here to stay, as I believe they are, we must learn to live in peace with them."

Koyen pressed the heels of his hands against his eyes, then turned to face Tall Otter. "You said there was something I could do. What is this thing?" Something better than spying, he hoped.

"You can speak the white man's words, the British words. There is a British man much esteemed by the Mohawks." Tall Otter glanced to the east and back again. "His name is William Johnson."

"I have heard of him." Everyone had. The man's fame had spread wide and long.

"It is said he has taken Molly Brant, a Mohawk woman, as his wife. He lives among the Mohawks, but the British trust him as well."

"What has this to do with me?"

"The Mohawks are Iroquois too, but they are Mohawk first." Tall Otter shrugged. "It would be good to have a Seneca who spoke the language close to William Johnson. To speak for the

Seneca. To speak for peace with the British instead of war." His eyes met Koyens. "There were more ways than one to meet an enemy."

As much as Koyen didn't want to admit it, his mother and Tall Otter were probably right. Fighting against an enemy many times larger and many times stronger was foolish. But it still rankled his spirit.

Koyen turned his attention back to the river. It was the one constant near his people, always flowing, always providing both food and water. And yet, it changed too. At one time—before the days of his grandfather's grandfather—it had cut the deep gorge that hid Devil's Hole. A flood, a drought, a beaver's dam, and the mighty river could alter its course.

The British were more disruptive than a flood, a drought, or any beaver's dam.

He rose and lifted the fish basket. "I will think on your words."

Tall Otter nodded but stretched back on the grass and let Koyen return to the village by himself.

Maybe Koyen should take a trip to the Mohawk village and see for himself the esteemed man called William Johnson.

Chapter 17

Returning with a small bowl of salt pork scraps she'd begged the cook to save for Dance, Abigail had her key in the lock of her room when Uncle Corne stepped into the corridor.

"What is this?" He scrunched his nose at the bits of meat trimmings in the bowl "Are you not eating enough at meals?"

"'Tis for Dance." The confusion on his face was too comical, and she couldn't suppress a giggle. "Come meet her."

She opened the door, and the gray-and-orange kitten rushed toward her, or perhaps toward the bowl she carried.

"A cat?" He took a step backward.

"'Tis exactly w-w-what I needed to keep my room free of p-p-pests."

He raised one eyebrow at the gangly kitten, who had attacked the bowl of scraps as soon as it touched the floor.

"Where did you get it?"

"Lurana Quinn keeps a cat in the bake house to p-p-prevent mice from getting into the flour and other s-s-supplies."

He frowned in earnest then. "Indeed, about Lurana Quinn." He cleared his throat. "I will not forbid you from continuing to learn from her on Fridays." He raised a finger. "Only on Fridays, mind you. However, if the Indian girl comes again, you must inform me immediately."

"Red Beads?" Her stomach dropped. "W-w-why?"

"I am given to understand that she speaks English. She must be questioned, of course."

"You w-w-would not lock her up, w-w-would you?"

"If 'twould keep you and me and the garrison safe? Of course I would." He patted her shoulder. "But I do not expect that to be the case."

"But Red Beads w-w-was w-w-with me all last Friday. No one s-s-spoke of the fort activities w-w-while w-w-we w-w-worked. No one. S-s-she could not have overheard any p-p-plans."

"Then she has nothing to worry about from me, I assure you." He pointed at Dance, who had finished her scraps and was cleaning her whiskers. "That one either, if you keep it out of my way."

Abigail scooped up the kitten and cuddled her as he left, closing the door behind him.

"W-w-what s-s-should I do, Dance? S-s-she is my friend. At least, I think s-s-she is." She stroked the soft fur under the kitten's chin, bringing forth a rumbling purr.

"I hope s-s-she is."

But the seed of doubt that had been planted during the attack had taken root. A tentative root, but a root just the same.

———

THEIR MOTHER BRAIDED RED BEADS HAIR AS SHE HAD when the girl was young, but with fingers that trembled slightly. Koyen wanted to argue with her, but his previous attempts had fallen on stubborn ears. And he had no authority over a clan mother. None.

It rankled.

He took some grim satisfaction that his sister's face was pale and her knuckles white in her lap, hands squeezed together, lips firm.

She ought to be afraid. Returning to the fort had been foolish. Even though those who had attacked hadn't come from their village, they were Seneca. And without a scout left in the fort, who would tell Sergeant Hagerman the attacking Seneca had come from villages to the east? No one.

They would assume Red Beads was a spy.

Koyen was glad he'd sent Walks Fast away so that his sister hadn't seen him. She wouldn't have identified him, he was sure, but neither could she keep her face from giving away her knowledge. His sister had no guile.

He shot a glance toward Shining Day. That one had enough guile for both sisters. But she was also smart enough to stay away from the fort.

Red Beads stood, smoothed the front of her shirt—a cloth shirt like the white women wore—tucked into her buckskin skirt. Already that one had a foot in both worlds.

If Koyen made the trip to the Mohawk lands to see William Johnson, it could end with him having a foot in both worlds as well. He'd talked at length with his mother the evening Tall Otter had suggested it. She'd been much happier about his going east than she was about her daughter returning to the fort.

But she was allowing it. Koyen had demanded to know why, which had been the exact wrong tactic to take, and she had refused to answer him. Or maybe—he searched his mother's face—maybe she didn't understand her reasoning either. Maybe she was following an intuition. The clan mothers sometimes did.

And most of the time they turned out to be right.

"I am ready." Red Beads picked up her basket and looked at Koyen.

He rose, nodded to their mother, then followed Red Beads out of the longhouse. They traveled the path under the tall trees accompanied by the whispering of the wind through the pines. He stopped before they approached the fort.

"If you have trouble, go to Mourning Dove." He almost bit his tongue as the name slipped out.

"Mourning Dove?" Her brows pulled together.

"The one called Abigail Aldridge."

"Oh." Her eyes widened. "Oh!"

"Her hair and eyes, they reminded me of a mourning dove."

"I did not know my brother noticed such things in a British woman." The hint of laughter in her voice grated against his ears.

"I am not blind."

She laughed outright then.

"Do not be foolish either." He clasped her shoulder and gave it a shake. "They could take you captive. You may never see our mother or sister again."

She lifted her chin. "I do not believe that will happen. Lurana Quinn will watch out for me and so will... Mourning Dove."

He growled low in his throat. It was born of frustration and exasperation in equal measure. But a part of him grudgingly admired his sister's courage. Could he have walked back into the fort after being released from captivity? He would have, to save her when he'd feared she'd been taken captive, but without that provocation? No. He would have been happy to remain in the village or the forest... or maybe even join with Farmer's Brother.

The journey to see William Johnson gave him another option. While it lacked the glory and honor of a battle well fought, he'd come to see the wisdom in Tall Otter's words.

There were more ways than one to meet an enemy.

Perhaps Red Beads had reached that conclusion before him.

He continued along the path, watchful and listening, but they met no one and soon arrived outside the gate. He stepped into the clearing, in full sight of the soldiers on the palisade, keeping Red Beads behind him.

"Sister come for Lurana Quinn."

"That you, Koyen?" George Swan shouted back.

"Yes."

George waved a hand at someone behind him. "Send her in. She bakes bread."

"I will return for you. Do not leave without me."

"First you worry that they will keep me, and then you tell me to stay." She gave him a sassy smile that trembled only a little as she strode away.

The gate opened, and Mourning Dove waited for Red Beads on the other side. For a moment, their eyes met.

"Care for her," he signed.

"I will. Always."

He had to snap his mouth shut. Where had she learned that? He'd only made the gesture to comfort himself.

She'd answered him.

In his people's language.

"You wait for me." Red Beads said as she walked beside Abigail toward the castle.

Abigail stopped and faced her friend. "My uncle w-w-wishes to s-s-see you. He w-w-would s-s-sp-sp—"

"Use hand talk."

Of course. Abigail took a deep breath and signed, *"He would speak with you*"—she didn't know the next motion—"about the attacks."

"I answer questions." Her response was without affront, without a hint of defensiveness. And her face was as open and honest as it always had been.

Abigail drew in another deep breath, one of relief. Her friend had nothing to hide. She shouldn't have doubted it. She linked her arm through Red Beads's and they continued to the castle.

Lurana Quinn watched from the bake house doorway, and Abigail freed her arm to sign, *"It is good."* It wasn't exactly what she'd wanted to say, but it was close enough. The Onondaga woman nodded and retreated into her domain.

They reached the door to the castle, and Ensign Tharp stepped aside for them to enter, then followed them up the stairs to Uncle Corne's room. He reached around them and thumped on the door. "Your niece and Scout Koyen's sister, sir."

"Enter."

"Her name is Red Beads," Abigail hissed at him as she passed. He could have taken a moment—spoken to Abigail—and asked. It annoyed her greatly that he hadn't. That he hadn't spoken to her at all, and that he'd treated her friend as if she were of no consequence.

Abigail had been treated that way for most of her life.

She took Red Beads's arm again and marched to the front of her uncle's desk. "Reporting as ordered, s-s-sir."

His brows hiked at her tone, and she regretted it.

"I am s-s-sorry, Uncle. 'Twas not you who has vexed me."

"Indeed, well." He rose. "Introduce me to your friend, Abigail."

At least her uncle knew how to be a gentleman. "This is Red Beads of the S-s-seneca. Red Beads, my uncle, Captain Hayward."

157

Uncle Corne bowed slightly. "A pleasure, Red Beads."

Red Beads glanced at Abigail, then dipped into the curtsy that Abigail had shown her during one of their baking Fridays. "A pleasure, Captain Hayward."

He sank back to his seat and folded his hands on the desk before him. "Good. I had heard that you spoke our language well. As does your brother, I know."

Red Beads nodded.

"I need to ask you what you know of the attacks that have happened outside the fort. Attacks during which five of our soldiers have been killed."

Abigail clenched her hands together. So much depended on what was said next—on what was believed.

"I know they happen. I know warriors from my village not take part." Red Beads's voice was calm and sure, even as her knuckles whitened as she gripped the sides of her skirt.

"And how do you know this?" Uncle Corne asked.

"All in village know this."

Her uncle pinched the bridge of his nose. "Then where did the warriors who attacked come from?"

"Other Seneca from east. I not know more."

He leaned forward. "Would others in your village know?"

Red Beads paused, her lips pinched into a line. "I not hear anyone say. Some maybe. I not know."

Abigail released her breath and loosened her fists, her fingers almost numb from the strain.

Uncle Corne leaned back against his chair. "Thank you, Abigail, for bringing your friend here." He waved toward the door. "Enjoy your day with Lurana Quinn. Perhaps you'll bake something special for your old uncle?"

"I w-w-will." She sent him a grateful smile, then marched past Ensign Tharp and into the corridor.

Uncle Corne believed Red Beads too—and that was good enough for her.

———

"I CANNOT BELIEVE HOW QUICKLY YOU LEARN THE hand talk." Lurana Quinn beamed up at Abigail. "As if you were born to it."

Abigail almost burst with pride, but she answered truthfully, "It does not have all the bothersome little w-w-words that s-s-speaking does." It didn't. It lacked the connecting words that made full sentences, but yet it was easy to understand. For her, anyway. She added the little words in her head.

"Now we like sisters. Know two languages," Red Beads said. "One hers, one mine."

Like sisters.

The thought made Abigail pause. Red Beads was nothing like Susanna, who barely recognized their relationship at all. A full sister to Bartlett and older by two years, she lived in Boston but had somehow managed to avoid Abigail for years. Deloris, her sister-in-law, was a small improvement. She may have treated Abigail like an imbecile at times, but at least she acknowledged her existence. To be a real sister to Red Beads, however, she'd have to marry the Indian girl's brother.

Heat surged to her cheeks. Where had that thought come from?

Lurana Quinn laughed. "We have embarrassed her with our praise."

"Only a little." Abigail resisted the urge to fan her face with the skirt of her apron. Better they think that than know where her wayward mind had drifted. She glanced out the door. "Come, 'tis best if w-w-we hurry to the fort's gate."

They stripped off their aprons and hung them up, then Red

Beads slipped a cloth-wrapped loaf of bread into her basket, and Abigail wrapped another cloth around a stack of shortbreads for her uncle.

"I will see you both back again next week." Lurana Quinn stood by the door as they left. "Come early and we will bake something new."

Abigail turned around. "W-w-what?"

The Onondaga woman grinned. "Molasses biscuits."

Red Beads's eyes rounded, and Abigail's mouth watered. It would be a long week to wait for that. She turned and tucked her arm around her friend's when a thought occurred to her.

She was looking forward to baking almost as much as to learning hand talk.

She—Abigail Aldridge—enjoying herself in a bake house surrounded by heat, flour, the constant aroma of yeast, and trickles of smoke from the fire. She clicked through the dates in her mind. It'd been scarcely two and a half months. How could she be so changed from the Boston Abigail?

Red Beads chattered about molasses and how much she enjoyed it, something she'd never tasted until coming to the fort. Abigail half-listened as they approached the gate. It was open, with soldiers visible on the wall and several others close by. A movement outside caught her attention and caused a hitch to her step.

Red Beads looked up and smiled at her. "My brother. He come take me home." She leaned close and whispered. "He call you Mourning Dove."

Abigail gasped. He called her that? Why? She stared at him on the far side of the gate, not at his bare chest or legs—it being the heat of summer, he'd stopped wearing leggings and was covered only with his breechclout and moccasins—but into his eyes. They were not the cold, hard bits of onyx she'd become used to in her uncle's room. Yet something fiery burned in their dark depths.

Something that stole her breath away.

Red Beads giggled. "He mean no harm, I promise." She squeezed Abigail's arm before dropping it. "I see you again." She ran to her brother without a backward glance, but his eyes didn't leave Abigail until he followed Red Beads into the forest.

Abigail hugged the shortbreads to her middle and turned toward the castle.

"A girl like you, miss, should have a proper escort." The man who had leaned against the bake house and watched her with Red Beads the week before stepped out from the shade of the palisade. His clothing was a combination of leather and cloth like the sutlers wore, and on his feet were moccasins, not boots. His skin was darkened by the sun. If not for the reddish tint to his dark hair, he might have been an Indian.

"I s-s-shall be fine crossing the p-p-parade grounds, sir." She sidled to the side to pass by him, but he stepped into her path.

"Allow me to see you to the castle." Without warning, he clamped his fingers around her upper arm and leaned close. Too close. His hot breath, reeking of fish and tobacco and decay, assaulted her. "Your brother asked me to speak to you, dearie He wants you back in Boston, and he's prepared to pay a pretty penny to have you delivered."

She jerked but could not free her arm. "Unhand me, s-s-sir, or I s-s-shall s-s-scream."

"And disturb the soldiers? For what? For a gentleman offering you his protection?" The laugh that followed was low and... evil.

"You, s-s-sir, are no gentleman, and my uncle w-w-will hear of this."

He let go of her arm and took a step back before touching his hat to her. "Another time, perhaps, dearie. Your brother, he was most insistent that I find a way to return what he has lost."

Indignation battled with fear to stall her tongue as the man walked away. She should tell Uncle Corne, of course, but…

What if he agreed to let that odious man return her to Bartlett?

She couldn't risk that.

Chapter 18

I t was a white man's house.

While that shouldn't have surprised Koyen, it did. William Johnson was so highly praised by the Mohawks that it seemed odd he would choose to live in a white man's house. It was nestled in a forest opening far enough from the Mohawk village to be secluded. The structure was flanked by a barn and several smaller buildings, but still, it appeared lonely.

Was it not better to live among one's clan? To have family and extended family nearby? To be a part of something bigger than one's self? That was the Seneca way.

Not the white man's.

Koyen watched for a while as dawn broke over the scene before him, content to rest and learn before he walked into the open. A part of him still chafed at walking away from Pontiac's war, but the first fires of battle that had stirred his blood had been quenched. Quenched by the wisdom of his mother and Tall Otter and even Lurana Quinn. And if he would be honest with himself, quenched by the relationships he'd formed—however unwillingly—within the fort.

George Swan was a good man, white or not. Sergeant Hagerman, while gruff and blustery, was a good man too. Even Mourning Dove's uncle had always treated him with respect.

Mourning Dove. The woman pecked at his thoughts far too often. Her actions, more than all the others, had doused his eagerness for a fight. That she had gone out of her way, even endangered herself, to protect his sisters was something he struggled to understand.

They were enemies. They should be enemies. But she refused to act like one, even as he sensed her fear of him.

Koyen shifted on the hard ground. The earth needed a good rain to soften it and to cool things off. He squinted into the rising sun. The sun was barely up, and it was already hot. He glanced back at the house as the door opened.

A woman emerged with a babe strapped to her front. Her hair was black and braided, but she wore a dress of cloth as wide as Mourning Dove's and as colorful. Two small children scampered after her, both naked and laughing, as Indian children of that age would in his village. Then behind them came three dark women in plain cloth dresses.

Koyen had seen the dark slave man owned by Major Wilkins at the fort. Slavery was a common practice among Indian tribes as well, but these slaves were different. Their skin was as dark as a beaver's tail. Their black hair was as woolly as the hump of the great bison. He'd heard they came from across the salt water, as did the English and French.

How many types of people must live there?

His mother's words about scooping the sand returned to him again. He could not deny her wisdom, nor the evidence before his own eyes. With a resigned sigh, he stood and let himself be seen.

The tallest child shouted and pointed to him.

Koyen raised his hands away from the knife and tomahawk at his belt and the musket strapped between his shoulders.

The woman said something that had the two children scurrying for the house. One of the dark women moved to the doorway, as if to protect them. The other two moved to each side of the woman who was obviously in charge.

"Nyah-weh-sgeh-noh!" Koyen called the traditional Seneca greeting, well-known among the Iroquois tribes.

The woman with the babe stepped forward and returned the greeting.

Koyen moved forward, still keeping his hands clear of his weapons. "Is this the house of William Johnson?" he asked in the Iroquois language. Not that he had any doubt, but politeness required he ask.

"It is. I am Molly Brandt."

The Mohawk wife.

"Is your man home?"

"He is." The masculine voice came from behind the house.

Koyen stopped halfway across the clearing, searching for the owner of the voice. A tall man with the long, narrow nose sported by so many of the British—but without the white wig worn by most men of importance, led a horse around the house and in front of the women. He held a pistol at this waist.

"Who looks for me?"

"Koyengquahtah"—Koyen switched to English—"Seneca Wolf Clan, from near Fort Niagara."

"Welcome to my home, Young King."

"Soldiers call me Koyen."

The man laughed. "I suppose they do. The Anglican version of your name would not be acceptable to them. They recognize only one king, George III. Come." The man waved him forward and then tucked the pistol into his belt. "Tell me what is happening near the fort. I have not been there or heard from Major Wilkins in too long."

Koyen nodded toward the horse. "You travel?"

"'Tis nothing that cannot wait." He handed the reins to one of the dark women, then turned back to Koyen. "Come. We will visit, and you can tell me what brings a Seneca here onto Mohawk lands."

Molly Brandt called to the children. She and two of the dark women herded them toward the fields planted with corn, beans, and squash beyond the outbuildings. The other woman disappeared around the house leading the horse.

Koyen joined William Johnson, following him to the broad porch of the house, where he was offered a chair. The man entered the house and returned in moments with two tankards, handing one to Koyen.

He sniffed the contents.

The other man laughed. "'Tis not spirits, my friend. While I may enjoy a bit on special occasions, 'tis far too early in the morning for that." He took a long drink from his tankard.

Koyen did the same. It was water, pure and fresh and cold.

"We have our own well at the back of the house. Nothing as fancy as the inside well at the castle."

"I know the well there." It was one of the features, along with thick stone walls that would not burn, that made the place almost invincible.

William Johnson leaned back in his chair and eyed Koyen. "Tell me," he said at last, "what news do you bring of the fort?"

Koyen eyed him for a moment. Surely this was a man he could speak to. A man esteemed by two peoples. A man with an open face, a steady eye, and a ready grin. A man with a wife and children and servants who were willing to stand between the Iroquois and the white man. To help the Iroquois—which included the Seneca. Not a man who threatened.

He liked what he saw in William Johnson.

Abigail smoothed her dress, checked that her hair was neat beneath its linen cap, and then pinched her cheeks. She couldn't see color in her reflection from the window —the room having no looking glass—but it would have to do. Then she scooped Dance from the bed and snuggled her close for a long moment, breathing in the faintly dusty odor that clung to the rapidly growing cat.

"Keep the room free of mice w-w-while I am away." She toed the square basket, lined with strips from an old petticoat, until it rested in a sunbeam, then placed Dance inside.

The kitten circled twice, her claws snatching and releasing the fabric until it conformed to her standards before she curled into it.

"Be s-s-sure to leave one eye open w-w-while you s-s-sleep."

A face-cracking yawn that exposed the cat's back teeth was her only answer.

Abigail unlocked the door and stepped into the corridor, locking it again and pocketing her key. Then she faced Ensign Tharp. The man had barely acknowledged her since sneaking the Indian girls outside the fort. She couldn't blame him, but she needed him again. And felt more than a little guilty over it. After all, he'd endured some form of punishment from her scheming already. But she pulled in a fortifying breath and pasted on a smile.

"Ensign Tharp."

He flashed his eyes toward her and away again so fast she almost missed it. "Miss Aldridge."

"W-w-would you be s-s-so good as to escort me to the gate to meet Red Beads? And then escort us both to the bake house?"

His blue eyes snapped back to her, suspicion almost palpable in their depths. "Escort you?"

She kept the smile firmly in place and nodded. It wasn't that she wanted his company, but he would be a positive deterrent to that odious man Bartlett had sent. Abigail hadn't said anything about him to her uncle. She'd stayed within the walls of the castle for the past week, fairly certain that the man would not try to sneak her out from within the fortress.

"'Twould depend upon the wishes of Captain Hayward, of course, miss."

"Of course." She crossed the corridor and rapped on the door.

"Enter!"

She opened the door wide enough to poke her head inside. "Uncle, can you s-s-spare Ensign Tharp long enough to escort me to the gate to meet Red Beads?"

"What?" Uncle Corne raised his head from the scattered paperwork strewn across his desk. "What's that?"

"I s-s-should like an escort this morning, if you can s-s-spare the ensign for a few moments."

"Indeed, of course, my dear." He made a shooing motion. "Whatever you need." Then his attention fell again to whatever lay before him.

Guilt pinched her, but only for a moment, at leaving him when he was buried in work. After all, she'd be back at his side the next day. She closed the door and turned to the ensign, opening her mouth—

"I heard." The words were stiff and short, but he extended his arm, and she rested her hand upon it.

"I do appreciate it, ensign, I assure you."

"At your service, miss."

Those words were a little warmer, and she squeezed her fingers against the thick wool of his coat sleeve. "There w-w-was a man last w-w-week w-w-who..." How much should she say?

The ensign bent a smidgen closer. "Who what, Miss?"

"W-w-who unsettled me. He w-w-was an unpleasant s-s-sort w-w-who made s-s-so bold as to approach me."

Ensign Tharp straightened, becoming the picture of a perfect soldier, head high, eyes sharp and alert, steps crisp and precise.

"I feel s-s-so much better w-w-with you at my s-s-side." She glanced at him. "And I mean that s-s-sincerely, ensign. I am not attempting to manipulate you in any w-w-way." He ignored that, but she needed to clear the air. "W-w-what I did w-w-was inexcusable, and I regret it deeply. I s-s-see now that I s-s-should have gone to my uncle and not entangled you in the matter. I am s-s-sorry."

"'Tis in the past, miss." But his words held less edge.

Abigail wouldn't push it any farther. That small thawing between them was a start. They left the castle and made it to the gate without a glimpse of the man who had accosted her. Red Beads waited, but it wasn't her brother who lingered at the forest edge. It was the other scout—former scout—who had come to Uncle Corne's room.

She and Red Beads linked arms and walked toward the bake house, Ensign Tharp falling in step behind.

"The w-w-week has been long, w-w-waiting to taste Lurana Quinn's molasses biscuits."

"Been long for me too." Red Beads glanced around then whispered, "Brother gone to see William Johnson."

So that explained his absence. "W-w-who is he?"

Red Beads tilted her head. "I thought you know. He important man to British. To Iroquois."

"I have not heard of him, but I w-w-will ask my uncle."

"Is good Koyen go there, Mother say. He maybe work at peace, not war."

Her uncle's words came back to her—*As soon slit our throats as take our coin.* Perhaps he had misread the Seneca scouts—Koyen in particular. The idea pleased her more than it should, but before she could delve into it more, they arrived at the bake house.

Lounging against the wall outside was the man who had all but threatened her the week before. She glanced back at Ensign Tharp and nodded when his eyes met hers, then turned back to find the man striding away.

Ensign Tharp stepped closer. "Was that the man?"

"'Twas him, I am certain." They stopped at the door. She let go of Red Beads's arm and touched his coat sleeve. "Your p-p-presence w-w-was enough to s-s-see him gone. I am grateful."

He gave a short bow. "At your service, Miss." Then he strode away in the direction the other man had taken.

Had she been foolish to point the man out? Would word get back to Uncle Corne? It was too late now to change it, and Red Beads was already inside. Abigail followed, but some of the excitement for the day had been spoiled.

***

THE ROCK HELD THE DAY'S HEAT EVEN THOUGH THE sun had disappeared behind the trees. Koyen drew his legs up, rested his forearms on them, and shut his eyes. He could think more clearly in his special place.

He'd left William Johnson's house two days before and had run much of the way, arriving home almost a full day faster than on his trip out. He'd stopped only to drink during the day, eat a handful of pemmican, and sleep a few hours each night. All along the way, the white man's words had tumbled in Koyen's thoughts. It was as if the man had opened his eyes. And yet, what he'd seen—understood the man to say—had been things he'd never imagined. Things that needed to be mulled over.

Were the man's words true? Could he be trusted?

It always came down to that.

He opened his eyes and searched the darkening forest around him. His stomach grumbled over his decision not to return directly to the village. But his mind kept him on the rock.

William Johnson had painted a picture with his words. A picture of a life that might be if the Iroquois and the British learned to live together. Learned to work together. Learned to respect each other.

Koyen respected some of the British at the fort. That was a start. But did any truly respect him?

Once more, it was Mourning Dove who came to mind.

Watching William Johnson with Molly Brandt and their children had opened Koyen's eyes in another way. He'd once seen a white woman who'd been a captive in another village. She'd been nothing like Molly Brandt. That white woman had been broken, her shoulders slumped, her hair and clothing neglected, her face never rising to see what was around her. She'd not belonged in a Seneca village.

Molly Brandt had stood proud in the white man's house. She'd obviously been in charge—not a captive. The dark slaves and children were both quick to obey her, and she'd honored Koyen as a visitor, even preparing a pallet of hides and blankets for him to sleep on the floor of her house.

While she dressed like the British, she'd spoken to her children in both languages, and allowed them to run naked as the Indian children did. On her wall had hung many things such as would be found in a longhouse. She had merged her life with William Johnson's without losing who she'd been born to be.

Could other people do the same? Would they want to?

Most importantly, did he?

Chapter 19

"Uncle, I meant to inquire if you know of a man named W-w-william Johnson." Abigail fidgeted with her handkerchief in front of his desk. She hadn't forgotten as much as procrastinated asking her question. After all, she may learn something she didn't wish to know about Koyen. Something had changed between them when Koyen had put her in charge of his sisters. Something important to Abigail, even if she couldn't put a name to it. But after three days of mulling it over, she decided to ask. Even if it showed him in a bad light in the end, she needed to know.

"'Tis *Sir* William Johnson, and indeed, I know him." Uncle Corne looked up at her, his eyebrows drawn together. "How do you?"

"Red Beads mentioned that her brother, the s-s-scout w-w-who used to come here, w-w-went to meet w-w-with S-s-sir W-w-william."

Her uncle dropped the quill in his hand to the paperwork below and leaned back in his seat. "He did, did he?"

"'Twould s-s-seem s-s-so. Is that s-s-significant?"

He rubbed his hand down his face and cocked his head. "It could be. Did she say anything else?"

Abigail shook her head. "W-w-we s-s-spoke no more of it. I believe he w-w-was with S-s-sir W-w-william w-w-while Red Beads w-w-was here, because the other s-s-scout escorted her to the fort."

"You will see her again at the end of the week?"

"I w-w-will."

"Ask her how that meeting went. Ask what Koyen said about it." He steepled his fingers, the index pair tapping against each other. "It may be significant indeed."

"Then I w-w-will learn w-w-what I can on Friday."

"Very good." He sat forward. "Have you finished those letters?"

"Only just." She grabbed the papers from her desk and passed them over.

"Splendid. I shall be in meetings most of the rest of the day. Please finish those reports for me, and compile the list of necessary supplies that Sergeant Morland requested."

"S-s-straight away."

He rose and went to the door, but stopped with his hand on the knob and turned to her. "I honestly do not know what I would do without you, my dear Abigail. You have relieved your old uncle of much of the drudgery of my position."

"'Tis my p-p-pleasure, Uncle."

"Indeed, you have spoiled me for my next post." He nodded and left.

Abigail's stomach dropped. His next post?

Why had it never occurred to her that Uncle Corne might leave Fort Niagara? Another possibility she hadn't planned for when she'd decided to come west. She'd been so terribly naive when she'd stepped aboard the *Huron.*

What if he were transferred back to Boston?

Abigail pressed her hand to her middle against the wave of anxiety that hit there. To go back to her half-brother's house, to once again be the object of pity or ridicule, to leave this place where she'd found a purpose… and friends.

How could she bear it?

"YOU KNOW I AM NO LONGER WELCOME THERE." KOYEN paced in front of Walks Fast. "None of the scouts are."

"Farmer's Brother needs information." The other man squatted near the base of a huge pine and cocked his head. "Does your sister still enter the fort?"

Koyen stiffened. "My sister is not a spy. Leave her out of this."

Walks Fast leaped to his feet, standing almost nose to nose with Koyen. "We need every Seneca to do their part if we are to push the British off our land."

The man's hot breath hit his face, but he didn't back away. "Not my sister. She is no warrior."

"She is Seneca."

"She is barely out of childhood." Frustration gnawed at Koyen. "Tell Farmer's Brother that I will not be passing on any more information. I cannot bring it myself, and I will not use my sister in such a way."

"He will not be happy."

"Then he will have to be unhappy." Koyen clipped off each word and left the other man, stalking back toward the village.

In truth, Koyen had no more desire to help Farmer's Brother and his followers. William Johnson's words—his example—had taken root. In the days since Koyen's return, he'd spoken with his mother, the chiefs, and several others, including Tall Otter. While some were still disgruntled over the British in general, none seemed inclined to join with Pontiac's cause. Most, like his mother, saw the cost to the Seneca being too high.

Perhaps even devastating.

After meeting William Johnson and listening to his words about the British, how many and how mighty they were, Koyen agreed.

He would not spy again on the British—even if he could. He certainly wouldn't allow his sister to spy. And yet, he also wouldn't betray those with Farmer's Brother, even if he knew their plans. He had come to believe that they were wrong in their actions, but they were still his people.

He, Koyengquahtah, would walk the line between, the line William Johnson had chosen. He would remain neutral in regards to the war, but would be active in finding a way to live peaceably with the British.

A way that would benefit the Seneca.

He may not be a true young king, and certainly not a chief, but that didn't mean he couldn't be a leader in a different way. A way like William Johnson had found. A way that mingled the best of the British with the best of the Seneca.

There had to be such a way.

THE WEEK HAD DRAGGED ON. EVER SINCE UNCLE Corne had mentioned a *next post*, Abigail had hardly slept. During the day, she was busy enough to push her fears aside, but at night she tossed and turned, disturbing Dance so that the kitten had jumped down and slept in her basket for the first time.

She leaned closer to the glass. Even in its murky reflection, she looked wrung out.

But it was Friday, and she was due to collect Red Beads, so she'd better get moving.

Ensign Tharp escorted her again. Since the previous Friday,

the air between them had warmed considerably. They exchanged the usual pleasantries and then chatted about the weather while walking to the gate. He was a good man, one she could trust.

Would he, too, be moving on to a next post?

A glimpse of blue and gold shirts pushed the thought aside. Not only had Red Beads come, but Shining Day as well.

Abigail dropped the ensign's arm and rushed forward, signing, *"It is good that you are here."*

Red Beads grinned at her, and Shining Day mustered something of a smile. She appeared to be trying, at least. That warmed Abigail's heart. Then over the top of their heads, Koyen's dark eyes met hers.

He had returned.

Why that added to her happiness, she didn't want to ponder, so she grasped each sister by an arm and hurried them toward the bake house, Ensign Tharp following.

She had to free her hands to sign, *"Shining Day, I am happy to see you."*

"It is good to be here."

Red Beads added, *"I have told her to come before, and she has refused. Today, she said she would join us. It surprised me, our mother, and our brother."*

"Miss Aldridge?"

Abigail turned around, walking backwards. "Yes?"

"What is all the arm waving?"

She laughed. "'Tis a w-w-way of s-s-speaking that the s-s-sisters have taught me. It means I can s-s-speak to them w-w-without s-s-stammering."

The expression on the ensign's face froze somewhere between disbelief and disapproval, but she laughed again and turned back around, fully happy for the first time in days.

It was amazing how much bread the fort needed, what with the steady stream of new soldiers arriving to replace those who had ventured west to support Fort Detroit. Abigail wiped her brow with the back of her forearm. It was the end of July and the days were steamy, especially so in the bake house with the heat and smoke from the oven.

Red Beads lifted the last perfectly round loaf from the oven with the broad wooden paddle Lurana Quinn called a peel. She slid it onto the cooling board and glanced at Abigail. "These the last. We have time before Koyen arrive. We do more faster every week."

Lurana Quinn had stepped out a while back, but Abigail had learned where things were and how to make several items on her own. "There are a few early yellow apples s-s-someone brought in. W-w-we could make apple s-s-scones for the officers." She glanced out the empty doorway. "And p-p-perhaps extra for you to take home."

Within moments, Shining Day was peeling and chopping apples, Red Beads was cutting butter into the flour, and Abigail was grating cinnamon and sugar. They worked well as a team. Boston Abigail would never have believed the scene before Niagara Abigail. Would never have believed how happy—truly happy—the work and the company made her.

If only things didn't have to change. If only the Indians and forts to the west could stop fighting and make peace. If only her uncle could stay in Fort Niagara for many years to come.

But life wasn't *if only*.

She'd put off asking Red Beads questions all morning and well into the afternoon, but time was running out, and she'd promised Uncle Corne. She cleared her throat, hands still busy with the grating, but she looked at Red Beads.

"You s-s-said your brother visited S-s-sir W-w-william John-son, but I s-s-saw him outside the gate this morning."

"Yes. He return."

"Did he s-s-say anything about his trip?"

Red Beads paused, her head tilted for a moment, then she gave it a shake. "Not to me. He speak to Mother for long time when he return."

That wasn't helpful.

"He less restless now. Perhaps he find answers there. He troubled before."

"W-w-what was troubling him?"

Shining Day, unable to hear, looked between them and frowned. But with their hands busy, they couldn't sign. Abigail smiled at her, but it didn't shift the frown.

"War to west trouble us all. You British think trouble, yes?"

"Indeed, very much."

"Mother not wish for war. She not wish Seneca—any Seneca —fight. Village chiefs no wish fight."

That was something to tell Uncle Corne, at least. She fished around in her thoughts for something that might prompt another tidbit of information.

"P-p-perhaps S-s-sir W-w-william w-w-was of help to your brother in s-s-some w-w-way." Oh, signing would be so much easier once her hands were free.

The other young woman shrugged. "Koyengquahtah do not tell me." She snorted. "He see me little sister, not young woman." She flashed Abigail a glance, then to the empty doorway and back again. "He meet with other Seneca away from village. I know. I see."

Abigail's heart dropped. It was *other Seneca* who had attacked the fort. Could Koyen be caught up with them after all? Did he mean the fort harm, and therefore, mean her harm?

Would he have entrusted his sisters to someone he meant harm? That didn't make sense. And for whatever reason, she didn't want to believe it of him. Partly because he was the brother of her new friends. Partly because he had given her a responsibility without regard for her faulty tongue. And partly because he was... he was a puzzle she couldn't solve. One moment fierce and dangerous like a leashed lion, the next dark and brooding with an air of mystery she had to admit...

Intrigued her.

———

KOYEN'S SISTERS APPROACHED THE FORT'S GATE, ONE on each side of Mourning Dove. Red Beads laughed, a merry sound reminding him of when she was a little girl. Always full of life, that one. Shining Day was silent, of course, her expression brooding. That sister kept her thoughts to herself. She'd been the opposite of her sister even before the spotting disease had blocked her ears. Quiet, thoughtful, purposeful, she was the steadfast one.

It was the woman between them that held his attention. Taller than his sisters, graceful despite her awkward clothing, with skin so fair she'd never be able to hide in the night. Their eyes met as the women neared the gate, hers light and bright and widening slightly as they remained steady with his.

What was it about her that fascinated him?

He was ready to admit—to himself—that she did. She was a white swan next to his dark goose sisters, standing out by her coloring, but even more by her bearing. There was something about her that proclaimed she was destined to become important to her people, as a clan mother was important to his.

Shining Day spotted him and ran to his side. Red Beads stopped and spoke with Mourning Dove for a moment more.

Shots rang out from nearer the river.

Koyen pushed Shining Day in the other direction, toward the

forest, motioning for her to run. He watched just long enough to see her obey, then ran to the gate.

"That you, Koyen?" George Swan shouted from the top of the palisade.

"Yes," he answered back. "I come for sisters."

"We have to shut the gate. Best call them out."

He nodded to the man, glad it was him and not another who might challenge his presence there. George Swan was a good man. And he knew Koyen's sisters.

"Come," he shouted for Red Beads, who was clinging to Mourning Dove as screams rose above the pop of muskets.

The British woman spoke words he could not hear, but it was clear she was urging Red Beads to join him. His sister—ever the contrary one—hesitated, glancing back at the castle.

"Red Beads. Come with me," he shouted again as the massive gate started to close.

A roar filled the fort, and smoke belched from the high windows of the castle. Red Beads dropped her basket and flew to him, her braids streaking out behind her.

Koyen met Mourning Dove's eyes again, tipping his chin in the direction of the castle.

She picked up the spilled basket, took a step back, then another, before turning and running for the stone structure. Then the gate slammed shut, cutting off the sight of her.

Red Beads reached him, and he grasped her arm, racing with her for the safety of the forest. Hoping no one on the wall would shoot at them, two Seneca running for their lives.

Another attack. Another wedge driven between his people and the British. A month ago, it would have made him happy, but now?

A second roar filled the air behind them. There was nothing the Seneca or the whole of the Iroquois had that could face those cannons and win.

Koyen deftly swatted branches out of his way as he plunged through the screen of brush at the edge of the forest with Red Beads at his heels. He ran on pure instinct, ever watchful, feet sinking silently into the deep bed of old pine needles that littered the forest floor, mind whirling.

Was William Johnson right? Was peace the best option for both sides? And was the man right that Koyen—a warrior of no significant standing—could help turn that tide?

He had no idea how—but he had to try.

Chapter 20

"My dear, would that I could shield you from the contents of this letter. 'Tis most distressing news." Uncle Corne set a blank sheet of paper on Abigail's desk, his bushy brows drawn together. "But Major Wilkins's scribe was one of those injured during the attack last Friday."

"W-w-was he s-s-shot?"

"What? No." Uncle Corne grimaced. "A horse backed into him in front of the castle and knocked him over. Another soldier stepped on his writing hand."

The poor man.

"'Tis imperative we send word to General Amherst with all haste," her uncle continued. "There can be no mistakes." He spread his hands. "And you know the state of my handwriting."

"Of course, Uncle." Abigail took the sheet, the quality far above what she normally handled. She dipped her quill as her uncle paced in front of her, hands behind his back, eyes on the stone flooring.

When his words tumbled out and Abigail dutifully transcribed them to the paper, she understood his concern. Major Wilkins was convinced that an Indian attack would occur during a supply run along the new wagon road.

She'd never been there, of course, but she'd heard the men talking of widening an Indian footpath into a proper road that wagons could traverse. The road led from Fort Niagara to Fort Schlosser and allowed them to move more goods and supplies to that lower fort on Lake Erie at the other end of the Niagara River. From there, men and supplies could be sailed to Fort Detroit or all the way to Fort Michilimackac.

"Sign it, Major John Wilkins, Commander at Fort Niagara." Uncle Corne stopped his pacing. "He would have dictated it to you himself, but he thought such distressing words would be easier for you to hear from me."

"I am not s-s-so delicate as you all assume, Uncle." She sanded the paper to dry the ink. "Have I not p-p-proved my ability to adapt to fort life?"

"You have indeed, my dear." He shook his head. "So like your mother. How I miss her."

Abigail tapped the paper on its edge, dislodging the sand and exposing her crisp, neat script. She offered the letter to her uncle, but he held up his hand.

"Please make an exact copy for the major's files, and then I shall deliver them both."

"S-s-straight away." She fished out a single sheet of clean paper, one of her last, and bent over it while Uncle Corne returned to his desk. But her thoughts were south of the fort. She might not have a military mind, but even she could picture the scene painted in the letter. A deep drop-off to the west, dense—almost impenetrable—forest to the east, and a line of wagons spread single file between them, open to attack. Indians hiding in that forest could rush the wagons and overpower them. There would be no way of escape.

She shivered.

Back in Boston, people spoke of soldiers and Indians as if they were just stones on a draughts board. But since arriving at the fort, to Abigail, they had become faces and names. Not just the soldiers, but the Indians too.

She sucked in a quick breath. When had she stopped thinking of the Indians as heathens and savages?

She finished the copy of the letter, sanded it, and rose. "Here you are, Uncle. All finished."

"Thank you." He took both copies, gave each a cursory glance, and dropped them to the desk. "In all the hurry and scurry of the past three days, I have not asked you about your friend's brother and William Johnson. Did you learn anything more of it?"

Abigail nodded, fingers fiddling with a loose bit of lace on her cuff that needed to be repaired. "Very little."

"But?" He had a look that said he knew she was holding something back.

She shifted her weight from heels to toes and back again. "He has returned. Red Beads s-s-said he s-s-seems less troubled s-s-since his return." She looked at the troublesome bit of lace then back to her uncle. "S-s-she also s-s-said he has met with S-s-seneca from outside their village."

Uncle Corne leaned back in his chair and steepled his fingers.

"But he w-w-was here at the time of the attack. S-s-surely if he had known of it, he w-w-would have fetched his s-s-sisters beforehand."

"Perhaps." Uncle Corne rose and picked up the letters. "I will think on that. 'Tis likely I shall be with the Major the rest of the day. You should take the time to yourself, my dear. Perhaps mend that poor bit of lace before you shred it, hm?"

He left the room, and she let out a long breath. Had she done Koyen a disservice by telling Uncle Corne what she'd learned from Red Beads? Had she done her friend one as well? Yet, surely, she owed Uncle Corne her loyalty first.

She walked around his desk to the window, the sun sparkling through its many squares of glass. Soldiers were occupied with their usual tasks around the parade ground. Smoke rose from the bake house and streaked across the sky. The tops of the pines waved, blown about by the wind.

Her fingers caught in the lace, and she grimaced. Uncle was right. She needed to mend it. She left his room and fished her key from her pocket. Ensign Tharp must have left with Uncle Corne. She unlocked her room and entered, greeted by Dance with a meow and ankle rubs.

"Hello, my love." She scooped up the cat and cuddled her for a moment, her purr deep and steady against her ear.

Someone knocked on the door.

Abigail stared at the key she'd sat on the chair when she'd picked up Dance. She'd never forgotten to lock it before. What it if were that odious little man or someone like him?

"Yes?"

"'Tis Judith."

Relief washed over her, and she set the cat aside to open the door. "How good to s-s-see you."

"Mr. Spooner mentioned that the officers would be gathered for most of the day. I thought perhaps you would like to join the ladies for a change." Her voice lifted at the end, making it something of a question.

"I w-w-would love it. I need to mend a few of my garments." Abigail pulled a clean dress from one of the pegs on the wall. At least the castle had its laundresses off the kitchen, and she needn't worry about that chore. "Let me change." She wagged the sagging lace where Judith could see it. "And I w-w-will join you."

"Very well." Judith's smile was infectious and genuine, warming Abigail's heart. Red Beads, Shining Day, and Lurana Quinn were women she enjoyed being with, working beside, and learning from, but... She shut the door and looked at Dance.

"I have missed s-s-spending time w-w-with w-w-women like me, Dance."

The cat rolled onto her back, begging for attention. Abigail rubbed the exposed tummy a moment, then changed her gown and gathered the other items needing attention. For that day, at least, she'd relax and enjoy the company of her own people.

"IT IS TOO DANGEROUS." KOYEN SPUN AROUND AND faced his mother. "They did not shoot at us the last time only because the attack happened at the other side of the fort. What if this time, it happens nearby?"

"Do you know there will be another attack?"

"Of course there will be."

His mother calmly cut wild onions into the kettle between her feet. "Do you know that it will be today?"

He ground his teeth together. "How can I know? Have I not told you that I have no more contact with Farmer's Brother and his followers?"

"You have said, but things may have changed since you told me that."

How could she remain so calm? So determined to see her daughters at the fort? In harm's way.

"Lurana Quinn will watch out for them, and you will escort them." She craned her neck to see him standing over her. "Nothing is certain in life, my son. We cannot hide from every potential danger."

"This is more than potential danger. You know it, and so do I. Why are you so intent on sending the girls?" There, he'd finally asked the question he needed the answer to. What was in his mother's heart and mind in regards to the British and his sisters?

"Red Beads." She called the girl over, and Shining Day followed.

His mother both spoke and signed, including the younger sister in the conversation. "Why do you wish to go to the fort?"

"To learn more from Lurana Quinn about how the British live," Red Beads said. "To bring home bread for our family."

"Is that all, my daughter?"

Red Beads glanced at the tops of her moccasins, then back to her mother. "No. I wish to spend time with the young woman who joins us in the bake house, Mourning Dove."

Koyen almost cracked his molars.

"Mourning Dove?" His mother's eyebrow rose. "Who is this? Is she Onondaga like Lurana Quinn?"

"She is the British woman, Abigail Aldridge, who purchased our baskets. Koyengquahtah has named her Mourning Dove."

If his mother's eyes had been musket shot, Koyen would have dropped dead where he stood.

"She is my friend, Mother. And she also brings an escort to the gate to see us safely across the inside of the fort. A man named Ensign Tharp, although Mourning—Abigail Aldridge calls him Viking."

"*Much of his face is covered in red hair,*" Shining Day signed. "*He is ugly.*"

"*He is not,*" Red Beads shot back, then turned to their mother again. "I am learning so much. I do not want to stop."

"It is good that you learn." She looked at Koyen again. "We all must learn if we are to live in peace. Gather your things, girls. You leave with your brother soon."

The girls obeyed, Red Beads with a wide grin, Shining Day reluctantly. At least one of the women in his life showed good judgment.

"This Mourning Dove, she is pleasing to gaze upon?"

Heat climbed Koyen's neck and attacked his ears, as used to happen when he was a boy and his mother caught him doing something he shouldn't.

"She looks British."

"Huh." His mother went back to cutting wild onions. "I wish my people to live in peace with the British. I do not wish them to live *with* the British." She glanced at him. "It would be a good time for you to visit High Clouds in her village."

THEY WERE DONE IN THE BAKE HOUSE, BUT ENSIGN Tharp was nowhere to be found. Abigail scanned the fort's grounds. She hadn't seen the odious little man who had threatened to return her to Bartlett in a fortnight, not since the ensign had followed him away from the bake house. Most likely, the man had returned to Boston, assured that she would never go with him.

Red Beads stepped into the doorway beside her. "We safe on our own. Brother waits beyond gate."

"I w-w-will accompany you that far." Abigail stepped into the courtyard, the day gray and gloomy, promising rain later. If it broke the August heat and humidity, it would be most welcome.

Shining Day followed a step behind, making no effort to keep up or converse with them. Gone were last week's attempts to be friendly. The younger girl was all scowls and sullenness again. Red Beads had confided that they'd had words with Koyen over being in the fort that morning, so perhaps that was the root cause. Abigail perfectly understood dealing with an overbearing brother.

They arrived at the gate, but no one waited on the other side. A niggling of alarm teased the back of Abigail's neck. She turned so that both young women could see her. *"You should wait until he comes."*

Shining Day ignored her and marched through the open gate without a backward glance.

Red Beads gripped Abigail's forearm for a moment, a gesture that had come to mean friendship between them. "We meet him on path. All good." And then she hurried after her sister who was already out of sight.

Abigail smiled at the soldier guarding the gate, then turned and retraced her steps to the bake house to collect the bannocks she'd learned to make earlier. They were an interesting flat bread made with oatmeal and flour, something like a scone without any sweetening. Lurana Quinn had also poured her a cup of milk to take to Dance.

She had put her hand on the side of the open doorway when someone grabbed her arm and shoved her inside.

"Keep your mouth shut else I will shut it for you."

Smelly breath assaulted her as she twisted and faced the man Bartlett had sent. "W-w-what do you w-w-wa-wa..."

"Want?" He bared his decaying teeth at her. "Money, mostly." He ran the back of his finger down her cheek. "But if your brother does not keep his word, I will take you instead."

The urge to spit in his face was strong, but it would serve no purpose other than to enrage him and get her hurt. "I w-w-will not leave w-w-with you."

"Perhaps you will have no choice, Miss High-and-mighty."

"P-p-perhaps you do not know about the Indian attack." The words came before she could think them through. But they might be her best chance to get away from him. "I w-w-wrote a letter for Major W-w-wilkins, dictated by him," indirectly, at least, "w-w-warning General Amherst."

The man released her arm and took a step back. "Wilkins himself?"

"Indeed. He expects the attack at any time."

"Afterwards, then, you and me will head back to Boston."

"I w-w-will never—"

"You did not tell your uncle that your brother sent me. Bartlett said you would not. Why else do you keep my secret other than to be reunited with—"

Lurana Quinn's muttering to herself drifted into the building before she arrived, looking flustered. The man grabbed one of the bannocks from the table and turned, holding it up for the Onondaga woman to see.

"Thank you for the bread, ma'am." And then he was gone.

"Come with me." Obviously distracted, the baker woman grabbed Abigail's hand and pulled her outside and around the corner of the building.

"W-w-what?"

"Shining Day is at the river gate. She says she must speak with you."

"I left them at the other gate only moments ago."

"She is in quite a state. Hurry. Something is terribly wrong."

Chapter 21

The river gate was small but boasted a very large bar to hold it in place. The soldier guarding it appeared relieved when Abigail and Lurana Quinn arrived. He shoved the bar out of its brackets and pulled the gate open.

Shining Day's hands flew as she signed, *"My sister has been taken by a soldier,"*—she jerked her head toward the one guarding the gate—*"like him. You must come."* She grabbed Abigail's sleeve.

Abigail looked from the young woman to Lurana Quinn and back. *"What can I do? We should alert an officer."*

"No!"

If an Indian sign could be a shout, that one was.

"I do not understand—" Abigail spoke to Lurana Quinn.

Shining Day grabbed her by both arms and gave her a shake, then signed, *"Speak to me. You know my language. My sister's life is in danger from a soldier. He would listen to you, a British woman. You must come now."*

Lurana Quinn signed, *"No, it is too dangerous. Abigail Aldridge is right. We must alert an officer to bring Red Beads back."*

But Shining Day yanked on Abigail's arm and drew her away from the fort.

Abigail glanced back at the baker woman. "Tell my uncle." She stumbled and almost fell, but Shining Day steadied her.

"Come back!" Lurana Quinn yelled behind them.

Abigail heard her, but the younger and undeniably stronger Shining Day couldn't have. And she didn't slow down, half guiding and half dragging Abigail behind her.

But if Red Beads was in danger, could Abigail have stayed behind? No. Koyen had left the girls in her care, and she'd allowed them outside the fort without him to escort them.

She'd failed.

Determination gave speed to her feet, and she ran alongside Shining Day. They followed the river into an area Abigail had never been before. Water rushed over rocks and swirled near the shore. Wind rattled the leaves and carried the scent of impending rain. In the distance came the faint rumble of thunder.

The river ran along the fort's west side, and so they must be running south, while the Seneca village was somewhere to the southeast. How had Red Beads been caught and brought so far? How did Shining Day know where to go? If only the other girl could hear. Even though Shining Day had dropped her grip on Abigail's arm, they couldn't sign while running. Eyes were needed to watch where feet were placed on the rugged ground they covered, and Abigail needed her hands to keep her skirts lifted out of her way.

She had no idea how long or how far they'd run, but the stitch in her side made her grab the other woman's arm and slow to a stop. Her breath burned in her chest as she gasped for air. She dropped her skirts and used her hands.

"How do you know where Red Beads is?"

"Red Beads signed to me where he was taking her."

"Is it far?"

"Not very. We must hurry." The Indian girl grabbed her arm again and pulled.

Abigail hiked her skirts and followed.

Thunder rumbled closer, and a gust of wind whipped the linen cap from Abigail's head. She yelped but had no time to grab for it or she'd lose Shining Day. The younger woman had already plunged into a thicket ahead of her, vanishing behind a screen of brambles. She almost cried with relief when she pushed through the thorny vines and caught sight of Shining Day again.

Why didn't she wait? Calling her name would do no good, but surely the girl could see that Abigail's strength was failing. The thought of Red Beads in the hands of a soldier—hadn't Uncle Corne warned her that first day not to trust them all?—kept her pushing forward.

Vivid white slashed the sky above, followed shortly by a crash of thunder. The wind picked up, howling between the trees. Abigail stumbled on an exposed root, then steadied herself against a huge tree.

The forest grew darker.

Where was Shining Day? Her buckskin skirt would blend into the forest, but her blue shirt should have caught Abigail's eye.

It didn't.

Abigail pressed her hand over her mouth. Yelling would do no good and might alert the soldier who held Red Beads. Shining Day must have run ahead to be certain where her sister was.

Another slash of lightning split the sky. The tree trembled against Abigail's side when the thunder answered. Rain soaked her hair as darkness enveloped the forest.

Shining Day would return for Abigail.

Wouldn't she?

"WHY DID YOU NOT WAIT FOR ME?" FRUSTRATION bunched the muscles between Koyen's shoulders as he stomped toward Red Beads on the trail. "Our mother has told you not to travel this path without me. I have told you. Why do you not listen?"

"You were not there."

"Shining Day said…" He scanned the area around and behind Red Beads. "Where is your sister?"

"Did you not pass her already? She ran ahead of me."

What was going on?

"What did she say?" Red Beads asked.

He scanned the area again, but there was no flash of blue, and the forest was quiet around them, as if waiting for the storm he scented in the air. "She said to come later, that you had much to do today."

"She said that?" Red Beads's brows folded together. "Why?"

"How would I know this? You were the one with her."

Thunder grumbled in the east. As much as he didn't like it, he'd have to send one sister on alone to search for the other. He'd have seen her if she'd been on the path to the village, so she must be closer to the fort.

Had someone snatched her? She had a voice, although she never used it. Would she even think to call out?

"Run to the village," he said. "Do not stop until you arrive. Tell our mother what has happened. I will find Shining Day."

Red Beads nodded, eyes wide and uncertain, but she sprinted past him and didn't glance back. Assured she would obey, he ran in the opposite direction.

Where was his little sister?

Had it been Red Beads, he would be angry. But Shining Day was the compliant one. Quiet and unassuming, she would not have gone off on her own. Someone must have stopped her. But who? A British soldier or one of Farmer's Brother's warriors, or perhaps a warrior from another tribe.

None of the options were good.

He ran, but only as fast as he could while scanning the ground and surroundings, watching for any sign. He was almost to the fort when a tuft of bent grass caught his eye. Dropping to the ground beside it, he pressed his fingers against an indentation in the old pine needles that could have been from a small moccasin. The tuft of grass bent toward a narrow rabbit trail. Koyen followed it, finding a few disturbed leaves, enough to convince him that Shining Day had been on the path.

Thunder rumbled closer, nearer the fort, promising an onslaught of rain. Rain that would wipe away any sort of trail.

He moved as quickly as he could while still watching for signs. There were moccasin prints, but not many visible on the dry ground.

And then there were none.

Grinding his teeth, he turned back. He must have missed where she'd left the trail. He paused, hand on a tall sapling. He'd only seen small moccasin prints.

No boot heels.

No large moccasins.

Shining Day was alone.

She'd warned him away that morning, telling him to come later than normal. How had she acted? He closed his eyes to better remember. Sullen, but she so often was. And maybe... eager? Eager for what? To run away?

It wasn't in Shining Day to run away. That one would be happy to settle down with a husband and a circle of children. She wasn't attracted to the British ways as Red Beads was. She harbored a deep resentment toward them for bringing the disease that stopped her ears. She even seemed antagonistic to Mourning Dove—

Despite the humid air, a cold sweat broke out across his shoulders.

But there was only one set of tracks and no heel marks.

A set of tracks on a trail that would lead to the river side of the fort.

Lightning flashed overhead, and the trees swayed above him in a dizzying display before the crash of thunder.

Koyen abandoned the trail—the rain would erase it soon enough—and headed for the far side of the fort. He ran on instinct more than coherent thought, toward the sound of rushing water. Then a flicker of white caught his eye. He raced toward it. Caught on a branch was a linen cap.

Mourning Dove's.

He'd seen her wear it often enough. The wind blew from the southwest, and the fort was north of where he stood. Mourning Dove was farther downriver from the fort. Why?

He angled in that direction as the rain sluiced down, slicking his hair to his head and washing his bare shoulders and back. It was a warm rain, but for a woman swathed in layers of fabric. She would be a sodden mess.

Lightning streaked above the trees four heartbeats before the thunder.

A frightened, sodden mess.

He must find her and return her to the fort. Could he do that before she was missed? And could he do it without implicating his little sister?

Or himself?

AN UGLY TRUTH TRIED TO PENETRATE ABIGAIL'S thoughts, but she pushed it away. Shining Day had said that Red Beads was in trouble. She had to take the young woman at her word. Friends must trust each other. She must press forward.

But to where?

The rain came in sheets, whipped by the wind, driven with enough force that Abigail had to lean into it. She'd not donned her straw hat after working in the bake house, her cap had blown away, and the pins holding her hair had lost their battle with the wind and rain. Her hair hung beside her face and straggled down her back.

She lifted her skirts, heavy with rainwater, and pushed forward, keeping along the river so she didn't lose her bearings. If all came to naught, she'd be able to follow it back to the fort.

And look a proper fool.

Lurana Quinn would have rushed to her uncle—as she should. It was likely that soldiers already combed the area looking for her. They may shout her name, but she'd never hear them above the wind and rain.

Another earth-trembling peal of thunder surrounded her.

With the sound came more doubts. She'd been very foolish to leave the fort with Red Beads and Shining Day before. That point had been driven home by Uncle Corne, and he'd restricted her to quarters. What would he do after this?

Find a way to ship her back to Bartlett.

Lightning split the air with a simultaneous roll of thunder followed by a wrenching crash as a tree not far ahead of Abigail exploded into two toppling halves.

Hands clasped to her ears, she dropped to her knees and shrieked.

A TREE AHEAD TOOK A DIRECT HIT BY LIGHTNING, THE air zinging with its power, raising the wet hairs on Koyen's forearms. Or maybe it was the other sound.

He charged in that direction, heart hammering against his ribs, feet skidding on the wet ground. It had been a woman's voice—but only one. Shining Day would have felt the thunder, but would she have called out?

Or was Mourning Dove alone?

Before he could ponder that, a woman came into view, huddled on the ground, hands pressed to her ears, British gown puddled around her.

He jumped a fallen tree and rushed to her side where he landed on one knee. "Abigail Aldridge?"

She gasped and pulled back, dove-colored eyes wild with fright. "Koyen?"

She knew his name. In the midst of everything, that thought settled deep in his heart, but it didn't answer his questions.

"Where Shining Day?" he yelled.

Blinking, she dropped her hands from her ears. "W-w-what?"

The wind, the rain, and her ears were likely still ringing from the lightning strike. He leaned closer. "Where Shining Day?"

"I do not know. S-s-she ran ahead of me…" Her face crumpled. "I lost her."

Koyen snorted, the picture of what his sister had done becoming all too clear. "I take you to fort."

She stood, looking around. "No, we must find Red Beads."

"Red Beads?"

She turned back to him, fear in her eyes. "S-s-she w-w-was taken by a s-s-soldier."

How could his compliant little sister have done this? He grasped Mourning Dove by the shoulders and brought his face close to hers to be heard above the wind and rain. "Red Beads safe in village. I see her, talk to her."

She shook her head.

"It true."

"S-s-shining Day s-s-said—

"I deal with sister after take you to fort."

"Red Beads is s-s-safe?" Relief warred with reluctance to trust him in her eyes.

"Yes."

"S-s-shining Day..." Mourning Dove shook her head, eyes locked with his. "S-s-she p-p-played a p-p-prank on me?"

A prank. Hardly. His little sister wasn't given to playing pranks. And looking into Mourning Dove's eyes, she knew it too. Yet she was willing to cast his sister's actions in that light. Willing to deflect a more sinister motive away from Shining Day.

An admiration he'd been trying to quell for a long time rose for the woman in front of him. Dripping wet, bedraggled, and clearly frightened, she would defend one she wished to call a friend.

A Seneca.

His sister.

That a British woman showed such character in spite of his sister's actions humbled him. It also filled him with an even greater desire to protect Mourning Dove.

"Come. I take to fort."

"Lurana Quinn w-w-will have alerted my uncle. There w-w-will be s-s-soldiers out looking. I think you s-s-should not be s-s-seen w-w-with me, lest they misunderstand. They might s-s-shoot."

She'd cared about his sisters from the beginning, even beyond her own safety. And now she seemed to care for him.

"I take to fort." And proudly be seen with her.

BETRAYED.

Abigail struggled with her skirts, using both hands to keep from tripping on them. She tottered while stepping over a thick branch, and Koyen gripped her elbow to steady her. His hand was warm even through the soaked fabric of her sleeve. She looked up at him through the rain, blinking it from her eyes.

"I thank you."

"I owe you debt."

She stopped. "W-w-why?" He'd rescued her from her own foolishness—again—and he felt he owed her a debt?

"Twice you in danger for sisters." He looked away and then back, the intensity of his eyes warming her in spite of the rain. "Now sister's *prank*."

She dropped her skirts and put her hand over his that still encased her elbow. "Did Red Beads know?"

"She not know." He grimaced. "Shining Day much to explain. Her *prank* punished. You have my word."

"Do not be too hard on her. S-s-she is young."

"Mother may think different. Up to her."

A shout reached them, followed by the sounds of people stomping through the brush.

"You s-s-should leave before they s-s-see you." What if the soldiers saw him and thought… what? That she's run off with him? The idea shocked her.

That she wasn't repulsed by it shocked her even more.

Chapter 22

K oyen hadn't expected to be prodded into the fort at gunpoint, but perhaps he should have. Ensign Tharp assisted Mourning Dove. She leaned on his arm, weary and miserable, all thanks to Koyen's little sister. A sister who would feel the weight of his displeasure as well as that of their mother, to have dishonored their family in such a way.

To have lied.

The three other soldiers in the group were strangers to Koyen. Likely men who had arrived since he'd left. News of each batch new arrivals on the great boats reached the village. Soldiers had gone farther west, some returned east, but always more had come. It was as his mother said, like sand to fill the hole.

The barrel of a musket dug into the skin between his shoulders.

He'd offered no resistance, and Mourning Dove had pledged his innocence in her disappearance, but they were taking no chances. Part of him respected them for it. The other part wished they'd quit prodding him.

The rain had settled into a steady drizzle by the time they reached the castle, the wind a tame reflection of what it had been. The view was clear enough that they'd been spotted. Captain Hayward burst through the doorway, his hat askew.

"Abigail!" he bellowed.

"Uncle Corne!" Mourning Dove summoned the strength to release the ensign's arm and rush to her uncle. He ushered her to the doorway where another woman waited, wringing her hands in her apron. The other woman urged Mourning Dove away from the door, but she stopped and glanced back at Koyen. "*Thank you,*" she signed.

"*I will see you again,*" he replied.

And then she was gone.

Lurana Quinn hurried from the bake house, a blanket over her head to keep off the rain.

Captain Hayward approached Koyen with a hand on the pistol at his belt. "What have you to say for yourself?"

"I find niece by river south of fort. Return to you when soldiers come."

"Is this true?" His gaze raked the faces of those who boxed Koyen in.

"Of course it is true." Lurana Quinn stopped beside the captain. "Koyengquahtah's word is good."

"Is it?" Captain Hayward roared. "When he is found in the woods—alone—with my niece?"

The little woman snapped her blanket in irritation. "I have told you, it was Shining Day who came for her."

"Have you not also told me that he"—he jabbed a thick finger at Koyen—"is her brother? How do you know he did not send his sister to lure Abigail away?"

"I know." She glanced at Koyen, an apology in her dark eyes. "Shining Day resents you British being here. And she resents that her sister is drawn to you, to the fort, to your ways. I have seen this resentment." She glanced down, then back at the captain. "I should have suspected she might do something like this. I accept the blame."

"'Tis all very well and good." The captain's ire had not diminished. "But my niece has been compromised." He jabbed his finger at Koyen again. "By him!"

"I find her. I return her to fort." Koyen jerked his chin at the soldiers surrounding him. "Ask them."

Ensign Tharp stepped forward. "They were on course to reach the fort when we came across them, sir. Miss Aldridge assured us—most fervently—that Scout Koyen had found her, not abducted her." He took a step back.

Captain Hayward's red face calmed to a lesser shade, but he glared at Koyen. "You swear this is the truth—all of it?"

"Yes."

The captain waved his hand at the soldiers. "Let him go." Then he drew the same hand down his face, wiping off the rain. "You have my gratitude." He turned and walked to the castle, transformed from an angry warrior to an old man in the space of a few steps.

The soldiers left, no doubt glad to be out of the rain.

Lurana Quinn grasped his arm. "You must be hungry. Come. You can tell me the story while you eat."

He followed her to the bake house, but his mind was not on filling his belly. It was on the woman in the castle.

A RUMBLING PURR NEXT TO HER EAR ROUSED ABIGAIL from an exhausted sleep. When her eyes fluttered open, Dance moved to stand on her chest, nose pressed to her nose, purring even louder. The poor animal. She'd slipped her only a crust of bread soaked in a dribble of milk the night before, what Judith had sneaked from the dining hall in a cup. Dear Judith, what a friend she'd turned out to be.

Abigail stretched, and the cat jumped from the bed. She swung her feet to the floor and brushed against something. Something furry, but not the soft furriness of Dance. She yipped and yanked her feet back under the covers. Then she leaned over the edge.

Dance gazed up at her, front feet kneading the threadbare rug while she stood over a dead mouse. A very large dead mouse.

Abigail pressed the back of her hand to her mouth, torn between a squeal and a laugh, she expressed neither. Dance had done her job, and at only half grown. The cat looked so pleased with herself that Abigail sucked in a deep breath and placed her feet on the floor again—not too close to the dead rodent—and reached out to stroke the cat's head. She responded by butting her fingers for more attention. "My p-p-protector."

What was Abigail to do with the dead mouse? Shouldn't Dance have eaten it? The thought had her stomach roiling, but that was what cats did, was it not?

She glanced around the room, at her rain-bedraggled dress hanging on a peg.

Heedless of the rodent or the proud feline, she hurried to pull on a fresh dress. She must speak with Uncle Corne. She glanced out the window at full daylight. What time must it be? Would he be at the Major's rooms, as he so often was these days? Was he waiting for her?

Or was he plotting to be rid of her?

In record time, Abigail settled her skirts and smoothed her hair into some semblance of control, then buckled her shoes. With a leather-clad toe, she nudged the mouse toward the door.

Dance, however, grabbed the offending rodent and issued an almost comical growl.

"Have it your w-w-way, but w-w-when I return, if you have not disposed of the thing, I w-w-will." She pressed her hand to her stomach and refused to dwell on how the cat would accomplish the task.

With one last steadying breath, she opened the door and hurried across the hall.

"Good morning, Miss Aldridge. I trust you slept well?" The air had thawed between her and Ensign Tharp over the past weeks, and true compassion softened his face as he greeted her.

"I did. I am much refreshed." She glanced at the door and back. "Is he in?"

He nodded and rapped on the door.

"Enter!"

The ensign sent her a sympathetic look as he opened the door.

Abigail nodded to him, lifted her chin, and stepped across the threshold.

Uncle Corne dropped his pen, stood, and rounded the desk to reach her. "My dear."

She fell into his arms and, much to her dismay, burst into tears. He patted her back, murmured inane words, and allowed her to finish her tears and dry her eyes. She pulled away from him, averting her face, ashamed at her loss of control.

"Sit, please." He pulled out her chair, then dragged his over to sit next to her. "Tell me what happened."

She'd given him the bare bones of the story before pleading exhaustion and the need for her bed the evening before.

"W-w-when S-s-shining Day s-s-said a s-s-soldier had taken Red Beads, I knew I had to try and help her." She met his eyes, kind and concerned, containing no trace of the anger of the previous evening. "Red Beads has become a dear friend to me, Uncle. I could not ignore her s-s-sister's p-p-pleas for help."

"You suspected nothing amiss?"

She shook her head.

"My dear, there is no guile in you, and so you cannot see it in others. It causes you to ask rashly, to put yourself in danger." He sighed and leaned back in his chair. "'Tis one of the reasons I must return you to Boston." He scratched the back of his neck. "Somehow."

She leaned forward, touching his knee. "I am learning. Every day I learn s-s-something new. I am no more the naive girl w-w-who arrived from Boston."

"Would that you were, my dear. 'Twould make me that much happier."

"No, Uncle." She scooted to the edge of her chair. "I w-w-wish to be here, w-w-with you."

"Things are going badly, I fear—

"Things always do, but w-w-we British p-p-persevere, do w-w-we not?"

He took her hands. "Do you not understand? You are in danger both physically and with your reputation. I believe the soldiers who found you will testify to your innocence—Ensign Tharp has ensured that—but you were alone with an Indian. My dear, 'tis not done." He shook his head. "Not even out here."

"Koyen was a perfect gentleman—

Uncle Corne scoffed, but it was half-hearted.

"Uncle, I urged him to leave me w-w-when w-w-we heard the s-s-soldiers approaching. He w-w-would not. Even knowing how close they w-w-were, he s-s-stayed by my s-s-side. His concern w-w-was for my s-s-safety above his own."

That pulled Uncle Corne's eyebrows to his wig's edge.

"Why would he?"

"I think p-p-perhaps because I had risked my s-s-safety for the s-s-sake of his s-s-sister."

"Indeed, well, perhaps." He shook his finger at her. "But you will have nothing further to do with that young woman, am I clear?"

"As you s-s-say, Uncle." He'd said woman—not women—so she could heartily agree. Because she had no intention of giving up her friendship with Red Beads. None at all.

***

"I HAVE GIVEN MY PERMISSION FOR RED BEADS TO continue at the bake house with Lurana Quinn." Koyen's mother glanced up at him as she worked on a pair of moccasins. "Even though I would rather she stay here with me in the village, with her own people."

Koyen drew his knife across the whetstone, then tested the edge with his thumb. "I thought you wished for our people to learn to live with the British."

She dropped her hands, still holding the moccasin, into her lap. "I wish for our people to survive alongside the British, not to be wiped out by them." Her voice was sharper than normal, her words quick and clear, her eyes directed toward her youngest daughter, dutifully tending the pot at the edge of the clearing, downwind of the longhouses. Shining Day stirred the stinking mess with a long stick, pausing to wipe sweat from her brow.

Tanning hides in the full heat of summer was a nasty job and left her isolated from the rest of the people, who avoided the stench. A fitting punishment for her actions.

His mother turned back to him. "It would not be my wish for my children to forget their upbringing and chase after the white ways." She cocked her head. "Or the whites themselves."

He wiped his blade and returned it to its sheath. "You speak of Abigail Aldridge."

"Mourning Dove."

He winced, which drew a grim smile across her face. It was time to come clean with his clan mother. "I admire her, that is true. Twice she risked her life for my sisters—your daughters—when she did not have to."

His mother set aside the moccasin and crossed her arms, then raised one hand, her finger tapping against her teeth.

"Mother, I can admire the woman without becoming less Seneca."

She shot him a narrow-eyed glance. "Can you?"

"Of course."

"Two moons ago you were wishing to do battle with the British at the fort, or to travel west to join that Ottawa, Pontiac. Today you are talking of admiring one of their women. What am I to think?"

"It was you, my wise clan mother, who encouraged me to rethink my path. It was you who agreed with Tall Otter's advice to seek out William Johnson."

"I did." She picked up the moccasin and bent over it, pushing a thin bit of sinew through a dyed porcupine quill. "But I did not encourage you to grow enamored with one of them. To forsake High Clouds in her village."

"I am not forsaking anyone."

"You have not visited her in many moons. Too many. You should go. Today."

Should he? When another woman occupied his thoughts? No. It would not be honorable. He would not want a man sniffing around his sisters whose heart belonged to another.

He glanced in the direction of the fort. Was that true? Is that what his mother had sensed? He faced her again, reading a bitter resignation between her brows, disappointment in the slash of her mouth.

Koyen rose and headed for his thinking spot, passing by Shining Day and receiving her glare as well.

Once out of sight of the village, he broke into a run. When he reached his rock, his sides heaved and sweat slicked his body. His muscles quivered as he gasped for breath. He'd pushed himself—hard—as if the exercise would rid him of his thoughts.

But it hadn't. Mourning Dove had come with him, her image firmly in his mind. The scent of her lingered in his nostrils. The sound of her voice whispered on the wind. He pulled his knees up and hugged his arms around them, dropped his forehead to his clasped hands, and tried to empty his mind.

Sometime later, a soft footfall alerted him, the swish of leaves against leather, the scent of woodsmoke clinging to hair.

"Brother?"

Red Beads. He sighed and uncurled his body. "What do you want?"

She joined him on the rock, scooting close until their hips touched. "I want to thank you for saving my friend yesterday."

"Our sister did a dishonorable thing. I tried to make it right."

She sniffed, a wet sheen to her eyes that unsettled him. "I love Mourning Dove like a sister." She turned to face him. "Is that wrong?"

Was it? If it was wrong for her, it was many times more wrong for him. Because he loved Mourning Dove too.

And not like a sister.

Chapter 23

He'd stayed away for a fortnight except to escort Red Beads, avoiding even the village gossip about the fort. Koyen stood at the edge of the forest and watched his sister scamper to the gate like a girl half her age. Mourning Dove waited, the ensign at her side. They made a striking pair, the tall red-haired soldier and the fair British woman.

The thought soured Koyen's stomach.

Then her eyes met Koyen's and she signed, *"I am thankful you are well."* The traditional Seneca greeting.

Without thought, he signed back, *"I am thankful you are well,"* followed by the British greeting, *"It is good to see you again."*

She smiled, a flash of teeth that did something inside of him he couldn't explain. Didn't want to explain. But he wanted to feel it again—and he shouldn't.

He turned back for the village, deep in thought about his mother, her wishes and wisdom, and the reaction of Captain Hayward should he ever suspect Koyen's emotions toward his niece. There was no future in such thinking.

William Johnson may have married a Mohawk woman, but her brother had given his blessing, knowing that Johnson, a powerful man, would protect her. Captain Hayward, on the other hand, would never consent to his niece marrying a Seneca and living in a Seneca village.

Mourning Dove would not adapt to a longhouse. She was used to a life of ease, with plenty of food and others to do much of the labor. She may help in the bake house one day a week, but Mourning Dove didn't manage her own fire or cook her own meals. She didn't even wash her own clothing. Koyen knew enough of the workings at the castle to know that. She'd never have sewn a pair of moccasins or tanned a deer hide.

She'd never survive in a village.

Any fanciful thoughts he had, he needed to lose them once and for all. For his mother's sake and his own. They could come to nothing. Better he sought out High Clouds and committed to her.

But not yet.

Not until his heart was free of Mourning Dove.

SHINING DAY'S PRANK STILL UNSETTLED HER, BUT Abigail had pushed the episode from her mind. Red Beads had come again, and they had turned out enough bread to feed the fort for several days. Lurana Quinn was pleased. She'd even complimented Abigail on the shape and texture of her treacle scones, one of Uncle Corne's favorites.

They were cleaning the bake house, putting away the last of their unused supplies, when a great shout broke out over the parade ground.

Fear clawed its way from Abigail's belly to her throat. Another attack? After several weeks without? She'd been so hopeful they were done.

Lurana Quinn and Red Beads hurried to the door as more

voices joined in. Voices raised in surprise and pleasure, not fear and dread.

Abigail joined the other two women. The forest gate was flung wide, and a group of soldiers lacking any spit and polish whatsoever marched through. The men looked as if they'd slept in their uniforms for many a night. But they were getting a heroes' welcome.

"W-w-who are they?" she asked.

"I recognize some of them. Men who left here to go to Fort Detroit." Lurana Quinn crossed her arms. "It is good they have returned."

No wonder they looked so worn. "Does it mean the w-w-war to the w-w-west is over?"

"I doubt it." Lurana Quinn returned to the bake oven. She pulled its wooden door away and raked to life its lingering coals before adding more sticks of wood. "But they will be hungry. I will bake a special batch of biscuits."

Abigail groaned but reached for the apron she'd already hung up.

Lurana Quinn waved her away. "You two go. I can do this on my own. I have for many years."

Red Beads grinned at Abigail as she tucked a loaf of bread into her basket. "We done early. Perhaps I visit Dance?"

Abigail nodded, then wrapped her treacle scones in a cloth.

She linked her arm with Red Beads and led her to the castle. But before they entered, a shout went up. A shout of alarm. Abigail leaned forward to see around her friend and looked into the pointing finger of one of the newly arrived soldiers, his shout clear in the heavy afternoon air.

"Indian!"

Red Beads froze beside her as several of the men raced toward them, several shouting, "Stop her!" and "Get the Indian!"

Two soldiers Abigail recognized also ran their way, stopping between them and the oncoming new arrivals. "Halt!"

The other soldiers slowed to a walk but kept coming.

Abigail moved in front of Red Beads, further shielding her from the angry faces before them. Their voices rose in protest and accusations.

Then Ensign Tharp appeared, charging out of the castle. "Swan, Baldwin." He addressed the two soldiers guarding Abigail and Red Beads. "What is the meaning of this?"

"'Tis them." Swan pointed his musket at the new arrivals. "They kicked up a fuss about Red Beads."

Thank goodness the regular fort soldiers knew Red Beads and her work in the bake house.

Ensign Tharp raised his hands and addressed the crowd. "We are not under siege here, men. Am I to understand that you arrive from Fort Detroit?" Several nodded, a few murmured agreements. "I can understand your anxiety seeing an Indian here in the fort, but I assure you"—his voice rose above the grumbling—"that Red Beads is no threat. She works here in our bake house. 'Tis by her labor that you will eat well tonight."

Tension seemed to disperse, although the crowd did not.

"The major will be out shortly to address you," Tharp continued. "Please wait here." He turned to her and Red Beads. "Ladies, if you will accompany me." He crooked his elbow.

Abigail took the offering. "W-w-we are most grateful, Ensign Tharp. Are w-w-we not, Red Beads?"

The other woman nodded, but her eyes were only for the ensign, her dusky cheeks flushed. It might have been from the near confrontation, but there was something of a ruddy hue to the man's face as well.

Abigail glanced from one to the other—but they didn't appear to notice her at all.

THERE WAS A BUZZ OF ACTIVITY INSIDE THE FORT when Koyen arrived. He hunkered down behind the forest's screen of foliage to watch for Red Beads... and Mourning Dove. The soldiers were used to him, wouldn't think twice about seeing him waiting, but they might get jumpy at his obvious interest in what was happening.

The activity inside was not in preparation for war. Men were milling together, their voices and laughter reaching him. He couldn't make out the words, but the tone was relaxed. Not triumphant as if a battle had been won, but something had happened. Something good—for the British.

Mourning Dove emerged from the castle, her dark blue dress filling the doorway for an instant. Red Beads stepped out behind her. Tharp followed, as he generally did, but much closer, not more than a full step behind and ramrod straight, every step pounding out his military authority.

Koyen's muscles tightened as he stood, sweeping what he could see through the open gate of the fort's interior for a possible threat, then sweeping the surroundings outside the palisade. When he glanced back, the ensign walked beside his sister with Mourning Dove on her other side. Unease crawled over his skin like ants over spilled maple syrup.

In sight of those guarding the walls, he kept his hands away from the knife and tomahawk at his belt. His weight was on the balls of his feet, however, his balance ready for whatever may come.

The trio reached the gate, and then Tharp spoke to Mourning Dove. She shook her head, but whatever he responded with caused her chin to dip in agreement. Koyen took a step forward but stopped when Red Beads and Tharp came toward him. Mourning Dove stayed at the gatepost and signed, *"All is well."*

Koyen's heels lowered to the forest floor, and he walked to meet the pair approaching.

"Scout Koyen, I bring your sister to you because there are others here not used to seeing an Indian inside the fort. They were understandably alarmed."

"Understandably?"

Tharp jerked his head to the south. "They arrived today from Fort Schlosser, and before that, Fort Detroit."

Soldiers from the fighting. "Is war finished there?"

Tharp shook his head. "Not yet, but it cannot last much longer. Supplies are getting through as well as reinforcements."

Like sand to fill a hole.

"I will meet you here next week to escort your sister and return her to this spot." Tharp cleared his throat. "At least until the new arrivals recognize her, 'twill be for the best."

Koyen glanced between Red Beads and the ensign. Both averted their eyes for a moment. What was happening?

"Go, Red Beads. I catch up soon." He jerked his head toward the path behind him.

She scurried past, still not looking at him.

"Is good you watch sister." Wasn't it?

"'Tis good that you watched out for Miss Aldridge." The man gave one brief nod and spun around, marching back to the fort.

"Thank you for watching over my sister," he signed to Mourning Dove.

"She is as a sister to me too."

How had the woman gotten so fluent with signing?

"I look forward to seeing her next week." Her arms dropped to her side just a heartbeat before she raised them and signed, *"And you."*

Tharp had reached her by then, and she took his arm, but with a last glance at Koyen. A glance that pooled in his belly and filled him with both warmth and regret.

DINNER WAS THE ONLY THING WITHIN THE FORT THAT reminded Abigail of Boston. The officers appeared in freshly brushed uniforms. Their ladies arrived in their best dresses without a hair misplaced. Manners were formal, stilted, stifling. And Abigail avoided speaking as much as possible.

How different it must be in the Indian village. Red Beads said they sat on the ground and ate with their fingers or a knife. The men ate first, and then the women, but she insisted it was better that way, as the women could speak freely once the men had moved on. Abigail wasn't sure about the sitting on the ground part, or eating with her fingers, but being free to relax, speak freely, and not worry about how others saw her held a certain appeal.

She took her seat and looked up as a striking young man joined those at the officers' tables. Striking in his thinness, his face so gaunt that his eyes and ears appeared much too large. His hair was unpowdered and clubbed back, but lacked any shine of good health. His skin was tanned and leathery, belying his young years. And yet, his smile in return to nodded greetings was relaxed and genuine. Friendly, even, in an atmosphere where that was a rarity.

"Gentlemen and ladies," Major Wilkins stood, "may I introduce to you Mr. John Rutherford, lately of Fort Detroit."

Muted gasps rose from some of the women.

"Mr. Rutherford, I shall let the others sort themselves out as the evening goes on. No need to memorize so many names at once." Major Wilkins gestured to an empty chair to the right of him. "Join us. We look forward to your story after the meal."

Some must have known his story beforehand, for the undercurrent of expectation smelled stronger than the steaming plate of venison Abigail selected a morsel from. She added two small potatoes, so fresh their skins were almost transparent, to her plate. The fort's gardens were producing beautifully, but excitement warred with Abigail's taste buds. To finally hear first-hand news of Fort Detroit was tantalizing.

The meal dragged on far too long. The lower ranking officers' tables were vacated and cleaned before Major Wilkins pulled out his pipe and waved the stem toward the rest of the high-ranking officers and their wives. "Men, we shall enjoy our pipes and port with the ladies tonight, who no doubt wish to hear Mr. Rutherford's fantastic tale."

The young man didn't stand, but he scooted to the edge of his chair. "Thank you, Major." He cleared his throat. "I was a civilian with an army scouting party heading up the river north of Fort Detroit when we were set upon by hostile savages."

Everyone listened with rapt attention as he poured out his story of capture and abuse, how he was then sold and eventually repurchased by his original captor, how a trader assisted in his eventual escape—a Frenchman, no less—and how Major Gladwin had tasked him to come to Fort Niagara and bring the news of what was needed to win the war in the west.

There were a few times when the young man's eyes had flicked to the major and back, and Abigail suspected there were parts of his tale omitted. Parts only the officers needed to know. Parts she may learn as she penned more letters for Uncle Corne. Or—she stiffened during one such brief pause—were they things not fit for the ears of the women at the tables? A delicate shiver raised the fine hairs on her arms.

Listening to the young man, watching his expression, hearing the strain in his voice as he related certain unsavory details, she couldn't help but wonder about the bits he'd left out.

Uncle Corne leaned toward her. "Are you well, my dear?" he whispered.

Abigail stopped rubbing her arms. "I am, Uncle. 'Tis a disquieting tale, to be s-s-sure."

He patted her hand. "We have it far better at Niagara, but make no mistake, the same could happen here." He raised his bushy brows at her before returning his attention to Mr. Rutherford.

His warning further unsettled her, but not as much as the thought of returning to Boston, and never as much as the thought of returning with that odious man who still lurked about the fort's grounds. She'd caught a glimpse of him as she and Ensign Tharp had returned to the castle after delivering Red Beads to Koyen several hours before dinner.

Mr. Rutherford's verbal portrayal of the Indian village where he'd lived and how he was treated sounded nothing like the idyllic village life Red Beads had spoken of. Would her friends have treated Mr. Rutherford as poorly as those Indians to the west?

Her friends. Plural. But not Shining Day, not anymore.

So… when had she begun to think of Koyen as a friend? Another shiver spiked her arm hairs, but this one didn't seem entirely rooted in fear.

Chapter 24

A great cheer arose from the parade ground and blew in with the wind ruffling the curtains.

"Huh? What is this?" Uncle Corne rose and went to the window.

Abigail hurried to his side. "W-w-what do you s-s-suppose?" More cheers greeted them, with several men tossing their hats into the air. They formed a circle around six riders on horseback. One of the horses reared in all the commotion.

Uncle Corne whirled toward the door. "Tharp!"

The ensign stepped inside. "Sir?"

"See what all the fuss"—he waved a hand at the window—"out there is about."

"S-s-shall I go w-w-with him?" Abigail asked. At her uncle's dubious expression, she hurried on. "S-s-should he be detained, I can p-p-perhaps return to you s-s-sooner." Oh, drat her stumbling tongue. It took her too long to spit out the words when she wanted to hurry.

"My dear—"

"I will remain at her side, sir."

Uncle Corne shot a glance at the ensign, then back to her. "Um. Well. Indeed, see that you do."

Abigail grabbed her uncle's hand and gave it a squeeze before scurrying for the door.

Once it was closed behind them, she leaned toward the ensign striding at her side. "Thank you."

"You have been shut in that room all week." He grinned down at her. "A bit of welcome news is an agreeable diversion from the drudgery, is it not?"

"'Twas my hope." They quit the stairs and were crossing the vestibule when the seedy little man who had threatened to return her to Bartlett slid out the front door.

He'd been inside the castle.

She pressed her hand to her middle to quell the nerves pinching there.

"Was that—?

"Indeed. 'Twas him." But Abigail plucked at the ensign's sleeve when he would have given chase. "Let him go."

"But—"

"He w-w-will not bother me w-w-while you remain at my s-s-side." She summoned a smile. "I feel quite p-p-protected in your care."

Ensign Tharp looked down his nose at her, one eyebrow hiked above the other. "Are you attempting to beguile me for another nefarious purpose, Miss Aldridge?"

Heat washed her cheeks, but she kept her chin steady. "I cannot blame you for asking, s-s-sir, but no. I w-w-wish only to hear the news and return to my uncle."

He gave a less-than-subtle snort and led her into the bright August sun. The men on horseback had dismounted but were still surrounded as they made their way to the castle.

"What news?" Ensign Tharp asked another ensign standing outside the door.

"Colonel Bouquet has won the day." The other man grinned from ear to ear. "Fort Pitt is no longer under siege. He has driven the red bast—" He cut his eyes toward Abigail and choked on the rest of that word. Then he cleared his throat. "He has driven the red devils farther west."

Abigail tapped Ensign Tharp's arm. "I w-w-will return and tell my uncle the news."

"Allow me to—"

"'Twill be fine." Better than Uncle Corne finding out and agreeing with Bartlett to send her back to Boston. "I am more than s-s-safe w-w-within the castle."

He squinted and scanned the area in front of the massive stone structure.

"W-w-we both s-s-saw him leave."

He gave her a reluctant nod before he was pulled along by the other ensign to gain more details.

Abigail climbed the steps and then paused outside her uncle's door. She was happy that Fort Pitt had been freed. She'd learned that the population of that fort had swelled to almost triple what it had been built to hold, that food had grown scarce, and that they had lived in fear of a massive full-force attack every single day. What a relief to them for Colonel Bouquet to have arrived and saved the day. That he had pushed the Indians farther west.

Would Red Beads and her village also be pushed west?

Surely not. They had no part in the siege of that other fort. Nor had her people attacked Fort Niagara, even though others had attacked its soldiers outside of the walls. But not Red Beads's village.

But would the army see the difference?

Abigail could change nothing by standing outside the door. She pressed her lips together and opened the door, giving her uncle her best smile.

"'Tis news of Fort P-p-pitt, Uncle. 'Twould s-s-seem Colonel Bouquet has fought off the Indians and ended the s-s-siege."

He surged to his feet. "Excellent news!" He scrambled to gather an armful of belongings, then passed her on the way out the door. "Oh." He spun around in the opening. "'Tis sure I will be with the major for the rest of the day. If you are finished with the supply lists, take the rest of the day to yourself. But"—he raised one finger while juggling the armload—"do not leave the castle. 'Tis unlikely Tharp will be available to escort you."

"I understand."

He gave a final nod and strode off.

Abigail finished her work in a few minutes, then cleaned her quill and corked the inkwell. She went to the window and gazed out over the high palisade to the forest beyond. Change was coming to all of them. She could see it in the new construction within the fort and in the gathering of more new arrivals in uniform. How much more change would come to those who lived outside the walls? To Red Beads and her people?

A somber feeling settled over her. She'd been driven from her life in Boston by the reckless desire to be more than just a spinster in the attic. That wasn't fair. Bartlett's spacious upper rooms were hardly an attic, however much she had felt them to be. But Red Beads might be driven from her home for... what? What would become of her friend in the forest? A friend who had come to mean more to her than anyone she'd left behind in Boston.

"THERE IS TALK OF AN IMPORTANT MEETING BETWEEN the Iroquois chiefs and William Johnson," Koyen's mother said as she served him a wooden platter of roasted rabbit. He pulled in an appreciative breath, the smoky goodness making his belly growl. He stabbed a piece with his knife and bit into it. Rabbits were fat and tasty even this early in the harvest season. He waited until he'd enjoyed a second bite before answering her.

"Why do you tell me this?"

She set the platter down, then sat on the ground beside him, watching other families in the village going about their evening meals. "The Seneca chiefs are not going to attend."

He stopped his knife halfway to his mouth for another bite. "I ask again, why do you tell me this?"

She turned her full attention to him, worry lines fanning from the corners of her eyes. Eyes clouded with concern for her people. And maybe for him. "The clan mothers are split on the decision."

"And you?"

"I would protect our people." She pressed a fist to her chest. "In my heart, I cannot see the Seneca surviving a war with the British."

He bristled at the idea. "You think they would defeat us? Do you think so little of our warriors? Have we not been successful in battle many times before?"

"We have, against other tribes. Against other warriors with bows and arrows. And against the British while fighting alongside the French who gifted us with guns and bullets and gun powder. To face the British without these gifts, to face their cannons and muskets with our arrows and lances..." She let her words trail off with a shake of her head. "No, my son. I do not think we could survive that."

Anger churned deep inside Koyen, the same anger that had sparked his interest in Pontiac in the spring. Who were these white men to come into Seneca land, to hunt Seneca forests, to fish Seneca rivers and streams? They brought their foreign ways, their killing diseases, and their metal tools and weapons. What right had they to come—to stay?

But there was no answering anger in his mother's eyes. In

their brown depths was only sadness, resignation, and sorrowful wisdom.

How much easier it would be to lash out in his anger, to rise up and fight. How much easier to die proudly in battle than to see beyond the battle to the empty longhouses, the fatherless children, the hungry wives of dead warriors. The pull to fight warred within him against the pull of his mother's wisdom.

Because deep in his heart—like it or not—he knew she was right.

"What would you have me do?"

She didn't hesitate, her answer swift and sure. "Go to the meeting with William Johnson."

He jerked slightly away from her, as if from a poisonous snake. "I am not a chief. It is not my place to go."

"Not a chief, but Koyengquahtah, our young king."

His name. Unlike most of the boys who earned a new name after their first successful deer hunt, which proved their step into manhood, Koyen had kept the name given him at birth. While it went against tradition, he had felt strongly that he was to remain Koyengquahtah. He'd been sneered at many times for thinking so highly of himself. The British would not say his name in English, as they recognized only one king, George of England. But in his heart, he'd always known that he was Koyengquahtah.

Perhaps for a time such as this.

"I will go and listen." He could promise no more. The chiefs may not let him near the talks, but maybe William Johnson would. Perhaps his trip to that man's house weeks past had been Koyen's first steps on the path that would lead him to such a meeting.

"YOU CANNOT MEAN TO RETURN, NOT AFTER ALL YOU have been through." Abigail chose her words carefully to avoid her stammer in front of Mr. Rutherford.

"Indeed, I do." Although the young man appeared rested, he'd not been at the fort long enough to add any weight to his frame. "'Tis my wish to bring relief to those who remain behind."

"You are very brave."

He ducked his chin. "I would not say that, Miss Aldridge, merely determined to do my bit."

"The army could use a young man of your attributes, Rutherford." Uncle Corne rose from behind his desk.

Mr. Rutherford gave a short bow and then straightened. "I hope to enlist after this voyage, sir. To follow in the footsteps of my uncle." He turned to Abigail. "You see, I have a most favored uncle in service to His Majesty as well."

"Most favored, indeed." She smiled at Uncle Corne.

"Huh? Well." Her uncle fussed with straightening the front of his waistcoat. "Have a safe voyage young sir, and Godspeed."

Mr. Rutherford inclined his head to Uncle Corne, and then to her, before stepping smartly from the room.

"The Crown could use a whole garrison of young fellows like him." Uncle Corne sighed and sank back into this chair.

"Sir?" Ensign Tharp stood in the open doorway. "If I may interrupt?"

"Come in, Tharp." Uncle Corne searched his cluttered desk for a moment, the glanced up. "What is it?"

"Sir, I would like your permission to accompany Mr. Rutherford and his detail to Fort Detroit."

Abigail smothered a gasp. Ensign Tharp gone? Who would escort her and Red Beads? She immediately squashed that selfish thought, embarrassed by it.

"To what purpose?"

"To aid in the relief, sir." If possible, the ensign stood even straighter. "To fight, if necessary."

Uncle Corne steepled his fingers, peering over the top of them. "Well I remember my impatience to join the fray, ensign. Indeed, I hardly think you will have long to wait here at Niagara."

"Perhaps not, sir, but Fort Detroit needs those supplies. 'Tis a small force to see them through."

"Indeed it is." Uncle Corne stood. "Very well, Tharp. I shall miss your presence here, as will my niece, I am sure." He tipped his head in her direction.

She summoned a smile, her heart heavy behind her stays. What if he didn't return? There had been soldiers killed weeks ago. She'd seen them from the window, their bodies draped across the backs of horses. But Ensign Tharp was... well he was too well known to her to be lost. He was a friend. She bit the inside of her lip to keep it from trembling as he pivoted and marched out the door, closing it with a soft click.

"Ah, my dear." Uncle Corne's eyes were full of sympathy. "Such is life in a fort. Men come and go." He cleared his throat. "At some point, 'twill probably be me walking out that door for the last time." He sighed again, looking older than he had before. "Whatever shall I do with you when that time arrives?

Abigail wasn't foolish enough—not anymore—to insist she would go with him.

KOYEN STOPPED RED BEADS IN THEIR APPROACH TO the fort, his hand on her arm. Mourning Dove waited at the gate —alone.

"Where is your soldier?" he signed.

"Gone west."

226

"Ensign Tharp? Gone?" A note of distress threated through Red Beads's voice.

Koyen said, "We should return to the—"

"No, Brother." His sister turned to him, her eyes pleading. "I will be safe. Mourning Dove waits for me. She would not if I were not welcome."

That was true. Mourning Dove had more than proved her loyalty to his sisters and their safety. He continued to the gate.

Mourning Dove's expression brightened. She'd been worried they'd leave. It wasn't lost on him that their coming meant so much to her. He should stop and let his sister continue on alone, as he normally would. It didn't matter that the ensign was gone. She would be safe crossing the open distance alone.

But he couldn't stop his feet.

"There is more you should know," she signed. *"The British have won the battle at the fort to the south."*

"You are certain?"

"I am," she signed before holding out her hands to Red Beads in the British style of greeting those women used. "I am glad you are here." Then her eyes sought his.

He had no right to interpret anything from their oddly colored depths, but the admiration needed no interpretation. He glanced over her shoulder at the inside of the fort as he spoke. "Ensign Tharp went west?"

"Indeed."

Her single word drew his attention back to her. Her lips were pressed firmly together. Of course, she dared not say more lest those close enough to hear think she'd spoken out of turn, just as she'd signed about the fort to the south. Fort Pitt, it must be. Soldiers stood above them, guarding the gate. She was intelligent, his Mourning Dove.

"I leave you." He turned and strode away.

His Mourning Dove.

He had to stop this fascination. Perhaps it would be best if Tall Otter escorted Red Beads in the future. He snorted. That man would demand to know the reason, and Koyen would not admit such a weakness before him.

Mother would be happy Tharp was gone, if the distress in his sister's voice had meant anything. Her happiness concerning him would have to wait, because he knew he'd be back for Red Beads.

And to speak with Mourning Dove again.

Chapter 25

Koyen had brought his sister to the gate again, as he had the week before. They'd exchanged few words, but Abigail still basked in the approval she felt from him. Other than her mother and Uncle Corne, nobody had approved of Abigail so openly. The feeling was quite... heady. Her steps were light as she and Red Beads headed for the bake house.

"You admire brother," Red Beads said.

Abigail stumbled and stopped, her face heating despite the overcast day and cool breeze blowing off the lake. "He s-s-seems to care for you, as a good brother s-s-should."

Red Beads laughed and linked her arm with Abigail's. "You admire as woman admires man." She leaned closer. "He good to look at."

Abigail opened her mouth, then snapped it shut. How should she answer? She didn't wish to insult her friend, but any admiration she felt for Koyen—and she couldn't deny it was there—could never be openly expressed. To do so would be to ostracize herself from all polite society. Even the fort's version of polite society.

"He appears as a w-w-warrior s-s-should, I s-s-suspect."

Red Beads huffed and pulled Abigail along toward the bake

house. "Tongue stumble. Eyes do not. He fine man. You see him."

"Even if I do, Red Beads, 'twould not be s-s-seemly for me to s-s-say as much."

"Why?" They'd reached the bake house and stopped by the corner of the building. "It wrong speak truth?"

"'Tis difficult to explain."

Red Beads glanced around them, then back at Abigail. "I miss Ensign Tharp. He fine man. Not difficult to say."

Abigail leaned closer, dropping her voice. "But w-w-would you s-s-say that in your village? In front of your mother and brother?"

The other woman dropped her eyes, shoulders pulling in.

"I think you understand w-w-what I mean by difficult." She took the other woman's hands. "W-w-we can admire, but there can be nothing beyond that. 'Tis not allowed, I think, in either of our cultures."

Red Beads's eyes flashed. "Lurana Quinn did."

"Yet her husband is dead. Killed by her own p-p-people."

"Do I have apprentices who are going to help me or am I baking alone?" Lurana Quinn stepped from the doorway.

Abigail's ears burned, but she was only half a step behind Red Beads to scurry through the door. Had the woman overhead their discussion? What would she think? Would she say anything to Uncle Corne?

Nothing would have her on a boat to Boston faster than that —even if she had to sleep on deck with the sailors.

Abigail dove into her apron and hurried about her normal duties without a word. Red Beads did the same. Their eyes met a few times, the other girl's face tight with worry. They didn't stop until past noon when Lurana Quinn returned from delivering one load of loaves to the barracks and another to the castle.

"It is time to eat." The little woman set the wooden tray onto the work table and looked back and forth between Abigail and Red Beads. "And talk."

Red Beads pulled the stools to the table, Abigail poured water into cups, and Lurana Quinn uncovered a plate of roasted pigeon she'd brought back on the tray, then broke a loaf into sections for each of them.

After Lurana Quinn and Red Beads sat, Abigail did the same, fairly certain no food would get past the lump in her throat, no matter how tasty it looked or smelled.

"I have never seen you work together without talking." Lurana Quinn squinted at Abigail. "No asking for more words in hand talk." She directed the look to Red Beads. "No asking how the British women do things."

Abigail peeked at Red Beads, who was focused on her meal, before dropping her eyes to the food in front of her—that she wouldn't be able to eat.

"What must I do to bring forth words? Hmm" Lurana Quinn tapped the table with one fingertip. "Must I pull them from you like rotten teeth?"

Abigail floundered for something—anything—to respond with, but Red Beads found her tongue first. "We talk of men."

"Ah. Men. Of course. Nothing stills a woman's tongue faster than a man. And Ensign Tharp is gone." The baker woman took a bite of bread and waved the rest of the piece between Abigail and Red Beads. "Am I to assume that you both favor that one? Did you quarrel over him?"

"No!" The word burst out before Abigail could think. Across from her, Red Beads's dusky face turned the color of new bricks.

Lurana Quinn took a bite of pigeon, swallowed, then said, "And why did I hear my name outside the door this morning?"

A pair of horses pulled a wagon past the bake house, their hooves striking the dirt, the wagon creaking under its load. A man shouted orders in the distance. But no sound came from inside.

"I cannot work with those who do not speak to me." Lurana Quinn pushed her plate to the side and leaned her elbows on the table. "Or with those who talk about me behind my back."

"It not that," Red Beads said. "I mention you, not speak bad."

"S-s-she is telling the truth." Abigail straightened on her stool. "W-w-we both respect you very much."

"Do you? Enough to tell me the cause of the silence?"

Red Beads nodded, glanced at Abigail, then said, "You married a white man. Abigail say not allowed—white or Indian —but you did."

The baker woman closed her eyes, nodded, and then glanced back at them. "And so I did."

"How?" Red Beads asked.

"You wish to know my story?"

Abigail nodded, the lump in her throat lessening as the woman showed no signs of taking offense.

"You will have heard that my father was also a white man. He lived among the Onondaga with my mother. I was raised Onondaga, except he taught me to speak English. Very good English." She clasped her hands on the table's top. "My husband was a cook in the army. He came to my village with some Onondaga scouts to trade for food in the harvest season. That is when I first saw him." Her eyes became unfocused. "And he saw me." She shook her head, seeming to come back to the hot and yeasty bake house. "On his third trip to our village, he asked my mother for me."

"That soon?" Red Beads asked.

Lurana Quinn smiled and cocked her head. "If there were meetings in the forest in between, I would not be telling you of those."

Abigail put her hand over her mouth rather than gape at the admission while Red Beads giggled.

"We got along well. He taught me to cook the white man's food." She pointed to the large brick oven. "To bake the white man's bread."

"And you loved him?" Abigail lowered her hand to ask.

"I did."

Red Beads leaned into the table. "And then?"

"And then he died." Lurana Quinn sighed.

"I am s-s-sorry."

Lurana Quinn raised her brows at Abigail. "I am not. I would do it all again. We did not have long together, but what we had was good."

"Is possible live together." Red Beads voice was barely above a whisper. "White man and Indian."

"Anything is possible." Lurana Quinn shot Abigail a knowing glance. "But not everything is wise."

Abigail swallowed against her suddenly dry mouth.

THE CIRCLE OF MEN SAT AROUND A CRACKLING FIRE in front of William Johnson's house. A black slave woman brought more wood and stacked it near the flames, while another stirred something in a huge pot at a smaller fire beside the house. Molly Brant and her children worked in the large garden past the barn. Beyond, wind shook the high leaves of towering trees that showed a hint of fall color. It might have been a peaceful scene if not for those gathered.

All were dressed in their finest for the meeting, in the traditional garments of the Onondaga, Oneida, Mohawk, Cayuga, and Tuscarora. Most faces were lined with wisdom only years could bring. Gray hair and gnarled hands attested to it.

Koyen had no legitimate right to be there, but turning back wasn't an option. Turning back would give him no answer to the question that had plagued him for most of the summer. Could the Seneca live with the white man and not be swallowed by him?

Pushing away from the tree he'd been resting behind, Koyen walked into the clearing that surrounded William Johnson's house.

"Ah! Koyen, you have joined us." William Johnson approached. "A pleasant surprise."

Koyen glanced at the stoic faces already gathered, chiefs and esteemed warriors of the six-nations confederacy—the Iroquois. There was no flicker of welcome and plenty squints of suspicion. As well there might be with no other Seneca in sight.

"Come, 'tis glad I am to have a worthy Seneca among us."

Koyen followed him to the loose circle around the fire and chose a position out of the way toward the outside near a pair of younger Oneida warriors. Each of the chiefs would have brought a few younger men to act as guards, of course. Koyen, having no one to guard, was as conspicuous as a snake in a goose nest.

A pipe was produced and passed among the chiefs. The formalities were recognized. Low murmurings filled the space. After a time, William Johnson rose and the gathering went silent except for the squabbling of chickens near the barn.

"My brothers, I have asked you here to discuss the distressing news from the west." A younger warrior in Mohawk clothing signed as William Johnson spoke. "Pontiac and his combined forces are wreaking havoc with the settlers and forts. He is building bad blood between the white settlers—the British —and the tribes there. My brothers, nothing good will come of it." He raised his hands, palms forward. "I tell you, even now the Indians are being driven further west by Colonel Bouquet, and Fort Pitt has been freed of the siege there."

Murmuring broke out again. William Johnson let it continue for a while as the news settled on those who had yet to hear it.

"You are Seneca, a guardian of the western gate," one of the Oneida close to Koyen said. "Did you know of this? Is it true?"

"It is. Word came to Niagara several days ago."

The Oneida turned to his companion and left Koyen to his own thoughts.

While Mourning Dove had given Koyen the news, details had reached the village over the next few days. Details of the British besting the combined tribes around Fort Pitt. Details of many Indians killed, many longhouses deprived of fathers and husbands and sons... just as his mother had predicted.

Details that had cemented Koyen's resolve to attend the meeting before him.

William Johnson finally spoke again, "You can see, my brothers, why this is bad for the Iroquois." He went on at great length about building a partnership between the British and the Iroquois. It was eloquently spoken, tactful, yet direct. He painted a picture of what life would be like if there were endless wars between the British and the Iroquois. Then he painted a different vision, where the two cultures learned to live in harmony as brothers.

Koyen watched those listening. More than one of the older men nodded at certain points. More than one young man scowled.

When William Johnson stopped speaking, questions arose. These he answered while Molly Brant and the black slave women brought food and cider and served those around the fire. Koyen'd had cider before and enjoyed the tangy liquid, but some of the men asked for rum or whiskey, which William Johnson claimed not to have.

During the endless discussion that dragged into the afternoon, the Oneida once again leaned toward him.

"Why are you not with your people?"

"I have come to hear William Johnson."

"So you will not join with those who plan to attack the soldiers between the forts on the river?"

Koyen froze, mind whirling before turning more fully to the man. "I have not heard of this."

"Talk reached us many days ago."

"When? Where?" The distance between Fort Niagara and Fort Schlosser was half a day's run.

The Oneida man shook his head. "I do not know. I only heard that an attack was planned by the Seneca." He faced the fire again as William Johnson answered another question.

When the meeting finished with the chiefs—to a man—agreeing to stay out of Pontiac's war, Koyen left but waited in the forest out of sight until the rest of the Indians dispersed. He might not get another chance to speak with William Johnson, so he would bide his time.

As darkness smudged the eastern sky, he walked into the clearing again. One of the black slaves saw him and hurried into the house. In moments, William Johnson appeared and came to meet him halfway across the clearing.

"Koyen? Why have you returned?"

"I ask you question without ears of others."

"Shall we sit?"

"Not take long."

"Then speak freely, please."

Koyen glanced around the clearing once, but they were alone. "Oneida warrior say Seneca attack planned between Fort Niagara and Fort Schlosser. You know?"

The man sighed and shook his head. "I do not, but neither would it surprise me. Farmer's Brother has made it plain that he will join Pontiac's efforts." He thrust his arm toward the smoldering fire. "He would not come and listen. I had hoped that other Seneca chiefs might." Then he clamped his hand on Koyen's shoulder. "I am heartened you did."

"I not chief. I not speak for my people."

"Maybe not as one in authority, but even one man can make a difference."

"How?"

William Johnson turned and looked over his house and barns and gardens. "I am but one man, and I have made a difference. I welcome men with like minds who would see our two cultures live in peace. We both come from proud traditions, but 'tis only by taming such pride that we can learn to live together."

Molly Brant appeared in the doorway, framed by the lanterns lit inside. She stood proudly in the house she must consider her own, with her head high. She and William Johnson lived outside of both cultures while being respected by both. They were a bridge between the Indian and British worlds.

Perhaps the key to learning to live in peace was the building of more such bridges.

A bridge.

Of course. The newly widened road that bridged the narrow gap above Devil's Hole. It was the perfect place to attack soldiers traveling between the forts. The perfect place for an ambush.

"Must go. Much to think on."

"Come again, Koyen." But William Johnson's words were almost lost in the wind that whistled past Koyen's ears as he raced into the forest. It would be dark soon. It was a four-day journey to reach the river, three and a half if he pushed himself.

Would he be too late?

Chapter 26

Rain smacked against the window, its panes rattling from the force of the wind. Abigail sanded the fresh ink on the paper before her, then eased her fichu higher up her neck against the chill in the room. She rubbed her hands together and blew on her fingers.

"Are you cold, my dear?" Uncle Corne asked. "Should I lay a fire in the hearth?"

A fire would have been nice, but with Ensign Tharp away and no replacement to be had, her uncle would need to see to the task himself. She hated to add to his duties when she should be lessening them.

"I am fine, Uncle. 'Tis likely to w-w-warm up on its own before long."

"If you say so, but 'tis no bother." Yet even as he said the words, his voice drifted off and his attention was toward his papers again, an almost-permanent frown creasing his brow.

News of Colonel Bouquet's victory east of Fort Pitt had brought a hearty swell of relief to those at Fort Niagara, but it hadn't erased the memories of the eight other forts which had fallen, their garrisons slaughtered. Nor did it guarantee that Fort Detroit would survive.

Voices rose from the front of the castle. A mule brayed. Wagons creaked and sloshed on the muddy ground. Those poor men, having to make the trek to Fort Schlosser in such a driving rain. But they carried vitally important supplies that would be loaded onto boats and sailed to Fort Detroit. Time was of the essence, as Abigail well knew from the reports and letters she'd copied.

Fort Detroit was manned by too few men with too few supplies and surrounded by hundreds of Indians from at least four different tribes. At Niagara, they had only the Seneca to worry about, and not all of them were unfriendly. Red Beads and her village were peaceful, unlike those who followed the one called Farmer's Brother.

She suppressed a shiver, but not from the cold. The reports said it was Farmer's Brother who'd been behind the attacks on the fort's soldiers. Killing men who were simply cutting wood for fires. That was not fighting honorably, as British soldiers did, on a field of battle. It was... it was barbaric.

The voices outside rose as another gust of wind rattled the panes. Abigail went to the window. Through the rain-streaked glass, the early morning scene was gray and dreary. The detail started moving toward the gate, horses and mules leaning into their harnesses as the heavy wagons left deep marks in the mud. The poor animals would be weary to the bone by the time they made Fort Schlosser sometime around dark. The teamsters driving the wagons huddled deep into their oiled coats with hats pulled down low. Tarps protected the cargo. On one load, a boy sat with a piece of tarp pulled around his shoulders. Imagine, taking a young lad on such a journey. But then, the mounted soldiers riding alongside the wagons were heavily armed and able to keep him safe.

Uncle Corne leaned back in his chair and pinched his thumb and finger on the bridge of his nose, eyes closed.

"Is there anything I can do for you, Uncle?"

"Make the Indians go away?" He peered up at her with a wry grin.

"P-p-perhaps fetch a fresh p-p-pot of tea?"

"That would be lovely, my dear." He sat up straight again. "And then, you should spend time with the other women. I monopolize you far too much."

"Nonsense. I w-w-wish to assist you as much as I can."

"I know you do, my dear, but 'tis no life for a young lady. You should be swathed in fine dresses and circled by dashing young men."

Abigail issued a very unladylike snort. "As if s-s-such w-w-would look twice at me once I opened my mouth."

He shook his finger at her. "The young men of Boston are a foolish lot for letting you get away."

His words warmed her better than any fire in the hearth. "I w-w-will bring your tea."

"Yes, do. And then off with you. Spend the day with the ladies. It should be quiet around here until that detail returns."

Abigail slipped out of his room and down the stairs for the kitchen. She'd made it across the vestibule when a voice stopped her cold.

"Where you be going in such a hurry, dearie?"

She swung around. It was Bartlett's man. Why was he still in the fort? Why hadn't someone thrown him out on his ear? She glanced around the vestibule.

They were alone.

"W-w-what do you w-w-wa-wa…"

"Want?" The smugness in his voice had her hands curling into fists. "I already told you. Your brother promised a right tidy sum were I to return you."

"'Tis been months. W-w-why do you not leave me be? I have no w-w-wish to return to Boston."

"Be that as it may, 'tis your dear brother's fondest wish to be reunited."

"You care nothing for my brother or for me." She drew herself as straight and tall as she could, doing her best to mimic a Boston matron. "Be gone. There is nothing for you here." It pleased her that she managed the order without a stammer. But her courage flagged when he stepped closer.

"Rumor is there be a ship coming soon. I be watching for it. And when it comes, I may be speaking to your uncle, dearie. Seems to me, he would be as pleased to see you safe aboard a ship as your brother."

"S-s-stay away from my uncle." She took a step back. "And me."

She turned and raced for the kitchen, ignoring his laughter bouncing off the stone walls behind her. Uncle Corne would like to see her returned to Boston, but surely he wouldn't entrust her to that nasty little man.

Would he? She didn't think so, but in her heart, she wasn't convinced.

KOYEN STUFFED THE FEW ITEMS HE'D NEED INTO THE leather bag and slung it over his head and shoulder, letting it hang beneath his left arm. He wore a shirt to shed the worst of the rain and leggings to keep his legs dry. He'd greased his moccasins to seal them against the mud. He wouldn't have minded one of the white man's hats, the kind with a wide brim to shield his face from the driving rain.

"I do not think it wise that you go alone," his mother said, not for the first time since he'd returned two days before.

"I agree." He picked up his musket. "But there are no others who will come."

"I know." Disappointment hollowed her words, matching the disappointment in his heart.

The entire length of his run home, he'd hoped to persuade the village men to stand with him against Farmer's Brother. To meet the other Seneca—not for battle—but to convince them of the folly of their plans. To convince Farmer's Brother to meet with William Johnson. For two days he'd talked himself hoarse, but to no purpose. Then word reached the village at first light of a line of wagons preparing to leave the fort.

He was out of time.

Though he suspected if he'd had an entire year, he wouldn't have shifted the chiefs. They wished to stay out of the conflict in every way. He agreed with them in principle, but it wasn't practical to believe that, if Farmer's Brother waged war against the fort that blame wouldn't spill over to all Seneca.

"Keep my sisters in the village if I do not return."

His mother gripped his forearm and squeezed. "I will." Then she let him go, defeat in the sloped line of her shoulders.

His throat tight, he left her fire and stepped into the wind and rain.

He'd barely entered the forest when footsteps splashed behind him. Tall Otter, dressed and armed, ran at his heels. They didn't speak—the time for words had passed—but Koyen's steps were lighter for having a friend at his back.

They'd run almost due south for a full hour before Koyen stopped. He rested his hands on his knees and pulled in deep breaths of the wet air.

Tall Otter did the same, then lifted his face to Koyen. "What is your plan?"

"To stop a war."

"That simple. I see." The older man smirked before mopping water from his face.

"Have you any idea where they might be camped?"

Tall Otter shook his head, but squinted into the distance. "I do not know, but if I were Farmer's Brother, I would pick a place with shelter from the rain."

"Do you agree that they will attack above Devil's Hole?"

The other man snorted. "He would be a fool to pick any other place, and Farmer's Brother is no fool."

Koyen shielded his eyes and scanned the sky he could see between the treetops. "This rain will continue all day. The wind will be fierce at the top of the cliff."

"You think it may put him off from an attack?"

Koyen shrugged. "The wagons must return by the same route."

Tall Otter rubbed his jaw. "You make a good point. I would prefer to attack when the footing was not muddy and slippery. Especially on top of a cliff."

"There is a dense cedar grove that is not too swampy a short run southeast of the cliff."

"I know it. A good place to hunt rabbits."

"A good place to conceal many warriors and keep them reasonably dry."

Tall Otter adjusted the straps across his shoulders. "What do we wait for?"

Koyen led the way at a trot and held that pace until they closed in on the area. He left the narrow path and melted into the underbrush, Tall Otter following silently. The Seneca would have sentries, even in the rain. Koyen hoped to spot them before being spotted. Before a knife or arrow headed their way. They crept through forest, the wet ground absorbing the sound of their footsteps, and rain covering any brush of leaves or needles against clothing.

"Who are you to think you can sneak up on true Seneca warriors?"

The voice caught Koyen off guard, a shaft of dismay at being so easily spotted echoed in the expression on Tall Otter's face. Koyen moved his hands away from his weapons and turned to the speaker, a man he didn't recognize.

"I am Koyengquahtah."

"I am Tall Otter."

The warrior looked down his nose at them, ignoring the rain that washed his face. "Why are you here?"

Koyen took a step forward. "I would speak with Walks Fast."

"He knows you?"

"He does."

The man turned and nodded to another sentry, who had remained hidden until then. The man left.

"How do you know Walks Fast?"

Koyen glanced around them but saw no other sentries. Not that it meant they weren't there. After all, he'd not seen this one. "I was a scout at Fort Niagara."

The man shifted, his hand staying close to the hilt of his knife.

"Farmer's Brother asked me to spy for him. I relayed information to Walks Fast."

"Why are you not with us then?"

"Those reasons I will say to Walks Fast." Who would relay them to Farmer's Brother. It was unlikely the leader himself would listen to Koyen or Tall Otter. The best chance was to get Walks Fast to take him a message. Farmer's Brother might listen to him.

The wind picked up while they waited, whistling through the trees. Koyen turned his back to the worst of it, as did Tall Otter. The sentry never moved, as if to show them who was the tougher man. The true Seneca warrior.

That bit at something deep inside Koyen.

Did being a true Seneca warrior mean standing face-first into the wind and rain? Or being smart enough to turn his back?

Only by taming such pride can we learn to live together. Pride in itself was not a bad thing, but pride taken to the extreme—that was what William Johnson had meant. That was what Koyen witnessed in the warrior before him.

The warrior's eyes flicked to something behind Koyen and Tall Otter a heartbeat before Walks Fast stepped into view.

"Koyen and Tall Otter, what brings you to the camp of Farmer's Brother?"

"A cold camp with no fires." As quickly as he'd arrived, Koyen and Tall Otter must have almost walked into the camp. They should have been able to see a few fires beneath hides stretched between trees.

"A warrior's camp." The spymaster straightened to his full height, well below Koyen's.

"Word came that a line of wagons has left Fort Niagara bound for Fort Schlosser." He might as well get to the point.

"So we have heard." The smaller man's eyes narrowed. "Why does this bring the two of you?"

Tall Otter half-lifted his hands and let them drop. "Our village is the closest to the fort. What you plan here, it will blacken the whole of the Seneca."

"What do you know of what we do here?"

"The Oneida have heard that you plan to attack the soldiers moving between the forts," Koyen said. "It was one of them who told me."

"The Oneida?" The sentry stiffened, eyes shifting to scan the forest. "Where did you meet him?"

"At the house of William Johnson."

Walks Fast barked a laugh without humor. "You attended that meeting, did you?"

"I did."

The spymaster pushed his face close to Koyen's. "Why?"

Koyen didn't hesitate, the words coming on their own,

worked out by months of thinking and watching and waiting. "Because I wish for the Seneca to survive."

"You think these white men can win against the forces we have gathered here?" the sentry asked, his nostrils flared.

"I think you will be triumphant in this battle—this ambush. But it will not stop there. The British will keep coming. There is no end to them. They are like sand on the shore."

"Sand is tossed and turned by the waves. We Seneca"— Walks Fast thumped his chest with his fist—"we are the waves."

"Waves are driven by the wind," Tall Otter said. "Captive to its whims."

"We are captive to no one." The sentry took a step closer.

Walks Fast held up his hand, stopping the sentry. "So you will not fight. Are you here to talk of peace, or to warn the British?" A warning flashed in his eyes.

"I cannot betray my people." Koyen looked to Tall Otter, who nodded for him to continue. "Not by warning the British—nor by attacking them. I have come to ask Farmer's Brother to meet with William Johnson, to listen to him."

"Farmer's Brother has no need to hear the words of a white man." Walks Fast crossed his arms. "He has no need to hear the words of any who will not fight beside him. Go home. Hide in your village with the women and children. The true Seneca will fight."

Tall Otter's hand on Koyen's arm kept him from responding. It would be a waste of words. Farmer's Brother and those who followed him could not be reasoned with. The time for fighting had come.

The Seneca might win one battle—but they could not win the war.

Chapter 27

"You can do nothing by going back there."

Koyen's mother was right—and he knew it—but he could not sit in the village any longer. Two days had passed, and no word of an attack. It was likely the teamsters had waited the extra day in Fort Schlosser to rest the horses and mules and allow the road to dry.

In some ways, Koyen was still surprised that Walks Fast had allowed him and Tall Otter to leave. The sentry would have had them bound and guarded. Walks Fast had not assessed them as a threat. That still rankled. But he'd taken Koyen at his word.

Which Koyen fully intended to keep.

"Stay, my son. Keep watch here in the village. Once the attack has happened, the soldiers will come. If you are here, they will know you played no part." His mother stood at the opening of the longhouse with him, eyes fanned by worry lines. "You can do no one any good there."

Red Beads plucked at his sleeve. "Warn the fort, brother. Please."

"You know I cannot do that."

"But—"

"Even if I did, little sister, there are not enough soldiers there to make a difference. Farmer's Brother's warriors are too many."

"But—"

"Go inside, Red Beads." Their mother gave the girl a gentle nudge to get her moving, then turned back to Koyen. "One more time I will ask that you not leave the village."

He hated to go against her, hated to disappoint her—his mother and clan mother—but the pull to go was too strong within him.

"I have to see what is happening. I have to know."

"Why?"

He closed his eyes for a moment, then blew out a long breath and looked at her. "I came to understand at the meeting that William Johnson is a bridge between two people. We must have more bridges if we are to live in peace with the British. A bridge must know both sides to which it is attached, or else its attachment will be weak and unstable."

She wrapped her hand around his upper arm and leaned into him for a moment, then straightened. "When did my son become so wise?"

"When he started listening to his mother."

"Go. And do what you must."

Without a backward glance, he strode from the longhouse and into the forest, his musket strapped to his chest alongside his bow and arrows.

IT HAD BEEN AS QUIET AS UNCLE CORNE HAD predicted, and for longer than he'd thought. The fort was waiting for the return of the supply detail to Fort Schlosser and the news it would bring of fighting to the west. There was an almost palpable expectation in the air, everyone hoping for news that Fort Detroit stood strong against the siege there.

Abigail rolled onto her side on the narrow bed, earning a one-eyed glare from Dance who snuggled next to her.

"I am s-s-sorry to disturb you, my p-p-princess, but 'tis my bed after all. Yours is over there." She pointed to the practically unused basket on the floor. Not that Abigail minded her furry friend sleeping beside her, just as long as the gifts of dead mice stayed on the floor. She peeked over the edge to make sure nothing awaited her bare toes.

Nothing but a roll of dust and cat hair. Ugh. She needed to clean her room. For a brief moment she allowed herself to miss the luxury of a maid to do that for her. She stretched and then sighed, enjoying the morning sunbeam slanting through her window. A cheerful sight after days of rain.

Surely that foretold of good news to come.

It took her little time to dress and tidy herself before she hurried to the kitchen, hoping for a bite of whatever she could find. She'd slept through breakfast, a rare thing for her and only because Uncle Corne had said he'd be busy with the other officers until at least noon.

"Good morning, Miss Aldridge," said the cook, a man almost as broad as he was tall. He ruled the kitchen with the same authority as Lurana Quinn ruled the bake house. Those two had an uneasy agreement not to meddle with the other, but both were friendly to Abigail.

"Good morning."

"Lurana Quinn brought those infernal oat cakes over last evening." He pointed a dripping ladle at a tray on the table. "Help yourself if you can stomach them."

Abigail took two, sliding one into her pocket and biting into the other. Delicious. She swallowed the bite. "May I have a cup of milk to go w-w-with it?

"Help yourself." He pointed the same dripping ladle toward a pewter pitcher on the corner of the table.

Abigail took a large cup from the shelf and filled it. She drank half while finishing her oat cake. She'd share the extra with Dance. Then she went into the storage room and gathered a clean rag, a scrub bucket, and a broom. She grabbed a second rag. She might as well clean Uncle Corne's room too.

Balancing all that and her cup of milk, she went to the vestibule and drew a bucket of water. Only then did she remember the soap. Well, the floors would get a nice rinsing today. She'd worry about soap the next time.

Carrying the bucket of water was much easier than the first time she'd had to do it. Come to think of it, she was never winded by climbing the stairs anymore either. She flexed her grip on the bucket's coarse rope handle, proud of her new muscles.

She went to her room first and crumbled half of the oat cake from her pocket into the cup of milk. Dance wove between her ankles and purred, all but pouncing on the treat when Abigail set it on the floor. "There you are, my s-s-sweet and hungry friend."

"Who are you talking to, Abigail?"

Abigail jumped and whirled, hand slapped to her chest.

Judith rushed into the room. "Pardon me, I did not mean to frighten you."

Panting to regain her breath, Abigail raised her hand. "'Tis not your fault. 'Tis just that I never leave my door open, but my hands w-w-were full and I..."

"I am sorry."

"You caught me quite by s-s-surprise." Abigail laughed. "I must have looked a s-s-sight."

"You did, rather." Judith's lips twitched. "What are you doing this morning?" She glanced down at Dance, who was finishing her breakfast undisturbed by the women talking over her. "Other than feeding your cat."

Abigail toed the offending curl of dust and cat hair. "'Tis p-p-past time to clean my room and Uncle Corne's."

"If only we had maids."

"I was thinking the s-s-same w-w-when I awoke, but cleaning is not s-s-so bad." Abigail smiled, determined to make the best of it. "After all, we need not w-w-worry about anyone s-s-snooping through our things."

"True. Well." Judith planted her fists on her hips. "You have inspired me. I shall follow your good example and get my own room in order. Mr. Spooner never complains, but I suspect were I to look closely, I would find similar dust balls under our bed."

"W-w-without the cat hair."

"Definitely without the cat hair." Judith waved as she left the room.

With Dance done eating, Abigail set her on the bed, out of the way, and attacked the floor with the broom. Even though the morning was cool, she opened the window when the dust billowed. She swept the length of the room from the window out into the hallway. The castle staff swept that at rare intervals and could whisk her dust away.

With the dry rag, she wiped her trunk and chair, having nothing else to collect dust, then dunked the rag into the scrub bucket, wrung out the excess water, and set to mopping the floor. When she reached the doorway, she wiped her hands and stood.

"W-w-what do you think, Dance? Is it not much better?" Abigail looked at the empty bed and then glanced around the room. "Dance?" Where was her cat?

HE'D ARRIVED TOO LATE.

Koyen had gone straight to the river south of the Lower Landing and picked his way along the riverbank, coming close to the cave known as Devil's Hole. He'd figured Farmer's Brother and his warriors would not venture below the cliff. He'd had to talk himself into going there. The Seneca had believed for generations in the evil spirit that dwelled within its dark depths. It was said only one man who had entered the cave had survived. And he had been transformed into a raving, white-haired lunatic. Others had entered never to be seen again.

But in front of Koyen was something that pushed such legends from his mind.

Wagons, broken and twisted from the fall, lay in ruins along the bottom of the cliff. Between them were scattered the bodies of men and horses and mules. Men in uniform. Too many of them.

Wind moaning through brush and trees that clung to the face and foot of the cliff was all that broke the silence.

A mournful sound.

Appropriate.

The fighting was over. The British lost. And all that filled Koyen's heart was a great sadness. Gone was his desire for what spread out before him. He couldn't have stopped what had happened. He couldn't have betrayed his own people. Yet failure rode heavily on his shoulders.

But he'd needed to see this. As he'd told his mother, he could not be a bridge without seeing both sides.

Someone would be coming for the bodies, and it was best he not be there. The soldiers would shoot him on sight, and he wouldn't blame them. Not after seeing the carnage.

He'd backed up a couple of steps when a sound caught his ear. Could someone have survived the fall? A horse or mule maybe, but surely not a human. Even so, it would be a kindness to put the animal out of its misery.

Scanning the bodies for any movement, he crept forward. Then he heard it again. A whimper? He didn't know much about horses or mules, never having owned one himself, but he was pretty sure they didn't whimper.

A flicker of motion. A flash of blue. Something behind a twisted wagon.

Koyen drew his knife and advanced. A soldier would see him only as the enemy, and while no one would have been able to retain his grip on a gun during that fall, a belt knife was something else. He didn't want to face a wounded soldier unarmed. In three long strides he cleared the broken wagon wheels and tongue, and pushed a board out of his way.

A boy stared back at him, huddled under a blue coat, eyes wide and glazed, blood smeared down the side of his face.

Koyen sheathed his knife. "You hurt?"

The boy shook from head to toe, perhaps in fear, but more likely in shock.

"I not hurt you. I take to fort."

"Why?" The word came through swollen lips, half the boy's jaw was discolored.

Koyen glanced up toward the cliff's edge. "I not part of battle."

The boy blinked, eyes still glazed and uncertain.

"You stand?"

He shook his head.

Koyen knelt in front of him. "Can move arms? Legs?"

The boy blinked again, then winced, but moved all his limbs.

"Climb onto back. Will carry."

"My father…" The boy glanced around.

"Soldiers return soon." Which was why he needed to get the boy on his back and get moving.

The boy looked as if he might balk, then blinked, but this time, it was due to moisture. "He is dead." It wasn't a question.

Koyen nodded, certain that nothing else moved amid the wreckage, and slipped the musket and bow from his back.

The boy reached for Koyen.

It took a couple of tries, the boy's movements clumsy from pain, but soon he was settled across Koyen's back, arms wrapped around his neck. Koyen picked up his weapons and headed for Lower Landing, which was closer than Fort Niagara. He briefly considered Fort Schlosser, but news would reach Fort Niagara quicker if he could reach Lower Landing.

He'd barely cleared the wreckage when the boy went slack on his back. Passed out, whether from the shock or pain from the fall, Koyen couldn't know. He hunched over a bit, helping to balance the boy's weight better, and gripped his thin wrists together with the hand not holding his weapons. If he ran into either warriors or soldiers, Koyen would be defenseless.

But so was the boy.

He'd been negotiating the riverbank with his burden for a short time when the sound of gunfire reached him. He froze. The boy still hadn't roused, but Koyen lowered him to the ground beneath a pine tree with concealing branches that brushed the ground. He tapped the boy's face. When his eyes opened, Koyen put a finger to his lips. Gunfire, as well as war cries, raged to the east of them. Terror contorted the boy's face, his mouth opening. Koyen cupped his palm over it and shook his head. The boy blinked, understanding clearing his eyes.

Koyen removed his hand and rose to a crouch. "Wait here."

The boy grabbed his arm in a surprisingly strong grip, shaking his head. Koyen could almost smell the fear coming from him. He couldn't be more than ten summers. A child. And to have witnessed what he had. It was no wonder he was terrified.

Koyen squatted beside him again. He could do nothing in the battle that raged beyond them, but he could protect this one child.

He could add this one connection to the British side of his bridge.

"DANCE?" ABIGAIL HURRIED DOWN THE HALLWAY, looking under the benches posted at intervals along its length. "Dance, w-w-where are you?"

The cat was nowhere to be seen.

How could she have been so irresponsible? Leaving the door open—even to sweep and clean—was just asking for the curious feline to escape. How long had she been gone? How far could she have gotten?

Heart racing, Abigail flew down the steps to the vestibule. It was empty when she skidded to a stop on the flagstone floor by the well. "Dance?" What if her cat had fallen down the well? She leaned over and called down the shaft, "Dance!"

"That be a funny place to look for a dancing partner."

Abigail's skin crawled at the voice as she righted herself. It was Bartlett's man. How did he manage to find her here alone, in an area that more often than not had soldiers passing through? But maybe he'd seen Dance.

"I am s-s-searching for my cat, Dance."

"About this big?" He held his hands a distance apart, about the right height for the cat.

"Indeed, you have s-s-seen her?"

He rubbed his jaw, then glanced toward the corridor that led to a small door on the river side, not far from the gate she'd used to search for Red Beads. "I saw something running that way, about that size, but I did not get a good look at it."

What else could it be but Dance? "I must find her." Abigail eased past him and started down the corridor.

He followed, but she couldn't worry about that. Dance was out there alone somewhere.

There was a light up ahead, and she hurried toward it. The door was open. Dance must be outside. Ignoring the footsteps behind her, she darted for the opening. "Dance!"

A few steps into the sunshine, she spun in a circle, searching for the gray-and-orange cat. Shouts came from the direction of the main gate. Men were running across the parade ground. But there was no sight of Dance.

"There." Bartlett's man reached across her and pointed to the fort's river gate.

The gate hung a full handspan above the ground. Even shut, Dance would have no trouble slipping under it. Abigail ran to the gate, vaguely aware that no guard stood nearby. She pushed on the crossbeam that held it shut, and then Bartlett's man was beside her, helping to shove it out of its brackets.

Abigail stepped out and had sucked in a breath to call for her cat when a hand slapped over her mouth.

Chapter 28

The battle raged for a short time. Too short. Followed by war whoops from the victorious warriors.

Koyen waited until long after the last whoop had echoed in the distance, then he rousted the young boy, who had mercifully blacked out again. He tapped the boy's cheek until his eyelashes flickered. "Awake, boy."

The boy stiffened in alarm.

"Fight over. We go now." Koyen turned his back and tapped his shoulder. "Come."

Thin arms wrapped about his neck, and the boy's slight weight covered his back. Koyen crept from under the sheltering pine and stood.

The sun had barely passed the middle of the sky. It didn't seem right that so much could have happened in just half a day. Adjusting the boy's weight, Koyen set off for Lower Landing again. The soldiers had probably come from there, those who had gone against Farmer's Brother in the second battle. They would not look kindly on him—a Seneca—appearing at their gates, not even with a British boy on his back.

He changed direction enough to bypass that fort and head directly to Fort Niagara. News of the battles would arrive before

257

him, but at least he knew some of the soldiers there. Some that might listen to him instead of shooting him on sight.

He hoped.

The forest floor was still damp and marshy in many places, but he didn't worry about leaving a trail, and his moccasins made no noise on the soft ground. Where he had a wide and clear enough path, he trotted, the boy bouncing on his back without complaint. He'd not said a word since Koyen had awakened him.

Would he ever speak again? Some children who witnessed a horror such as he had never did. But this boy was perhaps old enough to overcome what he'd been through. Koyen hoped so. The boy had courage enough to trust him—a Seneca—when he could have refused. The world would need more like him in the years to come. He might grow into a British man who could also be a bridge.

Koyen slowed when they neared the fort. The main gate was shut. Word of the battles must have reached them. He stayed by the river and under cover of foliage, hoping to recognize one of the soldiers on the top of the wall. The boy remained silent, but by the renewed grip around Koyen's neck, he recognized where they were.

"I find man who know me," he whispered over his shoulder. "Soldiers alert. Not give reason to shoot."

The movement behind him may have been the boy's nodded agreement. Koyen hoped so. Things could go horribly wrong in a hurry should the boy call out.

He continued along the river, placing each foot with care, stopping to look between the branches and bushes every few steps.

A muffled gasp reached him, followed by a muttered curse.

The boy stiffened on his back, then pointed over Koyen's shoulder. Koyen couldn't see anything, but the boy was higher and had a different range of vision. He moved in the direction the boy pointed until a break in the foliage exposed a sight that resurrected Koyen's desire for battle. The desire to kill.

Mourning Dove, a gag shoved in her mouth, was seated in front of a sapling tree. Her hands were not in sight, probably tied from behind. In front of her, a white man not in the uniform of a British soldier was bent over, rubbing his knee. When he straightened, the pure evil on his face made Koyen's blood boil.

He crouched and disengaged the boy's arms from his neck, never taking his eyes from Mourning Dove. Trusting the boy to remain still, Koyen notched an arrow in his bow, drew it back to his shoulder, and aimed the tip at the man's heart.

The boy pressed against his side with a shudder that cut through the red haze in front of Koyen.

A bridge. He was to be a bridge. Breath whistled lightly between his clenched teeth as he clung to that thought.

Then the man took a step toward Mourning Dove and drew back his hand.

Koyen adjusted his aim and released the arrow. It flew straight and true and sunk deep into the man's buttock. It didn't bring the satisfaction Koyen wanted, but it had stopped the blow from reaching Mourning Dove.

The unearthly howl that followed would bring soldiers down on top of them.

ABIGAIL HAD BRIEFLY ENJOYED THE CRUNCH OF HIS kneecap against her heel, but when he approached with his hand drawn back and murder in his eyes, she fully expected to die from the blow. His scream that followed ran her backbone like a blue crab across the sands in Boston. He arched his back, hands clawing at something behind him, and when he turned—

An arrow protruded from his—um—nether regions.

Abigail averted her eyes from years of training in social decorum as Koyen came through the forest with a bow in one hand.

A bow.

She glanced back at Bartlett's man, who didn't appear to have seen Koyen yet, with the arrow sticking out of his... She almost choked on the gag as she sucked foul-tasting air through it.

Koyen had shot him!

And then he was beside her, knife in hand, slicing through the cloth that bound her hands, then removing the gag.

"What?" Bartlett's man roared.

Koyen flicked a glance at him, but otherwise ignored him. "Mourning Dove, soldiers be here soon." He helped her to her feet and then reached behind him, bringing forward a young boy. "Go to fort. Take boy. He see too much today."

Bartlett's man pulled a knife from his belt. Koyen spun, his heel catching the man in the jaw. The man collapsed without a sound.

Koyen gripped Abigail's forearm and looked her square in the eye. "I not fight battle."

"W-w-what battle?"

"You hear soon." He stepped back. "Go, take boy. Tell uncle." He pointed at Bartlett's man in a heap on the ground.

Was he dead? "W-w-what about—?"

"He live. Soldiers find him. Tell uncle. He keep you safe." Koyen backed into the forest as he spoke while the noise of someone approaching reached them. "Go."

And then he was gone.

The boy looked up at her but didn't speak.

Bartlett's man groaned and tried to roll over, but the arrow must have hit something or twisted deeper. He yelled a curse as two soldiers burst into view, muskets raised.

"Miss Aldridge?"

She resisted the temptation to search for Koyen behind her. Miss Aldridge?

Koyen had called her Mourning Dove.

"I am s-s-sorry, Uncle." Abigail hung her head as she stood in front of her uncle's desk. "Of course, I s-s-should have come to you s-s-straight away."

"Why did you not?" His voice had settled from its initial bellow to a bewildered hoarseness.

"Because he s-s-said Bartlett had s-s-sent him to return me to Boston. Had offered him a handsome amount to do s-s-so." She fiddled with the edge of the fichu against her neck. "And I did not w-w-wish to go. I w-w-was afraid you w-w-would force me to leave w-w-with him."

Uncle Corne snorted, then ran his hand down his face. "My dear, while I would love to see you safely returned to Boston, I believe myself to be a better judge of character than that."

"Yes, Uncle. Of course you are. I s-s-simply w-w-was not thinking clearly." She hadn't been thinking at all. Yet another rash decision that had almost landed her in trouble... if not for Koyen.

"Equally unsettling is Koyen stepping in again." He slapped both palms on his desk. "It presses the bounds of believability that he *just happens* to be in the right place at the right time to rescue you—twice."

"But he w-w-was, Uncle." She shuddered. Uncle Corne had already confirmed that a boat was anchored off the fort. It was obvious the odious man had intended to sneak her aboard after dark. "He s-s-saved me."

"It simply rubs one the wrong way that in a fort full of His Majesty's finest soldiers, an Indian should return you to my care, not once, but twice."

"I am forever grateful that he did, Uncle." There was a wobble on his name that she couldn't control.

"Oh, my dear." He rose and came to her.

She fell against his waistcoat, ignoring the prod of his metal buttons.

"May I extract one solid promise from you?" he asked when her silent shivering stopped.

She nodded against the wool of his clothing and then lifted her face to see him peering down at her. He looked... older.

"Would you be so good as to remain within the walls of this fort from now on?" He raised a finger. "No matter what friend or feline might go astray?"

"I p-p-promise." And she meant it. She'd learned her lesson. Lessons.

Dance, on the other hand, merely blinked at her from across the room. She'd found her way back and invited herself into Uncle Corne's room. Another lesson learned. The cat would return when she was ready.

"Now." Uncle Corne stepped away and paced in front of the door. "Tell me again—exactly—what Koyen said."

"He s-s-said he had nothing to do w-w-with the battle. But, Uncle, I know not w-w-what battle he s-s-spoke of."

"'Tis not a pleasant topic, but you will hear of it soon enough." He stopped and faced her. "The detail to Fort Schlosser was attacked this morning on return to this fort. They were wiped out."

Abigail's mind spun, trying to absorb his words. All those men... gone?

"At least they got the supplies through for Fort Detroit. Combined with the supplies the detail with John Rutherford took, Fort Detroit should be fortified. 'Tis not a small thing. The soldiers' mission was met."

"But at w-w-what cost?"

"Almost every life." He put both hands on her shoulders. "The boy who came in with you, he was a survivor. One of only three who have made it to the fort."

The boy. A picture flashed through her mind of a boy huddled under a piece of tarp on a wagon leaving in the rain. "I remember s-s-seeing him w-w-when the w-w-wagons left."

"Indeed. The question is, how did he come to be with Koyen... if 'tis true that Koyen wasn't there?"

It was true. It *had* to be true.

THE CHIEFS AND CLAN MOTHERS GATHERED AROUND A central fire in the middle of the village. Others ringed them several people deep. What Koyen had to share could—most likely would—impact all of them. None more than himself.

A baby wailed from one of the longhouses. Children raced around the circle of their elders, a half-grown litter of puppies romping with them. Old dogs found spots of sunshine to stretch out and warm their bones. Young women tended pots over their fires. A pair worked on a deer hide stretched across a frame. A gnarled-fingered old woman wrapped in a blanket rocked back and forth where she sat in front of a longhouse, eyes closed in her wrinkled face.

Normal life in the Seneca village. The life he'd grown up in. The life of those who'd come before him for as many generations an any could remember.

Would it be forever changed by what he was to say? Not that

his words themselves could create the change, but the impact of the actions of those Seneca at Devil's Hole surely would.

The oldest chief motioned Koyen forward.

Part of him was reluctant to take those steps, knowing that at the least, he would be forever changed in the eyes of those around him. Knowing his words would cut his time in the village short. But also knowing that his path was already set, and it remained only for him to walk it.

"Speak, Koyengquahtah. Tell us what you have seen and heard."

"I left at first light to see for myself what Farmer's Brother and his warriors would do. I arrived too late. The battle was over. I had chosen to follow the river and arrived near Devil's Hole."

Startled gasps accompanied the shaking of many heads.

"I did not approach the cave. I did not have to. The wreckage of wagons, animals, and men was littered across the ground before it. All broken, smashed in the fall. But as I turned to leave, I heard a noise."

He could almost feel the collective holding of a breath as people leaned forward to hear his words better—or perhaps faster.

"It was a young boy. How he survived, I cannot imagine. Yet he did." Koyen shrugged. "I could not leave him there. He was maybe ten summers, no older. A child not unlike those surrounding us here."

Some nodded, some frowned, but it was his mother's slight smile that caught his attention. Her approval was plain to see. It strengthened his resolve, and he told the rest of the story, the second battle and finding Mourning Dove—the niece of an important soldier in the fort—gagged and tied and how he'd freed her. When he was finished. He sat and listened to the others speak.

Agreement ran through the crowd that the soldiers would come to the village if they did not send someone to the fort first. Someone to answer their questions. Someone to represent the village. Koyen felt the weight of many eyes upon him as the talking continued for a long time. He listened, but in his heart, he already knew what he would do. What he must do.

"Koyen." The oldest chief addressed him. "You were there. What do you think our best action should be to remain peaceful with the British?"

Koyen stood and glanced around at the faces. Faces he'd known his whole life. Many he was related to. Some he would please this day, and some he would disappoint.

"Because I speak the language and have a history with the fort, I am the one who should approach it for our people."

Heads nodded, several people murmuring in agreement.

"I will tell them what I saw, and that no one from this village fought in the battles."

"You will be in danger," one of the clan mothers said. "They may keep you, or torture and kill you as an example."

Koyen drew in a deep breath. "What you say is possible. This I know. But it is a risk I am willing, more than willing, to take. It is a risk I feel led to take." He spread his arms. "For my people to live, to prosper, we must learn to live with the British. If we fight them, we may win many battles, but in the end, we would be no more."

A hotheaded young man rose and shook his fist. "We are strong enough to fight. We should fight. This is our land. They have no right to be here."

It was like hearing his own words from the spring thrown back at him.

"We are strong enough." Koyen thumped his fist against his chest. "We are brave enough." He let his words settle over them for a moment, then added in a lower tone, "But we are not many enough."

The hothead continued. "Then we will band together like the tribes to the west that follow Pontiac."

"Those tribes have lost the battle at Fort Pitt. Many were slaughtered by soldiers led by a man named Bouquet. Many longhouses will be empty of fathers, brothers, and sons this winter. Many children will go hungry." Koyen pointed to the west. "Even now, Fort Detroit is holding strong against Pontiac himself and his combined forces of four tribes—not villages—tribes. Yet it is not enough."

Silence followed his words.

His mother, eyes dimmed by a sheen of dampness, nodded her approval.

Chapter 29

A bigail penned the words on the final notice for Uncle Corne. Guard duty was required of everyone regardless of rank, with the exception of the cook and brewer, beginning immediately and continuing until further notice. She sanded the wet ink and set it aside to dry.

Uncle Corne was taking his turn while she finished up the notices.

Yesterday's events had flipped everything upside down in the fort. She'd written letters that were already aboard the boat that might have whisked her away with Bartlett's man. Letters warning the rest of the army about the massacre—for it could be called nothing less—that had happened so close to the fort.

So close to her.

Two or three men killed here and there during the summer months had been tragic, of course, but yesterday... She tapped off the sand and placed the notice on top of the others that were ready to be posted.

For the first time since she'd arrived, Abigail seriously considered returning to Boston when safe passage could be found. There was no place for a woman alone on the frontier. She'd hate leaving, of course. Red Beads had become like a sister to her. No. Much closer than she'd ever been to Susanna, or Deloris following her marriage to Bartlett.

But it wasn't Red Beads who'd occupied her thoughts and interrupted her sleep throughout the night. Abigail propped her elbow on the desk and sunk her chin into her palm.

It was Koyen.

It may not make sense that he'd saved her life—or at least potentially saved her life—twice. Uncle Corne may be right about that. But she couldn't deny that he *had*. She didn't for one minute believe that he'd been part of the massacre. He was far too… far too…

She stood and walked to the window, pressed her forehead against the cool glass and gazed over the palisade to the forest beyond. Leaves with their edges touched by bronze, gold, and red fluttered in the morning light. Even they, in their untamed and untrimmed glory, reminded her of the Seneca man.

Koyen wasn't like anyone she'd ever known. He would fit in Boston like a bear would fit in a cow byre. He was wild and free and strong next to the pampered and kept society men she'd grown up around.

Could he have fought beside those who had committed the massacre? A part of her sensed that he could have. That maybe, under different circumstances, he would have. He was a warrior and no mistake.

But he was more than that.

He was a man who saw something in her that he'd trusted. Her. Abigail Aldridge with her stumbling tongue who was overly rash and ignorant of everything she should have known before arriving at Fort Niagara. But he treated her with respect.

He called her Mourning Dove.

Between him and Bartlett's man, there was no comparison. Yet in the eyes of the civilized world, Koyen was the savage.

Bartlett's man was on the boat headed for Boston. In chains.

Uncle Corne had made sure of that. And with him went a terse and pointed letter to the magistrate for dealing with the odious little man. Had he been a soldier, there was no doubt in her mind that her uncle would have had him flogged on the spot. But since the man was a civilian, the best Uncle Corne could do was turn him over to the authorities in Boston.

He'd also sent a letter to Bartlett, but he'd written it himself and hadn't allowed Abigail to read it. Not that she couldn't guess its contents... nor even disagree with them. With the massacre practically on the fort's doorstep, the truth Uncle Corne had tried so hard to make her see was now too plain, too stark, for even her to ignore.

Her dream of a life on the frontier, a life with Uncle Corne, a life of purpose and contentment—independent of Bartlett—was not to be hers.

"I FEAR FOR YOU, MY SON. I AM PROUD OF YOU, BUT I fear for you."

Koyen stuffed his leather bag with a clean cloth shirt, an extra breech clout, and his spare leggings. His mother had mended his old moccasins the evening before, so he added them to the top and closed the flap and slung the strap over his head and across his shoulders.

"I must go."

"I know." She touched his arm, then drew away, as if afraid she'd cling to him if she didn't. "Perhaps I have always known you were destined for something greater than our village. Perhaps that is why I named you Koyengquahtah."

"A name the white man cannot pronounce and will not say." He gave a dry, short chuckle.

"I think—very soon—it is a name they will know well."

He snorted and glanced out the door of the longhouse. "One way or the other." Would he be allowed to walk into the fort on his own, or would he be taken captive? Would Mourning Dove's uncle speak for him, after seeing her safely returned to the fort twice? If he asked them to send word to William Johnson to speak on his behalf, would they? Or would they shoot him on sight?

Stepping out the door of the longhouse would change his life forever. He felt it to his bones, and his mother obviously believed the same. Would he ever see her again?

He reached an arm behind her and pulled her close. Red Beads and Shining Day appeared on his other side, each pressing against him. He was leaving them without a man to provide for them. He'd spoken to Tall Otter and been assured that they would not lack for meat or fish, but it wasn't the same as having a man of their own to watch over them.

But he couldn't stay. Not even for the ones he loved.

Or perhaps more correctly, because of the ones he loved.

"HE ASKED TO SEE YOUR NIECE, MISS ALDRIDGE, SIR." The soldier stood ill at ease in front of Uncle Corne's desk.

"Preposterous!" Her Uncle rose, chest out, every inch the British officer.

But Abigail rose too. "Uncle." She almost flinched at the fierce look he shot her. "He s-s-saved my life."

"As yet, we know not if he played a part—"

"I know." She took a step toward him, ignoring the soldier in the middle of the room. She didn't look away from her uncle's hard stare. "I do know, Uncle."

"No prisoner is going to demand anything of me or you, my dear."

"He did not demand." She glanced at the soldier for confirmation. "He asked. 'Tis not the s-s-same."

The soldier nodded, his Adam's apple bobbing as he faced her uncle.

"You s-s-see? 'Tis the very least I can do after w-w-what he did for me."

The silence stretched between them until it became difficult to breathe. So much depended on what her uncle would say—or do—next. Abigail wouldn't have a life here on the frontier, but she desperately didn't want to hinder the lives of those she left behind. Especially not Koyen's.

"Very well. I can see you are determined to go, but I will accompany you myself. Dismissed, soldier."

Relief poured through her, but also a twinge of regret. Of course she couldn't meet with Koyen alone, which wouldn't be proper even at the fort, but oh—how she wished she could. To ask him about Red Beads and if she'd return to the fort, to the bake house the next day. And Shining Day. Did she have any remorse for what she'd done to Abigail? And—deep down—she wanted to know if he'd had any knowledge of the massacre before it happened. She believed with all her heart that he hadn't taken part, but had he known? Could he have alerted the fort? That was a question that had plagued her the previous night.

The question she wouldn't voice to her uncle or anyone else. Anyone but Koyen.

"Fetch your shawl, Abigail." Uncle Corne pointed toward the open door. "The breeze off the lake is brisk this morning."

She hurried across the corridor, pausing only to give Dance a scratch under the chin, then whisked her shawl from its peg and joined her uncle. They descended the stairs, his boot heels breaking the silence. Once outside the castle, she clutched her shawl tighter against the wind. Uncle Corne held his hat in place with one hand. In another month, the wind would carry snow across the water and into the fort.

Would she be here then?

In light of all that had happened, did she still want to be?

They walked straight to the barracks, a building Abigail had never been in, and around to the narrow end where there were bars across a single window without glass and a heavy door barred from the outside.

"Open it," barked Uncle Corne to the soldiers standing guard.

One soldier hurried to remove the bar, while the other unshouldered his musket and stood ready to use it if needed.

The sight—and the thought of Koyen getting shot—put Abigail's heart in her throat.

The door was dragged open, and Uncle Corne entered first, then motioned for her to follow.

Koyen stood against the far wall, his hands bound in front of him, his head high, his bearing almost regal. There was nothing of a conquered foe in his stance or on his face. A sense of pride flooded Abigail. She was proud to know such a man. A man she'd first seen as a half-naked savage on the sands near the lake.

How little she'd understood. How much she'd learned and grown during her months at the fort.

If circumstances had been different—

"Scout Koyen." Uncle Corne clasped his hands behind his back, rocking his weight from heels to toes. "I have brought Miss Aldridge to see you, as you requested and at her insistence. Now, pray, tell me the meaning of this!"

"I know she listen to me."

"You knew." Uncle Corne shot Abigail a look she couldn't interpret in the dim light of the room. "How did you know?" Suspicion crept into his voice.

"She kind to my sisters, even one who betrayed her. She not understand my people, but she listen and learn."

Abigail did her best not to preen under such praise, especially since her uncle seemed not at all impressed by it.

"Say what you wish, then, and be quick about it."

Koyen turned his dark eyes on her. How had she ever thought them hard and sinister?

"I tell you true. I not fight in battle. I find boy at bottom of cliff. He alone alive. I carry him to Lower Landing, hear second attack. I hide him under pine, stay with him until fighting done. I bring here, find you tied."

"Why did you not take him directly to Lower Landing?" Uncle Corne asked.

"Soldiers in second battle come from there. I not walk to soldiers shooting Seneca warriors."

Which made perfect sense. Uncle Corne's scowl had lessened, so perhaps he saw that as well.

Abigail touched his sleeve. "W-w-will he have to s-s-stay here, tied as he is? S-s-surely you s-s-see that he tells the truth? W-w-would he have come if he did not?"

Her uncle pinched the bridge of his nose, generally a good sign, but then he took a step closer to Koyen and asked, "Did you know of the attack before it happened?"

"Yes."

Abigail's heart dropped, and she pressed her hand to her throat.

"And yet, you did not come to the fort? You did not report it?" The walls of the small room all but shook with her uncle's roar. The two soldiers in the doorway shuffled their feet behind her.

Koyen didn't move. His face gave away nothing of his thoughts. "You know soldiers plan attack my people—my village —you come tell me?"

Uncle Corne took another step closer. "That is hardly the same. You are a scout."

"No more."

"If you had an ounce of loyalty—"

"I return boy."

Her uncle opened his mouth, then snapped it shut. He crossed his arms. "Suppose you tell me why you did."

"I not see you as enemy, Captain Hayward. I talk to William Johnson—"

"'Tis *Sir* William Johnson."

Koyen nodded. "Same man. I think he right, that British and Seneca need work together, build peace bridge. I return boy, show peace."

"But you could have warned us of a coming attack, man."

Koyen cocked his head. "Want peace between our people. Not put British above Seneca."

"It was your people who killed our soldiers."

"No."

"The two men who survived have both sworn it was the Seneca."

"Not Seneca from my village. Come from east." Koyen shook his head. "Not meet William Johnson." He leaned forward slightly. "Not listen to me."

"S-s-so you tried to s-s-stop them?" Abigail asked, afraid to hear the answer, but unable to stop the question.

His eyes sought hers. "Yes. Tall Otter go with me." He looked back to her uncle. "If we tell you, it not change battle. More soldiers die. Fort left too few soldiers."

Uncle Corne huffed and drew himself to his full height. "Do you imply that the full force of His Majesty's finest would have been beaten back?"

Koyen nodded. "Not enough men to fight Seneca at Devil's Hole. Too many warriors."

"He is correct, Hayward."

Abigail whirled around at the voice.

Major Wilkins stepped into the room. "As much as I hate to admit it, he is."

"Major Wilkins." Uncle Corne straightened to attention.

The major waved a hand at him, but addressed Koyen. "You say your village is not a part of these attacks. What is your situation with the rest of your tribe?"

"Seneca split. Some follow Farmer's Brother, some not."

"And you obviously do not." Major Wilkins fingered the gold chain that hung from his waistcoat. "What are your plans?"

"Go to William Johnson—"

"*Sir* William," Uncle Corne corrected in a tight voice.

Koyen glanced at her uncle, then back to the major. "He meet with Iroquois chiefs."

"So I have been informed," the major said.

"I there. Only Seneca. We talk. I go back."

The major spoke over his shoulder to the soldiers standing guard. "Release him." One came forward and untied Koyen's hands.

He rubbed his wrists and watched the major.

Abigail couldn't take her eyes off him. So brave to have come to the fort and faced these two powerful British officers. So calm, a sign of his honesty and integrity. And so handsome. Red Beads had been right about that.

"When do you leave?" Major Wilkins asked.

Koyen flicked her a glance, almost too fleeting to be sure he'd meant to look at her at all. "Now."

The major nodded. "And when will you return."

This time Koyen's glance paused on her for two full heartbeats. "Maybe not return."

Chapter 30

Leaving her had been harder than Koyen had imagined. While he knew his path, the rightness of it, and the impact it would have on keeping his village out of the war, on keeping his mother and sisters safe, it had taken everything he had to walk away from Mourning Dove. Two days later, his steps came no easier. It would take him two more days of heavy steps to reach William Johnson's place in the Mohawk lands.

He had left Seneca lands behind at first light with a feeling of relief. Walks Fast had let him go once, but Koyen wasn't trusting that it would happen a second time. His tribe was split, his village on the side of peace while others were on the side of war, including the village of High Clouds, the young woman his mother would have him take for his wife.

That would never happen with his decision to join William Johnson.

Would his tribe ever reunite? Would the Seneca be one people again? Or was the chasm separating them too wide and too deep to overcome? It would grow wider and deeper as warriors were lost in battle. Only the strongest and bravest would be able to leap it.

Or perhaps it would take someone who could build a bridge

—his reason for leaving his village, for turning his back on Mourning Dove, for joining with William Johnson.

A noise alerted him, and he slipped off the well-traveled path into the forest, crouching behind a tangle of blackberry canes. Voices, men making no attempt to remain quiet, approached from the east. Koyen remained motionless, ignoring a bee that searched in vain for a late blossom among the canes.

A group of young women approached. They spoke a language he vaguely recognized as Cayuga, another of the Iroquois tribes. They carried empty baskets, and he caught the words for pine knots. As did the young women from his village, they would gather them from pine groves. The knots remained when the rest of the wood had rotted away. They burned hot and long in the winter fires.

They moved past, but still Koyen waited. His patience proved itself when a trio of young men, each armed with bow and arrows, came into view. He grinned. How many times had he been sent to shadow his sisters? Mothers were the same in every tribe.

Once they were long out of hearing, he returned to the path and broke into an easy run. The Cayuga were not concerned with the war, or their young women would not be out under such little protection. Their chiefs' words to William Johnson remained intact.

Perhaps, of the six Iroquois tribes, the Seneca was the only one divided by the war.

He ran until the sun slanted through the trees to the west, then found a place to rest where he could see the path but remain unseen. He pulled a round loaf of bread from his bag. Lurana Quinn had met him at the fort's gate and slipped four of them into his bag.

"You have changed much this summer, Koyengquahtah," she

had said. "You have grown into a man of wisdom. A man with far sight. A man your people need."

He broke the loaf in half, tucked one half back into his bag, and ate the other. He would miss Lurana Quinn's bread.

But not nearly as much as he'd miss seeing Mourning Dove.

IT WAS DIFFICULT NOT TO GAPE AT THE CHANGE IN the young man standing in front of Uncle Corne, but Abigail did her best. John Rutherford, who had left with high expectations of delivering relief supplies to Fort Detroit, was now little more than a scarecrow. His clothing hung like washing from a bush, his bones poking against the fabric like branches. He'd had no weight to lose when he'd left them weeks before, and now looked barely fit enough to stand.

She tucked her head and scribbled as many notes as she could while he made his report to Uncle Corne. The detail he'd left with had run into trouble after just one day out on the lake when their sloop took on water. No amount of pumping helped, and they feared the worse. But just when all appeared to be lost, they ran aground on a sand bar. The dangers didn't end there, however. They managed to get ashore with many of the supplies and used the barrels and bundles to build a crude shelter. They were attacked by Indians and lost a number of soldiers. It'd been many days before help arrived. And then, returning to Fort Niagara, they passed the bodies of more soldiers still strewn around the cliff above Devil's Hole.

The poor man's voice gave out as he finished his report. Uncle Corne sent him to the infirmary, and when he'd left, her uncle rose and went to the door.

Ensign Tharp waited there, nearly as skinny as Mr. Rutherford, but standing straight and tall, ready to serve his captain.

Before Uncle Corne stepped out, he said, "Please tidy those notes into a report, my dear. I must speak with Major Wilkins."

"W-w-what can be done for Fort Detroit now?"

"I know not. I wish I did." He paused, then turned to face her. "It is not impossible that I may have to join the next exposition to the west."

Abigail rose. "You might leave?"

"Indeed, my dear. That has always been my fear at having you here, that I might be assigned elsewhere. And no"—he held up a hand as if to stop her—"there is no way for you to accompany me."

"No, uncle. I can s-s-see that."

"But what is to be done with you?" He rubbed the back of his neck. "I will not leave without a plan in place, that I can assure you. What it will be?" He sighed. "I only wish I knew."

"P-p-perhaps I could s-s-stay under the p-p-protection of Lurana Quinn."

He straightened as if to bluster and deny that possibility, but then didn't. Instead, he placed one hand on the doorframe and leaned there a moment. "I hope it will not come to that." Then he was gone.

Come to what? Being under the protection of another woman? Of a half-Indian woman? Or of having to work daily in the bake house to earn her keep in the fort?

She pressed shaking fingers to her temples.

Everything was falling apart around her. Everything. Red Beads hadn't come to the fort for baking the day before. Uncle Corne might have to go west. Her future was more uncertain than ever.

And Koyen was gone.

"When I first came among the Mohawk, Koyen, I lived with them. I lived as one of them in their longhouses. I slept as they slept, ate as they ate, hunted alongside them. It taught me how they saw the world. How they saw us British and the French. In short, it was an experience I needed to be useful here." William Johnson leaned back in his chair near the fireplace in his house.

Koyen sat in the opposite chair, its enveloping depth of padded leather foreign to his backside. Its high arm rests bumping his elbows. But the fire—although surrounded by bricks—was like his mother's fire in the longhouse. Warm and inviting.

William Johnson and Molly Brant had welcomed him into their home, but Koyen still struggled to understand the man. Not the language itself—the missionaries had taught him well—but its deeper meaning. He seemed to talk in circles around what he truly wanted to say.

"How this matter to me?" Koyen asked.

The other man almost jumped forward in his chair, landing with his elbows on his knees, a wide smile across his face. "Do you not see? As I went and lived among the Mohawks, so you must live among the British."

"I scout for—"

"Ah, but you did not live in the fort, am I correct?"

"I not live there."

"You returned to your village every night, back to your people, and remained steeped in their ways." When Koyen would have spoken, he held up a hand. "They are not bad ways, to be sure, but if you wish to understand the British, you must" —he smacked his knees with the palms of this hands— "immerse yourself in their ways."

"I come here. I learn from you."

William Johnson sighed and slumped back in his chair.

Koyen had always thought of chairs as a device to make men soft by avoiding connection with the hard ground. After watching the other man move around so much, he was rethinking his assumption. Perhaps a chair allowed a man to express himself in ways he could not while seated on the ground. He would need to ponder that when he had more time.

"In the long term, I believe you can and you should. However, a stint living inside the fort would educate you far faster than I can here in the ways of the British." He motioned for one of his children to come closer. "Tell your mother I require paper and ink to pen a letter."

The young boy scampered away.

"I shall write to Major Wilkins and request he allow this. He will, of course. He may not be the best military mind in His Majesty's service, but he is clear-headed. And when the time is right, when you are comfortable understanding the soldiers at the fort, I wish for you to return here. I will have a cabin built across the way." He waved toward the front door and the clearing beyond. "We will work together to broker a lasting peace—a friendship—between our people." He slapped the arm rests of his chair. "By jove, 'tis the best plan."

"A cabin?" Koyen looked around the room and through the doorway into another. The walls were straight and thick with windows, a few containing glass, others with stretched hide so thin and well-oiled it let in light. It reminded him too much of the room he'd been kept captive in at the fort.

"Indeed. Oh, not as large as this." He paused and squinted at Koyen. "Unless, of course, you have a woman to share it with you?"

He shook his head. The only woman who would matter to him, the only one he could picture in a cabin...

That woman was off limits to Koyengquahtah.

It was too quiet in Lurana Quinn's bake house. Abigail kneaded the huge ball of dough into submission, something she could do without thought anymore. How she missed Red Beads and her steady stream of chatter. What had once been fun, mixing and forming the loaves, was now drudgery.

"Such a long face this morning," Lurana Quinn said from the other side of the work table. "What is on your mind that has stilled your tongue?"

"Red Beads." The answer slipped out with a sigh that stirred a puff of flour from the work surface. She looked up at the older woman. "I miss her."

"As do I." The truth of that showed in the worry wrinkles that gathered in the far corners of her eyes. "But it would not be safe for her to be here now. The soldiers, they see an Indian behind every rock and under every tree."

"S-s-surely you understand w-w-why?"

"Of course I do." Lurana Quinn paused to test the loaves in the oven. "But I miss the girl too."

Abigail sucked up the courage to ask what she hadn't been able to voice before, even though the question had gnawed at her as she'd worked across from the Onondaga woman the week before, just a day after Koyen had left.

"You s-s-spoke to Koyen before he left."

The woman's sharp eyes snapped back to Abigail, dark and piercing.

Abigail swallowed against the dryness in her throat. "W-w-what did you s-s-say to him?"

Lurana Quinn placed her palms on the table and leaned forward, never breaking eye contact. "What does that have to do with you, Abigail Aldridge?"

"P-p-perhaps nothing, but I w-w-wish to know."

"Why?"

Why, indeed? Abigail refused to glance away. "Because he is my friend."

The little woman cocked her head, then turned back to the oven and removed the finished loaves. She slid them from the wide wooden paddle onto the cooling shelf with a practiced flick of her wrist. Then she placed six more loaves into the oven, dusted off her hands, and returned her attention to Abigail.

"I told him that he had grown into a man of wisdom with the gift of far sight, and that he would be important to his people."

"Because he w-w-will keep them out of the w-w-war?"

"Perhaps."

Abigail thought back to her original assessment of Koyen on the sands by Lake Ontario. "W-w-when I first s-s-saw him, I w-w-was afraid of him."

Lurana Quinn gathered the ingredients to make molasses biscuits. "He is a warrior among his people, a man to be respected." She shot a glance at Abigail. "Even feared."

"But he is against the w-w-war, is he not?"

"He is… now. But it was not always so."

"W-w-what changed his mind?"

The other woman shrugged. "Who can know the mind of a man? But Koyengquahtah is wise beyond his years, and he listened to those even wiser. Sometimes the greatest measure of wisdom is in listening."

"Is that w-w-why he w-w-went to S-s-sir W-w-william?"

The baker woman gazed toward the east, her eyes unfocused as if seeing things far beyond them. "I do not know."

"W-w-will he return?"

Her dark eyes found Abigail's again, understanding all too evident in their depths. "I do not know that either, but perhaps it is best he does not."

Because friendship with Abigail was unwise? Of course it was. She knew that herself. Yet she couldn't stop thinking about him. Wondering if he'd arrived at Sir William's. What he might learn or accomplish there. If he'd return.

If she'd ever see him again.

Abigail returned to her labors, dividing the dough and forming more loaves. The warmth of the oven was comforting, not stifling, as the cool wind blew in from the north across the lake. September was almost gone.

Would Uncle Corne remain at Fort Niagara through the winter? Armies rarely moved during the severe months when cold and mud and ice added to the dangers of everyday travel. Would that buy her some time before she was forced to return to Boston?

Stilted, lifeless Boston, where people were cruel behind their sophisticated facades. At least on the frontier, one expected a certain level of cruelty. A certain level of danger. One understood that life was fragile and peace even more so. Where strong men ruled—not those with powerful families.

Men like Uncle Corne... and Koyen.

But without such men, a woman had no place. Not yet. Perhaps never in her lifetime.

Chapter 31

K oyen approached the fort with caution. They'd let him go the last time, but would they again? He'd had the same thought about Walks Fast and Farmer's Brother while traveling to William Johnson. Would he forever be a man between two worlds? Looked at with suspicion by both sides?

Was that all he had to look forward to?

He took a detour to his favorite thinking spot, his rock in the forest. Even with his breach clout and leggings, the coolness of it seeped into his backside and legs. Women would be harvesting the last of the gardens around the village, his mother and sisters extra vigilant to pluck every edible part they could to dry and store against winter's pinch.

But if he wintered at the fort—as William Johnson wished— he would be close enough to hunt for his family. If the British gave him leave to come and go. If they didn't take him captive again, or restrict his movements.

So many ifs.

And yet, the bright spot was always Mourning Dove. Against all reason, his better judgment, and his mother's outright disapproval, he could not deny his feelings for the woman. Knowing nothing could come of them didn't matter. They were still...

there. Deep in his heart. So deep he knew he would take no other wife. His life would be a solitary one, as befitted the role he'd accepted.

The man between two worlds.

The sun was halfway to the western horizon when he arrived at the fort. The British flag snapped in the wind. Soldiers moved along the top of the palisade. The massive forest gate was shut.

Koyen watched for a while, then stepped into the clearing that surrounded the fort, a newly enlarged clearing judging by the tree stumps still bright and fragrant. He kept his hands away from the weapons at his waist, his bow and musket strapped to his back.

A shout went up along the wall. Feet thundered along the wooden walk behind the pointed tops of the vertical logs.

He stopped and waited, offering no threat.

"Koyen?" George Swan shouted from the wall. "Is that you?"

"Yes."

"Do you come in peace?"

Would he be standing here, an easy target, if he didn't? "Yes."

Orders were shouted and the gate opened just enough for a man to step through. Koyen accepted the invitation. As he entered, he was surrounded by five soldiers, but none grabbed him or his weapons.

"What is your business here?" George Swan asked, his face —in the past an open and friendly countenance—remained stern.

"William Johnson send me. I speak to Captain Hayward. Have letter for him."

The name Sir William was muttered between the soldiers. A name they recognized, and more importantly, a name they respected. How long would Koyen have to trade on that name? How long before Koyen's name would be both recognized and respected? He was jarred by that thought, even as the soldiers escorted him to the castle.

Is that what he wanted? Recognition and respect? Well, didn't every warrior—every man—strive for some form of those? Yes. From the people important to them, at least.

He glanced at the window of Captain Hayward's office, then entered the castle and walked the familiar route to his room. Ensign Tharp stood outside the door, his brows lifting as Koyen and his guard approached. He nodded to Koyen, then knocked on the door.

"Enter!"

When the door opened, Koyen glanced first at Mourning Dove, leaned over her desk, quill scratching on paper. She looked up, and their eyes met.

She smiled.

At him. As if she were glad he'd come.

He sucked in a quick breath and jerked his attention to her uncle. The man seemed to have aged a year in the ten days Koyen had been gone. Ten days to spend two nights with William Johnson only to be returned where he'd started.

Captain Hayward slapped his hands on his desk. "Did you not go to William Johnson after all?"

"I go. He say I return."

"Return? Here?" Disbelief colored his half-shouted words.

"He say I live with British for time. Learn British ways before work alongside him." Koyen reached into his bag, ignoring the stiffening of the two soldiers who had entered on either side of him. "He write letter." He handed it to the captain, glad that he'd convinced William Johnson to address it to the captain and not Major Wilkins.

"Preposterous." The man rose and snatched the paper from Koyen's fingers. He broke the seal and scanned the words written there.

Words Koyen couldn't read. He could speak British words, but not read or write them. It was something he wished to learn. While he knew he shouldn't, he shot a glance at Mourning Dove. She read and wrote well enough to work alongside her uncle. If she would teach him—

"It says you have agreed to partner with Sir William." Captain Hayward snorted. "Partner. 'Twould seem he has grand plans for you." He tossed the letter onto his desk, then paced in front of the window. "I shall have to consult with the major, of course. Until then"—he wagged his finger between the two guards—"watch over him. Do not let him out of your sight. And take those weapons from him. He'll have no need of them here in the fort. He can wait in the brig."

Koyen unstrapped his musket, bow, and arrows, handing them to the soldier at this right while the other soldier slipped Koyen's tomahawk and knife from his belt. He felt naked in a worse way than being naked felt. But if he were to be a man of peace, then he should get used to being weaponless. At least some of the time.

"Uncle?" Mourning Dove rose. "P-p-perhaps these s-s-soldiers could w-w-wait w-w-with Koyen in the vestibule. 'Twould be more convenient for you w-w-when you receive the major's decision, w-w-would it not?"

"What? Oh." The captain's frown didn't soften at his niece's suggestion. "I suppose. Carry on, men. To the vestibule."

Koyen was nudged toward the door, but he turned in the direction of Mourning Dove and returned the smile she'd given him when he'd entered. Then he allowed himself to be escorted below to wait by the round stone well.

And marvel at the smile he'd gotten in return before he'd left the room upstairs. If nothing else worked out for him at the fort, that smile alone had been worth the journey.

ABIGAIL PACED THE LENGTH OF HER ROOM ONE LAST time, then collapsed onto her bed. Dance hopped into her lap, rumbling and catching her claws in the fabric of Abigail's dress.

"Oh, Dance. I w-w-want s-s-so much to go to him. But 'tis not a thing I can do." She rubbed the cat's vibrating throat, and Dance closed her eyes. "How I w-w-wish it w-w-were. I hope the major w-w-will allow him to s-s-stay, and not as a p-p-prisoner. 'Twould be w-w-wrong w-w-when he is here to do good—not ill."

At some point during her speech, her fingers must have stopped. Dance butted her head against Abigail's chest.

"W-w-what w-w-will become of any of us, Dance?" She stroked the cat's velvety fur. "W-w-what of Koyen? W-w-what of me?" She lifted the animal's chin to look into her eyes. "And w-w-what of you, my darling?" Indeed, what would become of the cat if Abigail were shipped back to Boston? Perhaps she could crate the little beast for transport, but Bartlett would never allow a cat in his house. Dance would know nothing of the dangers of Boston streets. A carriage wheel would be the end of her, no doubt.

Abigail blinked back moisture.

When so many lives hung in the balance across the width of the frontier, why was it a cat's fate and that of the Seneca man below that saddened her so?

Because they had both come to mean so much to her. Too much, probably, but there was no help for it. She lifted Dance and pressed her face against the gray-and-orange fur.

"I s-s-shall do my best to s-s-see that you are taken care of w-w-when I leave." When—not if. "P-p-perhaps Lurana Quinn w-w-will take you in, or that man in the stables." Thankfully, he was one of the three who survived the massacre near Devil's

Hole. "Either w-w-way, you w-w-will be more s-s-safe than you could be in Boston."

Defiant of her blinking, one tear traced a path down her cheek.

Yet, even in this moment of sadness, Abigail could not be sorry for the impulse that had brought her to the fort. She'd grown closer than ever to her beloved uncle. She'd grown in ways she'd never have imagined back in Boston. She could bake bread and clean her own room. She'd even done a bit of cooking in the bake house, simple things Lurana Quinn had shown her that they'd eaten for their meals there. And while she hadn't done any laundry, she'd seen enough of it to understand how it worked. She'd also developed a firm understanding of the British army, its many integral parts, how they fit together, and what it took to run the vast entity that kept the British Empire on top of the world.

Abigail lifted her head and dashed the wetness from her face.

She may be going back to Boston, but she wouldn't be returning in defeat. Nor would she allow herself to be pushed aside or treated like an imbecile any longer. No. Abigail Aldridge would return in triumph with her head high, her accomplishments her badge of honor.

Bartlett better be ready. He'd be getting a very different half-sister than he was used to.

It was Friday. Koyen knew that by the calendar on the wall in the barracks. Not that he could read the words— yet—but he'd memorized where the column for Fridays was. Every morning, one of the soldiers marked an X across the box for the day that had ended. And that morning, the next open box was a Friday box.

He still felt naked without his knife and tomahawk, and he hadn't been outside the fort yet, but at least he wasn't held as a prisoner. The barracks weren't that different from a longhouse, except for the smell. The longhouse always smelled of smoky fires, cooking food, and the dried herbs that hung above each family's sleeping area. The barracks smelled of dirty socks, unwashed men, and the oil used to clean muskets. There was no hint of womanly softness within its walls. No sense of home. But it was dry, and Koyen—as William Johnson had anticipated—was learning much.

The first thing he'd learned was how to lose money at dice and cards. The second thing he'd learned was not to play those games with the soldiers. Unfortunately, he didn't learn that before his meager supply of coins had run out.

He suspected the soldiers had a good laugh at his expense, but he wasn't angry. After all, had they come to live in the village, the men there would best them with their Seneca contests and games.

It was a warm morning for fall, but he pulled on both shirt and leggings anyway. The third lesson he'd learned was that soldiers were less tense around him when he was fully clothed. He couldn't learn from men who were wary of him, so putting them at ease seemed the smart thing to do.

But it was Friday. His fifth day back at the fort and bake house day for Mourning Dove. Would he see her crossing the grounds from the castle? Would he find a reason to visit the bake house? He could if Red Beads came.

"What are you doing today, Koyen?" asked Martin Hagerman, the sergeant who had been in charge of the Seneca scouts before they'd been banished from the fort.

"Learning British ways." He grinned at the man. At first his smiles had been met with squinting eyes and shifting feet. Perhaps he'd never smiled when he was a scout, but it was an expression the British used frequently. And it put men at ease almost as much as wearing clothing. "And perhaps seeing my sister, if she comes to bake bread with Lurana Quinn."

"I have not seen her for more than a fortnight. Not since… before." The men rarely mentioned the massacre, which was fine with Koyen. He didn't need thoughts of it bringing suspicion back on him.

Koyen didn't really expect Red Beads to come, but he hoped she would. He could send word back to their mother, let her know where he was and what he was doing. Let her know that he wasn't a captive, even if he was confined within the walls.

The men—those not on duty—filed into the middle room of the barracks for their morning meal of porridge, bread, and tea. While no men had been sent out hunting, food was plentiful in the fort. Koyen had helped unload barrels from a ship the day before and stack them by contents in the storage room. Barrels packed with salted pork, salted fish, wheat flour, rye flour, dried peas, and even barley for the brewer. There had been smaller casks of molasses, salt, sugar, and tea.

How could Farmer's Brother hope to topple a people who had no need to provide for themselves? The Seneca must hunt, fish, gather, and garden or leave their families to starve during the winter. For the British, everything came to them aboard a ship.

Koyen ate the filling—if largely tasteless—porridge, and dunked a wedge of dry bread into his tea as those around him did before biting into it. The freshest loaves probably went to those who ate in the castle, not the lowly soldiers of the barracks. Perhaps he could charm a fresh loaf from Lurana Quinn later.

When the soldiers left the building for whatever duties awaited them, Koyen followed them outside. His duties were his own, or rather, were to follow William Johnson's suggestions.

Learn how to act and think as British as he could. Learn to understand not only their ways, but their whys. To do that, he must watch and listen and ask questions.

That morning, he could watch and listen from the corner of the barracks, in view of both the castle's door and the forest gate. It wasn't hard to listen. Many of the soldiers grumbled about the food and low pay—even though no one went hungry and their needs were furnished.

The white man was soft but also stubborn and smart. And numerous.

Koyen squatted with his back to the wall of the barracks and waited, watching for either Mourning Dove or Red Beads—or both—before making any further plans for his day.

Chapter 32

U ncle Corne stood in Abigail's doorway, long lines drawn deeply into his cheeks, his eyes clouded. Tendrils of fear climbed her like ivy clinging to the stones of the castle.

"Uncle?"

"'Tis not good news, my dear. I thought it best to tell you here."

"Come in." She swept her shawl off the only chair and hung it on its peg before sitting on her bed. "P-p-please, have a s-s-seat."

Her uncle removed his hat and sank to the simple chair with a hoarse release of breath, somewhere between a moan and a muffled expletive.

Dance came from under the bed, stretched, then jumped into Abigail's lap. Her uncle studied the cat's movements as if doing so would postpone what he'd come to say. Abigail wished it would. Whatever news he brought would not be to her liking. Far from it. She steeled her heart for the worst.

"My dear, it grieves me, it truly does, but I must tell you that I am commanded to travel west with Major Wilkins." He twirled his hat around one hand. "To Fort Detroit."

"Oh!" The only thing worse than being sent back to Boston was knowing Uncle Corne was heading into greater danger. "Oh, Uncle, I am..." Words fled from her like leaves before the wind. What could she say?

"I will speak to Lurana Quinn today on your behalf, to arrange for you to live with her in the bake house. You cannot stay in the castle without me, I am sorry to say. But 'twill only be until transportation to Boston can be arranged. May that be as soon as possible." He shook his finger at her. "Tomorrow begins October, and travel on the lake will be more treacherous soon."

"From the Indians?"

"Storms. You have not experienced the early winter here, but the storms are tremendous, unpredictable, and a grave danger to our schooners. 'Tis imperative that a berth be found for you within the fortnight."

"But Uncle, w-w-will you not also be on a s-s-schooner? Also in danger?"

He leaned forward and patted her hand. "I am an old soldier, my dear, not a beautiful young woman. 'Tis different for me." He cast troubled eyes toward the window and the lake beyond. "Every time I step onto a boat, I do wish I had taken the time to learn to swim." He sat back and slapped his knees with his palms. "But enough of that. To the bake house with you. Let Lurana Quinn know I will speak with her as soon as I can. And bake some of my favorite scones." He stood, his face once again pulling into long lines. "I will miss you. You have no idea the ray of sunshine you have been to your old uncle."

She put Dance aside and stood, taking his hands. "You have no idea how much I have loved being here w-w-with you." She swallowed against the tightness threatening to choke her. "W-w-when do you leave?"

"In four days."

"Then"—she squeezed his hands—"w-w-we w-w-will s-s-sp-sp…" She took a deep breath, willing the words to come. "S-s-spend every minute w-w-we can together."

"Would that we could, but I will be with the major all day. Go and bake my scones, speak with Lurana Quinn, and we will see each other at supper tonight. I may have news about a boat by then."

A ship to take her away from all she had come to love at Fort Niagara.

THE FOREST GATE OPENED BEFORE THE CASTLE DOOR. Koyen stood as Red Beads slipped through the opening. A feeling of relief flowed over him. Not that he had seriously thought harm might come to his sisters—or his mother—due to his decision, but seeing the evidence eased his conscience none-theless.

He strode toward her. When she noticed him, she stopped and stared. He must look different without his weapons and fully clothed on a day that didn't require it.

She ran to him. "Brother! I did not expect to see you here," she said in the Seneca language.

"I hoped I would see you." He nodded toward the closed gate. "You did not travel alone, I trust. Or without our mother's approval."

She shook her head, long braids dancing against her dress. "Tall Otter brought me. It was not easy to convince him, but since Mother approved, he relented."

"He is a good man."

"Yes. He is." Was that a blush staining his sister's cheeks? She'd averted her head too swiftly to be sure. Perhaps their mother had no need to worry about her daughter and the British soldier, Tharp. Koyen could think of no one he would approve of more than Tall Otter. He was older, but Red Beads could be a handful. An older husband would suit her well, and Tall Otter would see to her mother and sister.

"There is Mourning Dove." Red Beads pointed, then scurried off without him.

But in four long strides, he caught up with her. After all, escorting his sister was a perfectly acceptable reason to visit the bake house.

Mourning Dove arrived at the doorway first but had seen them. She waited, one hand clutching the flimsy cloth most white women wore around their necks and shoulders. The breeze ruffled the white fabric of her cap, loosening some hair that escaped around her ears. Her eyes, almost the same color as her hair, were soft and clear.

Only years of training kept his face stoic. His insides were a different matter, like a pair of bobcats quarreling over a rabbit.

"Koyen." She spoke first. "'Tis good to s-s-see you again, and not locked away."

"I treated well." He shrugged. "If not trusted."

Red Beads grabbed his arm and squeezed close to him for a moment. "I trust you, brother."

He grunted, one side of his mouth refusing to remain still. "As you should, little sister, for all the times I have kept you from harm—usually from yourself," he said in Seneca.

She dropped his arm with a huff and went to the door. "Come, M... Abigail, before he says more."

But Mourning Dove didn't follow. She met his gaze fully, openly, honestly. "I admire you for w-w-what you are doing."

"Doing what?"

"Trying to s-s-stop a w-w-war." She shrugged. "I know not

how one man w-w-will achieve it, but if anyone can, I believe it w-w-will be you."

"Not one man." He glanced to the east then back. "William Johnson work to stop. I join him. Bring Seneca back to rest of Iroquois people."

"You are very brave to w-w-walk away from your village, your p-p-people, to do this."

"You very brave come here, away from Boston village and people."

She laughed, but it wasn't a happy sound. "I may have thought s-s-so, once, but I have learned much in my time here. Enough to know I w-w-was much more headstrong than brave. P-p-perhaps s-s-some w-w-would s-s-say foolish."

She fumbled on the last words, so he switched to signing. *"You are not foolish."*

Her eyes widened, her mouth opening before stretching into a smile. *"I am glad you think so well of me."*

How quickly she had learned—mastered even—the sign language of his people. *"I think of you often."*

"Abigail Aldridge." Lurana Quinn appeared in the doorway behind Mourning Dove, hands planted on her hips, eyes shooting sparks at Koyen. "Did you come to bake or did you not?"

"Indeed." With a parting glance at Koyen, she slipped past Lurana Quinn and into the bake house.

"And you"—the baker woman signed to him—*"have no place here. Go away. Leave the girl be. She is not for you, and you know it."*

He did… didn't he?

———

UNCLE CORNE PACKED—THEN REPACKED—HIS TRUNK and a large canvas bag with his belongings. He'd leave in the morning. Abigail's throat tightened. She dipped her quill and scratched out the list he'd asked her to write.

Her last official duty for him.

It was her final night in the castle. The next morning, she would move into the single room Lurana Quinn would share with her until a ship arrived. Sergeant Moreland—the quarter-master—had agreed to see her on the next ship heading to Boston. No more soldiers were allowed leave to return east, so there would be a cabin. He'd assured Uncle Corne that it would be less than a fortnight.

How would she bear it? Saying goodbye to her uncle and then goodbye to the fort. To Lurana Quinn and Judith Spooner, to Red Beads and... Koyen.

For the past few days, since they'd spoken at the bake house, he'd signed to her several times. Once she'd spied him from Uncle Corne's window, and he'd signed a greeting, which she'd returned. The day before, she'd seen him from the kitchen doorway of the castle when she'd fetched Uncle's tea and Dance's milk. He'd signed another greeting.

He'd been closer that time. His dark eyes saying more than his hands. Things that stirred something deep within her. Something she ought not to think about. Ought not to wonder over.

But she did.

That very morning, he'd been in the vestibule when she'd gone for a bucket of water. He hadn't signed anything. Soldiers had gathered there, and he'd hung back against the wall. But his eyes had followed her. Watched over her. Made her feel safe, even in a room filled with men.

When her uncle was gone, she knew Koyen would watch over her. He'd not said so—would likely never say so—but she knew.

"Blast it, Abigail." Uncle Corne stood and scratched his

neck, knocking his wig slightly askew. "I cannot find my portable desk. Might you—?"

He broke off as she pointed across the room to the top of his armoire.

"Gads." He whisked it from its hiding place, showered with dust in the process. "How I will miss you, my dear. I have come to rely on you far too much, I assure you."

"I w-w-will miss you, Uncle." She cleaned the nib of her quill. "More than you can know."

"Now, now." He came to her, towering over her as she sat at her desk for perhaps the last time. "'Tis likely my last posting, you know. Your old uncle is almost ready for retirement. 'Twill be my great pleasure to retire to Boston and purchase a house down the street from Bartlett."

Abigail straightened. "And could I, p-p-perhaps, come and live w-w-with you there?" She held her breath awaiting his answer.

"I would have it no other way."

"And Dance? May I bring Dance w-w-with me?"

He rubbed his chin. "Do you think to take the cat when you leave?"

"I do." And Bartlett could either accept a cat in his house or see the back of her as she walked away. She'd decided that if she had to leave all else behind, she'd at least take Dance with her.

"I am certain I can purchase a house large enough for you... and your cat."

Abigail came around the desk as he opened his arms. In their warmth, she pressed her face to the stiff wool of his uniform.

There was hope for a better future. A future with Uncle Corne and not Bartlett.

"KOYEN!" MARTIN HAGERMAN CALLED FROM HALFWAY across the parade ground. "Captain Hayward requests your presence—now!"

The summons was unexpected, and it caused the small hairs on the back of his neck to prickle. What could Mourning Dove's uncle want with him, on the eve of the army's march to Fort Schlosser and from there, on to Fort Detroit on a fleet of boats?

The fort would be left undermanned until the next boat arrived with replacement soldiers. Major Wilkins had ordered upwards of four hundred men to accompany him from Fort Niagara, and would add men from both Lower Landing and Fort Schlosser before taking to the boats. Koyen had heard they expected to sail with a force of seven hundred.

Did the captain worry about taking so many soldiers out of the Niagara area?

Koyen did.

He climbed the stairs and knocked on the captain's door, faintly surprised that Sergeant Hagerman hadn't escorted him, that Ensign Tharp wasn't standing by. But then again, everyone was scrambling to prepare for the next morning's departure.

"Enter!"

Mourning Dove sat at her desk, but her hands were still, her eyes on him.

He snapped his attention to her uncle as the man stood from behind his desk.

The older man eyed him up and down, his mouth twisting in something close to a grimace, but not quite. "Twice you have safeguarded my niece in a time of need."

Unsure how he was expected to respond, Koyen gave a shallow nod, more a simple tip of his chin.

"Indeed. Well." The captain cleared his throat. "As you know, we pull out tomorrow after dawn. I would ask you—once again

—to watch over Miss Aldridge until she is secured on a boat and under sail for Boston."

Mourning Dove was leaving.

The realization hit like a kick to the stomach, even though he should have known she would. Without her uncle—with no family at the fort—it only made sense that she return to her village. Her people.

"I will."

"Good." The captain walked around the desk and approached Koyen, his hand extended.

Koyen stared at that hand for a moment, then grasped it, as the white man did, accepting it as the seal of a bargain. When he'd been a scout, such an action would have been unthinkable, but Captain Hayward was offering him something more. The respect of a fellow warrior.

"There should be a boat within the fortnight, and I do not anticipate anything going amiss in my absence, but…"

"Major leave fort with too few soldiers."

He cleared his throat again. "Just so." Then he shot Koyen a sharp glance. "Have you heard anything about hostile intentions?"

"No. I come from William Johnson straight to fort. Saw no one, speak to no one."

"And you would tell me if you had?"

Koyen lowered his head, studied the toes of his moccasins, then looked back at the older man. His back was straight, his head high, but in his eyes there lurked… what? Fear? Maybe. But not for himself. He was too much the soldier. Koyen glanced at Mourning Dove, who was watching silently, her lip caught between her teeth. Then he turned back to her uncle. "Yes."

The captain's release of breath was audible.

"You have proven yourself, Koyen, at least to me. Oh"—he held up one hand—"I may not have believed you when you first brought Miss Aldridge back to me, but"—he waved toward his niece—"she has assured me you are a man to be trusted. And that, as you well know, is not easy in this time and in this place."

She trusted him. He'd known that, of course, but hearing it confirmed filled him with something like awe. Then the full force of what he was being asked to do crashed down on him.

"I see her safe to boat for you, Captain Hayward."

But it would cost him.

Chapter 33

Raising very little dust but shooing Dance from under the makeshift cot, Abigail did her daily sweep of the small room she shared with Lurana Quinn. The room she'd shared for ten days, each day expecting word that a schooner had arrived to take her away.

Each day expecting it to be her last at the fort, her trunk and baskets packed and ready, a newly fashioned crate for Dance on top of them.

But it was Friday, and Red Beads would arrive soon, a bright spot in Abigail's uncertain life. The other bright spot undoubtedly lounged outside the bake house.

Koyen.

True to his word, he was always close. Always watching. Protective.

Which annoyed Lurana Quinn for reasons the Onondaga woman would not discuss.

Dance pounced on the meager pile of dust and broken bits of dry leaves that had been tracked into the room since the day before.

"S-s-shoo, Dance. Let me s-s-sweep."

But the cat only danced away, living up to her name, before pouncing again.

Abigail laughed.

"You spoil that cat," Lurana Quinn said from the main room of the bake house. "Give her a swat and send her on her way. There are mice to catch."

Abigail stooped and rubbed Dance's throat, drawing a deep rumble from its depths. "S-s-see w-w-what you do? You get me into trouble," she whispered. The cat curved and twisted around Abigail's legs, bumping with her head for more rubs.

The door to the bake house burst open, startling Abigail to her feet.

"Boat here." Koyen's voice sliced through the yeasty air.

Abigail straightened her skirts, touched her cap to make sure it was properly set, and then walked into the main room. Head high, she pulled in a calming breath, even while her stomach knotted and pinched.

"You have s-s-seen it?"

His eyes met hers, dark and burning. "Yes. It approach now."

She nodded, glanced at Lurana Quinn, and then pulled her apron from its peg and wrapped it around herself. "'Twill take them hours to unload. Until then, w-w-we have s-s-soldiers to feed, do w-w-we not?

Approval warmed the nod from the baker woman.

Koyen glanced between them, then backed out of the building. He'd let her know when she was to board. He'd given his word to Uncle Corne. He would not break it, of that Abigail was certain.

Red Beads arrived a short time later, out of breath and eyes wide. "A boat!"

"We know," Lurana Quinn said, then pointed to the aprons. "More mouths to feed."

"But"—Red Beads grabbed her apron—"mean Abigail must leave?"

"Eventually." The word was heavy on her tongue, but Abigail kept her hands busy kneading the dough in her bread bowl. "'Twill not be s-s-soon. And as Lurana Quinn s-s-says, it means more mouths to feed."

And with that, they settled into the routine of the bake house as if no ship sailed toward them, as if her future wasn't about to take a turn for the worse, as if she wasn't about to leave behind all she'd come to love—the people and the place.

Yet she wasn't as miserable as she thought she'd be.

The chatter with Red Beads and Lurana Quinn kept its usual ebb and flow. She joined in, smiled, and even laughed a few times. She enjoyed the morning. Truly enjoyed it.

It wasn't until they were eating their noon meal, surrounded by crusty loaves, flaky scones, and sweet biscuits that it hit her.

She'd matured in a substantial way since arriving at Fort Niagara.

She wasn't returning to Boston the same woman who had arrived on the shore of Lake Ontario half a year ago. She no longer dreaded a life in Boston, a life lived in Bartlett's shadow. The half-sister in the attic that everyone felt sorry for.

The one she—Abigail—had felt sorry for.

Months with her uncle's love, a gruff sort of love as befitted a bachelor soldier, but still deep and abiding. Months getting to know and respect Lurana Quinn, Red Beads, and Koyen, Indians she would not have made eye contact with back in Boston. Back then, she'd thought them savages and heathens.

But Abigail had learned one lesson very well during the past five months. People were not always what they seemed.

Neither was she. No longer would she allow her affliction to define who she was. Nor would she allow Bartlett to do so.

Never again. Abigail Aldridge would return with her head held high, in charge of herself and her future.

But a piece of her heart would always remain at Fort Niagara. A substantial piece.

———

THE FORT'S SMALL BOATS BROUGHT LOAD AFTER LOAD of soldiers to the shore, far more than Koyen would have thought could fit on such a vessel. Then came the barrels, kegs, casks, and crates to feed them all. Those were dumped onto the sand as snowflakes swirled in the air. The first of the season. Nothing that would stick to the ground but just a warning of things to come.

Koyen had hoisted a crate to his shoulder when a loud-voiced sailor dragged one last boat ashore.

"That be the lot of them. Make haste. We have no time to dawdle."

The rest of the sailors joined him in the small boat belonging to the schooner, and the last sailor shoved them off the beach. Oars slapped through the waves, and the little boat was underway, returning to the vessel bobbing a distance from shore.

Without Mourning Dove.

Koyen dropped the crate in the sand and approached Sergeant Morland, the fort's quartermaster, who had overseen the offloading.

"Sergeant?"

"What?" The man glanced up from his ledger, squinting at him. "Oh, 'tis you, Koyen. What do you need?"

"Miss Aldridge not board schooner?"

"That was the plan." He slapped his ledger closed. "But the schooner is taking on water and repairs cannot be made here.

They must sail to a proper port with the materials they require. They will not return straight to Boston."

"Miss Aldridge..." Koyen waited, almost seeing the calculations race across the sergeant's face.

"Will have to wait for the next schooner." He tucked the ledger under one arm. "And hope another comes before the ice."

Part of him wanted to whoop and toss something into the air, but he merely nodded, then returned to the crate and hoisted it again.

Mourning Dove wasn't leaving. Not yet.

He followed the rest of those carrying supplies and stacking them in the storerooms. His own plans might be thwarted. He'd given his word to Captain Hayward to watch over Mourning Dove and see her onto a boat. He couldn't—wouldn't—leave the fort before she did.

Even though it wasn't required of him, he worked alongside the soldiers until the beach was cleared and the storehouse bulging.

He returned to the bake house, its yeasty aroma overcoming the flurries that lingered in the air. Opening and stepping through the door, he was met with warmth and the full force of delicious smells. The women sat on stools around the work table, eating their noon meal.

His stomach growled, long and low.

Lurana Quinn rose and poured tea into a fourth cup. "Come. Join us." She pointed to another stool against the wall.

He carried it to the table and sat, feeling like a vulture on a limb suspended so high above the floor. Sitting on chairs and stools and the like was going to take him some time to adjust to.

"Must Abigail leave?" his sister asked, distress in her voice and written across her face.

Mourning Dove's face was serene. She broke off a small

portion of bread, then chewed it while watching him, waiting for his answer. As if she didn't have a care in the world.

"Yes. Not on—" He tipped his chin toward the lake "—boat. It gone."

The serenity flickered in Mourning Dove's eyes. Was she not as calm as she appeared? She'd learned to mask her emotions well since arriving at the fort. He remembered their first meeting on the sand when her outrage and disgust had been plain to see. Outrage and disgust aimed at him. There was no sign of either now, but a glimmer of... relief?

Lurana Quinn glanced between him and Mourning Dove, a frown marring her brow. "What has happened?"

"Boat leak. Sailors must fix. Not go Boston." He shrugged. "Go somewhere else."

"And they could not make room for Abigail?" Lurana Quinn's voice rose at the end.

"They w-w-would not." Mourning Dove pushed her plate aside. "The only p-p-ports between here and Boston are not p-p-places that w-w-would be s-s-safe for me. And I could hardly s-s-stay on a boat overrun w-w-with men making repairs, now could I?"

"Does this mean she can stay the winter?" His sister's eyes glimmered in hope.

"Not know." He took a bite of the bread, still warm, the fresh yeast tangy on his tongue. He hated to admit it, but when he left Fort Niagara, he would miss Lurana Quinn's bread. Bread make of ground corn was nothing in comparison.

"Am I w-w-welcome to s-s-stay longer w-w-with you?" Abigail asked Lurana Quinn.

The older woman nodded. "It seems you have no choice."

Unless she went with Koyen to William Johnson's.

He nearly choked, coughed, then took a drink of the tea,

scalding his throat. Where had that thought come from? And why did it wrap around his chest like a hot, wet blanket?

"Chew your food, Koyengquahtah, do not inhale it." The baker woman pushed another wedge of bread his way. "There is plenty. We have been busy this morning." She cocked her head at him. "How many soldiers came with the boat?"

A much safer topic than his thoughts. "Many small boats full."

"As many as those who left with the major?"

"No. Enough make fort safe."

"Well then." The baker woman stood and dusted off her hands. "We have more work to do." She speared Koyen with one of those looks he couldn't read—one probably best unread. "And you have learning to do. Elsewhere."

Mourning Dove smiled at him, and Red Beads grinned.

He grabbed one more chunk of bread and left the bake house, but he didn't go far. He settled against its wall under one of the windows, the building shielding him from the wind and snow. There he finished his bread and listened to the voices inside. He couldn't make out the words through the heavy glass and stone, but he relaxed and enjoyed the cadence of the sound.

And let his mind play with the outrageous idea of Mourning Dove joining him in the cabin at William Johnson's.

HER UNCLE'S WARNING ABOUT STORMS ON THE LAKE in the fall had come true. Abigail walked along the far side of the castle, under the window of what had been her room just a month past. The first few snows had not amounted to anything, but the last one had left a couple of inches on the ground. Even though the wind had died down, waves crashed upon the shore relentlessly. The pounding matched the headache she'd awoken with.

Koyen matched her steps. Ever her protector. Silent, as he mostly was.

She stopped and turned to him. "Do you think a boat w-w-will make it through before the ice?"

He searched the waves for a moment. "Not know boats. Canoe not make it." He glanced back at her. "Wait and see."

Waiting. It wore like a skirt of fresh nettles. Not that she wanted to return to Boston, truly, she did not. But she was prepared to go. The not knowing *when* was what caused her headache. The instability of her situation—

The distant roar of a cannon cut off her thoughts.

Koyen grabbed her arm and raced back to the bake house. She did her best to run beside him, but it was his strong grip on her upper arm that kept her from falling more than once.

The sound came again, still very distant.

"W-w-where is it coming from?" she asked, panting to draw in enough breath.

"Lower Landing."

So far away... and yet.

They arrived at the open bake house door. Lurana Quinn stood there with a blanket wrapped around her shoulders.

Soldiers raced here and there. Horses stomped and snorted while being saddled. And far above, along the castle's steeply pitched roof, shutters slapped opened and the noses of cannons rolled into view.

"Are w-w-we under attack?"

"Not us." Lurana Quinn lifted her chin to the southwest. "Not yet."

"Do you think w-w-w-w..." She shook her arm free of Koyen's grip and signed, *"Will we be attacked here?"*

"*I do not know.*" She detected a thread of uncertainty in Koyen's motions.

Lurana Quinn must have noticed it as well. She signed, "*What do you know, Koyengquahtah?*"

"*I know nothing, I have not left the fort. I have not seen any of my people other than Red Beads. And I have spent much less time with her than you have.*" His motions grew clipped. Had the question angered him?

Because he wasn't trusted?

The soldiers didn't fully trust Koyen, and neither did Lurana Quinn. It seemed as though Abigail was the only one who trusted him. And she did. Completely. Uncle Corne had trusted him, too, right before he'd left. He'd put Koyen in charge of her.

That thought brought on feelings she shouldn't be contemplating. Not while Lower Landing was under attack. Not while it was possible Fort Niagara itself could come under attack. Not... not ever.

He was Seneca. She was British. And that was the end of it.

Chapter 34

With dexterity brought on by months of practice, Abigail slid two crusty loaves of bread from the oven using the broad wooden peel. She positioned them over the cooling ledge, and with a flick of her wrist, jerked back the peel, leaving the hot loaves perfectly placed.

"You do good as Lurana Quinn." Red Beads held out her hand for the peel. "Let me try."

Her friend's last attempt hadn't ended well, but the baker woman had stepped out, so Abigail handed over the peel. "Have a care."

"I do."

Abigail moved out of the way and held her breath as Red Beads scooped up the last two loaves in the oven. She turned, balancing the loaves carefully, positioned them exactly, and then—

"What do you think you are doing?" Lurana Quinn rushed into the bake house.

Red Beads jumped, overbalanced the peel, and sent both loaves tumbling to the floor. The noise startled Dance, who streaked across the floor, between Lurana Quinn's feet, and out the door.

"Dance!" Abigail moved to follow.

"Let the cat go." The Onondaga woman folded her arms and frowned at Abigail and Red Beads. "Who thought this was a good idea?"

Red Beads hung her head. "I want try again."

Koyen appeared behind Lurana Quinn, the gray-and-orange cat tucked in his arms.

Abigail sighed in relief. Dance went outside often since they'd moved into the bake house, but seeing her run away in fear had spiked the memory of when she'd left the castle and Abigail had followed, only to be caught by Bartlett's man.

And saved by Koyen.

Dance looked ridiculously small in his arms, yet Abigail envied her.

Shouts broke out behind Koyen. He released the cat into the bake house, then stepped outside. Abigail followed, the other two women right behind her.

The forest gate was being thrown open—wide open—as shouts and even some cheers greeted them. Then a line of men marched through the gate. As they entered, the cheers died away.

Abigail clutched her fichu, the tightness in her chest more distressing than the mid-November cold.

The men entering looked exhausted, heads down, shoulders slumped, feet more dragging than marching. The man at the head of the column, minus a powdered wig... she gasped.

Major Wilkins.

He should be at Fort Detroit. Why—?

Where was Uncle Corne?

Abigail grabbed a handful of her skirts and apron and shot from the bake house, racing across the parade ground, barely aware of Koyen running beside her, step for step. She struggled to pull in one breath after another. Where was Uncle Corne? As the detail's second-highest-ranking officer, he should be there.

She stopped a short distance from Major Wilkins. He stepped to the side and waved the others on, then approached her.

"Miss Aldridge."

"W-w-where is my uncle?" She barely recognized her own voice, so hoarse and low.

"I regret to inform you that he was among the casualties on this ill-fated mission."

Abigail would have collapsed had not Koyen caught her by the elbows. He stood behind her, out of sight, but as always, her protector. Lurana Quinn appeared at her side.

"How?" It was the only word she could press between her clenched teeth. And if she unclenched them, the racking sobs behind would overpower her.

"'Twas a terrible storm. The boats we sailed were inadequate to the task. We lost seventy of the King's finest soldiers, Miss Aldridge, but the greatest loss by far was your uncle."

She looked around the major at the soldiers still filing into the fort. "Where is he?"

"Buried on the other side of the lake with his fellow soldiers." The major shifted his feet, glanced away, and then back. "I regret there was no way to bring him back to you."

Your uncle—among the casualties—terrible storm—buried. The words swirled in the fog of Abigail's mind. Uncle Corne couldn't swim. He never should have been on a boat. And yet... soldiers went where they were commanded. Even so close to their retirement.

Ensign Tharp, his features drawn beneath his whiskers, appeared in front of her as the major strode away. "Miss Aldridge, if there is anything I can do..."

Do? Uncle Corne was dead. There was nothing anyone could do.

There would be no house in Boston down the street from Bartlett. No morning tea in the parlor discussing world events—a shockingly unfeminine topic, but one they would have relished together. No evening strolls to see the boats in the harbor. No... no Uncle Corne. A single, wrenching sob escaped the hand she'd pressed over her mouth.

"Come." Lurana Quinn turned her around, one arm across her shoulders. "Come back to the bake house."

The bake house.

She managed to move one foot in front of the other, vaguely aware of Red Beads at her other side.

Always aware of Koyen at her back.

Crushingly aware that Uncle Corne was lost to her... forever.

———

HE'D FAILED. THOUGH HE KNEW IT WASN'T DUE TO neglect or inaction on his part, Koyen still felt the burden of failure. Mourning Dove should be in Boston, or at least on a boat heading that way. He glanced toward the lake. Although he couldn't see it from where he stood outside the bake house, the crash and frothing of the waves were a constant rhythm.

Mourning Dove hadn't emerged since Lurana Quinn had taken her inside the day before after the horrible news.

Koyen also felt the loss of Captain Hayward. A few months ago, he wouldn't have. A few months ago, he may have celebrated the loss of seventy British soldiers.

Not anymore.

His initial pull toward Pontiac and the war had been strong, a powerful urge to fight for what he held dear. For his people and their traditions, their way of life. For those he loved and respected. But some of them, the very people he would have given his life for, had made him see that there had to be a better way.

A way of peace.

And then there was Mourning Dove. A British woman, ill-equipped to survive at Niagara, who had befriended his sisters. Safeguarded them, twice endangering herself in the process. It had opened his eyes further. Enough that he'd met with William Johnson. Enough that he could see the vision William Johnson saw. A world where the Iroquois and British could live side-by-side.

In peace.

Captain Hayward was dead, and Koyen was honor-bound to see to Mourning Dove's safety. He couldn't return her to Boston, even had he known how to get there. It was too far for her to journey overland. And it was unlikely more boats would come to Fort Niagara before the spring.

Koyen could not join William Johnson until his duty was met. Until Mourning Dove was on a boat. Until then—

The bake house door opened, and the object of his thoughts stepped into the fading light of evening. She saw him, her eyes searching his face. What did she see there?

He stepped closer, fumbling for words. He didn't know how the British handled such things. "My heart sorrows for you."

Her mouth trembled, but she dipped her head in acknowledgment. Then she came closer until she was almost touching him. He didn't move, even though everything in him wished to draw her into his arms.

She sighed, a wispy sound. "I w-w-will always miss him."

"He great man." He meant it, having come to respect her uncle more than he'd once thought possible. She must have sensed his sincerity and inched even closer, her dress and shawl touching his buckskins.

"I do not know w-w-what I s-s-shall do now."

Come away with me. Be my wife. Work alongside me with William Johnson to build a bridge between our people. But he bit back the words. He'd promised to see her on a boat. To see her returned to her brother's care in Boston.

"Spring come, boats come again. You sail to brother."

A tremor shook her, one so slight he'd not have noticed if they hadn't been toughing.

"Half-brother. I have no w-w-wish to return to him, to Boston, to any of it."

"Your uncle say go."

"Indeed." She sighed again, the wispy sound catching at his heartbeat. "But he is... gone... and I am not." She turned then, looking up at him, the last remnants of the sun's glow glinting in her fair eyes. Fair eyes that pleaded with him.

For what? Could it be?

They didn't move as darkness gathered around them. He touched her elbow, then let his fingers slide to her wrist. She didn't move. He took her hand, and her fingers curled around his. They may as well have curled around his heart.

SHE'D NEVER IMAGINED HERSELF A WANTON WOMAN, but at that moment, she almost wished she had the nerve to be one. Oh, not truly wanton, but forward enough to make herself clear to Koyen. Then his hand slid over hers, and her fingers curled through his, and something changed.

The spark that had smoldered between them for months flared.

The heat of it took her by surprise. From the way his breathing changed, it'd caught him out as well.

Her uncle was lost to her. His protection gone. A woman

needed protection on the frontier. Maybe not Lurana Quinn, but she was Onondaga, not British. A *British* woman needed a man's protection.

The fort was filled with men. Logic said she could marry any who would ask her. Loneliness on the frontier all but guaranteed some would. But the only man she wanted was the one staring down at her. At one time, such a thought would have shocked her to her core. But the Niagara Abigail saw not an Indian, she saw a man—she saw Koyen.

His dark eyes held a promise she didn't understand, but wanted to. His broad shoulders, clad in a linen shirt and covered with a buckskin coat, blocked her from the wind. His hand clasped hers with a gentle strength that weakened her knees. His face, strong planes and defined edges, framed by hair blacker than the night, robbed her lungs of air.

"I know not how British do such things." His voice was a husky rumble, her midsection tightening in response.

"I know not how the S-s-seneca do s-s-such things."

"We find new way. Your way and mine."

"Indeed."

He lowered his head by inches, giving her all the time she needed to back away. Instead, she released his fingers and clutched the front of his coat, rising to her toes. When their lips met, her quiet gasp mingled with his muted groan.

When he lifted his head and the cold rushed between them, she secured the hold on his coat, unwilling to let go. Unwilling to lose him. Especially after that... her first kiss.

"I go join William Johnson soon. He build me cabin of logs."

"You w-w-will leave me?"

"I take you with me." He rested his forehead against hers. "You come?"

No words of marriage. No words of love. *A new way. Your way and mine.* What would his people say? She knew well enough what hers would. She sucked in a deep breath and leaned away far enough to see his face, shadowed as it was in the darkness.

"W-w-wh-wh…"

He loosened her fingers and moved her back a step to sign, *"Speak this way."*

"What will your mother say? Your sisters? Those in your village?"

He touched her cheek, fingertips warm against her skin. *"Mother will be unhappy, Shining Day angry, and Red Beads will beg to come live with us, I think. Unless Tall Otter wins her heart."*

"My brother will be angry, but he already is, so that is no different."

"This." He pointed from her to him and back again. *"This is different."*

"Indeed." She glanced out over the parade grounds, bare and quiet under the blanket of night. There was one thing he needed to understand. She was no Molly Brant. She wouldn't be… that way… with him. She didn't know how to sign what he needed to understand. "I w-w-will not be a kept w-w-woman."

Confusion pulled lines across his brow. "What mean?"

"I w-w-will not go away w-w-with you unless w-w-we are p-p-properly married. Unless you are my husband and I am your w-w-wife."

The lines melted away. "Yes. Come with me. Be wife."

Oh, dear. How to make him understand?

"The army's chaplain w-w-would marry us."

"What I bring him?"

"Bring him?"

"Bride gift."

"Oh, dear." Abigail pressed her fingers to her lips to suppress the giggle that threatened. She'd not begun to imagine how different their traditions were. At least she needn't worry about her dowry or lack thereof.

They had a lifetime to sort out their differing traditions. To make their own. "The chaplain is a… w-w-well… a holy man.

He s-s-speaks the holy w-w-words for marriage, and then w-w-we s-s-sign a p-p-paper—

"Cannot write." There was a note of anguish in his voice.

"'Tis fine. You can make your mark. Many do."

"Then married?"

"And then, w-w-we are married. Joined together for life."

He reached for her, but she took a step back and held up her hand. "One more thing."

Confusion—or was it frustration—wrinkled his forehead.

"Dance must come w-w-with me."

"Cat?" Disbelief colored his voice.

"A log cabin must have a good cat to keep away the mice. 'Tis essential."

"Bring cat." He glanced at the castle's hulking shape under the full moon and then back. "How British agree to marry if not bride gifts?"

Feeling more emboldened than she'd ever imagined—perhaps even a little wanton—Abigail gripped the front of his coat again and tugged him toward her. His lips met hers more forcefully this time—as if claiming her. It wasn't an unpleasant sensation at all. Then he broke away, pulling her to his chest. "Heart sorrows for uncle. Happy you be wife."

He hadn't actually asked her to marry him. It was on the tip of her tongue to say so, but she didn't. They were not British or Seneca, but something new. Her childhood fantasy of a handsome knight, armor shining in the sun, roses in one hand and kneeling at her feet... That was never going to happen.

She had a handsome warrior instead. A man she could trust. One who would protect her. Uncle Corne had seen that in the end. When he could have charged any soldier to watch over her, he'd chosen Koyen.

Abigail chose him as well.

Bartlett would disown her, of course, but she didn't care.

Society—even those here in the fort—would shun her, but she didn't care. The chaplain would marry them when she threatened to go without his blessing, she was certain. That was all that mattered. The rest? Well, she and Koyen would have to figure things out one day at a time. She was at peace with all of that.

And together—under the tutelage of Sir William Johnson—perhaps they could make a difference on the frontier, could make a place for themselves.

She backed out of his embrace. "I love you, Young King. 'Tis the British w-w-way for those w-w-words to be s-s-spoken between a man and w-w-woman before they marry." At least, in her book it was, even as she struggled to get the words out.

Koyen's hands moved in a gesture she didn't know.

She leaned closer as he did it again. "W-w-what does it mean?"

"You are heart of me, Mourning Dove."

She mimicked his motions in the courtyard outside the bake house with the moon resting behind the castle. Her heart was as full as the moon.

Author's Notes

Major John Wilkins was the British officer in charge of Fort Niagara at the beginning of this story. He would become a less-than-stellar officer in the King's service later in his career and leave the colonies for England to try and salvage his reputation.

The fore-and-aft schooner *Huron* was commissioned by the British and built in 1763. I have no evidence that it ever sailed to Fort Niagara, but it certainly could have.

Moravian missionaries Bishop Cammerhoff and Rev. David Zeisberger came into the Iroquois territory in 1750. I found a short note that they spent some time with the Seneca, but have no evidence that they actually taught there.

The castle at Fort Niagara does include a circular well in the vestibule. Even if put under siege, those inside would have had an unlimited supply of fresh water.

Sir William Johnson was the superintendent of the British Indian Department. He took a Mohawk woman, Molly Brant, the sister of the well-known chief, Thayendanegea (English name Joseph Brant), as a common-law wife. On his deathbed, it is said that he married her to give legitimacy to their eight surviving children. He was much respected by the British and the tribes of the Iroquois Nation. He worked hard to keep the tribes out of Pontiac's Rebellion, but a segment of the Seneca joined the war anyway.

Fort Sandusky fell to Ottawa and Huron warriors on May 16.

The 15-man garrison was killed, and their commander, Christopher Pauli, was taken prisoner. He escaped, however, and managed to meet up with a relief force heading to Fort Detroit some time later.

Farmer's Brother was the Seneca credited with leading the warriors who attacked the British at Devil's Hole. However, in later years, it was reported that he worked to promote peace between the Seneca and the Americans. Whether or not he led the attacks outside of Fort Niagara from mid-June to the end of July, 1763, is unknown but possible, so I used him in that way in this story.

On June 24, 1763, three men were killed just outside of Fort Niagara. From then until the end of July, a total of fifteen soldiers—often men sent out to cut firewood—were killed by Seneca warriors close enough that their screams could be heard inside the fort.

On August 1, 1763, Major Wilkins predicted a major attack on the newly constructed road that led around the worst of the rapids on the Niagara River near Devil's Hole in a letter to Sir Jeffery Amherst, British commander-in-chief in America.

John Rutherford's tale of capture and eventual escape, and all he suffered during that time, are recorded in his own words in *John Rutherford's Captivity Narrative* written just a few months after his ordeal. John Rutherford was seventeen years old at the time of his capture. He arrived at Fort Niagara on August 20, 1763, and left again with provisions for Fort Detroit. Only one day out of Fort Schlosser, their sloop developed a leak and the crew managed to reach the shore where they were attacked by Indians. Rutherford survived twenty-four days until help arrived, along with those of the original company not lost to the Indians. They never reached Fort Detroit, but returned to Fort Niagara, arriving three days after the massacre at Devil's Hole and becoming eyewitnesses to its carnage. John Rutherford then joined the British army where he rose to the rank of lieutenant.

Devil's Hole was well-known to the Seneca who believed that an evil spirit dwelled there. It was said that no Seneca had survived entering that cave except one, who emerged a lunatic with his black hair turned snow white.

On September 12, 1763, a band of Seneca thought to have been led by Farmer's Brother gathered at Ga'-a-no-geh and camped without fires awaiting the British. There was a fierce storm at this time, but even so, a detail of soldiers and teamsters left Fort Niagara with much-needed relief supplies for Fort Detroit. They made the trek to Fort Schlosser using the newly widened road on the cliff above Devil's Hole. The Seneca did not attack that day.

The battle of Devil's Hole occurred on the detail's return trip to Fort Niagara on September 14, 1763. Somewhere between 300 - 500 Seneca waited until the line of wagons—which had to go single-file—stretched across the cliff above Devil's Hole. They attacked from the forest, but also had warriors on both ends of the wagons. It was a slaughter. Of the twenty-four-man detail, only three people escaped, John Stedman, the porter master, who was likely out ahead of the main line, a young boy who was thrown from an overturned wagon, and a soldier who somehow survived. John Stedman was able to reach Lower Landing, north of Devil's Hole, where the British 80th Regiment of Light Armed Foot had camped. They also engaged the Seneca but were beaten back, losing eighty men in that second battle. Reinforcements were also attempted from Fort Schlosser, but seeing the carnage and realizing they were vastly outnumbered, they retreated to the safety of the fort. They returned days later to find and bury the dead.

The young boy in my story is purely fictional but based on the account above.

In August of 1764, William Johnson persuaded the Seneca to deed the land along the river—including the road above Devil's Hole—to the British in an attempt to make amends for the massacre there.

On November 1, 1763, nine men on a woodcutting mission within sight of Lower Landing were killed and scalped—one beheaded—by Senecas. The garrison fired its six-pounder cannon, but in the process, blew out a section of their palisade.

Major Wilkin's expedition to Fort Detroit was a total failure. They left Fort Schlosser in mid-October in a collection of smaller boats and were caught in a storm on Lake Erie. They lost seventy men, several boats, and virtually all of the supplies intended for Detroit before landing on the Canadian side, after which they made their way back to Fort Niagara.

The castle at Niagara still stands today and is open to the public as one of New York's parks.

Details about Fort Niagara at this time were more scarce than details about either Fort Pitt or Fort Detroit. I did my best to piece together the time-line and geography, but any errors made in that are fully mine, and I apologize for them.

About Author

Pegg Thomas lives on a hobby farm in Northern Michigan with Michael, her husband of *mumble* years. They raise sheep and chickens, plus keep a few barn cats and Murphy the spoiled rotten dog. Pegg is published in six Barbour historical romance collections, **won the 2019 Romance Writers of America FHL Reader's Choice Award**, was a **double-finalist for the 2019 American Christian Fiction Writers Carol Award** for novellas, a **finalist for the 2019 American Christian Fiction Writers Editor of the Year Award** and a **finalist for the 2021 Romance Writers of America FHL Reader's Choice Award**. When not writing, Pegg can be found in her barn, her garden, her kitchen, or sitting at one of her spinning wheels creating yarn to turn into her signature wool shawls.

www.PeggThomas.com

JOIN PEGG'S NEWSLETTER

writing updates | sneak peeks | fiber arts updates | personal content
www.subscribepage.com/PeggThomas

Made in the USA
Las Vegas, NV
30 April 2023

71372913R00199